LOLA GRANDE

To Perry

Embrace Change!

Linda

LINDA RAKOS

Lola Grande
Copyright © 2024 by Linda Rakos

Tellwell Talent
www.tellwell.ca

ISBN
978-1-77941-757-2 (Hardcover)
978-1-77941-756-5 (Paperback)
978-1-77941-758-9 (eBook)

Dedicated to my
family and friends,
new and old,
who have supported me,
and encouraged me,
throughout my journey.

Family Tree

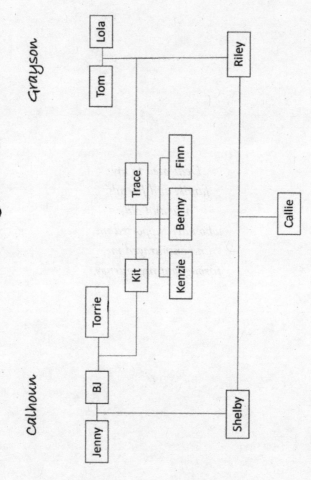

Calhoun

Grayson

Tom — Lola

Trace

Riley

Kit

Kenzie   Benny   Finn

Callie

Torrie

BJ

Jenny

Shelby

PROLOGUE

The Calhoun family was a well-known and respected family who had lived in the area for years. Generations of Calhouns were born and raised on the original homestead and dedicated their lives to ranching. Their forefather, Albert Calhoun, the original homesteader, had followed his dream to freedom and fell in love with the wide-open spaces of Alberta. He believed they had settled on the sweetest piece of land east of the Rocky Mountains. He saw the beauty that lay in the valley. Land and livestock were what Valley View became noted for. The Calhouns ran a first-class cattle business and were known for raising quality beef.

Will Calhoun, his wife Sadie, and his brother Buster were the present-day residents who lived on the original homestead. Buster was a widower and lived in the original house while Will and Sadie lived in the second house that was built as the Calhoun family grew.

When the Graysons moved to Alberta, they pulled into the Calhoun yard in a beat-up pick-up pulling a holiday trailer. The Graysons had lived a nomadic lifestyle, making do with the bare necessities. Tom was looking for work. It was late winter and the Calhouns would be gearing up for their busiest time with spring just around the corner, but they weren't looking to hire for a few more weeks and they usually tried to hire locals.

The Grayson family lived a transient lifestyle due to the fact that the father, Tom Grayson, never held a job for long even though he was a hard worker. Verbally, the man was smooth, but his manner was bold. Physically, he was a bull of a man. Lola Grayson, his wife, was a beautiful woman who didn't play on her beauty. It came from within. Lola's manner was polite, but cool. She looked tired and desperate. Trace, the older son at sixteen, had the Mexican features of his mother. He was dark and reserved like her but the look in his deep blue eyes was always direct. He had no problem keeping eye contact, unlike his father. The younger son, Riley, was an earnest looking youth. He had the fairer colouring of his father. With his wavy red hair and mischievous blue eyes, he was boyishly handsome. His look was too cautious for one so young.

Will and Buster didn't trust the drifter, but they quickly realized this family needed the stability they could offer. Tom Grayson became employed at Valley View. The Graysons lived in their tailer next to the bunkhouse where single part-time wranglers stayed during the busy season. Lola continued to homeschool her boys. Both Trace and Riley became part-time employees at the ranch. They mucked stalls, hauled bales, pitched hay, and mended fences. They did whatever they could to help.

The transient lifestyle had taken its toll on Lola. Disappointment had chipped away at her spirit year after year, move after move. Because Lola had been conditioned by their transient lifestyle, she remained reserved and aloof. She didn't want to get close to anyone, knowing it was just a matter of time before they moved on. But it was impossible to refuse Sadie's friendship. They quickly became close friends. Coming to Valley View, and her friendship with Sadie, restored Lola's sense of worth.

Only months after the Graysons arrived, Tom died. Lola and her sons remained living at Valley View. They moved into Buster's home, and Lola became his housekeeper and caregiver. Lola had a place to raise her boys and give them the home life they deserved. Their transient lifestyle had come to an end. The fear of the unknown was gone. They were able to put down permanent roots and plan a future.

Trace independently started Caballo Stables, his horse training business. After graduating from high school, he ran it under the umbrella of Valley View. Riley graduated from Olds College and worked with the Calhouns and their cattle operation.

As life played out, a couple of years later the Grayson family moved to their new home, Lola Grande. Together, Lola Grande and Valley View became partners and operated C&G Ranching, a huge cattle operation. Lola Grande became their dream place. The Graysons were able to put their mark on their own land and restore Lola Grande.

*****

For twenty-four years Kit Bennett believed her father was dead, due to an evil secret kept by her mother, Torrie Kennedy. Finding Torrie's journals and her birth certificate in the attic, Kit's world crumbled around her. After recovering, Kit went in search of her father, William Joseph Calhoun, better known as BJ. Her search was about revealing the truth and finding family. There was never a question that he was Kit's father. She was the spitting image of BJ Calhoun. What Torrie did wasn't fair to either one of them and Kit believed he deserved to know he had a daughter. Kit needed her father to fill a void in her created a long time ago by a mother who made her believe she wasn't good enough to warrant love.

Trace Grayson had been training one of his horses at Valley View the day Kit Bennett arrived looking for her father. Trace immediately believed Kit was a single mom who was looking for a handout or for someone to take care of her. He felt she was a gold digger who followed the rainbow to the Calhoun ranch. From the day Trace met Kit objectivity hadn't been an option. Never had he allowed a woman to get to him like Kit did. He couldn't deny that for some reason Kit kept getting under his skin, a distraction he couldn't ignore. She irritated and attracted him at the same time. That attraction continued to grow between them. He had never met a woman like her. She was feisty and spirited one minute, vulnerable the next. On one hand she was tough, argumentative, and stubbornly independent. On the other hand, she was genuine, brave, and honest. She was everything a man could want. And more. The fact that Kit had a three-year-old daughter complicated things. The thought of becoming a father scared Trace. He didn't have much of a role model growing up. Nothing in his early life had taught him anything about being a good father. In spite of that, there was an emptiness inside him that was almost unbearable. There was no more denying the feelings Kit stirred in him. Lust he understood. It was easy to satisfy and move on. Love, on the other hand, was an emotion that could interfere with a man's judgement and commitment to goals. Trace had seen the negative effects often enough to want to avoid it. A woman was capable of either consuming a man or smothering him.

Kit's first encounter with Trace wasn't any better. Her dislike for him was instant. The first moment she saw him the sparks flew. Trace had strutted toward her, carrying himself with a definite swagger, topped off by the arrogance of self-assurance. His shirt emphasized his solid muscles, and broad shoulders. Muscles strengthened and toned by a lifetime of working with horses and cattle. Kit could tell he was bold and sure of himself. Some might even say cocky. She definitely thought he was cocky. The dark stubble covering his strong jaw only emphasized the rugged planes of his face. His eyes, Kit noted, were sharp and observant. Kit found him to be arrogant, insufferable, and narrow-minded. Yet, there was a draw to him even though he continually annoyed her. Despite the fact that everyone was skeptical about her sudden and surprising arrival, Trace's attitude seemed irrational.

It was a big shock to BJ to find out he had a daughter. It was an even bigger shock to find out he was a grandfather. In short time, Kit was accepted by the Calhouns. It took Trace longer, but he soon had to admit his preconceived ideas were unfair and unjustified. When he got to know Kit better, Trace couldn't help but be impressed with her. Kit won his reluctant admiration and earned his respect. Even though they wanted each other, they wanted completely different things. Trace knew Kit would never entertain a casual relationship. She would want the full commitment of marriage. Marriage and family were not in Trace's future. He was a loner by choice and intended to stay that way. He wanted no personal commitments. Trace wasn't the marrying kind, and Kit wouldn't settle for less. She wanted forever with a husband and a father for her daughter. Funny how the right woman could change a man's way of thinking. Trace remembered the day he realized he wanted Kit and Kenzie to become his family and make his life complete. A thriving ranch meant nothing without someone to share it with. Kit opened his heart to new dreams. Trace wanted a lifetime with Kit and wanted to expand their family. His confession of his love to Kit had been exciting and terrifying at the same time. Trace didn't question his decision, just the challenges that would follow. Getting married carried a new sense of responsibility for someone, rather than just for something.

The next spring, Trace and Kit were married outdoors at Valley View. Mother Naure had worked her magic. Thin white clouds drifted like ribbons in a sapphire blue sky. The gentle breeze in the trees whispered promises of hope. A sunny glow crept across the land, encircling those present with a warm embrace. Trace stood spellbound under the trellis, astonished again by the miracle that this beautiful woman was going to be his wife. Kit was a vision as her veil flowed behind her like a cascading waterfall as she walked down the path with her dad. Trace stood waiting, his familiar grin curving his lips. When Kit reached the front, she took the hand of her daughter. The three of them stood together as the bride and groom exchanged their meaningful vows. After they exchanged rings, Trace reached into his pocket and pulled out a ring for Kenzie. He vowed to love her and be her proud dad. They walked back down the aisle as husband and wife, father and daughter, A family. At the end of the day, they went home to Lola Grande where future generations would be raised.

CHAPTER ONE

Lola Grayson, matriarch of the family, had been a widow for many years, and she lived independently in the suite above the detached garage next to the house. When Lola inherited Lola Grande, she knew there was no other place she wanted to live. This was where she had let go of the past and put down permanent roots. Their transient lifestyle had finally come to an end. The suite had been built above the new garage preparing for the future. Trace and Kit now lived in the main house. Lola made sure Kit understood that Kit was to make it hers and Trace's without guilt or hesitation. Although Lola and her sons had lived there, it was now the home of Mr. and Mrs. Trace Grayson and their family. Hopefully, it would be filled with more children. Kit had appreciated Lola's thoughtfulness. Lola quickly became the mother Kit never had and she became Lita to her new granddaughter. There was more than one way to say grandmother in Spanish, and because of her Mexican heritage Lola wanted to be called Lita.

Everyone had settled in at Lola Grande and life was wonderful. The changes Kit and Kenzie brought to Lola Grande filled the house with life and love. Right after the wedding Riley moved to Valley View to oversee the cattle business and prepare for the eventual position as foreman of their ranch.

Kit looked out the window and saw Trace down at the corrals with Kenzie. Even now he could make her heart beat faster. Her eyes lingered on Trace out of habit. She enjoyed watching the man who worked hard and was a good provider. He had adapted to the role of father and Kenzie loved him to pieces. His gentleness with Kenzie came naturally. He was a wonderful father. Kit couldn't believe how happy she was. She called out to them to come in for supper.

A few minutes later, Trace and Kenzie traipsed into the kitchen. Kit was standing at the stove. Trace told Kenzie to wash up, while he let his eyes rest on his young wife. He was astonished, not for the first time, by the magnitude of his love for her. Trace was amazed this beautiful woman was his wife. She gave meaning to everything else in life. Kit had opened his heart to new dreams. Kit was his life. Today, her mysterious gray eyes smiled back at him, but he remembered too many times when they challenged him in anger. She still challenged him, but he had learned how to deal with that. Even casually dressed in jeans and a plaid shirt, Kit had the same effect on him. His wife still took his breath away. He went over and put his arms around her waist, "Sure smells good in here, Mrs. Grayson. I would have married you sooner if I knew how domestic you were."

Kit looked up at the man with the cocky grin and was touched and amused at the same time. The sparks that brought them together were still there. "You would have married me sooner if you had any sense at all," she teased back and kissed him with passion.

Lola often joined them for supper instead of eating alone in her suite. She smiled as she entered the kitchen and overheard Kit tell her son he was still too charming for his own good. "Trace has the gift of charm like his father. I couldn't resist him either." Both women laughed.

Trace took a seat next to his mother. They had a close and comfortable relationship. They looked alike in many ways, since Trace had the Mexican features of his mother. Lola was still a striking woman with natural beauty, so makeup was something she usually kept to a minimum. Like usual, her hair was pulled back and knotted at the base of her neck. Having lived in Alberta for years, Lola had adapted to the causal western attire.

Conversation was light throughout the meal. When they were finished, and the dishes were done, Lola headed back to her suite. Usually, they sat and chatted over a second cup of coffee, but Lola had plans. Trace turned to Kit, "Let's drive over to Valley View. I want to talk to Riley, and you can visit with the women. I know Sadie has been missing you. Sadie said the new batch of barn kittens have grown enough so if we want, we can bring a couple home. We could use a couple of mousers."

When Kit arrived at Valley View, she had lived with her grandparents, Sadie and Will Calhoun, until she married Trace. She missed her grandmother as well. They had spent many evenings in the kitchen talking over a pot of tea while Will watched TV in the living room. Kit nodded and went to the cupboard to see what dishes she was willing to relocate to the barn. Kenzie was excited about getting a pet but pouted a little, "I will love the kittens, but I really want a dog." Kenzie was sweetness and charm when she wanted something and had the ability to wrap her dad around her little finger. Today, Trace shook his head and Kenzie let out a long sigh.

When they got to Valley View, Riley and Trace went to the office while the others headed over to the barn to decide which kittens should go home with Kenzie.

"It's still weird seeing you settled down to family life. Kit is exactly what you needed. She has brought out the best in you," Riley commented.

Trace merely raised an eyebrow. His life had definitely changed. "There are still times I shake my head wondering what I got myself into by marrying Kit. When are you and Shelby going to tie the knot?"

"I have the ring," Riley confessed. "Over the last year Shelby has finally reached a level of maturity and is ready to settle down. We all know her parents were rather lenient at times and gave her too much freedom. It took a few hard knocks to help her grow up. Your wife was responsible for a few of them. At least they get along now. Everyone knows I've loved Shelby since I was fifteen, but as weird as it sounds, I'm scared."

"I was afraid, too," confessed Trace.

"Afraid she'd say no?" Riley enjoyed teasing his brother.

"No. Afraid she'd say yes. Was I really ready for such a huge personal commitment?" Trace held Riley's gaze, "I have never regretted my decision for one day. I plan on living a long, happy life with Kit. So, what are you waiting for?"

"Next week is Shelby's birthday and we're going to Banff for the weekend. I plan on proposing then. Like you, I will let her plan the wedding once we decide on a date."

"You're assuming she'll say yes," Trace teased back, a grin on his face.

"I'm surprised she hasn't proposed to me. She's been waiting for a long time, and we all know she isn't known for her patience. Will you be my best man?"

"Of course. You do realize they don't change. Shelby will still be giving you grief when you're eighty. Women are difficult."

Riley's gaze never faltered, "I love Shelby. Even though she can be selfish at times, she is also generous. She is impatient, opinionated, and stubborn. Sometimes to a fault, but I wouldn't change Shelby for the world."

"Your efforts would be futile," Trace commented quietly. He grinned as he held his hand to his ear, "What's that I hear?" Riley cocked his head but didn't hear anything. "I think I hear those wedding bells coming your way."

"You're still an ass, Trace. Don't say anything to Ma."

"I won't. It's your news, not mine. Ma will be excited. Heck, everyone will be. Even though marrying Kit was the best thing I've ever done, women are too much trouble."

Riley pretended to swallow hard, "And we can't live without them." The two brothers shared a hearty laugh as they left the house and headed to the barn.

*****

It was always a rush getting Kenzie ready for school in time to catch the bus. Kit waved as the bus pulled away. She leaned against the verandah post thinking how quickly her little girl was growing up. Trace came out to the verandah holding two cups of coffee. "Let's have our coffee here before I start my day. I want to talk to you about something. Do you remember when we told Kenzie I was going to be her daddy and she said maybe this daddy would get her a puppy?"

Kit nodded. Kenzie had been asking for a dog ever since she could talk. "She loves the kittens, but she really wants a dog."

"Now that we are settled what do you think about making our little girl really happy. Garth Harvey said his dog had a litter of pups and they are ready to find a new home. I know it's sooner than we planned but I'm okay to do this if you are."

They looked at each other and smiled, "What breed are they?"

"Border Collies. Garth says they are even-tempered and known for their obedience and loyalty. They are also a barking breed, which is okay. It will make an excellent watch dog, especially when we are away from the ranch."

"It sounds like a good choice. Kenzie will be ecstatic."

With their decision made, Trace and Kit went into town and purchased the necessary supplies so they would be prepared when they brought the new puppy home. They hid them away along with the doghouse Trace had already built knowing Kit would say yes to getting a dog. Lola would set everything out after they left to pick up their new family member.

As soon as supper was done, Trace said, "We're going for a drive."

Always inquisitive, Kenzie wanted to know where they were going.

"It's a surprise."

Kenzie pouted because they wouldn't give her any hints, so she was surprised when they pulled into a stranger's farm. They got out and headed straight to the barn. Kenzie could hardly contain herself when she saw all the puppies. There was seldom a time when Kenzie wasn't smiling but nothing could compare to her smile when she was told she could pick one of the puppies as her own and take it home. Kenzie's face took on a serious expression as she examined each and every pup. Looking concerned, her eyes settled on the runt of the litter whimpering in the corner. "I want that one over there. It's all alone, so I think it should come home with us." Kenzie went over and picked it up. It stopped whimpering as soon as Kenzie held it close. Their bond was instant. The pup began to lick her face and Kenzie began to giggle as she grinned at her parents. "This is the one I want. Is it a boy or a girl?"

Garth answered, "He's a boy. Do you want to give him his name?"

"Buddy," Kenzie answered without hesitation. The early excitement in her voice had been replaced with a note of despair, "I don't have a brother or a sister and everyone needs a buddy. Now I have a buddy of my own. Oh, I already love him more than anything."

Kit felt guilty. She knew her daughter had been lonely at times. Kit kissed her darling daughter on her cheek. "You made the perfect choice. Buddy is a lucky boy."

As soon as they arrived home, Kenzie jumped out of the truck with Buddy. Even though Kenzie had spotted the doghouse she wanted her puppy to stay in the house.

Trace shook his head, "He's a farm dog, Kenzie. He will live outside."

Kenzie's voice filled with dismay, "He'll be cold." Tonight, the air was crisp.

"This is the best kind of dog to have. He likes cold and hot weather. Besides, he's already used to living outside. He was living with his mom in the barn. Here he has this nice doghouse."

Kit was surprised by the tenderness in Trace's voice. There was always an aura of power that surrounded Trace, but he had a sensitive and caring side he tried to keep hidden.

That seemed to appease Kenzie, especially when she looked inside and saw the blanket and dishes filled with food and water. She set her pup inside and Buddy immediately began to explore, sniffing into every corner and making himself at home.

CHAPTER TWO

What had been a regular day changed the minute Kenzie got off the school bus. By the time she was coming up the drive, Kenzie was having a major meltdown. Familiar with her daughter's dramatics, it could be anything, so Kit wasn't overly concerned. "What's upset you, baby girl?" Kit still called Kenzie that when her daughter needed comforting. It had been her childhood nickname since she was born.

Tears poured down Kenzie's cheeks as she flung herself at her mother. She was such a drama queen when she was upset. "Lucy Rose told me she's going to be a big sister because her mommy and daddy are going to have a baby. I want to be a big sister, too." Kenzie looked down at Buddy, who always greeted her when she got home from school. "All I have is a dog." Still upset, Kenzie didn't give Buddy his usual greeting, so Kit bent down and patted him.

Kit smiled knowing that was about to change. She hadn't said anything to anyone, not even Trace. She wanted to wait until she knew for sure. She would pick up a pregnancy kit the next time she was in the city. If Kit got one in town, the grapevine would have it spread before she even got home.

It was another week before Kit got to Calgary. As soon as she got home, she took the test. It was no surprise when it showed positive. The next morning, she told Trace and laughed at his stunned expression. A moment later he was grinning from ear to ear.

"You're pregnant. I'll be damned; we're going to have a baby!" Trace grabbed his pregnant wife and twirled her around. As soon as he set Kit down, she ran to the bathroom. Morning sickness was ugly. By the time Kit got back Trace had sobered. Mixed emotions had taken over. His expression changed to one of apprehension. His voice became serious, and his dark eyes were anxious. He felt helpless. "You realize I have no idea how to handle a newborn. What if I don't know what to do? What if it cries and I don't know why?"

"I told you it comes naturally. You love them and they sneak their way into your heart before you can blink."

Trace couldn't supress his feelings of self-doubt, "What if I can't figure it out? What if I make mistakes?" Trace asked with increased concern.

"I've made my own, and there will be more. We have to remember that we are not perfect, and we won't raise perfect kids. We just do our best. Parenting is a big responsibility, but it is something we do every day. Like ranching, it becomes a part of who you are. If what we do is out of love, it can't be wrong."

Trace took Kit in his arms. He knew she was right. Kit had been successful in helping him to calm down. "Thank you, wise one. Our kids will have the best mom."

"Still the charmer, Trace Grayson." Kit closed her eyes, waiting for her nausea to pass. It didn't, and she ran back to the bathroom.

Trace was still in the room when she returned. "I was worried because I thought you were sick, and you didn't want to tell me. Boy was I wrong. Feeling better?"

Kit managed a weak smile, "Not much."

"I'll get Kenzie off to school this morning. What can I make you for breakfast?"

Fighting nausea again Kit chocked on her response, "Just dry toast. Once my stomach settles, I'll come down. I like you spoiling me."

"Don't get used to it. How long does morning sickness last?"

"With Kenzie, it lasted the whole first trimester, but every pregnancy can be different. I'm already eight weeks and it has started to get better. At least it's not every day and only a few smells make me want to vomit." The smell of greasy bacon still turned her stomach. "It won't be long and I'll start showing, so we'll have to tell our family soon. I'm sure your mom has already guessed but hasn't said a word. Kenzie will be so excited she might burst."

Once Kit's morning sickness passed, her pregnancy was normal, other than the mood swings. Those were something Trace was not prepared for. He raked a hand through his hair in frustration when he mentioned it to his mom. "We were watching a family movie last night with Kenzie. A commercial came on and for no reason Kit started crying. Kenzie gave me a dirty look like it was my fault."

Lola laughed, "That's not unusual. You notice I didn't say it's normal because there is nothing normal during a pregnancy. Does Kit have any unusual cravings?" Trace shook his head. "With Riley I craved bananas. Now I hate bananas, can't eat them to this day. Can't even stand the smell. With you it was spicy foods."

Trace offered up his killer grin, "Maybe that's why I'm so hot."

Lola hugged her son, "You're not doing anything wrong. Just try to be patient and put up with her mood swings. Patience and long walks help."

Some days, poor Trace was beside himself. There were also the wonderful days. Like the first time he felt the baby move. Trace was speechless and so overwhelmed he had to wipe his eyes. Moments like that made up for all of Kit's mood swings. Kit and Trace were sitting together on the couch. They called Kenzie over. Kit reached out and placed her daughter's hand on her stomach. Kenzie's mouth dropped open, "I felt the baby move." Kit and Trace smiled at the thrill on their daughter's face.

The next morning Kit's friend, Maggie Walker, stopped by for a visit, They had met shortly after Kit's arrival at Valley View and Kit liked Maggie the minute she met her. Maggie had been Kit's friend since then, and their husbands were best friends since high school. The two families were close friends, often spending time together. Kit and Maggie sat out on the verandah comparing pregnancies. Maggie shifted uncomfortably, "I saw the doctor yesterday. He told me to have my suitcase packed because our son can come anytime. We think we have his name picked out but aren't saying anything. Lucy Rose's name got changed the day I had her."

"Trace and I have chosen not to know. I'm sure Matt is excited to be having a son to carry on your family name. Trace hasn't said anything, but I know he would like a son. If we also have a boy, our sons can become best friends like Kenzie and Lucy Rose. And us. Last night my hormones were completely out of wack. I snapped at Trace for no reason. He said sorry. I start to cry. He said sorry, again. The poor man had nothing to be sorry for other than having a hormonal wife. This pregnancy has been so different. I find I've been more irritable than usual." Kit was glad to share this with a friend who could understand.

That night Kit was more tired than usual. These days everything was an effort, and she was always uncomfortable.

"Go and put your feet up. Kenzie and I will clean up the kitchen."

"I told you I would get fat. I can't even see my feet," Kit complained as she waddled off to the living room. She could hear Trace chuckling.

*****

Three weeks later Benjamin William Grayson arrived. He was named after Benjamin (Buster) Calhoun, Trace's mentor while growing up and William (BJ) Calhoun, Kit's father who was named after his father. They were going to call him Benny for short.

Trace was deeply moved as he looked down at his son. "Thank you for wanting to honor Buster." Just then Benny grabbed Trace's thumb with his little hand and smiled. A shiver ran down Trace's back as he felt Buster's presence and smiled, "I would like Riley and Shelby to be his godparents."

His request came as no surprise and Kit readily agreed. Baby Benny was a precious child. He was the tie that would bind every member of both families together. He belonged to everyone.

Both Lola and Kenzie were waiting on the verandah when they arrived home from the hospital. Kenzie was jumping up and down, unable to contain her excitement. "Can I hold him?"

"Yes, darling, but let us get in the house first."

"He is beautiful, Mommy. Little Benny Bear is my very special brother."

"You are special, too, Kenzie. You will always be my baby girl but now you have a special role. Only you can be a big sister."

When Benny began crying, Kenzie wanted to give him back. Kit suppressed a smile as she took Benny. She cuddled her infant for a moment before handing him to Lola.

Lola looked down at the black-haired baby who gazed up at her with intense blue eyes. "Benjamin Grayson, you are the spitting image of your daddy as a baby." Lola laughed softly as she kissed his cheek. "If you have the Grayson charm like your daddy, there won't be a safe female in the county."

That night Kit sat down in the rocking chair and looked down at her innocent baby. Memories held at bay for a long time stirred inside her. She allowed herself to drift in thought, silently reliving the past. Her grandmother, Lou, had bought this chair when Kit's mother had discovered she was pregnant, but it was Lou who had spent hours rocking her precious granddaughter because her own mother had left. It was the chair that had brought comfort to Kit during her own pregnancy, knowing there would be no father to welcome her baby because her husband Mike had died. Kit missed her grandmother but was grateful to now have Lola and Sadie in her life. Kit would make a point of telling Benny all about these people and the wonderful people living on the neighbouring ranch. She looked down at the sweet face of her infant son and kissed his plump cheek, thinking she was the luckiest woman in the world.

CHAPTER THREE

Benny, now two, pulled at his mom's leg to get her attention. Kit knew he wanted to go outside with his dad, but the day had dawned cloudy and there were dark clouds gathering on the horizon. Heavy snow was forecast for the foothills by tomorrow, but Trace was sure it would start sooner than that. There was already frost in the pastures. Realizing his mommy wasn't going to help him, Benny went over to his dad. Trace smiled down at his son who was now sitting on the floor trying to put his boots on. Benny had Kit's stubbornness and Trace's perseverance. Sometimes a combination of both. Trace squatted down to his son's level, "Not today, Benny. Daddy has things to do before the snow comes."

The weather worsened and the dark clouds were closing in. There was a biting north wind and the temperature had dropped. The threatening storm, now forecast to be much worse than predicted, created a beehive of activity. Kit was outside gathering firewood to take inside. It would be needed to keep the house warm if the power went out. She breathed deep and saw her breath as she exhaled.

Trace glanced over at Kit, "Alberta winters come with cold winds and mountains of snow, but spring storms can be just as severe. I think we're in for one hell of a spring storm, so we better prepare for the worst. You can see the snow blowing in from the north." Even as he spoke, the first flakes of snow began to drift through the air. Trace had lived in Alberta long enough to know they were in for a heavy blizzard before the storm was over. "Ma is closing up her suite and is going to hunker down with us.

Don't be surprised if we lose power. I've already filled the kerosene lamps. I'll take a couple and put them in the birthing stall. When Doc was out yesterday, he said Ginger would probably foal early. He thought another day or two, but Murphy's law says it will come tonight." Trace wanted to be prepared. He had settled Ginger in the birthing stall earlier and would be checking on her throughout the day.

Within the hour the weather turned. The wind suddenly picked up and the temperature dropped even more. By mid-afternoon the wind was blowing the heavy snow with frightening fury. If this kept up it would be impossible to see anything, especially once it got dark. The way the wind swirled the snow through the yard made Kit nervous as she watched Trace tether a rope from the house to the barn. By nightfall there was nothing to see from the window, but a curtain of white draped heavily over the land. There was no sound outside but the howling wind.

After supper, Trace began layering up to head back outside. Trace knew Ginger would give birth before the night was over. "Ginger picked a fine night to have her baby. It may take a while, but I'll stay with her now." Trace was glad this wasn't Ginger's first birth, but it was an ugly night if she had problems. There was no way, on a night like this, that the vet could make it out to the ranch if there were complications.

It had been hours since Trace had left. Kit had become both antsy and concerned. The kids were in their pajamas and settled in front of the crackling fire in their sleeping bags. Despite her own concern, Lola tried to reassure Kit, "I'm sure they are fine. Trace has done this before and so has Ginger."

Logic was all well and good but worry trumped logic. Ten minutes later Kit had filled two thermoses with steaming coffee and put them in a backpack along with sandwiches. She threw on a heavy sweater, her barn coat, and boots so she could join Trace. The minute she opened the door the wind slapped snow in her face. Kit pulled her scarf up over her nose and pulled her hood lower. Another strong gust of wind whipped the snow around Kit and took her breath away. It was a miserable night. With a blizzard like this it would be easy to lose one's way, even in a short distance. Kit grabbed the rope Trace had strung earlier. With her flashlight in one hand, she hung tightly onto the rope with the other. Trace had shoveled a path from the house to the barn, but it had drifted over. Kit's breath was laboured as she trudged slowly through the snow-covered path. Nearly stumbling in the deep snow Kit braced herself and grabbed the rope tighter. The footprints she left behind quickly drifted in. It seemed to take forever to make her way to the barn. She was relieved when she saw the light cast by the kerosene lanterns. Kit struggled with the barn door and called out, hoping Trace could hear her. She was relieved when the door opened.

"What the hell are you doing out here, Kit?" Trace asked in exasperation as he quickly closed the door.

Kit looked up at him, snowflakes clinging to her long lashes. "I've never seen anything like this. It's really bad out there," she admitted.

Trace could smell the hot coffee and even though he was mad at her he was grateful. It had already been a long night and he would enjoy her company. They quickly walked back to the birthing stall. Ginger snorted in discomfort. She was panting heavily, sweat streaming down her swollen sides.

Kit poured Trace a coffee and handed it to him. "Everyone is bunked down in front of the fire. I was worried about you and Ginger. How is she doing?" Kit dropped to her knees beside the distressed mare and caressed the swollen stomach that clenched beneath her hands. "Poor mama. I know it hurts but it will soon be over." Kit continued to talk to Ginger in a soothing voice as she gently patted the labouring mare's neck.

"It won't be long now," Trace said, as he rubbed his hands over the exhausted mare's side. They sat together, soothing her with words and hands. Ginger's contractions gradually grew longer and harder. She whinnied louder, then pushed with an effort that racked her body. A couple more pushes and her foal was born.

"You have another beautiful baby, Ginger. Good job." Kit had tears in her eyes. The birth of any baby was such a miracle.

"You were a big help, Kit. You have a nice touch with horses."

Kit smiled up at him. She appreciated the compliment. "We could call her Stormy, but let's call her Coco. She is the color of hot chocolate which I could use right now."

"Coco, it is. Why don't you go back to the house and warm up. I'll join you soon." Kit bundled up and Trace watched as she left. Seconds later, she disappeared into a flurry of white. Trace smiled to himself. For a city girl, Kit had easily adapted to her life as a rancher's wife. She continually amazed him.

The drifts were knee-deep going back to the house. Kit entered the house covered with snow. She tossed her coat over a hook and stomped her boots on the mat. She was grateful for the light from the lit candle on the kitchen table. Kit walked into the living room. Benny and Kenzie were sound asleep in front of the welcoming fire. Lola was covered with a blanket sitting on the couch. "I'm going to make hot chocolate. Would you like a cup?" Trace had brought the Coleman stove in earlier. Even though they had a generator they only ran it when necessary. The power could be out for days.

Lola nodded. "Did Ginger foal?"

"We have another filly appropriately named Coco. I'll be right back." When Kit returned, she grabbed a spare blanket and curled up beside Lola. They chatted away until Trace joined them. It had been quite the night.

It was hours before the storm was over, but the morning brought with it a sense of reality. Even though the world around them was snowed in, Kit smiled. "It's beautiful isn't it. The whole world looks frozen in time and at peace, if only for a moment." As beautiful as it was with the sun glistening off the fresh snow, there was a lot of snow removal to be done. Trace bundled up and headed outside. The fresh snow sparkled but the air was cold. Trace shovelled snow until he was able to get the tractor with the attached snow blade out of the Quonset. Soon mounds of snow were piled high, which would be fun for the kids to slide down on their sleds. By noon the yard was cleared. After lunch, Trace went back out to shovel. He was shovelling the driveway as the vet pulled into the yard. Trace leaned on the shovel handle, grateful for the break. It was already late afternoon. Trace warmly greeted Dr. Jim Parker, better known as Doc to everyone. They were old friends. "That was a hell of a storm. How are the roads?"

Doc had closed his office for the day, knowing his services would be required elsewhere. This was his last stop before heading home to his own place. He followed Trace into the barn and over to the birthing stall. "Some areas were drifted in pretty bad. The plows have been busy, so most roads are plowed. There are places where you feel you are driving through a white tunnel. The pastures are buried, and livestock were lost. I stopped and talked to Riley. He said Valley View lost a considerable number of new calves. Let's check out that new baby of yours." After examining both horses, the vet turned to Trace. "She's another beauty, Trace. You continue to breed a strong lineage of horses."

"Kit will have coffee on. Want to come in for a cup before you go?"

Doc nodded. He had experienced an instant tug of attraction to Kit the day he met her shortly after she had arrived at Valley View. Both he and Trace were intrigued by the young lady, but she only had eyes for Trace. There was instant chemistry and the sparks between Trace and Kit were obvious from day one. Doc had quietly stepped aside but his attraction for Kit never faded. He had only buried it deep within out of respect for his two friends. Doc respected their marriage, but it didn't change his feelings.

Kit was cleaning the kitchen when they entered. "Daddy," Benny called out as he launched himself at his dad.

"Benny," Trace responded as he opened his arms and lifted his son high in greeting. It was their usual routine when Trace came into the house.

Kit took Benny and held him on her lap. He giggled when she gave him smoothie kisses on his neck before she set him down to go play.

Doc smiled at the little boy who enjoyed the cuddle from his mom, and it gave Doc an unexpected hunger for a family. A faraway look darkened his eyes. He envied the family life they had and was unable to dismiss the feeling of loneliness that assailed him. Some men weren't meant to be married. Today, he knew he wasn't one of them. Because he had always been enamoured by Kit, he wasn't willing to settle for just anyone.

After Doc left, the family bundled up and went outside to play. Kenzie was excited because the schools had been closed due to the storm. Trace was on his way back to the house when he spotted the kids behind the piled-up snow where Kenzie had stashed her arsenal of snowballs. He kept walking knowing he was about to get bombarded. As Trace got closer, he could hear them giggling. He bent down and made a couple of snowballs for his own attack. Trace was enjoying himself as much as the kids. Once they were out of snowballs, they began building a snowman. It was a great family snow day.

*****

Spring had brought everything to life. Kit pressed her forehead against the cool glass and watched her family down at the corral where Kenzie was practicing her barrel racing pattern. Now that Kenzie was eight, she was bored with the simplicity of gymkhanas. They were fun but gymkhanas were amateur competitions for all ages with various abilities. Kenzie had been riding horses since they arrived in Alberta, so she was well beyond being a novice rider. She had a natural grace and the physical ability to perform and wanted more of a challenge. This year Kenzie wanted to focus solely on barrel racing.

They had bought Kenzie an experienced barrel racing horse named Tilly. The owner's daughter had quit barrel racing when she discovered she liked boys more than horses. Barrel racing was all about technique and skill and involved hours of practice. It was a combination of the horse's athletic ability and the horsemanship skills of the rider. Their connection with each other was also a factor. Kenzie was just getting to know her horse, so they were still practicing at a slower pace. Kenzie was committed because she wanted to be able to compete in competitions next year as a youth. Both Kit and Trace were impressed with her progress.

On her way to join Trace, Kit waved to Lola who was working in the garden. Lola had revived the overgrown garden patch the year they moved to Lola Grande and had become an avid gardener. Trace watched Kit as she approached. Today, Kit's hair was pulled back in a ponytail that made her look as if she hadn't aged a day since he met her. He admired her willowy figure in her slim jeans and denim shirt. Trace's life had taken on more meaning now that he had this wonderful family. He turned back and praised Kenzie as she cleanly rounded the barrel.

"Kenzie loves horses as much as you do." Kit reached up and took Benny so Trace could focus on Kenzie. Trace smiled as he handed their son over. Trace still had the same effect on Kit. The devil was still in this man's smile, and she found herself smiling back. Kit only watched a moment longer since Benny was bored. Outside the house, Benny stopped and picked a flower from her flower bed. The dirt was still clinging to the root. Kit laughed, "Benny, you little stinker. I take my eyes off of you for a second and those little hands are busy." Her son may be cute and cuddly, but he was also a terror. Chaos followed the toddler around like his shadow. Gray clouds had gathered throughout the morning. They were likely in for a spring shower. Thunder cracked and Benny ran into his mother's arms. He was afraid of the sound of thunder. Kit didn't particularly like it either.

Over lunch Trace mentioned he needed to pick up an order in town, but he wanted to get a few things done before it rained.

"I'll run into town for you if your mom will watch the kids. If you're not in too much of a hurry, I'll do a couple of errands."

Kit was rewarded with a brief smile, "That would be a big help, but don't be gone too long. Those aren't friendly clouds building over the mountains." It was early spring, and everyone knew how quickly the weather could change.

"Don't worry," Kit said as she kissed his cheek and headed over to Trace's truck. She needed to take his to haul his order in the back. Trace headed to the barn.

It had taken Kit longer in town than she intended. It never failed, when you're in a hurry you always ran into someone who wants to talk and today was one of those days. By the time Kit headed home the wind had a bite to it and the sky had grown darker overhead. Minutes later the overcast sky opened, and heavy rain came pouring down. It was unsettling because Kit knew the road would soon be muddy and slick. The visibility became almost impossible even though she had the wipers on high. Kit was almost tempted to pull over, but she was so close to home. Having driven down this road many times, she knew a curve was coming up. Seeing headlights approaching, Kit slowed down to a crawl. A dark Hummer swerved at her on the tight curve and skidded as it roared away. Kit, in turn, swerved out of the way. Had the road been any slicker she would have ended up in the ditch. Kit was visibly shaken as she pulled over and stopped. Had the Hummer actually swerved at her on purpose? Kit couldn't shake off her disturbing thoughts, but she tucked them away until later. She had to focus on her driving. By the time Kit got back to the ranch, she was more mad then scared.

Once in the house all was forgotten. Everyone was gathered in the kitchen and Kenzie was helping set the table. The aroma of fresh buns was a delightful surprise and would taste great with the stew Kit had put in the crock pot before she left. Lola stayed and had supper with them.

Kenzie was still excited about her training session. "Lita, you should see how good Tilly and I are at going around the barrels. I just love Tilly." The adults exchanged knowing looks. Kenzie either loved everything and everyone or she absolutely hated it. She could go from one side of her emotional spectrum to the other in a heartbeat. "I have to practice a lot more so one day I can compete at the Calgary Stampede."

Kit kissed the top of Kenzie's head as she cleared the table and dodged Benny who was riding Poco, his stick horse, around the table. "You are a natural on a horse. Who knows, Kenzie, one day you might do that." The rain continued so no one was in a hurry to leave the table. They sat and had another coffee before Lola headed home. Kit didn't say anything about the incident on her way home until the kids were in bed. "Do you know anyone around here who drives a dark Hummer?"

"There are quite a few out here in the country. It's a popular vehicle with ranchers. I know Jackson Beaumont drives one. Why?"

Kit's underlying anger was clear as she told Trace what happened. "I'm sure the vehicle that swerved at me was a Hummer."

"Are you sure it swerved at you, or did it slide because of the muddy road? Maybe the driver entered the curve too fast for the condition of the road."

"I hope that's what happened," Kit said with resignation and left it at that even though she remained unconvinced. The more she replayed what happened, the more she felt it was intentional and her gut feelings were seldom wrong. Knowing the Beaumonts owned a Hummer didn't help. Had it been Jackson who swerved at her thinking it was Trace driving? He had a vendetta against Trace that seemed to be escalating. Kit forced herself to shake off her mood.

CHAPTER FOUR

C hanges happen as seasons come and go, but some things never change. Mornings were always hectic in the Grayson house. They had finished breakfast and Benny was squirming in his booster chair. "Hey there, little guy. Quit your fussing. I'll get you down as soon as I wipe those sticky little hands."

Kit was glad there were only a couple more months of school. She enjoyed summer holidays. Mornings were less hectic; days were carefree and filled with adventure. Kit turned to Trace, "Buddy has been barking more than usual the last couple of days and something has been in the garbage bin outside. Is it possible there's an animal rummaging in it?"

Trace grabbed his hat off the peg at the back door. "I'll check before I go over to the barn." Today, Trace was going to check out Darby, a magnificent colt from Brody Maddox's stock. He would begin training the young colt in a couple of weeks. Trace first met Brody when he showed up a few years ago looking for a new cutting horse. Brody bought Champ, Trace's own horse. Brody Maddox was well known in the professional cutting horse business, so it meant prestige, and recognition for Caballo Stables. There were riders like Brody who paid big dollars for a trained cutting horse for competitions. Champ had lived up to his name and as a result Trace's business flourished. It had taken years of commitment and determination to get where he was. He had paid his dues and was now reaping the rewards. Trace had earned a reputation for using a patient and gentle technique when training and it usually took him twelve to eighteen months of concentrated training before a horse was ready for competition.

Trace was grateful to have an indoor arena that allowed him to train year-round. He preferred to train outdoors, but even though the last Chinook had melted most of the snow the ground was still slick. Safety for the horses was always his prime concern.

Trace went around back to check the garbage bin. Sure enough, the lid of the bin was ajar, and the bag inside had definitely been torn open. He didn't see any animal prints but the area around the bin was disturbed. He would keep his eyes open for anything that was unusual. Buddy followed Trace across the yard to the barn. Inside, Trace's eyes were sharp and observant. Because the barn was shadowy, Trace wasn't sure if he saw movement in the farthest stall. He proceeded slowly, not knowing what to expect. It was a surprise when he looked in and found someone crouched in the corner hidden under a horse blanket. His hair was long and unkept, the ends curling over his collar. Trace pulled the blanket away. When Trace spoke his voice was deep and authoritative, "Who are you, and what are you doing in here?" Trace stared down at the startled freckle-faced boy who looked to be around eleven or twelve. The boy's piercing green eyes were enormous in his thin face. Trace studied him closely. The boy cowered when Trace moved closer, "You don't have to be afraid of my dog. Buddy is friendly."

The reassurance didn't help. It wasn't the dog he was afraid of. The youth stood up clutching his backpack tight, while looking around for a means of escape.

Before the boy could dart, Trace grabbed him firmly by the collar and led him to the house. The frightened youth kept trying to pull away as he glared up at Trace. "Here's your scavenger," Trace declared as they entered the kitchen.

The unkept youth was greeted by odd stares. Kit could tell the boy had been crying. His defiant eyes were rimmed in red; his manner guarded.

"Who's that," Kenzie asked.

There was no time for a response; the school bus driver was honking his horn. Kit scooted Kenzie out the door. Kit didn't miss much where her children were concerned. It was no different with this boy. What Kit saw was an angry child who looked scared to death. Kit's heart went out to the youth standing there in ripped jeans with his tattered backpack, looking miserable. "What's your name?"

"Finn." Trace remained standing next to Finn, his posture unyielding, expression stern. Finn experienced the full impact of Trace's steely blue eyes. When Trace stared him down, the youth said, "Finnigan Morgan Doyle." He slipped his hands into his pockets and shifted uncomfortably.

Kit threw Trace a silencing glance before turning back to the boy with genuine concern. "Well, Finn, my name is Kit, and this is my husband Trace. Our little boy is Benny, and that was our daughter Kenzie who scurried out to catch the school bus. I'll make you something to eat while you wash up. After you have eaten, we will talk. I'm sure you're hungry."

Finn was comforted by the warmth in her voice and felt better. "Yes," he admitted as his stomach growled. He was ravenous. The smell of cooked bacon still hung in the air.

"I'll show you where you can wash up." Without thinking, Trace touched him on the shoulder as he walked by and felt the boy pull away. The boy's look was heartbreaking, for it told a story of its own. Understanding childhood fears too well, Trace took a step back.

When Trace returned, he accurately stated, "He's obviously run away but how in heaven's name did he get out here? That boy better be ready to answer a lot of questions."

Kit gave Trace a warning look, "Don't pounce on him the minute he comes back. Wait until after he has eaten before you start asking questions." Kit didn't miss the open anxiety in Finn's expressive eyes when he walked back into the kitchen. His look was cautious as he headed over to the table and sat down. Finn wolfed down a double helping of breakfast while Kit and Trace remained sitting at the table.

With Trace the direct approach was the only way to deal with things. The moment Finn was done, in a demanding voice Trace asked, "How did you get out here?"

Finn remained silent, trying to cover his vulnerability with defiance even though he watched them with troubled eyes.

When Trace repeated the question, Kit glanced sideways at the boy and saw him squirm. She cleared her throat, cutting off Trace's reaction. "Trace and I need some answers."

Finn's gaze remained on Trace, "I hopped in the back of your truck when you were in Calgary at the gas station. It seemed like a good idea at the time, but now I'm not so sure. I didn't think I'd end up way out here in no-man's-land." Finn stared at the imposing man and regretted his impulsive actions, due to the unwelcoming tone in the large man's voice.

Kit drew in a shocked breath and was unable to keep the disbelief out of her voice, "That was three days ago. Weren't you afraid out there all alone?"

Finn shrugged in response, "I'm not afraid of being alone." Behind the façade of bravery, he was scared to death.

"Only because you haven't the good sense to be. Your parents must be sick with worry."

"I don't have any parents," Finn blurted out.

"What do you mean, you don't have parents?" Trace didn't believe him, whereas Kit was shocked by Finn's blunt answer. Her heart twisted painfully.

"I never had a dad, and my mom is dead. I live with foster parents. I ran away because they aren't nice people. I'm not going back." The eyes focused on them were dead serious.

"So, you have run away, and your foster parents don't know where you are." Trace's harsh voice reflected his aggravation.

Finn's mouth was set in a hard, thin line and his expression grew even more gloomy. "It's not like they would care. The only reason they would miss me would be because they won't get paid." There was so much hurt underneath the anger. Finn's eyes filled with worry, and was quick to add, "I'll run away again if I have to go back."

"That isn't the answer. You'll just become a tough brooding street kid who will struggle." Trace motioned for Kit to join him outside. "I hate to leave you alone with him, but I have an appointment I need to keep. I won't be back until suppertime. I tend to believe him about having foster parents. See if you can get more information out of him. He might actually be a little more open if I'm not here. I'll take Benny up to Ma's for a while, so you aren't interrupted, and I'll explain what's going on." Times like this, it was convenient to have Lola so close.

After Trace left, Kit sat down next to Finn in the living room. "You do understand we must report this to the authorities, but I want to know more before I do." One look at Finn and Kit realized she was going to be challenged not only by the situation but by the boy himself.

Past experiences had made Finn cautious. He looked at Kit with dread. "Where is your husband?" Finn was intimidated by the tall man with the gruff manner.

The frantic look in Finn's eyes broke Kit's heart. She understood more than Finn realized. "Trace is gone for a few hours so it's just you and me, but I want honest answers. Why are you in foster care and why did you feel you had to run away?"

Finn breathed an audible sigh of relief. His encounter with Trace had made him wary, but Kit had eased some of his fears. It didn't feel like Kit was prying, not like her husband who had interrogated him when he found him. "I became a ward within the system, essentially the government is my legal guardian." That was the beginning of years of suffering caused by others. He looked at Kit, his intense green eyes unable to hide the torment he experienced from all kinds of abuse. A spasm of sorrow washed over Finn's face, "My mom was all I had." Finn would never forget that morning. "I was only seven when she died, too young to understand what was happening. When I woke up, I went to her room to see if she had come home. She just lay there cold and not moving. I couldn't wake her up. There wasn't anybody to help her. Just me." He was unable to hide the pain he had buried for years.

Kit had to swallow the lump that had formed in her throat. She could hear the anguish behind his words. "Of course, you couldn't. You were only a little boy. It's not your fault."

Finn was quiet for a moment and then in a ragged voice he continued, "I remember crying and saying I was sorry. I couldn't find her phone so I couldn't call 911. I ran next door and the woman living there came back to the house with me. By the look on her face when she saw my mom, I knew my mom was dead. The neighbour lady stayed with me until the police came. After they were done asking me questions, they told her to take me back to her house until a social worker arrived. She helped me pack up some clothes. That's all I was allowed to take, and I was never allowed to go back to get anything else. I was really scared because I didn't know what was going to happen to me. I was so young, but some memories never leave." Finn became quiet once again. His face showed the anguish these painful memories brought back.

Kit watched as Finn struggled. Kit guessed he had deeper secrets. She remained silent, knowing the boy needed to talk. Kit smiled with encouragement.

When he finally spoke, his voice was flat, so unemotional. Finn's brow was creased with a frown as he took a deep breath, "My mom did the best she could, but it wasn't always good at home. Sometimes I would go to school with an empty lunch kit so the teachers wouldn't know there was no food in our house. I didn't want my mom to get in trouble. She was all I had. Sometimes, I didn't go to school because I had to take care of her. There were times she was so out of it she would sleep all day or vomit in her sleep. I didn't always know what to do. She left a lot, and I never knew how long she'd be gone. Sometimes she wouldn't come home at night. Sometimes she'd come back with a man. Mama used to be happy, but that changed once the men started coming around. There were lots of different men. I never liked any of them. They would drink and do drugs. One time one of them struck Mama with the back of his hand. I tried to stop him from hurting her, but she pushed me away and yelled at me to go to my room. I could hear him slapping her even with my door closed. I was too little to stop him. Other times, I would hear yelling, but I was too afraid to leave my room. Some nights I was afraid to go to sleep." Finn had lain awake many nights fearful of what might happen.

Kit fell into her own silence. She closed her eyes as the urge to cry swept over her. There was nothing Kit could say to ease the pain this young boy had experienced. When she spoke, she changed the direction of the conversation. "How old are you now?"

"Eleven, I will be twelve in a couple of months."

"Have you been in foster care the whole time?"

"No. I was in a group home for a while." His voice had dropped to an agonizing whisper.

"Was that better?"

Finn shrugged again, obviously uncomfortable with such personal conversation. "Yes and no. At least you weren't alone." The words were spoken with chilling indifference. They were no more than a statement of fact.

Kit felt Finn withdraw. "We all have things in our life that are difficult to talk about. When we share them, others can hopefully understand us better." When Finn remained silent, Kit asked, "Why did you run away and how did you get away from your foster home without them knowing."

Finn gazed at Kit with troubled eyes. With a look of despair he explained, "I planned it for days. I knew the rest of the family was going away for the weekend, and I wasn't included. They always had an excuse not to take me, but I was too young to be left on my own overnight. I overheard them talking about using a respite home. It's available if foster parents want a break. When Leo, another foster boy, left my first foster home to go to a respite home he never came back. Nobody told me why and I knew better than to ask. I remember thinking if I ever had to go to one I would run away. When I heard Mr. Unger say the case worker would be out the next day, I was ready. After they went to bed, I packed what I could in my backpack along with some food and waited until daylight and left." Finn sighed as he shook his head in resignation, "I thought the first foster home was bad. Living with the Ungers was worse." Finn's fears were deeply ingrained. He grew silent, declining to go into detail.

Kit had listened intently. She understood the impact of Finn's last words. She knew there was a lot left unsaid. She could see it in the desperate way he looked at her. The hardness in the young boy's voice stabbed through Kit's heart. "It's going to be okay. I promise."

Finn looked away. He had no reason to believe her. "I don't want to talk about this anymore," Finn said mournfully. There was enough snap in his voice to terminate the discussion.

"Then we won't. Just know what happened with your foster parents lies with them, not you." Kit turned away so he wouldn't see her tears. This poor boy had been abandoned before his mother had even died. Finn had endured a lot in his young life, and he was hurting inside. Kit wanted to hold him to comfort him like she did her own children but knew she couldn't.

Finn's tone changed, now laced with anger, "The whole foster care system is screwed up and you can't count on anyone. You grow up fast when you're an orphan. People are only nice when they want something. With the Ungers, it's all about the money." Responding to Kit's surprised reaction he said, "Just stating facts. You wouldn't understand. Your life is perfect. The perfect family. Mother, father, daughter, son." His voice carried a thread of resentment.

Kit's heart went out to Finn, feeling the boy's anguish, and hearing the resentment. Instead of being upset, Kit was understanding. "I'm glad you see us that way, but my life has been far from perfect." Kit had no desire to bring up painful memories but sometimes it was necessary. "I do understand. I didn't come from a conventional family. My mom was a party girl, and she didn't change after I was born. She had always been a rebellious child growing up and defiant when she became a parent. She wasn't about to let having a child change her life. Like your mother, she was unwilling to leave her world of parties. Unlike you, I still had my grandmother. I thought it was my fault my mother always left. She didn't love me enough to stay. She was never a real mother to me. She never accepted that role. Not everyone has a perfect mother." Kit paused, trying to deal with the unexpected wave of sorrow brought on by the memories. Some pain you can't bury deep enough. The bitterness toward her mother was gone but the hurt and anger occasionally surfaced. Today was one of those days. Kit resented being abandoned by her mother. Why did mothers continue to hurt their children with their selfishness? "My mother told me my father had died before I was born. She died when I was young, and I continued to live with my grandmother. After my grandmother died, I found my birth certificate and my mother's journals in the attic. She had lied about my dad being dead. Based on what I found I decided to come up to Canada to find my father. I had nothing to lose. If something were to happen to me what would happen to my daughter. Even though I was terrified, I had to find my dad if he was out there."

Finn was confused, "What about your husband?"

"Trace is not Kenzie's birth father. He adopted her when we got married. Kenzie was five by then. My first husband, Mike, was killed while I was expecting Kenzie. She never knew her dad either." Kit hoped by sharing some facts about Mike it would help Finn to trust her and open up more. "Mike was abandoned when he was young, and he grew up in foster care. I understand how bad some foster families can be. Mike shared his darkest secrets with me. He shared the horror stories about living with different families and eventually living on the streets. He grew up tough and angry, just like you. As soon as Mike was old enough, he joined the military. By the time I met him he had let his anger go but it took him a long time. You have to understand the choices you make now can have long-term effects."

Finn gave Kit another of his intense looks. His expression hardened. "You also learn tough lessons living in foster homes. I leaned you can't trust anyone."

Kit felt Finn suddenly withdraw. A wave of sadness washed over her. "It's important for you to understand when you have the right people around you and you know you are safe trust can be rebuilt."

Finn broke down. "Everyone kept telling me my mom was a bad person. My foster parents kept saying I better listen, or I'd end up like my mother. I thought that meant I was bad, too. I grew up thinking I didn't deserve love." The poor boy's emotions spilled over, and Finn wrapped his thin arms around Kit and cried.

"It's all right, Finn," Kit said gently. "You will stay here with us while we figure things out." It had been an enlightening conversation. Kit knew Finn would need all the compassion she could give him.

Kenzie was full of questions when she got home from school. After Kit filled her in with basic details, she heard Kenzie and Finn talking in the living room. Kenzie was drilling Finn with questions without much success. Kenzie may not have understood everything, but she knew Finn was scared. "You can stay here. Mommy and Daddy will take care of you."

Finn's face was bleak, eyes anguished. "That's not up to your parents but I won't run away from here." *Not yet anyway.*

Because Finn still looked sad, Kenzie asked, "What makes you happy?"

Finn said nothing because he didn't know how to answer. He couldn't remember the last time he'd been happy.

Kenzie, expecting a response, waited. Instead, Finn left and went up to his room. She stared after him, thinking he was rude. She was too innocent to understand.

That night when Kit tucked Kenzie into bed, Kit was searching for the words to explain to an eight-year-old child not everyone has parents who love them.

Kenzie's small face was serious with concern. Finn's arrival was impacting all of them. "Finn is really sad, Mama. I heard him crying in his room. Finn will be okay because you always know how to make us feel better. Can he stay with us?"

"Finn isn't a stray dog that we can keep." *But he's been kicked around like one.* "Dad and I will have to talk to some grownups to decide what is best for him."

Once the children were asleep. Trace called his mother to come over to talk. They wanted her opinion as to the best way to move forward. Trace and Kit were in heavy conversation when Lola arrived. Together, they shared the few details Finn was willing to share. "As you can see, we don't have a lot to go on. Kit was able to get the name of the Foster Agency and the name of his foster parents. Kit called the agency to make an appointment and was able to get one for tomorrow morning. Would you be able to watch the kids, especially the runaway, while we go into Calgary and talk with the authorities involved?"

Lola understood the complexity of the situation. An angry young boy's future was at stake. She was quick to agree, "Fortunately, it's harder to run away when you're stuck out here in the country. If any of his story is true, he is at least safe here. God guided us here with his hand. I think God guided Finn here as well." They all hoped the frightened boy upstairs was making most of this up and was only looking for attention. Kit prayed they were lies. If not, the boy's life had been a nightmare. Kit and Trace thought of their own children sleeping upstairs. As parents, they would give their lives to protect them.

After Lola left, Kit went upstairs to check on the children. She noticed that Finn's bedroom light was still on. She knocked lightly but there was no answer. Kit entered quietly. Finn was curled up, fast asleep and his undershirt had ridden up. The poor boy's back was bruised, and welts were visible. Kit gently pulled it down. Struggling to control her emotions, she covered him, leaned over him and kissed his forehead. Her heart hurt for the poor boy. "You're safe, Finnigan Morgan Doyle." The boy didn't stir, even as Kit wiped the tear that had fallen on his cheek. Vision blurred; Kit left the light on when she slipped out of the room. As Kit was going out the door, deep in thought, she all but collided with Trace. He noticed her tears and followed her as she walked back downstairs. They sat down beside each other on the couch and Trace took Kit into his arms. She told him what she had seen. What had this boy had to endure in his young life?

The vulnerable image of Finn crouched in the corner of the stall kept popping into Trace's head all day. Trace regretted his earlier abruptness with Finn.

They were silent for a long time, troubled by the events of the day. It had been an upsetting day. "I'm sure the next few days are going to be trying while decisions are made as to what to do with the boy." Kit was also dealing with anger due to the cruelty the young boy had experienced. She knew he had inner secrets, but she hadn't expected this. Long after Trace had gone to bed, Kit was still up. Her thoughts remained on Finn. She was concerned that tomorrow was going to be a hard day on all of them, life-changing for some. This was a complex situation.

Finn had spent a restless night thinking about the unknown future that lay ahead of him. What if he had to go back to the Ungers. His mind was filled with panic as he joined the Grayson family in the kitchen. The atmosphere was tense. Finn's immediate reaction to Lola was one of mistrust. A level of trust had not been established by anyone.

It was a quiet drive into the city. Trace and Kit didn't know what to expect or how to present a case on Finn's behalf. They had so little to go on. They were anxious as they entered the office at the agency. The woman who greeted them extended her hand, "I'm Margaret Sloan." She smiled but her smile didn't emit much warmth. "Please have a seat. Due to the urgency of this situation, I changed my calendar so I could meet with you this morning. I will be meeting with the Ungers after lunch. I was surprised by your call. The Ungers didn't report that Finn was missing. How did he end up at your place?"

Trace explained, but when he was done, he added, "Finn says he left because Mr. Unger is both verbally and physically abusive."

Margaret Sloan gave Trace a doubtful look, "The Ungers have been foster parents for years. They have dealt with problem children before. When it comes to foster children, we don't know what to believe. According to his file, Finn tends to lie, and his defiant behaviour gets him in trouble. He is always acting out, but this is the first time he ran away. You have already seen for yourself that Finn makes impulsive choices and poor decisions. Next time, it will be something else. We've been down this road before with Finn."

Both Graysons were disappointed by her response. Trace Grayson was a man who took nothing at face value, so he challenged back, "Did anyone ask Finn why he acts out? There has to be a reason. I'm inclined to believe Finn, at least about most of what he's saying. If his foster parents were loving and caring, why wouldn't they have reported him missing? Maybe the Ungers have kept other occurrences like this to themselves."

Margaret Sloan had to admit this was a valid point, one she would address with the Ungers when she met with them. This caused her to pause for a moment. Before either of the Graysons had a chance to voice further concerns. Margaret steered the conversation in another direction. "Has Finn told you anything about his past and why he is in foster care?"

Kit answered, "Finn didn't share a lot, just bits and pieces. He shared more about his mother, her lifestyle and how she died. Can you tell us a little about Finn's history after his mother died?"

Mrs. Sloan was surprised Finn shared as much as he did about his mother and his homelife. "Keeping family together is a priority, as long as they are safe. We know not every child is born into a loving, protective environment. Abandoned children are always a concern because they are often deeply troubled. The more traumatic their experiences have been, whether at home or in foster care, the worse their fears become. In the beginning they often go into group homes until we can find a foster parent. That's how Finn entered the system. The Ungers aren't Finn's first foster home. We don't always find the right fit the first time. We do our best but foster care is arguably one of the most broken systems in our country. Things slip through the cracks so often times foster kids end up in homes that neglect their basic needs."

A shadow crossed Kit's face as she thought about what she saw last night, "It's evident Finn is frightened and angry and he has every reason to be."

Margaret sighed heavily, "The issue is Finn is intelligent and familiar with the system. He knows a foster home is not a permanent home, and these children don't know where home will be if it doesn't work out."

The Graysons shared an anguished look before Kit interrupted, "No, the issue is Finn isn't safe with the Ungers. He has fresh welts on his back as well as bruises." Kit took out her phone and her hand shook as she showed

Mrs. Sloan the pictures, "Do you need more proof than this? Finn can't go back to the Ungers."

They could tell Margaret was affected by the grim pictures. "Many of these children have been silenced about the trauma they've suffered at the hands of neglectful case workers and horrible foster parents. I will talk to the Ungers this afternoon. We have to consider the possibility it might not have been the Ungers who did this."

Trace had always been a man of action once he made a decision. Taking a deep breath he lowered his voice, "We have not discounted that possibility, either. What if Finn is telling the truth? Under the circumstances, you have only one choice. For the sake of this boy, please let him stay with us for now."

Margaret Sloan could no more resist Trace's charm than any other woman. "I can tell you are both fair and understanding people. You have presented a valid case."

"Does that mean we can keep Finn at our home until me meet again?" With her stomach in knots, Kit clasped her hands together in her lap.

Margaret left the question unanswered for a moment while she considered her response. She recognized there were times unexpected adjustment needed to be made. "We will make an exception for the sake of the boy. Finn can stay with you tonight. My decision moving forward will be based on my interview with the Ungers. They deserve the same opportunity I have given you to present their version of what has transpired over the last few days. I want everyone back here tomorrow morning, including Finn. He will be able to present his version with everyone present. I need to be able to evaluate this case as objectively as possible."

Nothing was resolved, just delayed. They rode back in relative silence knowing they had no control over what happened next. They had presented their case and would have to wait until their meeting. At least for now, Finn could stay with them. Arriving home, Trace and Kit knew a serious conversation was about to ensue and they hoped Finn would be open and honest.

Finn was uneasy when he asked, "Do I get to stay here?"

Finn deserved an honest answer. They weren't prepared to lie, even if it would ease this poor boy's troubled heart. "You can stay tonight, but we are only your temporary guardian. Your file is being reviewed and there is a meeting with the Ungers this afternoon. I'm sure they will have a very different version. We will all go back tomorrow, and you will be asked some very specific questions. You need to be totally honest. That's the only way any of us can help you." Trace wanted to make the situation clear. Finn's answers would matter to all of them. Looking into Finn's eyes, they could see continued fear. He looked away, pretending it didn't matter.

Relief was quickly replaced by doubt. Life had conditioned Finn to expect the worst. He was close to tears as his disappointment surfaced. He knew he needed to share more with the Graysons if he wanted to rely on them for support. Once he opened up, the conversation became enlightening and heartbreaking. Occasionally anger surfaced. "The Ungers did provide me with the basic necessities but nothing more. I had a new set of clothes that were hung away until a case worker would come to visit. Otherwise, I wore their children's hand-me-downs, or we would go to the thrift stores to shop. I was painfully aware this family took me in for no other reason than the money. I was afraid to say or do anything in case I did it wrong and then get punished." Distraught, Finn ran to his room.

The severity of the situation caused Kit's voice to break, "It's repulsive this can happen in this day and age. The system is failing and how many more children are in the same situation?"

Trace was controlling his anger with effort. With a scowl on his face, Trace headed for the back door. He left the house without another word. The kids were in bed before he returned.

Kit could see the mental stress on Trace's face, "What's troubling you? You were gone a long time."

"You know I need to process things before I can make a decision. Things have really changed since yesterday."

Kit gazed up at Trace with tear filled eyes, "That poor boy can't go back to that family and what if his next family is just as bad. Or worse."

Kit might not have said it, but he knew what she wanted. Trace had been playing this scenario back and forth is his own head. "Are you suggesting we foster Finn? Things will change for all of us if we do. What if he runs away from here, too?" Trace's voice sounded a little panicked and full of doubt.

Kit was wise enough to know life could change quickly, and it wasn't always what you expected. Even though she shared Trace's doubts and had her own misgivings, she was willing to take a chance. She believed fostering Finn themselves was the right thing to do. "I don't think we have any other choice. We can't stand by and allow this. We need to be there for this poor boy. Here he will be safe."

Trace gathered Kit in his arms and took a long pause before continuing, "Are you sure about this?"

"Yes," Kit replied without hesitation.

The look Trace gave Kit was guarded, "It won't be easy."

Kit's mind was set. "When have our lives ever been easy? Remember your mom said God guided Finn here for a reason. We have to have faith. We are making the right decision."

Kit continued to amaze Trace. "If they allow it, we'll give it a try and see how accepting he is of us." Because they understood Finn's type of hardship all too well, they would work out the challenges.

Breakfast around the Grayson table was solemn. Lola had joined them since she would be watching Benny while they were gone. They were having their second meeting with Margaret Sloan and this time the Ungers would also be there. No one said it out loud, but they were all anxious.

The fear was back in Finn's eyes when he asked the question that was on everyone's mind, "Are you taking me with you because I'll have to go back to the Ungers?" Finn was terrified of what would happen today. What if everyone believed the Ungers instead of him?

Kit tried to reassure Finn, "That's not up to us, but we will do everything we can to prevent that. We want you to come home with us. Everything will be all right," she said with false brightness. Kit hoped she was right.

Finn drew a deep breath and prepared for the worst. If he had to go back with the Ungers he would run away again and this time he'd make sure nobody would find him. Finn ran his tongue nervously over his lips, "So, what do you think the Ungers will say?"

Kit was as anxious as Finn because she didn't know how to prepare for this any more than Finn did. Her tone was serious when she replied, "I don't know. My grandmother always said to have hope and believe in possibilities."

Trace added, "My mother believes in prayer. I'm sure she's praying for us right now."

The atmosphere driving into the meeting was tense. No one knew what was going to happen or what the final decision would be. Finn anticipated the worst. With his stomach in knots, he withdrew. Finn's face was solemn when they were led into Margaret Sloan's office, but Kit sensed his underlying fear.

The tension grew because the Ungers were twenty minutes late. Wilbur Unger, a tall, stern looking man, headed to the empty chair next to Trace. Hilda Unger, a tiny, timid looking woman, went and sat next to him. She was an expressionless woman with mousey brown hair streaked with gray. It was pulled severely back from her face. Her demeanor was one of submissive resignation. She looked extremely uncomfortable. Neither expressed an apology for their late arrival.

"You don't look very happy to see us, and here we were so glad to hear you were safe. We've been very worried about you." Wilbur spoke all the right words, but his tone was harsh.

Trace shook his head in disbelief. "Is that why you never reported him missing?"

The two men glared at each other. "This isn't the first time the boy has run away. He usually comes back the next day after he has come to his senses," Wilbur declared in a voice that was indifferent and lacked any emotion.

Kit annoyance surfaced, "The boy has a name. It's Finn."

Margaret Sloan raised a questioning eyebrow. "Why is this the first our office is hearing about this, Mr. Unger? Yesterday you implied this was the first time he ran away." Margaret was disappointed that Finn's file had not indicated anything amiss with the Ungers.

Wilbur fixed his gaze on Finn. "We're raising the boy the best we can. We didn't want our Finn to get into trouble. He often plays the poor orphan role. He may simply be playing all of you. He's sneaky and manipulative but we have always been able to deal with his antics." He turned to Finn and spoke with authority, "We're here to take you home."

Finn's face paled at the prospect. "You're not my father and she's not my mother. I won't go with you," he said with defiance.

"You will do exactly as I say," Wilber corrected. He turned to his wife, "Let's go."

Finn sat as far back in his chair as possible and didn't move. The others couldn't hide their startled expression.

Wilbur was unable to control his temper, "There, you saw it for yourself. This is the defiant behaviour we have to deal with."

"Is Finn always this defiant?" Margaret added, attempting to obtain more information. The whole time she had been observing Finn closely and had been aware of the boy's wariness.

Wilbur didn't hesitate to reply, "You have no idea."

Finn turned to Mrs. Sloan and threw caution to the wind. "If you make me go with them, I will run away again." His eyes were surprisingly direct and so were his words.

Margaret Sloan looked pointedly at Finn, "Will you run away from the Graysons if you go there?"

"No, I'm not afraid of them." His comment said it all and Margaret Sloan understood. A challenging spark remained in Finn's eyes as they shifted back to his foster parents. Finn was going to say something more but seeing the look on his foster father's face caused him to shrink back as Wilbur leaned forward.

Wilbur's eyes narrowed in an intimidating manner. Finn had seen that expression too many times. Finn was afraid when he got that look in his eyes. The tears smarting behind Finn's eyes were dangerously close to spilling over and Finn didn't want to give any of them the satisfaction of seeing him cry.

Margaret had been observing everyone closely, occasionally writing in her file. Even though the boy was openly defiant, she was seeing much more. She documented the panic she saw in the boy's eyes at the prospect of having to go back with the Ungers. She was stunned by the scene that was playing out in front of her. She struggled to keep her voice steady, "Finn, I want to hear what you have to say. You are safe here so you can tell me anything." She hadn't missed the increased fear that crossed Finn's face every time Wilbur Unger spoke.

Finn didn't deserve the abuse, but he had always accepted it from his foster parents because he felt like a burden and at least he had a home. Today, Finn took a breath for courage and opened up as resentment and anger from years of abuse poured out. The flood gates had opened. The bitterness in his voice was heavy as he confessed to the beatings he'd taken, the verbal abuse, the sparse meals.

"According to the Ungers, they said you were having trouble adjusting."

Finn offered no denial. "There was a definite divide in the house. Them and me. When I did complain, the case worker didn't take it seriously. My foster parents said I was a liar and she believed them. After she left, I was taught a hard lesson. It was the first time he hit me, but it wasn't the last time. I always wore long-sleeved tops and long pants to hide any physical signs of abuse." A familiar look in Wilbur's face made Finn want to flee, but he wasn't about to give him the satisfaction of intimidating him. Finn refused to react. He knew this was his only chance to speak the truth. Finn lifted his chin and continued, "When Mr. Unger was mean and abusive, Mrs. Unger would go to her room. I think he was mean to her, too." Finn's expression remained set and hostile.

Wilbur Unger was visibly infuriated. His face was red, and his breathing laboured. He glared at Finn, daring him to say anything more.

Finn met Wilbur's gaze with courage. He hesitated for a moment before continuing, "The Ungers were always very clear about how I was to behave when the case worker was there. There were lots of fake smiles and scripted answers. I was to say as little as possible and when they asked, I was to say I was happy living there. It was all a lie."

Trace was impressed by the boy's courage to not back down.

"That's a fine tale you're spinning, but I think everyone has heard enough. We're done listening to your lies." Wilbur got up and grabbed at Finn, "We're done here. Get up so we can get out of here and go home."

Wilbur's actions caught Finn off-guard. Fear flashed in Finn's eyes like an animal backed into a corner and he pulled away.

"Keep your hands off of Finn," Kit cried out in disgust. It never failed to amaze Trace the way Kit went after what she wanted. Today, she sought justice for the poor boy sitting beside her. The despondency in Finn's voice pained Kit. Her cheeks were flushed by held back temper, "Finn never displayed any fear with us, and we have seen the welts and bruises on Finn's body."

Wilbur looked at the Graysons, "You don't like me very much, do you?"

Trace was trying not to interrupt, but Wilbur Unger's behaviour had been grating on his nerves and he finally had enough. Trace took a deep breath for control, but his voice had a hard edge when he turned and faced the irate man. A muscle twitched in Trace's face, indicating anger that wasn't firmly under control. His face darkened, but he controlled himself as he shot the man a look of pure disgust, "You're wrong. We don't like you at all."

"Gentlemen, let's keep this meeting civil." Margaret's authoritative voice indicated that this type of confrontation was unacceptable.

"Can we take a ten-minute break?" Kit wanted to give Trace a chance to get his temper under control and not say something he'd later have cause to regret. A display of temper wouldn't help their case.

Margaret didn't reply. Instead, she pressed a button and a young lady entered. "Finn, this is Tanya. You can go with her while I talk with the adults alone."

Finn stood hovering in the doorway, directing his look to Mrs. Sloan, "I don't want to go if you're all going to gang up on me." The insecure child was back.

When Finn looked at Kit, she reassured him, "Nobody's going to gang up on you. Mrs. Sloan is doing her best to understand it would be best to have you come back with us." Everyone, including Trace, was shocked by Kit's declaration. The atmosphere continued to be tense. A flicker of hope followed Finn as he left.

Throughout the meeting Margaret Sloan had been studying everyone through eyes that missed very little. She entered another note in her file before focusing her gaze at the Ungers. With simple candor she stated, "There is no need to continue this meeting. Finn will not be going home with you. His case worker will be out to pick up his belongs."

Wilbur Unger's eyes went cold as reality hit. His voice rose with indignation, "Good riddance. He was too much trouble anyway." He turned to his wife who got up and meekly followed him out. She had not spoken a word.

Yesterday, Margaret had done her research on the Graysons to gather as much information on them as possible. She liked being prepared for any scenario when presented. She was not surprised when they asked if they could be Finn's foster parents. Her voice turned earnest, "Let's get down to business in regard to what is best for Finn. You have made quite an impression on Finn, especially you, Mrs. Grayson. You must understand if you're going to take over this responsibility you need to know what you may be up against. My purpose in telling you this is to make you both aware of the challenge you would be taking on. Finn has a lot of pent-up anger. Due to hormonal changes and his additional challenges, he may show mood swings, low self-esteem, depression, and aggression. There are also legal considerations. I'll do what I can to hurry it along but there are specific requirements to becoming a foster parent. Our organization will have to see if you are eligible."

"What does that entail?" Trace asked.

"The first thing will be for both of you to provide a criminal record check."

"We can do that on our way home and bring it back with us at our next meeting."

"You'll need first aid training."

"We both have that as well as CPR training. We have first aid kits in the house, out in the barn and in our vehicles. We also have fire alarms and extinguishers in all of our buildings."

Margaret was impressed. "I'm sure you're aware Finn can be very stubborn. It's not going to get better overnight. You have admitted he doesn't open up easily."

Kit was quick to reply in Finn's defense, "I think that's a natural reaction. Why would he trust anyone right now? You're doing the right thing."

Margaret refrained from comment. She thought the agency had done the right thing when they placed Finn with the Ungers. "Finn has issues, trust being only one of them."

Kit remained optimistic, "We will deal with his issues as they arise, just like we do with our own children."

"School is another problem. We will provide you with a copy of his school reports. They show Finn is behind academically."

Trace quickly entered into the conversation, "That won't be a concern. I don't think putting Finn into the school system right now is the answer. He will be dealing with enough changes. My mother lives at the ranch and growing up she often homeschooled both me and my brother. I'm sure she can get Finn caught up academically before September. Then Finn will go to the same school our daughter goes to. My mother is fearless, capable, and dogged. She will be the boss and I'm sure she will get Finn caught up in no time. Kit also earned a teaching degree before she moved to Alberta. We will all work together to help Finn adjust to his new home and our family life."

There was an intense expression on Kit's face as she added, "It's not Finn's fault that he's the way he is. I don't think he's a bad boy. My husband was vocal earlier because he felt protective for the boy. Trace is a fine man, and a good husband and father."

"How may children do you have?"

Trace responded with pride, "We have two children, Kenzie is eight and Benny is two. We are a mixed family. I married Kit and adopted Kenzie. Her real dad died before she was born. Kenzie has always known she was adopted but I am her dad."

"Finn is an untamed youth who is strong-willed and reckless. I don't know if that will change. He'll test your boundaries and push back on rules."

Kit smiled, "They do that at every age. We recognize Finn is confused and probably scared right now. He will need time to adjust to this new change. We all will."

Margaret comforted the Graysons by detailing her decision, "Finn will be assigned a new case worker. You will come back here to meet her and share how Finn adjusts. Finn will not be present, as we want you to be open and honest, especially in regard to his behaviour. Once that happens, she will go out to the ranch and follow up and see for herself how he is doing. There will be times when she will come unannounced."

"That will be fine. She is welcome anytime. What's going to be done about the Ungers?"

"Their file has been flagged. They won't be allowed to foster any more children." Margaret Sloan had a few final words for the Graysons. In a softer voice she added, "Good luck, I think you'll need it. The boy will be a challenge for sure."

"Thank you." The smile that crossed Kit's face was one of relief.

Margaret rang for Tanya to bring Finn back in. "You will go back with the Graysons to their ranch. You've been given a chance to live with a wonderful family. They are good people. You will be safe living with your new family. Make it work this time."

Finn didn't utter a word; he just nodded. The look on his face was thanks enough. His eyes no longer had a wounded look. Finn was able to hold back his tears, but he couldn't contain a tremendous sigh of relief.

After the meeting was adjourned and the Graysons closed the door behind them, Margaret Sloan sat back in her chair and wondered what kind of an impact this young boy would have on their lives. She hoped this would be a permanent placement.

That night Lola joined Trace and Kit and they shared the news with her. They filled her in on what happened at the meeting.

Lola was deeply affected. She would do whatever she could to help. Lola did have to wonder what kind of a challenge she had taken on with her offer to homeschool Finn.

Trace looked at his mom, "You know he's headstrong."

Lola smiled, "I'm used to that."

Later that evening, when Kit walked by Finn's room, she noticed the light was off. He was settling in.

CHAPTER FIVE

I t was Monday morning and Kenzie had already caught the school bus. Finn knew his school day was about to start as well. Even though he was glad to be reassigned to the Graysons, and he had met Lola who would be teaching him, he was filled with a new fear. He was afraid to confirm to anyone how far behind he really was.

Finn jumped when Trace spoke, "Everyone has chores around here. One of yours will be to take out the garbage since you already know where the bin is." Trace had hoped to coax a bit of a smile out of Finn with a little humor but failed miserably. Instead, Finn's scowl darkened. He grumbled when Trace handed him the garbage bag but didn't argue. "I'll walk you over to Ma's. You will be with her mornings from nine until noon and go back from one until four. She is going to work hard to get you caught up." Finn said nothing as they crossed the yard and walked upstairs to Lola's suite.

When the boy lingered in the doorway Lola told him to come in and sit down at the table. With a feeling of nervousness Finn obeyed and Lola went and sat in the chair next to him. Lola had reviewed Finn's school files and realized the notes were vague and most likely subjective. She would do her own assessment. "Your school file contains limited information so this morning we will try to determine where you are academically in your core subjects." Every subject she opened for review was met by defiant silence. Their gaze locked briefly, but Finn didn't back down. Finn refused to participate. Lola had expected him to be nervous. Instead, he was downright stubborn. Lola could recognize a challenge when she saw one. The boy had the better of her, for now. So much for her misplaced optimism. Lola didn't know who was more grateful when they broke for lunch. It had been a trying morning. There was no doubt that Finn was going to be a challenge. Because her efforts weren't working, disappointment swept through her. Over lunch, Lola prayed to find a way to get through the day and connect with the defiant youth. She had no idea what to do with him. Her own boys had never challenged her like this.

When Finn returned after lunch, Lola knew it wasn't going to get any better. She sat down next to him. He glanced at her. Fully aware of her displeasure, he crossed his arms over his chest. With firmly set lips, he continued to give her the silent treatment. His expression remained set and hostile, so the tension continued to build throughout the day. Finn was totally bored, but refused to give in. He continued to sit there like he was set in stone, and the hours passed painfully slow. The day seemed endless. Four o'clock didn't come quick enough for either of them. It brought a momentarily sense of relief, but tomorrow was another day.

Lola looked over to see Finn's shrewd gaze watching her. The boy had done nothing; therefore, she had achieved nothing. She threw Finn an exasperated look, which he ignored. Tired and discouraged, Lola stated coldly, "Well Finn, if I have to give you a grade based on today it would be an A for stubbornness. Understand this, you are stuck with me, and my perseverance will outlast your stubbornness. You can decide how tomorrow goes but you will be back even if Trace has to drag you up the stairs. Your only assignment tonight is to work on your attitude. See you tomorrow at nine." Lola added a hard glare so Finn would understand she meant what she said. She had anticipated there would be difficulties and she was willing to deal with anything. She hadn't anticipated this. Finn may be stubborn, but Lola was no less determined.

Lola had no sooner sat down when Trace knocked. It had been a long day for Trace. He had been wondering how Finn was with his mother. Trace noticed Lola's frustrated look as they watched Finn stomp cross the yard. "Problems with Finn?"

Lola nodded, too angry to speak. Lola thought she was prepared for this. She was dead wrong. Did she really need this stress in her life?

"What did he do?"

Lola threw her hands up in the air and gave an exasperated groan, "It's what he didn't do. He just sat there unwilling to say a word, let alone do anything. The boy is incredibly stubborn so that's my problem." Oh well, she'd dealt with stubborn before.

"You'll need more patience," Trace teased.

Lola made no attempt to hide her irritation, "This isn't funny, Trace. Besides, I have prayed for patience every day since the day you were born."

Trace laughed, but hadn't failed to notice her look of concern, "What do you think his problem is?"

"I'm sure Finn is embarrassed because he knows he's behind in his schooling. Beneath his rebellious behaviour, he's confused, and angry. I'm irritated with his behaviour and frustrated because I'm not sure what to do. Hopefully, I can figure something out by tomorrow. This is between Finn and me so don't confront him, just make sure he comes back tomorrow. Let me deal with this."

Trace nodded and gave his mom a quick kiss on her cheek. "Good luck." They all knew it would be challenging in the beginning.

Kit was in the kitchen preparing supper when Finn walked in. She smiled at him, "How was your day?"

"Great. Can't wait to go back," Finn snapped as he stormed off to his room.

The tone of his voice was unacceptable, but Kit let him go. She waited for the door to slam, which it did. She would find time to talk to Lola after supper.

Mealtime was tense. Finn was relieved that nobody mentioned school. He was surprised and confused knowing Trace had gone upstairs and had likely been filled in on how the day went. Finn didn't know what to expect tomorrow. Or even tonight.

After supper Kit slipped over to Lola's. They sat discussing Finn over a pot of tea. Lola vented, "I'm sure once we establish a level of trust his wall will come down. That in itself will be a big challenge. He hasn't had much reason to trust the adults around him. As they say, tomorrow is a new day," Lola said with a weary sigh.

After Kit left, Lola stared out her bedroom window at the darkening sky. She gazed toward the distant mountains, an expression of disappointment on her face. Lola hated the fact that the boy had gotten the better of her.

She thought having two boys and homeschooling them had prepared her for this. She replayed portions of the day in her mind. There wasn't much to recall and there was no glimmer of hope. Before she retired, Lola decided on her plan of attack for tomorrow. She would keep challenging Finn until he responded. She didn't care how. She just needed to connect with him. Lola was again optimistic.

Day two. God, please guide me, Lola prayed as she heard Finn coming up the stairs. Lola greeted Finn with a smile when she opened the door. It was a new day, a fresh start.

Finn's jaw was set stubbornly. He walked by Lola and sat down at the table. He looked at her and turned his chair, so his back was to her. Finn was too stubborn to concede. His expression remained set and hostile, but he sensed Lola watching him. He waited, not sure what she would do.

This was an unexpected move. Lola wasn't sure if she wanted to laugh or cry. She didn't know what to do, but she wasn't about to have another day like yesterday. Yesterday she had felt sorry for the poor kid. Today, she was mad. Lola decided to address the situation and get right to the point. Even though she took a deep breath, her voice came out more clipped than she intended, "We can have the same kind of day as yesterday. Your choice, but you're sitting there the whole time. And you're coming back again tomorrow and the day after that." The look on her face was uncompromising.

Finn made no acknowledgement that he even heard her. Aware of Lola's constant gaze but refusing to meet it, he spoke not a word all morning. Like a trained dog he returned after lunch and went and sat back in his chair.

Lola glared at Finn and the boy didn't flinch. *This kid doesn't give an inch.* She studied Finn with concern as she struggled internally. The minutes had to be dragging for him. They certainly were for her. The afternoon was the same as the morning, which was the same as yesterday. *A+ for stubbornness.* She looked at the clock, grateful to see that it was finally four o'clock. Another unproductive day filled with long hours. Two days in and it had already seemed like a week. Even though Finn had obstinately stayed quiet he hadn't managed to deter her, but Lola was definitely at the end of her patience. She didn't lose many battles, but

Finn was good. When Finn got up to leave and headed to the door, she blocked his way, "How can I help you when you won't participate? I need to know where you are academically to move forward." Lola was more than frustrated with his attitude.

"I'm sure you've read my files," Finn retaliated with sarcasm. The boy was not going down without a fight.

Well neither was Lola. She gave Finn an assignment. "Since you didn't do anything today in class time you have a homework assignment. I want you to describe family and I want it handed in tomorrow." Hopefully, that might reveal more to her. She had to try something.

For a moment, Finn's composure slipped. He hadn't missed the firmness in her voice. As usual he didn't respond and was glad to make his escape. He went up to his room as soon as he got home. He decided to let the Graysons know exactly what family meant to him. They might not like it, but he didn't care.

Lola spent another long night analyzing the last two days while trying to figure out an approach that would reach him.

Day three. God help me. Lola refused to admit she was failing; she just wasn't succeeding. As soon as Finn took his seat at the table, he folded his arms, refusing to meet her gaze. Lola decided today was going to be different one way or another. It was time to get real with the kid. She grabbed Finn's arm so he would have to look at her. The older woman's eyes challenged Finn. "I'll admit you have managed to frustrate me, but I'm done with your attitude. If you don't cooperate, they will take you away. You know who 'they' are."

Finn shot her a nervous look but didn't say anything. He didn't want that, but he was embarrassed because he didn't want them to know how stupid he was. All he had ever heard was that he was stupid. He didn't want to prove it to this family.

It was almost noon and Finn hadn't caved. Lola's expression was one of pure exasperation. "Whatever your feelings are toward me doesn't much matter to me. Is it that you don't like me?"

"I don't know you," Finn pointed out.

With a calmness she was far from feeling, Lola continued, "True enough. How about today you and I just talk. What are you interested in?"

"I don't like talking," was Finn's only response.

With a heavy sigh Lola leaned forward in her chair and rested her elbows on the table. "Since you choose not to participate, I am going to share a few things with you, and you can just sit there and listen. Growing up, my boys were teased and bullied. They had to deal with it all their lives. They wore thrift store clothes. Trace's younger brother wore Trace's hand-me-downs. Often the jeans had patched knees because Trace had already worn them through. Children have enough problems without being teased or bullied. My boys had to deal with it year after year. They were homeschooled more than once. Fortunately, they had me. You also have me, Finn. I'm not going to give up on you and you do need my help. Whether either one of us likes it or not, that's the way it is. If you talk to me, I can help. We all have difficulties throughout our lives. I would like to say that changes when you get older, but it doesn't. You just learn to deal with it. I found talking to someone does help. What's bothering you, Finn?"

Finn shrugged his shoulders, "Why should I talk to you about anything. Nobody listens. I finally got the courage to talk to my case worker, but she never did anything about it. So why should I believe you?"

Lola didn't miss the look of defeat in Finn's eyes, but she refused to overlook his continued rudeness. Lola threw it right back at him, "Why shouldn't you?"

Finn didn't know how to respond to that. He looked at the clock with a look of relief. He looked directly at Lola, "Since it's lunch time I think we are done." He glared at her with tears in his eyes and stormed out, escaping further questioning.

Lola's eyes darkened at Finn's angry retort. "This isn't over. Be back at one," Lola yelled after him as he stomped down the stairs. Lola took a deep breath and shook her head. Finn was proving to be more of a challenge then she imagined. Their morning had upset her. Her shoulders were tense, and she had a headache. Her approach this morning hadn't worked. She crossed over and gazed out at the mountains. She would have to remain just as rigid as they were, or she'd lose control of the situation. Lola did feel a surge of optimism due to the fact that Finn had finally opened up to her, even though it was in anger. Lola felt sorry for Finn, but she didn't deserve the attitude.

Trace was nearby and saw what happened. His lips were pursed, and his jaw was rigid as he made his way over to Finn before he could get to the house. Even though his mom had told him not to interfere, Trace stopped Finn. Lunch could wait. This conversation couldn't. "What's with the attitude?"

Finn shifted uncomfortably as he ignored Trace's question.

Trace gave Finn a challenging look, waiting for him to say something. Finn remained silent. Trace was disgusted with Finn's rudeness. "Your behaviour is unacceptable. My mother doesn't deserve this. This is a period of adjustment for all of us, not just you. You can start to make an effort."

Finn's distrust was evident, making him defensive, "Why do any of you want to help a screwed up kid like me?"

Trace remained irritated, "You are no more screwed up than I was at your age so lose the attitude, starting now."

Finn lashed out, "You can't tell me what I can or cannot do. You aren't my father and Kit isn't my mother. And that lady upstairs is worse than both of you put together."

Trace's expression hardened, "Are you purposely trying to irritate me? Despite the fact that my mother can be overbearing, you will not be disrespectful. You're hurting everyone by being stubborn, but you're hurting yourself the most. You would be better to learn gratitude to those who want to help you, so don't be giving my mother any more grief. She is under no obligation to put up with you. She is not getting paid to take your abuse. My mother is trying to help you, so the first thing you will do after lunch is go back upstairs and apologize."

Finn fought the urge to retaliate as he glared back at Trace, "Fine." He knew he was in no position to argue.

After lunch, Trace watched Finn stomp up the stairs. The boy continued to worry him. Trace hoped they hadn't taken on a challenge they couldn't handle. When Finn didn't come back out after a few minutes, Trace went back to work.

Lola looked up when Finn walked in.

Finn cleared his throat as he looked at Lola in defeat, "I've been out of line, and I apologize."

Lola stared at him with eyes that were sharp and aware and hesitated a moment before answering, "I accept your apology." Lola wondered what happened during the lunch hour.

Finn decided to relent even if it made everyone realize how stupid he was. "I do need help so if you are still willing, I'm willing as well."

Lola smiled with satisfaction. *Finally.* Now they could move forward. She figured the boy was smart. "Why don't you tell me why you are behind in your schoolwork."

Finn recognized the concern in her voice. When he raised his eyes, they were surprisingly direct and so was the anguished remark that followed, "I'm stupid."

Displaying a bit of temper of her own, Lola snapped at Finn in a voice he had never heard from her, "Don't say that."

"Why not," Finn challenged. "That's what everyone says. You've seen my files."

"You are not stupid." Lola grabbed her iPad and pulled up the definition of stupid. "The definition here says you would be lacking ordinary quickness and keenness of mind. It means you are dumb or unintelligent." She smiled wryly, "You may be dumb at times because that means lacking good judgement. By definition, you don't really believe you're stupid, do you?"

Finn finally accepted defeat and shook his head.

"Good. Now let's get down to business." Lola's voice held an underlying authority that Finn couldn't ignore. Lola attempted to help Finn feel at ease, so she asked a few general questions. Lola's thoughtfulness paid off and Finn began to open up.

Finn shared what his schooling had been like. "Before I went into foster care, I missed school because I had to stay home and take care of my mom. Near the end, I missed a lot of school and fell behind. The authorities were even threatening to take me away from my mom. After she died, I went into foster care. At the Ungers, their children had iPads and the parents had a laptop, but I wasn't allowed to use them. I didn't always have time to do my homework because I was forced to do a lot of chores. I fell further behind in school, so I was bullied and called stupid. The teachers comments said I was moody and lazy. School became a nightmare."

Lola took a deep breath and let it out. She realized Finn hadn't been given a fair chance. That was about to change. "Tomorrow morning you and I are going on a field trip. We will call it that so it can be documented as an educational day. We are going into the city, and we are getting you your own personal iPad. We aren't going to wait to go through the appropriate channels with your case worker. It would take too long, and we have already lost enough time. To start with, you can only use it for school-related work but at the end of every week we can assess and decide if you have earned some personal time. Does that sound fair to you?"

Finn's face lost it's mask of indifference and he smiled despite his low spirits, "What about at the end of every day?"

Lola met his gaze with a gentle smile. "Nice try. It will stay up here with me. Not because I don't trust you but because I don't want Kenzie or Benny getting into it."

Finn forced his attention away from his misery, "Why do your grandchildren call you Lita, when your name is Lola."

This question surprised Lola but she decided anything that could get Finn to open up to her, even a little, was a start. "Lita is one of the short versions of Abuelita, which is a way to say grandmother in Spanish."

"Are you Spanish?"

"No, Mexican." Lola decided to keep this conversation going. For the next hour she shared information about her past, her move to Canada with her husband and the transient lifestyle they lived until their move to Alberta. Lola was pleased she had finally found something that caught his interest. Maybe not what she expected but she could work with it.

"Would you like to learn Spanish." The boy's eyes finally sparkled with enthusiasm and intelligence. "How about every Friday afternoon we dedicate it to Spanish. It's becoming a language that is used more and more, even around here. The Mexicans are coming up to Canada to find work, In fact, friends of Trace's just hired Hector Ortiz to help on his ranch. I hear they have a son who is your age who will be starting school when you do."

This helped to put Finn at ease. He wouldn't be the only new kid starting in the fall.

By the end of the day, Lola felt they had made progress. Lola recognized Finn was a very intelligent boy. "When we get back from Calgary, we will commit to determining where you are academically. I think maybe you are smarter than your files indicate. I can get you caught up. It's up to you. Let's call it a day and I will see you tomorrow." Lola was exhausted but filled with the pride of accomplishment. If every day was like this one, there was hope on the horizon. Lola stopped Finn before he reached the door and asked for his assignment. Finn reached into his pocket and pulled out a crumpled piece of paper. The single sheet of paper had only five words on it. "Family. All dead. Assignment done." As impressed as she was with his cleverness, those few words spoke volumes. Her heart went out to him, but she kept her face impassive. It had been an intense couple of days. The door closed behind him with a gentle click. Nice change from all the other times he slammed it shut.

The next morning, Kit could tell Finn was excited to be going into town with Lola. Kit kept busy to help pass the time that seemed to drag while they were gone. She even baked cookies as a treat for the kids. It was later in the afternoon by the time Lola and Finn returned. Kit heard them and hoped their trip went well. She was relieved to see them both smiling when they headed up to Lola's suite.

Lola got down to business. This time Finn cooperated when Lola reviewed his academic skills. She was pleasantly surprised. She quickly realized most of the entries in Finn's file were vague and inaccurate. She was confident that Finn would be caught up by the end of summer. Today was a turning point. The afternoon remained productive, and Lola had a better idea on how to move forward.

That night after supper, Kit watched Finn outside playing with Buddy. He was clearly dying for affection but was terrified to accept it from them. She knew it would come in time. Kit also knew she would need patience and understanding. She just didn't realize how soon.

CHAPTER SIX

Kenzie wasn't used to sharing the attention and she didn't always understand Finn's teasing. They were beginning to develop a typical brother-sister relationship, but there had been a lot more squabbling between the two of them lately. Today was worse than usual. Maybe it was because it had been raining for the last couple of days and everyone had been housebound. They were both upstairs, but Kit could hear them clearly.

Kenzie was bored so she went to Finn's room to see what he was doing. She decided Finn spent too much time alone in his room, and he should play with her. The fact that Finn refused and wouldn't let her in was an invitation to trouble. Not that either of them needed an invitation. Kenzie was stubborn and strong-willed. When Finn didn't let her in, she began pounding on the door. "Why can't I come in?"

"Get lost, I don't want you in my room." Finn's voice cracked when he raised his voice. He was at that age.

"Your voice sounds funny. Now it matches your pimply face." Kenzie was purposely being cruel. She wasn't always sweet and loveable.

Finn was quick to react with a shot of his own, "Well, your face looks funny. You look like a Halloween pumpkin when you smile."

"It's not your room so you have to let me in," Kenzie ordered.

"You're not my boss. You're not even my sister," Finn taunted back. Today's fight had taken a nasty turn.

Kenzie had never managed her emotions well, so she became overdramatic. "I'm glad you're not my brother," she shot back.

When their fighting woke Benny from his afternoon nap, Kit had enough. Trace, who had just come in, also heard their raised voices from upstairs. "Sounds like it's just as stormy in here as it is outside."

Kit was far from amused so flashed her husband an angry look. "Those two have been at each other nonstop and now they've woken Benny. He's teething and has been cranky all day. I just got him down." Kit didn't miss Trace's smirk. "Yes, I'm cranky, too."

"Kids fight, Kit."

Trace's indifference made Kit madder. The man could be so infuriating. She was unable to control her flare of annoyance, "You could take this a little more seriously. I've had enough of them squabbling. Lately, that's all they do." Kit stormed upstairs and stepped between them and snapped, "Stop it. You should both be ashamed of yourselves. Kenzie, you can go to your room while I get Benny and take him to your father. You can both stay in your rooms until I come back."

The situation had escalated out of control. Finn's anger at Kenzie spilled over to include everyone. He still felt like an outsider and his feelings were hurt. "You're not my mother and Trace is not my father." Finn scowled at Kenzie as he slammed his door.

Due to sheer stubbornness, Kenzie didn't move. Kit raised her voice, "Get to your room, young lady." With a stubborn set to her chin. Kenzie turned and stomped away. Kit went and grabbed a now wailing Benny and went downstairs. She shoved Benny at Trace with frustration. "Here, watch this one while I go up and deal with the other two since you won't."

Trace merely raised an eyebrow and didn't reply but he knew Kit was now annoyed with him as well. He had always been careful not to get too involved. Besides, she would handle it better. Feeling no guilt, he began bouncing Benny on his knee who began to giggle with joy.

Kit headed to Kenzie's room first. She opened the door and Kenzie was laying face down on her bed. She rolled over and sat up, eager to explain how this was all Finn's fault. "I knocked on Finn's door and he yelled at me to leave him alone."

"Which you didn't do."

Kenzie paused only for a moment, "No. I pounded louder and told him he had to let me in. It's my house, not his."

Kit was unable to hold her anger, "Our house belongs to everyone in it."

Kenzie hadn't missed the note of disapproval. "Even if they aren't really part of our family?" she cried out in confusion.

Kit didn't know how to answer that.

"How come Finn is mean to me at times?"

Kit, grateful for the change of topic, asked her young daughter, "Do you ever tease Benny? Have you made him cry by being mean because you didn't want him around?"

"I suppose so," she admitted, but remained defensive, "Everything is about Finn since he got here."

Kit detected a note of resentment in her daughter's voice. She understood why Kenzie was having difficulty dealing with some of the recent changes in her life. Kit's expression wasn't one of anger but rather one of disappointment, "Do you remember when we brought Benny home. It took all of us time to adjust to our Benny Bear. He needed all our attention and as long as he was fed and dry and got that attention, he was fine. Finn's arrival has been another change for all of us. His arrival was unexpected and now all of us are learning to adjust, including Finn. It's harder for Finn. We have been a family for years and know and love each other. This is all new to him. Do you think it's easy for Finn as he tries to fit in here? He needs time to feel safe. You knew things were going to change for everyone. We've talked about this."

Kenzie loved being the center of attention. "I liked it better when I was the oldest."

"And you like it when I still call you, baby girl." Kit hugged Kenzie and gave her a kiss on the cheek.

"Why is growing up so hard?" Kenzie asked with real despair.

"It can be difficult at any age. We just learn to cope better with age and experience."

Even though Kenzie could be a handful at times, she was raised with good values and her fairness kicked in. She met her mom's gaze and bit back further words of protest. "I'll go say sorry," Kenzie said with great reluctance.

"I want to talk to Finn first. Go set the table for supper. You can come back up after Finn and I have our talk. I love you. You're forgiven for your behaviour, but don't let it happen again." Kit left and knocked gently on Finn's door.

Finn opened the door, walked away, and sat on the end of his bed and waited. Finn had nothing to say for himself. Something Kenzie never had a problem with.

"Kenzie has a history of making a scene and tends to be over dramatic. She has a quick temper and releases her anger without thinking. I heard Kenzie say some hurtful things."

A look of sadness darkened Finn's face, "It wasn't the words that hurt. It hurt because it's true. I live here but I'm not really family."

"We do think of you as part of our family. You do like it here, don't you?"

Finn nodded. The Graysons treated him fair. He even trusted them, but in reality, he wasn't family. His mind kept coming back to that fact. He wanted a real home with a mom, dad, brothers, and sisters. He could even learn to put up with a sister like Kenzie. A shadow crossed Finn's face, "I watch you with your family. I don't fit in?"

This was going to be more challenging than Kit thought. "What are you talking about?"

Over the past few weeks, it had become natural for Finn to confide in Kit. Finn's voice deepened as a flicker of emotion crossed his face, "You don't know what it's like to have no history or happy memories with your family. It didn't bother me so much before because I didn't like my other families." The pain in his voice was evident as Finn stated his truth. Interesting things come out in anger.

Kit hated the look on Finn's face, "Look, Finn, we are all learning how to accept each other. Understanding has to come along with change." Kit knew it was time to share more of her own past with Finn. "Let me tell you how wrong you are." Kit proceeded to tell Finn about her own arrival at Valley View and the struggles and disappointments she experienced in the beginning. "I was worried my father would reject me like my mother did. Even though my dad welcomed me right away not everyone else did, including Trace. I understand frustration and wanting to hurt back. What my mother did to me, and my dad, was despicable. The hurt she caused was deep, and I took my anger out on my dad. I also judged my dad unfairly because of my experiences with my mother. It was unfair but

I couldn't stop myself. Like you, I was scared." When Kit was done, she could see the conversation had a profound effect on Finn. "You are part of this family. You are safe with us, and you can stay with us as long as you want."

Once again his deepest fears took over and Finn gave Kit a long look before commenting, "I'm still not family. This isn't permanent. It never is. They can come and take me away tomorrow." He wished this really was his family, but there was no sense in wanting something that would never be.

Kit continued to talk to Finn in a soothing voice like she used with Kenzie and Benny when they were upset. When she was done, she returned to the reason she was there, "The behaviour between you and Kenzie was unacceptable. If you didn't try so hard to irritate Kenzie it would make it easier on all of us."

"Oh, I don't have to try hard at all." Finn confessed with a wicked grin.

Kit laughed, then told him Kenzie would be up to apologize and this time he was to let her in. Kit headed downstairs. Peace had been restored. Kit wondered how long it would last.

Kenzie was subdued when she headed up the stairs. Apologizing wasn't in her nature. This time she knocked gently before entering. "I'm sorry for being mean. Don't leave us, Finn," Kenzie begged, her jealousy forgotten.

Her apology sounded sincere, but Finn was still hurt. He fought the tremor in his voice, "That's up to your parents, not me." Kenzie looked so crestfallen that Finn felt bad. "I'm sorry for egging you on." He did feel like he was part of their family even though he really wasn't. They went back downstairs together and apologized to Kit and Trace.

Thinking he should take an active roll, Trace ignored the apology and snapped at Finn, "I know it takes two to fight but you are old enough to know better. After supper you can ..." Trace didn't get a chance to finish. An immediate stab of resentment caused Finn to react. The front door slammed on his way out, and they knew Finn was going out to the barn. When Kit groaned with frustration, Trace knew he had made a mistake. "I should have let it go since you had already dealt with it. I told you I'm not good at this parenting thing. I was a jerk, wasn't I?"

Kit nodded, still irritated. "Knowing your flaws is only half the battle. Changing them takes effort."

Trace let out an offended breath as his foul mood darkened. Now he was not only a jerk but also an idiot, according to his wife. "I'll go out and talk to him."

Kit gave him a warning look, "Give him a chance to cool down."

Kenzie didn't understand what was going on. "Is Finn in trouble again?" "Why?"

"Because you have your mad face on."

Kit managed a reassuring smile, "It's more a case of being troubled, Kenzie. Everything will be fine. Finn's living here requires patience and understanding from all of us. Some of us have more than others."

Trace knew her remark was intended for him. He also knew it was better to remain silent.

Kit continued, her voice serious, "You know what I think, Trace?"

This time, Trace was unable to control his flare of annoyance, "I'm not interested in what you think."

Kit narrowed her eyes; an expression Trace had seen more times than he could count. A thread of anger remained, "I'll tell you anyway."

No longer able to keep his voice calm, Trace snapped, "I don't have time for this. Besides, why would I even try to talk to Finn? It's like having words with a fence post. How come you and Lola are getting through to him and I'm not?"

Kit hesitated, knowing her next comment would anger Trace, "You intimidate him."

Trace shrugged his shoulders because he didn't know how to deal with Finn. He didn't want any part of this conversation. Trace started to walk away like he usually did.

"I'm not through talking with you. Besides, I think the barn is already occupied by someone else who is dealing with his frustration. You're going about this all wrong. Finn is like Diego. When you got Diego, he was young and needed to be trained. He was a temperamental stallion who was strong with a mind of his own. Well, Finn is also headstrong. I think at times your approach is wrong with Finn. You worked slowly with Diego because you didn't want to break his spirit. Like Diego, we don't want to break Finn's spirit while we rein him in. You need to go slow and have patience with Finn while you get to know him."

"There was an immediate connection between me and Diego that was tangible. Something I had never experienced before. Finn and I have no connection."

Kit's tone turned to one of concern, "You may not have that connection yet, but don't always judge Finn so harshly and so quickly. Go slow and give the boy time to adjust."

Their conversation ended when Finn came back in for supper. Hardly a word was spoken. After supper, Trace grabbed his hat. Without so much as a backward glance he walked out. Obviously, he still had a few issues to work out. Kit went into the living room with Benny and the two oldest escaped upstairs to their rooms. They knew things had been resolved between them but now the parents were mad at each other.

It was hours before Trace returned. He had been upstairs talking with his mom. He was grateful to have his mom to turn to. She was often his voice of reason.

Lola tried not to be judgemental, but she gave Trace the same advice Kit did. She followed up by saying, "For what its worth, you need to let Finn express his feelings and make personal choices you might not agree with. You do this as long as you know his choices won't hurt anyone, including himself. It will help him to mature and grow."

"Speaking from experience, Ma?"

Lola smiled, "Learn to save your energy for more important battles."

Trace's look was apprehensive, "Like the one I'm going to have with Kit when I go back home?" His mother's parting conversation replayed in his head as he walked home. Trace went in and sat next to Kit in the living room. It was later than he thought, and the kids were in bed. Like an anxious child he sat there waiting for Kit to speak. There was only silence.

When Kit finally broke the awkward silence, she was unable to keep the frustration out of her voice, "Parenting is an equal role, Trace. We're in this together."

"This parenting thing has gotten more difficult," Trace replied, shaking his head in a gesture of exasperation.

"Dealing with Finn is new to both of us. He's not a bad boy, Trace."

"No, but he still continues to be defiant and challenging. Don't let him take advantage of you, Kit."

Kit resented Trace's tone and her first reaction was to deny it but there was a measure of truth to his comment. She couldn't help but worry about Finn. That didn't stop her from saying, "Finn can't be blamed for all of this. Sweet little Kenzie is just as much to blame. I would be upset myself by her mean remarks. This is more than just about today. You don't see it all because most of your day is spent outside while I'm inside parenting."

Trace remained silent, which angered Kit. "You are completely ignoring the fact that I made a valid point earlier."

It was pointless to deny the fact he tended to let Kit deal with the kids in general. Tonight, he realized how difficult it was at times. "You're much better at this parenting thing."

Kit's tone took on a new intensity, "You could at least try more. The kids will continue to challenge us over the years. You need to step up. We are in this together. They will need both of us in different ways and at different times. You will have no choice but to get better. Those kids upstairs are keepers."

Trace hadn't enjoyed their conversation, but he did understand what Kit was saying. "You mean we can't sell them off like the horses," he said with a grin.

The tone of Trace's voice told Kit that he was trying to lighten the mood. Trace could annoy and charm her at the same time. This time, she was not swayed by his charm, but she did feel better now that they had talked. Kit remained troubled. What Finn had said earlier about them not being his parents had upset her. As Finn pointed out, 'they' could come and take him away anytime they wanted to.

Trace admired his wife's strong qualities and firm beliefs. It didn't stop him from saying, "You are still an exasperating woman, Kit Grayson."

CHAPTER SEVEN

Kit enjoyed the summer holidays and having the kids home every day. Days were filled with carefree fun and lots of adventure. Maggie and Kit were out on the patio watching the children play in the back yard. Finn watched from Lola's window. It might be summer, but Finn was still having to attend classes at Lola's every day, and lately on weekends. Extra time was required for the next couple of weeks. The homeschool curriculum had to be followed and Finn had a couple of assignments that had a deadline. He knew he was getting caught up so why couldn't he at least have the weekends off? Today, Finn felt he was being punished. Feeling it was unfair, he was in a bad mood. Lola had gone over to the barn to talk to Trace while he was stuck in her suite. None of them had a care in the world. Must be nice. The Graysons accepted him but times like this he really felt like an outsider. Despite being treated better than he had anywhere else, his time with foster parents had ingrained a certain caution. Finn kept waiting for things to change. The Ungers were nice in the beginning, too. Maybe the Graysons were getting tired of him. He hoped he had found a permanent home, but luck never was on his side. His bad mood lasted throughout the day.

It was almost suppertime and Finn still hadn't shown up. Trace had come in and was ready to wash up. Kit stopped him at the door, "Have you seen Finn?"

"Not since lunch. Maybe he's still upstairs with Lola."

"He left Lola's over an hour ago and none of us have seen him. Lola said they had a bad day today, and she lost her temper with Finn just before he left."

"Do you think Finn ran away?" Kenzie asked as she started to cry.

Kit forced a smile, "It's okay, baby girl. I'm sure he's around here somewhere. He promised not to run away." Inside, Kit remained unconvinced. Distraught, she began to pace.

Trace was annoyed. If Finn wanted to sulk and hide, fine. When Trace saw how upset both Kenzie and Kit were, he left and started calling Finn's name as he headed to the barn. He was deep in thought when he found Finn in the same stall he had found him the day he showed up. Trace's face was solemn when he walked over.

Finn looked up at Trace but remained seated. It was evident Trace was in a foul mood. "You thought I'd run away again, didn't you?"

Trace gave Finn a stern look, "Only for a moment; you do have a history."

Finn ignored the sarcasm. "I told you I won't run away. I just wanted to be alone."

"Do you like to be alone?"

Finn scowled, "I'm used to being alone. I told you the Ungers always left me home on my own. You don't know what it's like, always being on the outside of things."

"I'm sorry you felt that way growing up. We don't want you to feel that way here."

Finn had never been more serious when he asked, "Are you gonna make me leave?"

Looking into Finn's eyes, Trace could see the renewed fear due to his past experiences with foster parents. Trace recognized the signs of abuse and understood them too well. Trace became momentarily absent as he tried to think what Buster would have done in a situation like this, a tactic Trace reverted to when facing a dilemma. Kenzie had never caused this kind of grief. Finn had continually presented them with challenges since day one. Trace lowered himself next to Finn in the hay, his broad back now leaning against the weathered wood of the barn wall. He tipped his cowboy hat back and looked at Finn, his expression intense. "We are not like your other foster parents but out of fairness we have never had to deal with an angry adolescent. Our relationship with you is new to us. If you have a problem, come talk to one of us. There is no problem too big that we can't deal with it. Disappearing like you did today is unacceptable. Everyone was worried."

Trace paused, deciding how to continue. Looking into Finn's eyes he could see the deep hurt. Trace's voice became heavy with emotion as he carefully chose his words, "You keep telling me I don't understand. I'm going to tell you something I have only shared with two people, my younger brother Riley and Kit. I trust you to keep my secret." Trace hated sharing the dark side of his past but in order to help Finn he opened up. "Even at a young age I was a challenge to my dad. I hated how he treated our mom. She deserved better. From the time I was little my dad would whip me so I would understand he was the boss. He made sure no one could see any bruises or marks. If it wasn't physical, it was verbal. He would shout accusations, and utter threats. I was able to protect Riley, but I always had to be on guard. Fortunately, our dad only needed one whipping post. Ma never knew. It was our secret. One we've kept to this day. It would have broken her heart. I told Kit. There are no secrets between me and Kit." Talking about his dad caused Trace's eyes to darken. His voice trailed off, now deep in thoughts of remembering. The ghosts from the past had pushed their way through. Trace's face grew somber when memories he didn't want to recall took over. He wasn't willing to share anything more. His voice was solemn when he spoke, "The invisible wounds are the ones that hurt the most and last the longest. Sometimes, a lifetime. I can't make up for what happened before you got here."

Finn gave Trace a sideways glance, understanding that Trace was being honest. Finn did understand how difficult it was for Trace to share. Trace was a hard man to figure out.

"When I'm upsent and feel I need a time-out, I take off like you do."

"Where do you go?" Finn asked in surprise.

"I saddle up my horse, Diego and I go for a ride."

Finn's eyes lit up. "Is Diego that beautiful black horse I've seen?" He had watched and admired the stallion many times from afar.

Trace smiled but a moment later his face was serious again. "He is, but don't try changing the subject."

For a moment they were both silent. Finn didn't know what to think. "I'm going to get a punishment, aren't I."

Now it was time for Trace to get real with Finn. "In our home, our children are accountable for their actions. You will be too. There are always consequences for bad behaviour. It is never physical." Trace said nothing else for a moment as he thought back to his own relationship with his father. A man who was far too free with criticism and the back of his hand. He continued to share more of his own dark past. Things he rarely shared with anyone. "I can't begin to understand the continuous hardships you have endured in your young life, but you don't have to be afraid of us. You have to think before you act out because there are always consequences. What do you think your punishment should be?"

"How about I say I'm sorry."

"Are you?"

"Yes."

"Well, I accept your apology, but you also have to apologize to the rest of the family. We were all worried."

Finn was afraid to ask, "How do you punish your kids?"

"Kit and I will discuss what your punishment will be. Be prepared for a lecture from Kit. When she gets scared, she gets mad, and it can take her a while to get over it. So don't be giving her more grief. Even though we don't always agree, and we argue, we still love each other. There will be times when there are raised voices but there are never raised hands. We believe in a time out until everyone has a chance to think about what happened, but our children never get locked away. I'll head back to the house and let the others know you're out here and safe. Take a few minutes but don't be long. Supper is almost ready." Trace realized there was still a period of adjustment for all of them.

After a few more minutes of solitude, Finn left the barn. He no longer wanted to be alone. It was still a challenge having a new family. The Graysons were so different from his other families, especially when it came to punishment. If he was being honest, he really liked this family. This was where he wanted to be. Here there was a sense of family he'd been missing. Sometimes, he even pretended they really were his family, but they weren't.

Back in the house, Trace and Kit were deep in conversation. Anytime Kit was concerned about the kids, her anger lasted longer. "Finn needs to know he did something wrong. He is testing us and wants to know what we're going to do about it. This is a huge test, Trace. This time you are the one who has to deal with it and see it through. Usually, with something like this an apology is enough but not in this case. This was an open act of defiance."

Trace nodded. He would figure something out.

Finn was quiet during supper knowing Kit was still mad. Kenzie, of course, chatted away unaware of the tension around the table. The boy's eyes lit up with excitement when Trace told Finn they were going out to the barn after supper. His excitement waned when Trace added, "Since you want to be treated like our other kids, your punishment this time is to help me clean the stall I found you in."

Kit didn't consider this much of a punishment, but she would let Trace have this one.

Once they were finished in the barn, Trace placed a hand on Finn's shoulder, "We will keep this stall for you, it will be your personal place to escape to. We will forbid Kenzie from coming here as well."

Finn was excited when he realized he could be alone with no one bothering him. For the first time in a long time, Finn laughed freely. "Do you think she'll listen? I really am sorry about the fight I had with Kenzie the other day."

"It's about time you stood up to Kenzie." Trace knew he and Finn were slowly forming a bond. "Kenzie knows Kit and I are the boss even though she likes to boss everyone. It's a female thing. Don't tell Kit I said that. It's time to call it a day and head back to the house." That night, the barn became Finn's safe place.

After the kids had settled for the night, Trace was still troubled, despite his relief at finding Finn and dealing with his punishment. It wasn't long and he was putting on his coat.

"Where are you going?"

Trace's tall frame indicated continued annoyance as he met Kit's gaze. "I need time alone to think." Despite the new understanding between him and Finn, the angry youth had gotten to Trace. It wasn't long and Trace was heading upstairs to his mom's suite. They talked for a long time about Finn and family.

Lola wanted to reassure Trace, "It took me a couple of weeks, but I now have a good understanding of our young man. There is a reason for his troubled behaviour. Finn has an underlying fear of doing something wrong, fear of failure, fear of rejection. All of these could result in him having to leave here, which is his biggest fear. He has a lot of fears to overcome."

Their conversation continued with both of them reflecting on their own past. Trace shared most of what he had shared with Finn, and Lola was encouraged by Trace wanting to help Finn. As Trace was getting ready to leave, Lola walked over and took out a single piece of paper. It was Finn's homework about family. The few words revealed so much. When Trace looked at his mom she was crying, something she rarely did. Trace swallowed hard as he held her close. Over the years Trace had struggled with change. He figured they were in for another big one if he followed his heart.

*****

The next day Finn's case worker, Carrie Peabody, came out unexpectedly. They all liked her, and her reports indicated Finn was adjusting well. Lola joined them. She was always included in their meetings.

Carrie was quick to address her observations with both ladies. "I can see the positive change in Finn in the short time he's been here. I've seen for myself he's slowly coming out of his shell. He smiles freely and talks more. He was a difficult boy prior to coming here. It is evident he is doing better overall."

It was Lola who responded, and her voice had a definite edge to it, "That poor boy was only seven years old when he became an orphan. He spent years with foster parents who were abusive in more ways than one. It's no wonder he was an angry boy who didn't trust anyone. Trust has to be earned and it doesn't happen overnight. He was also labelled difficult because he refused to conform."

Carrie wasn't offended by Lola's truth. "Finn is lucky to have found a new home here. I can see you all love him very much. It seems you and Finn have made a special connection. You've made quite an impression on him," Carrie said sincerely.

"When it's just him and me upstairs in my suite he knows he can trust me with anything he says. Sometimes he talks and I just listen. When he opens up, I try to turn it into a learning lesson, not a lecture session. So, some days our lessons are unscripted and unconventional."

Carrie had to ask, "How is his schoolwork coming?"

"I knew right away Finn was intelligent, but he's also proven to be a good student. By the start of the new school year Finn will be caught up enough to enter the school system. If he needs additional help in some areas, I will continue to tutor him in the evenings. I hope you have documented his file he was behind due to circumstances."

Carrie nodded, and turned to Kit, "How is Finn getting along with your children?"

"He's beginning to fit in. We treat Finn like our own children. All of them have chores and they know what our rules and boundaries are. Finn does the chores assigned to him. Not always cheerfully, but he does them. Typical kid. We have all adjusted to having Finn as part of our family. Despite everything, he misses his mother. We all hang on to the image of the mother we wish we always had." Kit swallowed hard. She was speaking on behalf of both Finn and her.

After school, Finn asked Kit how the meeting went with Miss Busybody, his unkind nickname for his case worker. Finn was always concerned 'they' were going to take him away from here. He was still a young boy with a lot of distrust with the system.

"As always, Miss Peabody was pleased with the progress you have made, especially with your schooling. She loved your new room." It was a little dark for Kit's liking, but they wanted Finn to feel like it was his room. Not a room that was made over for the foster child.

The next afternoon, Trace and Kit sat together on the verandah having coffee. Finn was with Lola, Kenzie was watching television, and Benny was down for his nap. Kit had been quiet all morning. Yesterday's meeting with Finn's case worker, although positive, was troubling her.

Trace had been watching Kit, knowing her thoughts were far away. He took Kit's hand, "I've been sitting here patiently waiting for you to tell me what's bothering you. This has to do with Finn, doesn't it. Did something happen?"

"You do realize the Agency could come and take Finn away from us." Tears glistened in Kit's eyes.

"Yes." This was secretly a shared concern.

"Our family has never been a typical family. I think we should adopt Finn if he wants us. I believe in fate, Trace. When we had our meeting with Carrie, I said Finn is part of our family, I realized at that moment it should be permanent." Kit put a coaxing hand on his arm, "I love Finn as if he was our own son. More time won't make a difference."

Trace nodded in agreement, "No, I suppose it won't." They both started to laugh. Could their family get any more complicated? As much as Trace hated change, he knew it was something he had no control over. "Here we go again. Ever since you came into my life, Kit Grayson, my life keeps changing."

"For the better I hope."

"Absolutely. Together we can handle anything." A comfortable silence fell between them knowing they had made the right decision.

*****

The summer sun, hot and high, beat down from a clear blue sky. A gentle breeze offered little relief as Kit and Maggie sat outside on the verandah so they could keep an eye on the kids playing in the yard.

Kenzie called out as she pushed her brother aside, "Mom, the boys are wrecking our game. Do something with them."

Kit got up to grab Benny, who took off when he saw her coming. He had a definite look of mischief in his eyes when she caught him. "The girls don't want you and Rhett bothering them, so leave them alone. Go play in the sandbox with your trucks." Benny gave his mom one of his charming smiles as he and Rhett scooted off.

"Your Benny is a charmer. We know where he gets that from." They watched to see what their sons were going to do next. "You do realize our boys are always going to be a handful when they get together."

Finn, who had finished his time upstairs with Lola, had been watching. He went and got the wagon. "Come on, you little hooligans. Let's go for a ride." He placed both boys in the wagon and told them to hold on tight. Kit and Maggie watched as Finn pulled the wagon down the lane as fast as he could while the toddlers squealed with delight.

Maggie turned to Kit, "How are you all adjusting to your new family member? Is Finn settling in?"

"It depends on the day and who you talk to. He's less angry and more trusting than when he arrived. At first, I think Lola felt she had met her match. She has come to realize Finn is a very intelligent boy. Lola will have him caught up by the end of summer, but the homeschooling is continuing through the summer."

"How does he feel about that?"

"Finn isn't always happy about it, but he's been putting in the effort. Fortunately, he and Lola have developed a trusting relationship and Finn has worked diligently. He's a smart boy so he has had no problem getting caught up. In fact, this week they cut back to only mornings and no weekends. We felt it was important for him to have time to enjoy the rest of the summer like the other kids. It took time and a lot of effort by all of us, but he has come around. He was so hostile in the beginning and tried so hard to hide his vulnerability. Finn is a complex boy who is finally revealing another side to him. His sarcasm is slowly being replaced with humor and teasing. It's still a struggle at times, especially between him and Trace. I'm sure Trace intimidates the poor boy. Heck, there are times Trace can still intimidate me. Trace has always struggled with change but more so when the change is unexpected, and with Finn everything can be unpredictable."

Maggie heard the frustration in Kit's voice, "Trace isn't always the easiest man to understand. He doesn't bend as easily as a willow tree when the wind changes. As long as I've known Trace, he struggles with change, and you have to admit this was a big change to everyone's life. Kenzie seems to be adjusting well with Finn living with your family. Lucy Rose says she brags about having a big brother all the time."

"That novelty is starting to wear thin. He teases her relentlessly," replied Kit with a hint of laughter in her voice.

The conversation took a sudden twist when Maggie commented, "Did you know Olivia Beaumont is back? She returned last week. Her marriage failed again. This was her third. Number one and number two liked to use their fists. I never thought I'd say this, but I feel sorry for Olivia. Imagine marrying two men who both have a violent nature. I'm not sure why she divorced her third husband. She's living with her parents, and it looks like it could be permanent. Or until she finds herself another husband. Good thing Trace is married."

Kit wasn't pleased with Maggie's news. "I remember the day I met Olivia. She showed up uninvited to the Calhoun Labour Day barbeque. That was right after her first marriage failed and she came back home divorced and wanting Trace back." Kit's attention momentarily drifted back to that day when Olivia crashed the Calhoun barbeque. Her family lived in the area, so she was familiar with the annual event. Kit was chatting with Trace when Olivia approached. Kit thought the new arrival looked out of place. She was over-dressed in her maxi dress, but accented with fashionable cowboy boots and a designer denim jacket made it work. The woman was eye-catching. She was sophisticated, pencil thin and posh. Her platinum blonde hair was cut in the latest fashion forward bob. The look Olivia gave Kit was anything but friendly, but she greeted Trace with a dazzling smile. With her high and mighty attitude, Olivia nudged between Kit and Trace, forcing Kit to move over. It was clear Olivia wanted Trace's full attention. Olivia felt entitled to Trace and no one was going to get in her way.

Kit hadn't thought about Olivia in a long time. The news of her return left Kit feeling uneasy. "I don't think that would make a difference to Olivia. I know how obsessed Olivia has always been with Trace. When Trace and I were engaged, Olivia told me he regretted their breakup and wanted to get back together. She has a habit of stirring up trouble like a dust devil. She better not show up here."

"Do you really think she would?"

Apart from the fact that Kit disliked Olivia, she didn't trust her. The woman was cold and calculating. Kit didn't hesitate to respond, "That woman is as brazen as they come. Olivia can be extremely charming to your face but don't turn your back on her. There has never been a pleasant encounter between us."

In Maggie's opinion Oliva was a world-class bitch. "It wouldn't take any effort to hate Olivia. I can't stand her, never could. It's too bad Olivia took after her father and not her mother. Evelyn Beaumont is a lovely lady with a kind heart. She is what one would call a true southern belle. Evelyn is beautiful and always dresses in the latest fashions. In her younger years she participated in beauty pageants."

"Sounds like a shallow life."

"Raised in the south, that was the role of a southern belle. Evelyn is known for her southern hospitality and generosity and she's a leader in all the social events around here. She has a reputation for hosting elaborate dinner parties and is well-liked because of her graciousness. She is one of the kindest people I know. Any time my path crosses with hers, she is polite and sweet. When I saw her in town last week, she greeted me warmly and asked about Matt and the children. There is a natural dignity about her, a genuine lady who possesses inherent poise. Evelyn is still an attractive lady who has aged gracefully and has kept her charming southern accent."

"How did a delicate southern belle wind up with a ruthless businessman like Jackson Beaumont? Did she marry him for his money?"

"That's what many believed, but she came from old money. Her family is very affluent, and members of the upper class who revel in the social life. Back in the day, Jackson was suave and charming. They met when he was in Texas on a business trip, and he was immediately infatuated with Evelyn. He wooed her and swept her off her feet. He has treated his wife like a porcelain doll and has always been loving and faithful to her. Evelyn is well-bred and intelligent and knows and accepts her role in life. She never worked outside the home. Her time was devoted to her family, and she does a lot of volunteer work. When Evelyn needs a break from her domineering husband she escapes to their home in Florida or takes a winter cruise. She is often gone for months at a time, but for the last couple of years she has stayed home."

"A lot of her people thought Jackson married Evelyn for her money, but he was already well on his way to becoming a successful businessman. He made his money the hard way and he built his empire through grit and determination. He has always been business minded and for him business aways comes first. Olivia's marriage to her first husband allowed Jackson to diversify overseas. For Jackson it was a great business deal until the marriage failed. After the divorce, the business began to struggle but within a couple of years Jackson turned it around and was back on top. He still likes to purchase small independent companies. For Jackson, it isn't about the company as much as it is about the take-over. He can be ruthless to get what he wants. He will take advantage of the underdog to build his own enterprise without caring about others. It makes him feel powerful. Jackson enjoys flaunting his wealth and surrounding himself with opulence. Their home is a mansion, and as you know he has one of the finest horse facilities in the area."

Maggie continued, "Jackson doted on his wife but hardly paid any attention to Olivia. He always wanted a son and his disappointment was taken out on his daughter. There is a reason they say money can't buy happiness." Maggie's voice became serious, "Rumor has it that Jackson isn't well. There's talk going around he is no longer of sound mind and easily gets confused and angry. It seems any time the Grayson name is mentioned Jackson becomes unhinged. The man is seriously demented. Jackson keeps telling everyone that Trace stole his horses even though it was Jackson himself who suddenly sold all of his horses." Maggie flipped back to Olivia, "Do you think Trace knows Olivia's back?"

Kit's body tensed, "If he does, he hasn't said anything." Kit had to admit the conversation about Olivia bothered her. Olivia had a habit of showing up like a bad penny. If Trace did know she was back, why hadn't he said anything? Kit was unable to push that thought from her mind and began jumping to conclusions. She shook her head refusing to allow negative thoughts in. She refused to give Olivia Beaumont that power.

CHAPTER EIGHT

E ven though her mother had asked Olivia to come home, Olivia
had already intended to return. Her life was in shambles. Her third
husband had just divorced her, and she had nowhere else to go.
In fact, that was the driving force behind her return. What Olivia wasn't
prepared for was the mental and physical decline of her father.

Evelyn and Olivia were alone in the office. They wanted privacy,
and the staff knew never to enter Jackson's office unless summoned.
Evelyn, who was usually calm in any situation, was pacing nervously. The
dynamics within the Beaumont home had changed dramatically in the last
six months. Evelyn Beaumont was at a loss as how to manage the situation,
but she knew important changes were required.

Olivia could see her mother had been under a lot of stress and her
dad's behaviour had become rather bizarre at times. "What's going on
with Dad?"

Evelyn knew it was time to share the reason she needed Olivia at
home and the extent of Jackson's illness. "Your father has been diagnosed
with Alzheimer's. The specialists believe he's had dementia for years and
when I look back, I can see there were definite signs. When your dad kept
misplacing things, he would accuse me of hiding them. I could rationalize
this because it wasn't any more abnormal than usual. In the early stages
it was only impacting his short-term memory loss. I could excuse the
little things, thinking it was due to aging. As he got worse, he would get
angry and accuse the staff of stealing. The staff started coming to me
with complaints and threatened to quit. Some actually did. His mental

and physical capacity is declining quickly. He's still capable of everyday functions but his mind is confused. When it comes to logic, your father is sometimes incapable of distinguishing between what is real and what isn't. I'm sure you've noticed this even in the short time you've been home."

"Is that why he doesn't go into the office anymore and you stopped traveling?"

Evelyn nodded, "Your father has had poor judgement for months, and his periods of confusion are lasting longer. He isn't capable of running his business, so it has suffered. He began missing appointments. There were times he wouldn't go into the office for days. One time he called me to go and get him. He didn't know where he was, and he couldn't find his car. When I finally found him, he was agitated, and he pushed me when I tried to get him into my car. It was the first time your dad had ever been physical with me. That day, I made an appointment with his doctor and the tests began. I'm sure you've noticed his speech has been affected. He often seems to be at a loss for words, like he's searching for the right one and he often repeats himself."

Olivia was aware of this; now she understood why. "Yesterday he said something that didn't make sense and he repeated it again this morning word for word."

"That's where our patience is required. Even though it's frustrating for us, it's confusing for your father. This disease also effects his balance. He began stumbling and falling so he's using a walker most of the time."

Olivia was affected by the conversation. She felt sorry for her mom. She could see how much her dad had declined since the last time she was home, but she wasn't prepared for his diagnosis. Her father had always been such a strong and independent man. Nobody and nothing could get in his way. He had always been in control, including over her. "I suppose he refuses to admit there is anything wrong with him."

"It's been heartbreaking to watch his decline as his behaviour becomes more bizarre. Last month he sold all the horses and fired the men." This was a sad reminder of how confused Jackson had become. "He keeps saying Trace Grayson stole the horses. Do you know why he has become fixated on Trace? I know you dated Trace in your teens but that was years ago."

"In Dad's mind he has more than one reason. When Trace and I dated he defied Dad when he ordered him to stop seeing me. Dad didn't like

Trace because of his lack of breeding. A mere cowboy wasn't good enough for his little girl. That was the beginning of the turbulent relationship between them. After I divorced Burke and came home, Dad tried to buy one of Trace's horses. Trace said his horses were too good for Dad because we just had show horses. Dad doesn't like being refused anything. He offered Trace an exorbitant amount of money that no reasonable person would refuse. Trace still turned him down. Trace told Dad he couldn't be bought, and threats didn't work. He actually threw us off his property. That was the day Trace became an enemy in Dad's eyes. It seems everything bad relates back to Trace in Dad's confused mind. Dad's gotten really bad, hasn't he?"

Evelyn nodded sadly, "You know your dad as well as I do. At first, I could cope on my own. Now it takes so much effort and patience. I can't do this alone anymore. His symptoms will become more severe as the disease progresses."

"Is this why you hired Dolores?" In the short time she'd been home, Olivia could see her father's periods of confusion were happening more frequently.

"It gives me peace of mind having a full-time nurse living here and Dolores is very good with your father. I have set up a room for her on the main floor next to your dad's. Your dad had to be moved downstairs due to his immobility. We have a motorized wheelchair on order so it will be easier for him to get around the house. Everything worsens over time."

Olivia walked over and stood staring at her father's portrait on the wall behind his desk. Those cold eyes stared back at her. Her father's office always brought unpleasant emotions and unhappy memories. Like the day he ordered her to give up Trace Grayson because she was expected to marry Burke Benson, the son of her father's business partner. Burke had been sent to Calgary as the liaison between his father's company in England and Jackson Beaumont's company in Calgary. Jackson wanted a merger of families as well. Olivia was attracted to Burke, but she wasn't in love with him. His biggest appeal was he belonged to one of the richest families in London. Burke would continue to provide her with a lifestyle she enjoyed. She had been young and desperate to do anything to please her dad. She married the suave and wealthy Englishman. That hadn't gone well. Burke was more controlling than her father, so the abuse continued. Only with

Burke it became physical. Olivia stayed in her bad marriage for her father's sake and maintained the façade of being happily married. Olivia endured the physical abuse as long as she could. In the end her father relented to a divorce after telling Olivia she had been a disappointment from the day she was born. Jackson's verbal and emotional abuse continued.

Olivia turned back to her mother and shared her mental step back in time. "I was too young to challenge Dad's authority. When my first marriage failed, I tried again. I think I kept wanting to prove to Dad I was worthy of his love. If another man loved me, he should too. I wanted love from my own father more than anything. Little did I know I had repeated history by marrying another controlling man and that marriage was ended very quickly. You'd think I would have learned, but I married a third time. I prayed this marriage would be better. It was wonderful and I believed I had finally found the right man. He was kind and generous, a hard worker but not a workaholic, and he wasn't abusive in any way. When we decided to have children, I got pregnant right away. Everything was fine in the beginning, and we were going to have a boy. I hoped Dad would finally give me full acceptance if I gave him a grandson. Then complications set in, and I lost the baby. Because of the complications I had to have a full hysterectomy and couldn't have children. That was the final blow and the beginning of the end of our marriage. Neither Dad nor my husband forgave me for that. Like it was my fault. Daddy went crazy when he heard Trace and Kit had a son. Dad said their son would have been mine if I had married Trace instead of all the other losers I married. It didn't matter what I did; I continued to be a disappointment." Her voice registered her deep hurt. Most times she was able to bury it, but it had been so stressful since she returned home.

Evelyn understood all too well having also experienced a miscarriage. At least she had her beautiful daughter.

Olivia's hurt and disappointment was taken over by anger. "It has taken me years to realize the abuse started with Dad. He abused me emotionally for years. It would hurt but I'd go back for more. When I decided to come home this time, I decided I would not allow him to do that anymore. I'm strong enough to stand up to him and I don't need his approval or love." Olivia was finally able to own this.

Not knowing what to say, Evelyn remained silent. She understood. She had witnessed the ongoing conflict between father and daughter for years.

Olivia continued, her voice reflective, "In the past, if I defied Dad, I would pay the ultimate price. Did you know he threatened to disown me if I didn't marry Burke. My future was determined by my father because I was too young and too naïve to stand up to him." The huge divorce settlement helped dispel Olivia's sense of failure and ease the disappointment from her father. "I'm no longer a young girl who believes in happily ever after." After three failed marriages Olivia often wondered what life would have been like if she had married Trace. He may not have given her everything she wanted in the beginning but that would have changed over time. Olivia knew Trace had become a businessman and landowner who had moved up the class ladder and made the Grayson name mean something.

Feeling a great heaviness inside, Evelyn returned to her husband's health issues. "Sometimes decisions are made for you. Your dad's doctor says it's time to assign someone as his Power of Attorney and Personal Directive. Your father no longer possesses normal cognitive skills. I know I can't do both. Darling, you are a strong, independent woman. I don't know anything about the business, and I've never had to make important decisions. I want you to become the POA."

Olivia felt sorry for her mother as well as her father. As much as she loathed her father at times, Olivia hated seeing him like this. "You can trust me to step in and access the damage Dad has caused. Even though I have no experience working with Dad, I've listened and watched him strategize and manipulate for years. I have more knowledge about the business than he was aware of. I am capable of doing this and doing it well. Dad knew how to run a business, but he didn't know how to be a father."

"He gave you everything you wanted," Evelyn reminded her daughter.

"So did my husbands. I was given all the luxuries, but I paid for them in different ways. I can have all the plastic surgery needed to hide damages caused by physical abuse, but the hidden scars never go away. Even though Dad gave me everything money could buy, I never had his love or acceptance. I would have given up everything for that. I wanted him to accept me and be proud of me even though I wasn't Jackson Beaumont's son. Never once did he allow me to be a part of that life." Olivia had to ask, "The baby you lost, was it a boy?" Her mother's silence was answer enough. An agonizing moment of grief was shared by mother and daughter.

It took a minute for Evelyn to regain her composure. She knew how her daughter felt because she had also disappointed her husband. "Your Dad wanted to be able to pass everything on to a son. It was such a bitter disappointment to be told that due to circumstances I couldn't have any more children. Jackson was so used to getting everything he wanted in life. There are some things you just can't buy. Sadness and disappointment exist for all of us." She turned and walked out of the room.

Olivia's gaze turned to her dad's picture and she smiled to herself. Olivia was always a fighter and now it was time to take on her dad. That meant taking over Beaumont Enterprises. Life can only beat you up if you let it. An actual shiver of excitement went down her spine. In that moment, Olivia became the 'son' her father always wanted. She had found her calling. She was ready to step in and take over the family business.

*****

Olivia couldn't get Trace Grayson out of her mind. He had been such a fascinating summer fling. Over the years she had daydreamed about a life with Trace and now she was back, and it was worse. As a teenager Olivia had been captivated by Trace's ruggedness and hard-toned muscles on his six-foot frame. The hunk was a real cowboy who had become a landowner and renowned horse trainer who operated a thriving business.

Olivia headed over to Lola Grande, wanting to see Trace. She was sure he would be there. The man never stopped working. Olivia smiled, believing fate was on her side when she saw Kit pulling out of the drive. Kit wouldn't be there to interrupt them and with luck, Lola would be gone as well. Trace was replacing a broken board on the corral fence as Olivia drove into the yard. Her heart quickened at the sight of him. He was still as handsome as she remembered even though his face was more weathered from the sun and there were light crease lines at the corners of his eyes. The dark stubble emphasized his masculinity. As usual, he wore faded jeans, western shirt, and scuffed boots. Still the epitome of a real cowboy.

Trace looked up when he heard Olivia's vehicle and noticed she was driving her dad's black Hummer. He frowned when she pulled alongside and got out. As usual, Olivia had dressed to impress. She had kept herself fit and enjoyed showing off her ample curves. She walked slowly over to Trace, letting him have a good look. As enticing as Olivia was to look at, Trace had zero attraction to her. Darkness clouded the cowboy's eyes.

"I was passing by and took a chance you would be home." Olivia's lies flowed easily as she exercised her charm.

Trace was always amazed by the gall of the Beaumonts. "Kit told me you were back. Just visiting?" he asked hopefully. He was not smiling.

Olivia was disappointed by the unwelcoming look on Trace's face. "Gossip must not travel this far out. I've moved back home. My marriage didn't work out."

"Again."

Olivia chose to ignore his sarcasm but didn't miss the cool indifference in his sexy blue eyes. Olivia challenged him, "What about you? Have you grown tired of your ball and chain?"

Trace actually felt sorry for Olivia with her desperate hope for his unhappiness. He didn't bother to answer.

Olivia saw the joy in his eyes at the mere mention of Kit. Looking for sympathy and attempting to draw Trace in, she continued, "Mom asked me to come home. I don't know if you heard, Dad has Alzheimer's."

Everyone knew this. Some gossip traveled faster than others. Trace's mouth clamped in a hard line, "Is your memory getting as bad as your father's? I thought I told you to never step foot on my property again." There was something about Olivia that could quickly bring out the worst in a person.

"That's a cruel thing to say. Besides, I didn't think you really meant it. I don't understand this animosity you have toward me because of my dad. Here I am struggling to put the pieces of my life back together." Olivia moved closer to Trace. "I know you and I had our differences but I'm sure we can overcome them."

Olivia's intrusion in his life only infuriated him. Trace was tired of the Beaumonts. There was usually trouble any time one of them showed up. "Look, I get it. Things were tough for you, but frankly I don't give a damn. Deal with your mess and stay out of my life. You've always been a survivor. I'm sure you'll be fine."

Olivia paled at Trace's coldness. Nor had she missed the hard glint in his eyes and the firm set of his jaw. She gave Trace one of her best sultry looks. "I want to go back in time. We were so good together. I've never stopped thinking about you and what we had. You always did fascinate me."

Trace's sarcasm was heavy, "We all make mistakes. Some of us learn from them. When I met you, I was young and unsophisticated. Sadly, I believed you loved me. Instead, you were amusing yourself until Burke returned. You must have laughed at how easily I was manipulated by your charms and my willingness to spend time with you even though your dad despised me. Over time, I realized it was only teenage infatuation and physical attraction for me."

"Daddy wanted me to marry Burke."

"You had no problem making your choice," Trace said with no sign of emotion. It didn't matter to him anymore. "I wasn't good enough for your father. I was poor white trash who was a common labourer. He didn't want his daughter involved with a hell-raising cowboy." Back then Trace didn't measure up financially or in terms of sophistication.

Olivia's look was deliberate, "You've come a long way since then. You are a landowner and credible businessman. Daddy would approve of you now."

Trace shook his head, "I'm still a cowboy, Olivia. I always will be. For some people that's good enough."

The realization came to Olivia that the man she obsessed over would never love her. She could never have Trace, especially with Kit in the picture. At that moment, she understood the bitterness that festered inside her dad and how he could justify his actions.

Looking at Olivia now, Trace's only feeling for her was pity. She had three failed marriages. Seeing Olivia up close he realized she looked too old and hard for her age. Trace looked over at the Hummer, indicating it was time for her to leave. "Kit told me about a month ago a dark Hummer swerved and tried to run her off the road. Know anything about that?" By the shocked look on Oliva's face, Trace could tell this was news to her and was relieved.

Olivia was angry at the assumption that someone in her family would do such a thing. "Why do you always think the worst of my family?"

"Because you have given me good reason to over the years. I told you before to stay away. Go home, Olivia, I have a ranch to run." Trace turned and headed to the barn.

Alone in the barn, hurtful memories grabbed hold and took Trace back to another dark time in his past. The first time Trace saw Olivia Beaumont his gaze was fixed on the stunning blonde as if he was hypnotized. Despite her haughty attitude, he was immediately fascinated with her. He was eighteen and had more hormones than good sense. He was infatuated with this beautiful girl who represented all the glamour and excitement a young man could dream of. He knew she wasn't his type, but he wanted to see how rich folks lived. He didn't measure up financially or in terms of sophistication. They dated over the summer but for Olivia it was merely a summer fling. As soon as Burke returned, she discarded Trace in front of her friends and family. That was the first time he experienced how calculating and malicious Olivia was. It had taken Trace longer to get over her betrayal than Olivia herself. Trace realized his feelings had been more lust than love. Now, here she was again. Trace shook his head. He wished she would stay the hell away from him. He left the barn and went back to work. He looked down the road and saw Kit returning. He smiled in appreciation at having Kit in his life and the family they had together. What he had with Kit was real. She was his happiness.

Olivia headed home when she left Lola Grande. Today's visit hadn't gone as planned. As disappointed as she was by Trace's rejection, she had been shocked by what he told her about the incident Kit had with a Hummer. Olivia hadn't thought much about the recent damage to her dad's Hummer until Trace mentioned the incident Kit had. Vehicles were always getting damaged, and Olivia had taken it to the garage and got it fixed a few days after it happened. Now she knew why her dad wanted it fixed right away. If his actions were due to escalating Alzheimer's, it had to be addressed before he did something worse. Olivia stormed into the house and straight to her dad's office.

Jackson was sitting at his desk with a glass of whiskey in his hand. He was drunker than usual as he sat in his deeply cushioned chair. His portrait hung behind him like a trophy head.

"I just came from seeing Trace Grayson at Lola Grande."

Before Olivia could continue, Jackson roared at her, "Don't you mention that man's name in this house."

Olivia was not willing to let this go. "Trace told me that someone forced his truck off the road when Kit was coming back from town. Is that how you got the dent in your Hummer?"

Jackson cried out in anger, "What the hell. I've never known anyone but Trace to drive his truck. I didn't hit the truck because it veered out of the way in time. Damn unfortunate." Jackson took a moment to light his cigar with his gold-plated lighter. He sat back and puffed on his expensive cigar clasped between his stubby fingers. Ashes fell onto his shirt. "Here I thought I had taken care of him." He smiled; there would be another opportunity.

This venomous rage was a new experience and it scared both women. His out-of-control resentment was poisoning his view of everything and everyone around him. Enraged, Olivia yelled, "Your actions endangered the lives of his family. What if Kit had the kids."

Surprising everyone, Jackson started to cry, "I'd never do anything to hurt children." His words were slurred, and he began to shake. With great effort he composed himself and his mind totally drifted. "I'd go for a ride if I had a horse but that damn Grayson stole them." Jackson turned to Evelyn. "Get one of the men to hitch up the trailer so we can go get them back."

Olivia looked at her mother and rolled her eyes.

"Why don't you to go rest while I go talk to the men." Evelyn knew it was easier to agree and distract than fight and argue.

"I'm not going for no rest. Both of you get the hell out of my office and leave me alone."

Olivia was quick to retaliate, "You can't order me around like you did in the past. I'm not that young girl anymore. I've come a long way, Daddy."

The defiant tone in Olivia's voce affected Evelyn more than Jackson. It was getting to be a real effort to keep the peace between the two of them. Evelyn went to the desk and called for Jackson's nurse.

The arguing between father and daughter continued, "Have you forgotten whose house you're in?"

Olivia actually laughed, "Forgot! What an interesting word to use under the circumstances."

"Olivia, that will be enough." They both ignored Evelyn's cry of anguish.

Jackson had always been known for his quick temper but now he was unstable, and his ugly tantrums were more frequent. He stomped out his cigar, "Don't you dare raise your voice to me, young lady. I'm your father."

Olivia hadn't missed the firmness in his voice, but she was no longer afraid to stand up to him. "Some father you've been. You were never there for me unless it helped you in business. You actually married me off to close a deal. I was young and anxious to please, so I obeyed."

Hearing the knock on the closed door, Everlyn opened it to let the nurse in. "Please take Mr. Beaumont to his room. He needs a rest."

Jackson turned to Evelyn as he was being helped out of the room, "You are no better than your despicable daughter."

After regaining her composure, Evelyn turned to Olivia, "There was no need to treat your father like that. He's a sick man."

Sick or not, Olivia couldn't let this go. Any time her dad sought retribution it was never harmful. Was this a new stage that required institutionalization? Olivia's concern wasn't just for her father. Because his anger had taken a dramatic shift, Olivia was afraid of what he would do to others. In time, would he turn on her or her mother? This needed to be addressed immediately. "You know as well as I do it's time to take matters out of Dad's control before he really does hurt someone. If we don't get control of this now something bad is going to happen. We don't need any scandal or public embarrassment." They could deal with that, but harmful actions were another. Olivia decided to be direct, "We have to finalize making me POA immediately before Dad does something we can't change. I'm not saying this to be cruel, Mother. We have run out of time allowing Dad to remain in control of anything."

Composing herself with difficulty, Evelyn went over to her husband's desk and picked up the phone to call the lawyer. Oliva could hear the pain in her mother's voice as she left the room smiling.

CHAPTER NINE

Weddings were a community event everyone looked forward to. Today, Kit and Trace would be attending the wedding of Dixie Dawson, the daughter of Trudy and Lyle. Kit was delighted to get dressed up for a change and put in the extra time getting ready.

The family was watching television when Kit entered the room. Her pale-yellow dress floated past her knees like a daffodil waving in the wind. As always, she wore her grandmother's pearl necklace around her slender neck. She was a vision of loveliness.

Trace whistled and declared, "You better go up and change. You wear that and nobody will look at the bride."

"Then we will be the best looking couple there, you handsome devil."

Finn rolled his eyes, got up and headed into the kitchen.

Lola smiled at the happy couple. "Go enjoy the day. You'll see lots of friends and you can catch up on the latest gossip."

"I suppose the Beaumonts will be there since they are neighbours." Trace wasn't happy about the prospect.

Kit nodded, but it did not curb her excitement. She would simply avoid them.

Trace and Kit were already seated in the church when the Beaumonts arrived. Kit was shocked to see Jackson walking slowly with a walker. When she first met him, he was using a cane and was quite mobile. Olivia hadn't changed much. It was Evelyn Beaumont who Kit's eyes rested on and Kit had to agree with Maggie. The tall, elegant looking platinum blonde walked gracefully beside her husband. She was exquisitely dressed from head to toe. The woman was stylishly attired in a dress that stated its exclusiveness. Her jewelry was appropriate, and Kit knew the diamonds in the choker around her neck were genuine. Kit studied her for a moment. The woman emulated classic beauty, but she couldn't disguise sad eyes.

The bride looked enchanting, all fluff, frills, and sparkle. Dixie's veil and tiara were worthy of the princess she wanted to be. She glowed as she walked down the aisle. As the bride and groom's personal vows were being exchanged and promises made, Trace turned and gave Kit his sexy grin, remembering their wedding. Kit met his gaze and smiled back, her eyes sparkling. The look between them was intimate. Olivia, who was sitting a few rows behind them, witnessed the exchange. She sighed heavily as she silently accepted Trace would never be hers. She had been obsessed with Trace Grayson for a long time. She usually didn't give up until she got what she wanted. Today, she would let him go. Olivia never liked to admit defeat. In her own way, she was happy for Trace. He really was a nice guy.

Kit was talking to the mother-of-the-bride when she heard a delightful southern drawl behind her. She turned, knowing it was Evelyn Beaumont. Olivia stood rigidly next to her mother. While her mother was classy, Olivia's beauty was more artificial, making her look cold. She always wore an air of privilege and entitlement. As usual Olivia's perfect features were set in an expression of disinterest, and she looked through Kit as though she didn't exist. Neither Olivia nor Kit pretended social politeness. Olivia had to admit that Kit looked attractive. Today, smoky eyeshadow drew attention to Kit's beautiful gray eyes. Olivia always thought they were Kit's best feature. They were naturally accented by long, thick lashes.

With natural grace, Evelyn turned to Trudy, "Dixie was so beautiful walking down the aisle she literally took my breath away. I so love weddings."

That's good, thought Kit, *since your daughter had three of them.*

As if Kit's thoughts were spoken out loud, Evelyn said, "That's a good thing but it would have been nicer if we had a wedding for three daughters instead of three weddings for one daughter. I guess not all of us get lucky the first time." Evelyn's delightful laughter had those around her smiling.

"Whatever," commented Olivia, trying to hold her temper as she scowled at her mother.

Evelyn turned to Olivia, "Where are your manners? You should have introduced me to this beautiful young lady. I'm Olivia's mother, Evelyn. Please excuse my daughter's rude behaviour. She has been taught better."

Kit was unaffected by the intentional snub. Olivia always gave Kit the cold shoulder. She liked the natural friendliness of Evelyn Beaumont and introduced herself.

"It's a pleasure to meet you. I'm surprised we haven't met before now. I've heard a lot about you and your adorable family. Trudy told me your daughter is an excellent barrel racer for someone so young. It can be quite a competitive sport so she must be very committed. I hear your young son looks just like his daddy. He must be as cute as the dickens. I understand you and Trace took in a foster child as well. Your family must keep you busy."

Kit was surprised at this woman's sincerity. Evelyn was an engaging woman.

While Trace and Matt were standing in line at the bar Trace watched Olivia and Kit and he compared the two. Olivia's statuesque frame was wrapped tightly in a low-cut black dress. Her artificial coloring did not enhance her features as flattering as Olivia thought. Kit was beautiful in a natural, fresh way. Her bare skin had been warmed to a honey color by the sun. She looked healthy and wholesome. Trace was impressed that his wife always dressed appropriately but he thought she would look just as good if she was in her jeans and T-shirt. Kit fit into his world. She was his life.

Matt nudged Trace when he saw Jackson Beaumont, "There's been talk around town that Jackson is no longer of sound mind. He gets confused and angry and any time your name is mentioned he becomes unhinged. The man is seriously demented. No one knows how much of what he says is real or a product of his mental illness."

Trace had been aware of the man's presence all day and was doing his best to avoid the whole Beaumont family. He cringed when he saw the man approaching.

Seeing Trace ignited Jackson and he was determined to seek Trace out. He had become obsessed with ruining Trace, but it wasn't working. Contempt curled the man's lips as he spat out his accusation to Trace, "You are a thief. I want my horses back."

The commotion at the bar and Jackson's raised voice had drawn attention. "Oh damn," Olivia shrieked.

Evelyn put a hand on her daughter's arm, "Let's get your father and make a quick exit." The quiet authority in Evelyn's voice was evident and Olivia had no choice but to do as ordered. Both women looked stressed as they crossed the room, hoping to remove Jackson before he completely lost control.

Trace folded his arms across his chest and glared back at Jackson. Trace had never been intimidated by this man. "Nobody needs to listen to your rantings, and I don't like being accused of something I didn't do. I haven't been out to your place in years."

Jackson's accusations were bizarre and his animosity toward Trace kept escalating. Jackson's eyes narrowed, "You've lived here long enough to know how powerful I am, and you'll be sorry. I'm going to ruin you if it's the last thing I do." Jackson had a way of going after people who defied him.

Trace had experienced the man's threats before. Until now they had only been verbal, but tonight there was a menacing look in Jackson's eyes that Trace hadn't seen before. "Are you threatening me?"

The volume of Jackson's voice increased, "Damn right, I am, cowboy." Nothing could mask the fiery burst of rage that sprang up in his eyes. Jackson's temper was vile when lost.

Olivia thrived on attention but not this kind. She stepped between the two men and gave Trace an apologetic look. "Come with me, Dad, it's time for us to go home." Olivia took his arm and turned him away and led him to the door. She couldn't make her escape fast enough.

Jackson turned back and yelled, "I'm coming to get my horses back."

Evelyn hated seeing her husband like this. When he got this way there was no reasoning. She walked over to Trace, "I am sorry. Because Jackson was so good today, we thought he would enjoy getting out and seeing friends. Unfortunately, there are definite triggers that make him lose control."

That's an understatement. He's off his bloody rocker. Just last week Matt told Trace that when he was in town at the hardware store Jackson was also there. When someone mentioned Trace's name the man went berserk, started yelling, and was asked to leave.

Kit had now reached her husband's side, "Is everything all right over here? We could hear Jackson yelling from across the room."

Matt attempted to break the tension, "I'll get back in line and get us drinks. I'm sure you need one."

"Make mine a double, buddy."

Kit's compassion surfaced as she watched the Beaumonts leaving, "I feel sorry for Olivia and her mother. Nobody likes a scene. While Matt's getting drinks, let's go dance. If we don't make light of this, everyone will be gossiping about it for weeks. We both know what it's like to be the target of gossip. Let's not make it worse." As they maneuvered through the crowd, voices were buzzing.

Trace took his wife's arm and led her onto the dance floor. The newlywed couple passed by them, their arms wrapped around each other, the incident easily forgotten. "Word about what happened here tonight will get around pretty fast," commented Trace.

"When doesn't it? As nice as Trudy is she's a nonstop gossip. She'll be the first to start spreading what happened here."

Despite the drama it had been a wonderful wedding. Dixie was radiant all day, evidence that her special day was everything she had dreamed of.

"This may surprise you, but I like weddings. They remind me of the happiest day of my life when you became my wife. You changed my life for the better and I will love you until the day I die."

Misty eyed, Kit leaned in for his kiss. Kit and Trace left the wedding arm in arm.

*****

Olivia and Evelyn were in Jackson's office. Olivia had an appreciation for her mother, who was the moral compass of the family. She admired how her mother always planned and managed the social events when Olivia was growing up. She was efficient and organized but never relied on her daughter's input or assistance. Her mother didn't need her, and her father didn't want her. Olivia was aware that her mother's role had changed. Now Jackson needed his wife beyond the social setting. Evelyn would fulfill her new duties as efficiently as she had all her other duties. Olivia had stepped in for her father at work. He was unaware of her involvement and to the fact she was running the business. Olivia now had Power of

Attorney over his affairs while Evelyn was his Personal Directive. Evelyn knew Jackson would be furious when he found out. They had decided to share this with him when he joined them. The nurse was with Jackson in his room getting him ready for the day. Evelyn was distraught, "Do we really have to do it today?"

"We have to, Mother. Waiting won't change anything. We did what we had to. Dad is getting worse every day." Jackson had declined quickly over the last couple of weeks, and he was now confined to a wheelchair. "He is no longer competent, and he can no longer be taken out in public." His attendance at the wedding was an unpleasant reminder that it was time to confine him to the property. They turned when Jackson was wheeled in. He was in a foul mood, and they knew it would likely get worse.

Evelyn greeted him with false brightness, "Good morning, dear. I hope you slept well."

"Who can sleep when you have a business to run, and you have a bunch of idiots working for you. I'm going into the office to fire every one of them." His periods of confusion were happening more often along with more frequent outbursts.

Evelyn was anxious, "Now, Jackson, you know you don't go to the office anymore. Olivia goes to the office for you." The die was cast.

Jackson's hysteria surfaced, "What the hell are you talking about?"

"Mother is your Personal Directive, and she makes the decisions relating to your daily care and health issues. I have been given the role of Power of Attorney and I make the decisions and run Beaumont Enterprises."

"I didn't give permission for any of this."

Evelyn gave her husband a look filled with regret. "Not all changes are by choice."

Olivia wasn't as kind, "You have no choice. You no longer have the mental capacity to understand what is relevant to even made a decision. The company has suffered from the consequences of your poor decisions. I am running your business and control your financial affairs. You have no say at all." Olivia could be as malicious as her father. Her eyes went cold as she smiled triumphantly at her father.

His daughter's criticism only made Jackson madder, "This is what you've always wanted."

If Olivia denied it, it would have been a lie. Not that lying bothered her.

Jackson's anger erupted as he glared at his daughter. He was now in a full-blown rant, "I'm telling you; I am Beaumont Enterprises. What the hell do you know about business? What even makes you think you can run my business without me? It's a dog-eat-dog world out there."

Things had changed; she had changed. Olivia was no longer intimidated by her father. "Don't worry, Dad. I learned what I needed to by watching and listening to you for years. You showed me exactly how to be powerful and decisive." Victory was hers. More big changes were going to happen. Olivia understood if you want something go after it with everything you have.

Casting another speculative glance at his daughter, Jackson sneered, "If you think you can run my business, you're the one who is out of her mind. You'll run it into the ground in six months and I can't allow that." Jackson refused to admit defeat. "No lousy piece of paper is going to tell me different. You're fired."

Olivia laughed, "You no longer have any authority. I know you keep forgetting things, but I just told you I have been given Power of Attorney. That makes me Beaumont Enterprises. You have no control over Beaumont Enterprises and your control over me is over." She looked down at her dad with disgust, "You don't even have control over yourself." Olivia's manner was detached as she turned to her mother, "Dad needs to go to his room. He seems to be extremely upset. Dolores can give him something to settle him."

Before it could escalate any further, Evelyn rang for Dolores. There was no point in letting this continue. She hated it when the two of them would fight.

Resistance remained in Jackson's bulging eyes before he acknowledged her strategic moves, "By damn, you always manage to surprise me you conniving bitch." When the nurse arrived to take him away, he looked like a broken man.

Evelyn usually maintained the aura of helplessness, but she could be tough as nails when called upon. "Please take Mr. Beaumont to his room and give him a sedative." Evelyn had always been a caring person. She gently patted her husband's cheek, "A rest will do you good."

Olivia deliberately went and sat in her father's chair. Her life again had purpose due to her dramatic change of direction. She turned to look at her father's portrait and smiled. A calm settled over her, a calm that came from surviving her father's rant. Even though her father was incapable of doing any work, his desk remained exactly like he left it. There, or not, his presence was felt. In time she would make the office her own and the first thing she would do would be the removal of her father's portrait. Olivia turned back to address her mother, "I'm doing what I can in regard to the business. I have to rely on others, which is difficult because Dad never trusted anyone else. He ran the whole show on his own once he bought back the share of the business he sold when I married Burke."

"You're doing a fine job. I'm not surprised, and I am proud of you. You are smart and strong and capable."

Her father had never said those words to her. "Thank you, Mother. Dad would just be telling me all the things I'm doing wrong."

Evelyn could see Jackson in Olivia's eyes. "You have a lot of your father in you, Olivia." This was not a compliment. Her daughter was cold and calculating like Jackson.

Olivia grew up knowing they had lots of money. The only thing that impressed Olivia more than money was power. She always knew her dad was a good businessman but as she grew older, she began to realize how ruthless and cutthroat he was. "Dad's vision was to win at all costs. My goal is also to win, but you have to look long-term. I plan on being prepared rather than pay for mistakes." Jackson would go after things with no limits despite what he might lose. "Dad has made some drastic, and often unwise, decisions over the last few years. It cost us money and our reputation. He should have been removed from the helm way before this."

Olivia smiled. She loved the power and control. She discovered power to be intoxicating. She prided herself on how she had adapted to her working environment. Olivia had a lot of her father in her, so she adapted quickly to make the people around her do what she wanted. It was exhilarating. Olivia knew the staff called her Miss High and Mighty. She couldn't care less. Nothing and no one was going to get in her way.

Evelyn had been watching her daughter. "You like being the boss. It's in your blood, just like it was in your father's."

Olivia had a mission. She wanted the power more than the money. "Beaumont Enterprises is no longer the same company. It's time to take it back to its former glory and back to the forefront in the business world."

CHAPTER TEN

Kit enjoyed the long, slow days of summer, but they were counting down. The Calhoun Labour Day barbeque was next weekend. Maggie had come over and the women were enjoying the morning outside on the deck. Maggie's kids were at her mom's for the day and Trace had taken Kenzie and Benny to town with him. Finn was upstairs with Lola.

Maggie released a contented sigh, "I don't even feel guilty when I say I enjoy time without the kids. It's been a busy summer. I can't believe school starts next week. I must admit I'm ready to get back into a regular routine. Is Finn enrolled in school?"

Kit nodded. "Lola and Finn have worked hard, and he's caught up in the core subjects."

"You're going to the Calhoun barbeque, aren't you?"

"We are but I'm anxious for Finn. I remember how nervous I was when I attended my first barbeque just after I arrived here. It isn't easy being new and meeting a whole bunch of strangers for the first time."

Maggie smiled at her friend. They had met that day and had been best friends ever since. "All the young men were attracted to you. Especially Trace Grayson and Doc Parker. Matt and I laughed about it when we got home. Doc, as always, was respectfully attracted but poor Trace had been knocked to his knees and didn't know how to get up."

Kit laughed, "At the time, Trace had adamantly declared he and I could only be friends because he didn't want any commitments other than the ones he had with Lola Grande and Caballo Stables. I don't know if you remember, but I had gone out with Doc. I liked him but quickly realized how deep my feelings were for Trace. Doc is such a nice man. I'm surprised he's never married."

Maggie knew the vet still had feelings for Kit but didn't know if that was the reason. "Do you think the Calhouns would mind if we brought our hired hand's son, Cruz Ortiz, with us? He's the same age as Finn and will also be starting school this year as a new student."

"He'll be more than welcome. I hope the boys hit it off. Finn could use a friend." Kit knew it wouldn't be easy making new friends at school. Trace had shared how hard it was for him and Riley every time they changed schools. "I took Finn to Calgary last week to buy new clothes for back to school. I think he grew two inches over the summer. We made it a full day and the two of us stayed and had dinner. It did us both good to spend time away from the ranch and I believe he and I developed a stronger bond."

Kit allowed her thoughts to drift while Maggie took a call. The trip to Calgary had been a success in more ways than one. They shopped for hours and bought a pile of new clothes, right down to underwear. When they were done shopping, they went to Kit's favorite restaurant for dinner. Their conversation over dinner made for an interesting and revealing day. "Are you nervous about going to the Calhoun barbeque?"

Finn shrugged in his typical off-hand manner, not quite meeting Kit's gaze. "I didn't know I was going. I never got to go anywhere with the Ungers and their children."

Kit's face never faltered even though she was shocked. "Of course, you will be coming with us. You're part of our family, Finn." Kit saw the look of anxiety on Finn's face and understood what going to something like this meant. "I remember how nervous I was attending my first barbeque. I had just arrived at the ranch, and I didn't know anyone either. I'll stay with you until you feel comfortable just like my dad did with me."

Finn was relieved to hear this and appreciated Kit's thoughtfulness. It didn't make him any less nervous.

Kit decided to address another concern, "It's not easy dealing with a bunch of strangers and everyone seems to be dissecting your every move. I felt like that when I came to Valley View. I was afraid my father would reject me like my mother did. My dad accepted me right away and welcomed me into the family. It took longer for others to accept me, especially Trace. In time they did. I'm not saying that any of us don't accept you. I'm saying we all need time to adjust. I judged my dad unfairly because of my experiences with my mother. Don't judge us unfairly because of your experiences with previous foster parents. We aren't like them. Your arrival has had a huge impact on our lives. It takes some a little longer to accept change. Give us all some time, Finn, including yourself."

Finn refused to comment but Kit knew he was listening intently. He chose to change the direction of the conversation, "The Calhoun family and your family seem to be very close."

"Our families operate a joint venture called C&G Ranching. With the Calhouns we make a comfortable living with the cattle. They are the mainstay that helped Lola Grande get on its feet. Even before Lola Grande belonged to the Graysons, Trace started Caballo Stables as his own enterprise and began breaking and training horses right out of high school. His hard work has made it a viable independent operation and he has made a name for himself as a highly specialized trainer. Trace runs a first-rate operation training horses for cutting."

Finn had seen for himself Trace's skill with the horses. "You said you aren't from here. Did you grow up on a ranch?"

Kit had successfully drawn Finn into conversation. "No, I grew up in a city in the United States. When I arrived at Valley View, Trace kept calling me "city girl" and it wasn't a compliment. It's easy to judge someone knowing little or nothing about them. They all assumed I was just a city girl, so they also assumed I didn't ride. I knew how to ride horses because of my summer job at camp. I ride as well as I walk. I had the last laugh on that one."

"I've watched Kenzie. She's very confident on her horse."

"She's been riding since she was four. Benny is next. We have never discussed this. Do you ride?"

Finn was hesitant before expressing his longing, "No, but since I'm living with your family I'd like to learn since you all ride."

Kit hated the dejection she saw. They had been so focused on Finn's schooling they hadn't considered anything else. "I'll talk to Trace to see which horse would be the best for you to start with."

Kit didn't know if it was because they were away from the ranch and everyone there, but Finn continued to open up, which allowed him to make a confession, "You unconditionally accepted me into your home and as part of your family, but I don't think Trace likes me."

Finn's comment troubled Kit. She knew Finn was still apprehensive of Trace, but it was more serious than she thought. "There are many facets to Trace making him a confusing man to understand. He often appears rigid and aloof, so he isn't the easiest person to get to know. Trace is reserved and complex. I know it seems like he's hard on you at times. Believe it or not, that's his way of showing he cares."

Finn's face shadowed, "He always sounds so stern when he talks to me."

It was pointless to deny this. Facts were facts. "Trace was exactly like that when I met him. He struggles with change. Change can be scary, even for adults. We don't always have the answers and we don't have the experience or history of raising an older child, so we are still trying to figure this out. Give us time like we are giving you time."

"You do realize Trace is demanding and forceful. He's even worse than Lola. Is it a Grayson trait I need to keep watching out for?" Finn challenged.

Kit laughed and nodded. "You learn to deal with it. Trace is a hard man, often unyielding like the land. He isn't exactly the easiest person to get to know. But he is someone you can rely on and trust." She knew she'd have to have faith in both of them.

Finn intentionally changed the subject, "Trace loves working with the horses."

"He does. Trace knows more about training horses than most men and he's made a name for himself with his line of horses. He is a renowned cutting horse trainer, but if you asked him what he does he would tell you he's a cowboy who works on a ranch. He's an honorable man. The Graysons are a proud family."

"Do you think Trace would let me help with the horses even though I have no experience?"

Kit heard the yearning in the boy's voice and didn't miss the desperate searching look in Finn's eyes. He wanted to belong, not just fit in. "That's something you'll have to ask Trace. Why haven't you asked before?"

"I don't know how long I'll be here. When you're a foster child you always live with the fear your foster parents can give you back or the agency can send someone to take you away." He shrugged his shoulders, pretending it didn't matter.

Kit's words were sincere and heartfelt when she spoke, "We won't let that happen, Finn. Your bad memories will fade in time. We'll make new ones together and I pray they will be happy ones. It's hard for you right now because it still hurts so much, and everything is new." They got up and left.

The silence was heavy on the drive home. Kit knew Finn understood the significance of what she had shared tonight. Finn realized maybe everyone had things in their past that were difficult to talk about. Kit understood the significance of what Finn had shared. They were both learning new things about each other.

Lola was having coffee with Trace when they returned home. Kit grabbed a glass of water and joined them. Finn headed up to bed, avoiding more conversation.

"Kenzie and I made supper together. She's getting to be quite the helper. I must have read Benny at least five stories before he fell asleep." Lola loved the nights when she had this special time with her grandchildren.

Kit wanted Trace and Finn to develop a closer relationship. Lola had already made quite an impression on Finn. Actually, so had Trace but it wasn't a good one. Kit turned to Trace, "We had a great day but it's later than I intended. We talked a long time after our meal. You know Finn has been watching you for weeks with the horses. Deep down he wants to learn how to work with them. He'd like to spend time with you, and it will help you to get to know him better. He told me he has never ridden a horse. We all ride. It's time he did, too."

Trace had seen the yearning more than once when Finn had been watching him train.

Lola put her hand on her son's arm, "The boy has come a long way, but he still needs guidance. He also needs purpose. I know the commitment and determination Finn has. It's time to focus that elsewhere and he wants more than anything to fit in. Finn is a lot like Diego. Head-strong and stubborn. You will have to establish who the boss is while trying to understand the boy better."

"Speaking from experience, Ma?"

"Are we still talking about Finn?"

Trace was annoyed when they both laughed. "Very funny. I can't win with you two ganging up on me." Trace was feeling apprehensive. Since meeting Kit there was always one challenge after another. He understood a little better how Finn must be feeling. Trace shook his head, "You are aware I'm not exactly known for my patience."

"This will give you a chance to work on it." Kit lifted her chin when she wanted to make a point. With jaw set she had the last word, "You can start by talking to Finn tomorrow."

Trace failed to hide his irritation.

The next morning, Finn was drawn by the activity happening in the far corral. Trace was astride a young horse. Finn went over, crossed his arms on the top rail, rested his chin on them and watched. He stood in silence, fascinated by the ritual between man and beast as they worked the young calf. The horse's head was down, ears back, and everything about his body language told the calf he was the boss. Each time the calf feinted the horse shifted course, anticipating the calf's every move. The horse was following the cow's lead step for step, proving to be very athletic. When the horse snorted and pawed the ground with restless energy, Trace settled deeper into the saddle, concentrating on the task at hand. Horse and rider cut and dodged, gaining control that defined the skill level of both. Evidence of the practiced precision and patience learned from hours of training.

Kit stood on the verandah and watched as Finn stood alone. She walked over with Benny and joined him. Reaching up to climb and hold onto the top rail, Benny declared, "Daddy's going to teach me to be a cowboy." Today, Benny was wearing one of his dad's old cowboy hats although it was much too big.

They continued to watch until Trace was done and joined them. Kit wanted them to have time alone to bond. She was also hoping Trace would act on their conversation from the night before. Picking Benny up she said, "Well little cowboy, let's go find Poco and you can ride around the kitchen while I prepare supper."

Trace decided not to delay the inevitable but lead in with caution, "Kit told me the two of you had a good day in the city. Are you nervous about starting school?"

Even though living with the Graysons was better, Finn hated to admit he was nervous. He had too many bad experiences to relate to. The Graysons treated him like they treated their own kids and Kit had made arrangements to tour the school so he would know his way around. They kept doing unexpected things which helped to make him feel they were really his family. He knew he was lucky to have ended up here. "As much as I hated having to do it, I do appreciate Lola's commitment to get me caught up."

"I'm proud of you, Finn. Not everyone would have committed to a full summer of home schooling to catch up."

"I didn't have much choice," Finn replied, matter-of-factly.

"What do you think of ranch life?"

"I don't know much about it." Finn tried not to sound disappointed.

"Every season creates its own work on a ranch. No one is ever idle. Ranching, whether it be cattle or horses, is a job you do every day. Days are filled with hard work that isn't always productive, but the rewards make it worth the hardships. Four generations of Calhouns have dedicated their lives to Valley View. We are the first generation here at Lola Grande."

Finn didn't interrupt, he was thrilled because Trace was giving him more than just the usual time of day before walking out the door to go to work.

"It's been pretty hectic around here since your arrival. You with school and me with work. Spring is the busiest time of the year for ranchers. That's why you haven't met my brother yet. Riley works for the Calhouns at their ranch. You'll get a chance to meet him and the rest of Kit's family when we go to the Calhoun barbeque. My brother and I helped around the ranch when we arrived at Valley View. I was always hanging out at the corrals hoping to see the horses. I became a full-time employee right out of high school. I wanted to be more than somebody's hired hand. I wanted better than what our dad left us with. I had already established Caballo Stales and was training horses at Valley View. I kept moving forward with my dreams when my family got Lola Grande. Here, I have a great set up for my horse training operation right down to an indoor arena. I work hard, but at the end of the day, I am a cowboy. A cowboy lives to be free and proud of being his own man. Now that you are spending less time homeschooling. I could use help with the horses. What do you say?"

There were tell-tale signs of doubt on Finn's face. Trace was taken aback when Finn asked him if he was doing this because Kit asked him to. Finn could be as direct as Kit.

Recovering his composure quickly, Trace admitted, "We talked about you, and she was the one who suggested it. It's hard to say no to Kit."

"Yeah, I'm learning that." Finn's face remained apprehensive, and he didn't let it go. He had to know. "Are you sure?"

"I think you know me well enough by now to know I don't do something if I don't want to. I thought you had enough to deal with to fit in and get caught up with your schooling."

Finn's whole body was tense. He wanted this more than anything, but old fears run deep. He spent years being afraid to make mistakes because he would be punished. Pushing his fears aside, Finn nodded his head, "I might as well. There's nothing else to do around here." The boy still didn't give an inch or show how much things mattered.

"I don't see why we have to wait. Come with me. Once you're settled in school, we'll set up a new routine around here." Trace put his arm casually around Finn's shoulder and felt they were definitely making progress when Finn didn't pull away. Finn fell into step with Trace as they headed over to the barn. Trace knew where they would start. Finn's first few weeks of training would be spent either in the tack room learning about the equipment and how they were used or in the main stable mucking stalls. The chore of mucking would remain as part of Finn's ranch duties. They walked to the back of the barn to the tack room. "This is where my training began. Today I will explain every item and its purpose. When something is used it gets cleaned and put back in its place. That way everyone knows where it is when it is needed."

Finn was quick to realize that Trace's expectations were high, and his rules were rigid. It came as no surprise. Finn listened intently.

CHAPTER ELEVEN

The countryside had slowly transformed. The transition from greens to vivid autumn colors was complete. The days were getting shorter and cooler. The early morning air was crisp, often cold enough to see your breath, but the scenery was so stunning it could take your breath away. Calving season was over and harvest was done. It was time to celebrate.

Today was the Labour Day barbeque at Valley View. The Calhouns always celebrated the end of a productive season with an annual barbeque. The Grayson family was attending, along with other neighbours and friends. It was a big day for the Graysons. They would be introducing their foster son.

Kit took in the scenery driving over. It was a beautiful day. The morning dew had dissipated, and the air was warm. The gentle breeze blowing off the mountains helped wispy clouds drift aimlessly across the sky. Kenzie was talking nonstop anxious to see friends she hadn't seen all summer. Finn was quiet. The thought of meeting a bunch of strangers terrified him. Kit understood his nervousness.

Valley View was a bustle of activity. Groups had formed around the backyard and people were milling about. There were a lot of people, and a lot of activity. The informal setting was welcoming but Finn was still terrified. Kit saw the look of anxiety in Finn's eyes. He was having a hard time taking it all in.

Kit rested her hand on Finn's shoulder as her grandparents were making their way toward them. She was excited to introduce them to Finn.

"My grandparents are admirable people. My grandfather, Will Calhoun, appears stern and gruff, but he's a marshmallow inside. My grandmother, Sadie, may hug you to death. She is a lovely person who always sees the good in people."

As expected, Sadie pulled the boy to her and hugged him close. "I am happy to meet you. Welcome to our family."

Shelby strolled over and joined them. "This is Shelby, Riley's wife. You met Riley earlier." Shelby usually dressed to the nines in tight designer jeans and sparkly shirts. Today, she looked demure in a flowy empire-waisted maxi dress. She was beginning to look more like a mature young lady. As always, the long-legged blonde looked stunning and graceful. Looking closer, Kit could see her baby bump and wondered when her and Riley would share their news.

Finn thought Shelby was one of the prettiest ladies he had ever met. He flushed when Shelby gave him one of her radiant smiles.

Moving on to make more introductions, Kit approached Doc Parker. Doc's gaze was drawn to Kit. He wondered if he would ever find someone like her to share his life with. Doc greeted them warmly. He always had a relaxed and easy manner and welcomed Finn causally, trying to put the boy at ease. Doc was a good friend.

While they were chatting, Trace joined them. He looked at Finn, "I'm sure by now you're tired of meeting strangers, but I thought you might like to meet someone your own age. Cruz's dad works for my friend Matt, and he is also nervous about being here today."

Kit smiled. Finn was no less nervous but was putting up a good front. "Tell Maggie we will save a table next to ours when it's time to eat. Kenzie wants to sit at their table with Lucy Rose and if Cruz wants, he can join our table."

Trace always had a habit of showing up out of nowhere. Doc was annoyed, then immediately annoyed with himself due to the stab of jealousy he was experiencing. He envied what Trace had. Usually, he could control it. Today, he couldn't ignore the void he felt within. Doc's feelings for Kit were stronger than simple attraction. It was his secret that he was in love with Kit. He had been since the day he met her. He excused himself and left when another neighbour joined them.

After they were done meeting people, the two boys took off together and were soon mingling with other kids their own age. The boys were relieved to have endured the initial meeting of so many strangers. Kit continued to watch Finn throughout the day. At first, Finn had struggled in this social environment even though everyone was welcoming. Finn had met dozens of people, but his demeanour changed after he met Cruz. Now Finn's brooding looks had been replaced by newfound confidence. Finn and Cruz stuck together like Siamese twins for the rest of the day.

Shelby was resting in the shade. Seeing an empty chair, Kit went over and joined her. Kit finally began to relax and enjoy herself.

Shelby smiled, "I see Finn is doing okay. Do you remember your first barbeque here at Valley View? It was just after you arrived."

Kit nodded, "Like it was yesterday. My arrival here was met with animosity and open hostility especially by you. Trace wasn't any better."

"I felt threatened by you. You were getting all the attention I was used to getting. The Grayson boys began spending a lot more time at Valley View than at Lola Grande. I considered you a rival, but I underestimated your determination. Your Calhoun stubbornness was as strong as mine. I had met my match. You never backed down."

"You brought out the worst in me. I wasn't always nice either."

"I was mean to you so many times. I wanted you to go away. I was scared. More than I cared to admit. I was afraid Dad would love you more than me. I allowed my resentment to overshadow everything. I was raised with good values, but they seemed to go out the window when you arrived. It took me too long to find them again. Dad lectured me about my behaviour toward you more than once. I was too head-strong to give in."

"It was difficult dealing with your spitefulness while I was trying to fit in. I envied the loving relationship between you and Dad. I felt like an outsider, but I knew I had a right to be here. I was also jealous of you. You had Dad's unconditional love and I felt I had to prove to him I was worthy of it as well."

"My behaviour was deplorable. I took every opportunity to turn everything into a personal assault and I fought dirty."

"Everyone kept telling me your behaviour was out of character. I knew if we met under different circumstances, I would have liked you. You're exciting to be around, full of life and high energy."

They were glad they could both laugh over it now. Like Maggie, Shelby had become a friend.

A shadow crossed Shelby's face. "Riley waited patiently for me to grow up."

Riley always had an easy-going manner. "Your husband is a saint. Not like his brother. Patience isn't one of Trace's virtues and we know how he struggles with trust. So does Finn. There is still a lot of work ahead of us before Finn and Trace bond."

"Thank God Riley has more patience than Trace. I know I've tried his patience many times over the years. Our first year of marriage was challenging. I was still growing up. As you know, it takes me a while to think beyond myself. I must admit I enjoyed living in the world of Shelby growing up. As I matured my world began to feel more like an island and like always Riley rescued me. I love Riley more than anything. I've come a long way which is a good thing because we're going to be parents." Shelby's cheeks warmed as she placed her hands on her stomach. "We'll be welcoming a little girl before the new year."

"Congratulations, Shelby. I know you will be a good mom."

"I hope so. I know having a baby is a huge responsibility so Riley and I had to wait until we were ready to take on such a huge and life-changing responsibility. I had to grow up and be less self-centred if we were going to be parents."

Benny ran over crying. He had scraped his knee and needed comfort from his mom. Kit lifted him onto her lap and cuddled him close.

Unexpected tears formed in Shelby's eyes, "I have another confession, I was envious of you when I heard you and Trace were expecting with Benny. You know me, I want what everyone else has. Being more mature, it was a fleeting moment." Shelby had grown up.

Benny shifted, wanting down. He just needed a cuddle before he took off again with the other kids. Kit kissed his cheek and set him free. "Being a mom is the best job in the world, just not the easiest. Parenting will give you your highest highs and your lowest lows as your children challenge you. Every new stage brings on a new challenge." Her eyes wandered over to Finn, who was at the corrals with Cruz. "Just when you think life is back in balance you take on a new challenge. It has been an interesting summer, but Finn is fitting in with our family."

"We all had to learn to deal with change. I'll do my best to make Finn welcome, so he feels like he's part of both our families. There will be big changes ahead for all of us."

Kit looked around, watching her family. "There always are." A profound statement.

They looked over and Riley and Trace appeared to be in deep conversation. They guessed Riley was sharing his news with his brother.

Trace was watching Benny romp around with Rhett. "When are you and Shelby going to start a family?"

Riley smiled, "You and Kit are going to have a niece right after Christmas."

"Why didn't you say something sooner?"

"Shelby wanted to wait until she was in her second trimester. She also wanted to know as soon as possible what we are having. You know Shelby as well as I do; she has never been known for her patience. Needless to say, she was thrilled when she found out it was a girl. I have to admit it's very different having a pregnant wife."

"Let me give you the same advice Ma gave me. She said there is nothing normal with your wife during pregnancy. When you can't deal with her mood swings and unexplained tears, you go for a long walk."

Recognizing the responsibility facing them, Riley admitted he was nervous about becoming a parent.

Trace understood. "The minute I held my infant son I immediately understood Ma's unconditional love for us. I know you'll be a wonderful father," Trace said with true conviction.

"Thanks, Trace. That means a lot coming from you."

There were cheers when BJ started going around announcing it was time to eat. Kit looked up and Finn was on his way over with Cruz. "Trace has grabbed a table, and the Walkers pulled another table over next to ours. Follow me."

The rest of the day passed pleasantly. They headed home when others with young ones began to leave.

Kit sighed with contentment as she sat next to Trace when the kids had settled upstairs. "This was a big day for Finn. He managed it well. And he made a friend. He is fitting in."

"It was one day, Kit. We still have to expect bumps along the way." Kit just smiled up at him. Trace was familiar with that smile. She smiled at him to pacify him, but she hadn't changed her belief that everything would work out.

CHAPTER TWELVE

As the weeks passed, Finn developed a level of trust to go along with his newly found confidence. Finn began to let go of his inner fears and was developing into a confident young man. He had developed a strong sense of self-worth thanks to the Graysons. He finally had the courage he needed to ask Trace, "I kinda want to see if I can learn to do what you do."

"That's what we've been doing. It's all part of ranching." Trace knew what Finn wanted but he wanted Finn to be sure on what he was asking.

Finn's voice rose with excitement, "I meant training horses."

The fact that Finn was specific convinced Trace he was ready. Finn had proven to be a hard worker and followed orders well. "When would you like to get started?"

Finn was surprised by Trace's response. He took a deep breath before saying, "Whenever you have the time." Finn was a little hesitant to add, "I like horses and I'm not afraid of them, but I have never ridden one."

Trace stopped dead in his tracks. He had forgotten that Kit told him this. "Well, that's a big oversight on my part. Why didn't you say something sooner?"

"I needed to get to know you better. You scared me to death when I first came here," Finn replied with a cheeky grin.

"It takes time to build trust with the horses just like it takes time to build trust with people. I may come across gruff at times, but you don't have to be afraid of me."

Finn believed him.

"That fenced area over there is where we put the yearlings through their paces. Follow me. I have Charlie in there now." Finn was right behind Trace as he followed him over to the small paddock. Finn's gaze remained on the young colt who pranced freely in the confined area. Trace whistled and he pranced over to the rail. "This is Charlie. He was sired by Rebel, not Diego. Both are prime stud horses who continue to sire a fine lineage of foals. I'll start training him in a couple of weeks. Just because you don't have experience doesn't mean you can't learn to train them. When the time comes, I'll start training you at the same time. You can be Charlie's trainer." It would be interesting watching them. Two inexperienced and determined entities. "I love the challenge of training horses without breaking their spirit. It takes months of commitment and practice, but the end results are worth it."

Finn could tell that Trace wasn't complaining. This was him sharing facts relevant to the course of training. Finn was beginning to develop a new respect for Trace and could better understand what Kit had been telling him about this man. With gentle fingers, Finn stroked the yearling's forehead. The foal leaned in and nudged him.

Trace pulled out a sugar cube from his pocket and handed it to Finn. "You need to learn everything you can about horses before you can train them. You might as well get on the good side of Charlie right away. I'm sure you're tired of hearing this, but school comes first."

"I know," Finn replied without attitude." Lola had helped restore Finn's confidence. "I know I can do this."

"I have no doubt," Trace said with a note of encouragement. Trace's belief in Finn was solid. "When I began my training, the first thing I was taught was safety with the horses is the main concern and training horses means understanding them. Once you start to work with them, you will see horses have different personalities. But first things first; let's get you on a horse."

*****

Over the next couple of weeks, Trace continued teaching Finn the basics. He explained how to handle the horses and how to care for them. Finn was an avid student, taking in every word. The days passed, one day the same as the other. Finn was beginning to question if Trace was ever going to have him start training Charlie. That night, they headed over to the small paddock where Charlie was waiting. The young colt greeted Trace with a whinny.

"It's time to advance to a new phase. It will involve more work."

"Training?"

Trace nodded.

Finn grinned from ear to ear. He was nervous and excited at the same time.

So it began, just like it did years ago when Murphy trained Trace. Trace showed Finn how to slip a bridle over Charlie's head and attach a lead rope. "Start by leading him with a simple walk." Trace stood back and observed.

Finn straightened and with determination he began leading the colt. He turned Charlie and repeated the exercises as Trace instructed. Trace wanted to get a clear picture of Finn's confidence level and attention span.

Once the gait exercise was learned, Trace had Finn mount Charlie. "Keep your mind on Charlie. You have to always keep your connection with the horse. You have to put yourself in the horse's mind and stay there."

The boy's set jaw and rigid frame emphasized his serious concentration. Finn dug deep for the confidence he needed as he followed Trace's instructions. Finn reigned Charlie in, backed the yearling up, then squeezed with his knees. Unfortunately, Finn had applied too much unexpected pressure. Charlie reared up, throwing Finn to the ground, and pranced off.

Trace smothered the urge to laugh, instead easing Finn's embarrassment by saying, "When Kenzie was learning to ride, she fell off more than once. She would get up, brush off her pants, and climb back on. That takes courage and determination." Trace waited to see what Finn would do next.

A scowl darkened Finn's face. He wasn't about to be shown up by a girl years younger than him. He had to dig a little deeper for the courage to get back on Charlie. He wouldn't let Trace down by quitting. Finn glanced over at Trace, his expression intense and determined, and remounted Charlie. He focused harder and remained mounted.

The training continued and Trace offered words of encouragement. At the end of the session, Trace patted Finn on the back. "That's enough for today. When a horse is young, you don't want to overdo it. Too much exercise can hurt their joints. You did a good job considering it was your first day riding Charlie."

Finn shot Trace a look of frustration. "Even though I got bucked off?"

"There's an old cowboy saying. If you haven't fallen off a horse, you haven't been riding long enough. It has happened to the best of us. Go cool Charlie down."

*****

Trace had been busier than ever. Teaching someone else took twice as long as doing the training yourself, but Trace continued to give Finn the time he needed. The reward was worth it. Trace and Finn established a strong bond. Finn's confidence remained even when the training took on a dramatic twist. When the training became more intense, so did Trace. Kit observed this as she stood next to Trace and watched.

"Keep your mind on what you're doing at all times. You have to trust in your horse and trust in yourself. Your focus has to remain on your horse. Do not get distracted." Trace turned to Kit, "The boy has come a long way. Finn is a fast learner. He's making real progress. Charlie was a good horse to start his training with. Finn handles Charlie with confidence and command."

"Did you tell him that? A word of praise would go a long way."

Trace knew Kit was right. He hated it when she was right. "I don't want him to get too cocky like I was."

Kit laughed, "What do you mean was, cowboy?"

"I see a lot of me in Finn. He's a natural with horses."

"Hearing something like that from you would mean a lot to him. I admire your dedication and patience with Finn. You're doing a great job."

Trace could have laughed knowing the compliment was to prove a point. Which it did. His wife wasn't always very subtle. Trace called out to Finn, "That's enough for today. Go brush Charlie down and then come in for supper." Finn slowed Charlie to a walk and headed back to the barn.

By the time Trace and Finn made it back to the house, Kit was inside having a moment with Kenzie. Kenzie was old enough to know her behaviour was unacceptable, and Kit said as much to her daughter.

Kenzie didn't take her mother's chiding well, "Dad's nicer to Finn because he's a boy, and Finn's being mean to me because I'm a girl."

Trace and Finn walked in and heard Kenzie's last comment. "You're certainly whining like one," Finn taunted.

The kids ignored Kit's 'that's enough' look.

Kenzie's reaction was to attack back, and she tore into Finn. When he started to laugh it only made Kenzie madder. Usually, his teasing just annoyed her, today it made her cry.

Benny didn't help matters when he called her a cry baby.

"I hate you both," Kenzie cried as she stomped off.

It usually took Kenzie time to work through her moods. She ignored everyone during supper. When they were done, she asked her mother, "Can Lucy Rose and I stay after school tomorrow. Her mom can pick us up and bring us home before supper."

"No, you can come home on the bus like usual." Kit was sure the two girls had planned this, and Lucy Rose was asking her mom the same thing, only she was probably saying it would be Kit picking them up.

Kenzie turned to her dad, who she could usually wrap around her little finger, "Why not? I'm old enough and responsible."

"Your mother said no." His expression was uncompromising.

Trace's forbidding stare only silenced Kenzie for a moment. Her manner remained defiant, "You and mom say no to everything. You're just like mom."

"Then I'm doing a good job." Trace looked at Kit and winked.

"Maybe you're asking the wrong questions."

Finn's comment made Kenzie madder. "Shut up, Finn."

"Don't talk to your brother like that." Kit was tired of the bickering.

"He's not my real brother." Kenzie got up and ran to her room.

This was such an emotional and unpredictable hormonal stage. Trace looked at Kit, "Why don't you go see what's bothering her. Finn and I will clean up the kitchen and keep an eye on Benny."

As soon as Kit was upstairs Finn stated the obvious, "Usually Kenzie just chips away until she gets her own way." He knew Kenzie's remark was spoken in anger. It didn't mean it wasn't true.

Trace laughed. "Like mother, like daughter. Kenzie can be a real pain at times."

"Are you saying Kit can be a pain?" Finn asked with a mischievous grin.

Trace threw a tea towel at Finn, "No comment. You can dry the pots and put them away."

Finn looked at Trace. "I probably shouldn't have kept teasing her." Finn enjoyed teasing Kenzie, but he hadn't meant to make her cry. He felt bad.

Trace grinned. "That would be a wise lesson to learn early."

Finn grinned back, "A woman thing?" Trace nodded.

Kit knocked gently on Kenzie's bedroom door and entered. Kenzie was laying on her bed staring up at the ceiling but sat up when Kit entered. Kit went and sat down next to Kenzie and stroked her hair, hoping to find the real reason for her daughter's anger. Trace had been spending a lot of time with Finn lately and maybe Kenzie was feeling left out. "Your dad and I are concerned about your recent behaviour. Especially to Finn. That was a mean remark at supper."

"It's the truth, isn't it?" Kenzie challenged back. "The kids at school say he isn't really my brother. He's a foster child who lives with us. Someone can take him away any time they want to. I do love Finn and I don't want him to be taken away."

Kit realized some of Kenzie's anger was coming from fear of the unknown. "Nobody is going to take Finn away from us." Kit couldn't say why but she could promise Kenzie he would always be part of their family. The adoption process was almost final. Kit knew her daughter well enough to know this wasn't all that was upsetting her. "What else is bothering you? Are you having other problems at school?"

Kenzie sat there stubbornly, only replying when her mom nudged her. "Nothing."

"Do you really expect me to believe that?" Kenzie shook her head. "Are you upset because Dad is spending so much time with Finn?"

Kenzie's expressive eyes were still troubled. There was a long pause, "I've done a lot of thinking about this. I don't want to barrel race anymore. It takes so much of my time that I'm missing out on other things. It seems all I do is practice and go to rodeos. I want to do the things my friends are doing. There's a birthday party for Lindy Marsh next Saturday. They're going to Calgary for a movie and pizza, and the girls are sleeping over. I can't go because I have another rodeo." It was a relief to be able to confide in her mom after weeks of holding it in.

This caught Kit completely by surprise. "I thought this was your dream for the future." Like her dad, Kenzie had a natural ability with horses.

Kenzie looked at her mom hoping for understanding, "It was, and I have enjoyed barrel racing. I am good and I probably would continue to do well. You know I love winning. I always practice hard because you and dad say when you want something bad enough you don't give up. I'm not giving up, Mommy. I just don't want this anymore. I hardly have any time with my friends. I've missed out on so many things. I didn't even get to go to Lucy Rose's birthday party. I don't want this anymore." When Kenzie looked at her mom again, she couldn't stop the tears. "Will we have to sell Tilly if I quit?" Kenzie asked miserably.

Kit took Kenzie into her arms, "No, she will be a good horse to start Benny on. Next year Benny will be ready to start riding a real horse. He is quickly outgrowing Poco. We may have to sell Poco."

Kenzie laughed through her tears. "Do you think Dad will be mad?" There was a definite note of unease in her voice.

"Dad and I always want our children to try things and challenge themselves while committing to something. You did that and we are proud of your achievements. Not just the winning but the devotion you had for your sport and your horse. We will support you in whatever else you choose to do just like dad is now committing to training Finn because that is what Finn wants to do. Finn is committing himself to learn how to train horses and meeting the challenges that go along with it. It's important for you to understand there will always be changes in our lives. That's what growing up is all about. I'm proud you are confident enough to make a decision like this."

"Is growing up always this hard?" Kenzie asked.

"It can be difficult at any age. We just learn to cope better with age and experience. For your information, parenting isn't always easy either."

"Is it okay if I wait to tell Dad?"

"It would be easier if you do it right away. There's no sense putting it off and worrying about it. I'll go downstairs and send him up." *My baby girl is growing up,* thought Kit as she headed downstairs.

CHAPTER THIRTEEN

Today was a very special day. It was Finn's thirteenth birthday. Last year Finn's birthday was during the traumatic transition from his foster home at the Ungers, so it had been missed. Kit and Trace stood alone in the kitchen conspiring before the kids showed up for breakfast. They had been keeping secrets for weeks. Today would be a day of celebration as a new family.

"Can you take Finn away from the ranch after lunch? I need time to prepare. I'm sure he thinks we've forgotten about his birthday like last year." Trace didn't miss the excitement in Kit's voice or the tears in her eyes. Today was a big day. This was going to be one heck of a surprise party. "The women are bringing potluck, so Finn doesn't know what's going on." All of the Calhouns and the Walkers were coming to celebrate Finn's surprise birthday. They were in for a big surprise as well. Nobody else knew about the adoption.

"Is Maggie bringing her famous chilli?"

Kit nodded. "They all plan to be here just after two to help. Shelby said they'd come after Callie's nap."

"Did you say anything to Maggie about the adoption? I know you two share everything."

Kit pretended to be offended but it was true. "No, this is our secret. I can hardly wait to tell Finn."

"I told everyone to park in the Quonset so Finn won't see the vehicles."

Trace agreed to take Finn for a horse ride and show him their land after lunch. It was better to be far away from a kitchen filled with a bunch of bossy females. Kit was pouring a coffee for Trace when Finn entered the kitchen. A minute later Kenzie and Benny bounded in.

"What's for breakfast, Mommy?" Benny asked.

"Daddy wants pancakes. Is that okay for everyone?" Hearing a resounding yes, she told Kenzie to get ingredients out of the fridge while she started mixing up the batter. Finn grabbed plates and silverware. One of his daily chores was to set the table for breakfast and Kenzie had to clear the table afterwards. Benny's job was to stay out of the way.

Kenzie, who struggled to keep a secret, hadn't been told today was Finn's birthday. As usual, she chatted away, "Can we go over to the Walkers this afternoon? Lucy Rose and I would like to have a play day."

"Maggie and I will make sure you spend time together today." Kit smiled inwardly and looked over at Trace, who winked. The Walkers would be bringing Cruz with them. Finn and Cruz had become fast friends and shared a common interest in horses.

Finn, on the other hand, was very quiet during breakfast. He was thoroughly miserable. It had been a disappointing morning due to the fact it was the same as every other morning. Here it was his birthday, and nobody had remembered. His spirits did lift a little when Trace said they'd go for a ride after lunch.

Trace and Finn spent the morning in the barn, mucking stalls, filling feeders, and doing general maintenance in the tack room. Trace had promised Kit to keep Finn out of the house while she puttered in preparation for the party. Lola was upstairs in her suite making Finn's birthday cake.

Right after lunch Trace and Finn headed back to the barn and saddled up. Trace shoved his foot into the stirrup and with easy cowboy grace swung into the saddle. Diego neighed, anxious to head out. "I thought we'd ride into the hills and show you more of Lola Grande."

Finn leaned down to stroke Jasper's neck once he mounted. At least he would be doing something exciting on his birthday.

It was a perfect day for riding in the country. The dry wind carried the scent of the trees and grass, and billowy clouds gathered overhead. When they reached the ridge, they gazed out. Finn sat deeply engrossed in the unfolding beauty sprawled in front of him. He scanned the landscape stretching out on all sides, the rugged mountains a spectacular backdrop to the west. "The view is breathtaking. You can see for miles. Is this land all yours?"

Trace nodded. "There's no place like this. It used to be bigger, but we sold off a large parcel to the Calhouns. Lola Grande didn't need all the land for my horses and the cattle herd keeps increasing. Last year Mom and I bought out Riley's share of our ranch. He's fully invested at Valley View now that he and Shelby are married." Time passed unnoticed as they chatted. "We should head back." They turned from the view and headed back to the ranch.

For Finn it had been an awesome afternoon. Trace's talk about the joining of the Calhouns and the Graysons reminded him that he was still not family. They didn't even remember it was his birthday.

Trace recognized Finn had become more withdrawn the closer they got to home. Trace guessed what the problem was. The boy was in for one huge surprise.

While they were gone, Kit and Kenzie were busy. Kenzie was surprised when she was told today was Finn's birthday, and they were giving him a surprise birthday party. She was miffed that it had been kept a secret from her but if she was being honest with herself, she knew she couldn't keep a secret. Their time was limited even though Trace had promised to keep Finn away all afternoon.

Benny was fascinated with the balloons Kenzie was blowing up. "Benny, quit popping the balloons. We need them for the party." Benny giggled as he ran off with another one. Kenzie's excitement grew when Lola arrived with the cake and a helium balloon with 'Happy 13th Birthday' on it. The Walkers were right behind her.

Kenzie was even more excited, "This will be Finn's best birthday ever."

Kit knew it would have broken her daughter's heart if she knew Finn had never had a birthday party.

Kenzie could hardly contain herself when she heard Finn and her dad coming up the stairs. Everyone had gathered in the kitchen. As soon as the door opened, they all yelled out, "Surprise."

Trace put his hand on Finn's shoulder, "We have something to tell you before the party gets started. We won't be fostering you any longer." Finn stared at them in disbelief. Having misunderstood what was meant, fears from his past grabbed hold. Kit watched Finn's reaction through tear filled eyes. The poor boy's face had paled, and she thought he was going to cry. Before that could happen, Trace continued, "Because we have adopted you. We love you and want you to be part of our family."

Finn was so moved it was difficult to speak. When he did, his response reflected his shock, "You adopted me?"

"We love you as much as we love Kenzie and Benny, so we have officially adopted you, Finn Grayson. We hope you are happy to become a permanent member of our unconventional family." Kit kept chocking on her words.

Finn Grayson. The name he hadn't dared say out loud. "Will I be able to call you Mom and Dad?" Finn asked in a quivering voice, thick with emotion.

"You better, because that's who we are." This time, Kit did cry, along with a few others. Kit made a quick exit to get Finn's birthday cake from the pantry, and they all began to sing.

A huge smiled transformed Finn's freckled face when he saw the cake. "This is the first birthday cake I've ever had."

"Ever!" exclaimed Kenzie in disbelief.

Trace handed Finn his card, "You are now a Grayson in name. You were already a Grayson in our hearts. Welcome to our family." The outside of the envelope read, "Finn Grayson" The front of the card read 'Happy Birthday, Son.' Finn broke down even before he read his card.

Hoping to break the emotional tension, Lola said, "How many get a family for their birthday. Now I am officially your Lita." She went over and hugged Finn.

Finn had to make sure he completely understood. "This means they can never come and take me away. Right?"

"Right. You are a permanent member of our family. We have the final legal documents to prove it, son."

Kenzie went over and hugged Finn. "Now the kids at school can't say you're not my brother. Our mom didn't even tell me about the surprise. She knows I can't keep a secret."

Finn blinked hard several times to hold back more tears. It was amazing what a new day could bring. This was the best day ever. He had wanted desperately to be accepted. This was beyond his wildest dreams.

Everyone was surprised when Will spoke, "The Calhoun family is a close family. So are the Graysons. Both of us have complex family units but we also have strong family ties. Trace and Riley are extremely close as brothers. You now have a brother and a sister. There has always been a strong bond between the Calhouns and the Graysons. Consider yourself part of our family. Welcome to our family, Finn."

Maggie looked at the kids gathered around Finn. "They grow up fast, don't they?"

Kit nodded, "And now we have a teenager." Trace groaned. The others laughed.

The kids were all off playing. Lola placed a hand on Trace's shoulder, "I'm so proud of you and Kit. This is an honorable commitment you have made. You and Kit are two amazing human beings."

"We never know where our journey takes us and who we meet along the way. I dreaded it when Dad said we were moving to Alberta. It turned out to be the best thing he ever did for our family. Kit and I did what we felt was right, just like Buster did when he took us into his home after Dad died. It was an easy decision to make. It was harder to keep it a secret."

Sadie also took a moment to reflect on Kit's past, one similar to Finn's journey. "Kit's arrival resulted in some mighty big changes in all of our lives. Who knows what big change the future will bring next for any of us. No one knows when life takes a dramatic change. In time we learn to embrace the changes and accept what is."

Kit hugged Sadie, "You welcomed me, a stranger, no questions asked."

"You may have come here a stranger, but the moment we saw you we knew you were family. Finn may have come here an orphan, but he is now family. There was such anguish on BJ's face when he found out about you and such anxiety on your face wanting to be accepted. We all saw the anxiety on Finn's face when he arrived. Time and love erased his fears and today his last fear is gone. No one can take Finn away from your family."

It had been an exciting day for everyone. On his way to bed Finn hugged his parents. Nothing remained of the haunted, slightly vengeful youth who had first come to Lola Grande. "Good night, Mom and Dad."

Kit needed a moment and went out to the verandah. She always enjoyed the stillness of a perfect summer night. The gentle wind bringing cool air off the mountains was refreshing. The moon was only a sliver in the sky, but the stars sparkled brightly. Trace joined Kit on the verandah. They were both silent. All in all, it had been a memorable day.

CHAPTER FOURTEEN

The last two years had flown by. Finn was like a different boy since the adoption. Finn was able to let go of most of his inner fears. Fears were real even when unfounded. There was a new level of confidence in everything Finn did. "Before I was adopted, I was always afraid to do something wrong and that would be an excuse to send me away." *Or get punished.* At times, it was still hard to let go of his past.

Ever since Trace and Finn started working together Finn spent even more time down at the corrals. Trace could see Finn's love for the horses, especially Charlie. Trace decided it was time to take the next step and establish a new routine. "Saddle up Charlie and bring him over to the arena. You've done a good job training him and have reached a level of skill I'm satisfied with. I think it's time to advance to a new level. Maybe we should see if Charlie would make a good cutting horse. What do you think?" Trace knew Finn wanted to train horses for cutting. Finn had expressed this more than once.

"If he's ready, I'm ready." Finn's voice was confident, and his face beamed with enthusiasm.

Trace couldn't be prouder of Finn. Finn had proven to be a hard worker. "You're ready. It's time to alter your training to focus on the art of cutting. I don't have to tell you it takes commitment and determination with even more hours of training."

Finn knew the commitment required. He had lost count of how many times he had watched his dad in silence, appreciating the ritual between man and beast.

"Not all horses are suited for competition. Some horses are better suited for ranch life, and they get trained differently. Cutting is part of the regular work on a ranch. There are many times during the year when ranchers need their horses. I can tell within the early stages of training if a horse is better suited for the range, or for competition. Or neither. There are colts who have fun chasing something around. It's play, pure and simple. They don't have the knack to become good at cutting. Once they find out it's work with precision, form, and style, they don't want to do it. The horse I was on today belongs to Brody Maddox, a professional competitor. I've been training his horses for years. He actually bought my first foal sired by Rebel, who was the first horse I bought when I was still in school." Trace continued to tell Finn their history, finishing by saying, "Rebel has proven to be a successful stud horse for breeding. Both Diego and Rebel have produced generations of champion horses. Caballo Stables has more than just a reputation for training cutting horses. My breeding horses are another successful part of my business. My stud horses earn large fees for their services. I love my horses, but it is the training I enjoy the most. It takes a man with a lot of patience to train a cutting horse because it usually takes a minimum of eighteen months to prepare a horse for competition." Trace's look was serious when he said, "I think maybe it's time to take on an employee."

For a moment, Finn was dumbfounded. He wasn't prepared for this. Then Finn grinned at a foreseeable opportunity, "Does that mean I'll earn a paycheck, not just an allowance like Kenzie and Benny?"

Trace appreciated Finn's quickness to address the opportunity. He patted his son on the back, "I've never worked for free so why should you. We'll discuss pay later. We'll start in a couple of days. There's something else you might be interested in. As you know, there are things that must be done every day, but there are additional activities on a cattle ranch. Tomorrow BJ and his wranglers will be going out on the range to gather up strays. He invited us to go along. You can see trained cutting horses at work. We'll head over to Valley View as soon as the sun comes up. I'll hitch up the horse trailer tonight and load Diego and Jasper in the morning."

*****

Trace called out to Finn, "Charlie needs a light hand and a long look at the calf to build his confidence." Trace was teaching his son the same work ethics he had been taught.

When Finn nudged Charlie, he snorted and pawed the ground with restless energy. Finn settled deeper into the saddle, concentrating on the task at hand. Horse and rider cut and dodged, gaining control that defined the skills learned by both from hours of training.

Brody Maddox pulled into the yard and joined Trace at the railing. Brody was picking up his horse today. Trace had finished training Darby; the horse was ready for competition. Brody watched the activity in the ring with appreciation. "You do good work, Trace. With you it's a gift and an art. It's obvious who has been training the rider. He has the same training techniques and ease in the saddle as you. I can see he has established a real connection with the horse and has great hands. Who is he?"

"That young man is our adopted son, Finn. He started training Charlie when he was just a yearling and has been his primary trainer. He has become an excellent trainer and is becoming quite skilled at working a cutting horse."

"Skilled like his dad." Brody admired the boy's skills at such a young age. Brody could see Trace's gentle and patient technique had been passed on to his son. Brody was also impressed by the young horse. The horse's head was down, ears back, and everything in his body language told the calf he was the boss and he shifted course as he anticipated the calf's every move. The horse was following the cow's lead step for step, proving to be very athletic.

Trace waved Finn over. Finn slid off Charlie, looped the reins around the rail, excited to met Brody Maddox. Finn had been reading up on cutting horses and competitors, so he knew who he was. "I'm pleased to meet you, Sir." Finn was in awe.

"Call me Brody. You know, I bought my first cutting horse from your dad. He had just started up Caballo Stables over at Valley View. He wasn't much older than you, but he had already earned the reputation of being one of the best trainers in the industry. Your dad's skills with a horse come naturally. I can see he has passed his skills down to you. You're an exceptional trainer for your age. It's obvious you have worked a lot of hours with your horse."

Finn flushed, appreciating the praise. "Charlie is a great horse to learn on and develop my skills. Dad actually let me work with Darby a couple of times. It gave me experience at a more advanced level of training. You have a smart and talented horse."

"And a good trainer, or should I say two? Keep up the good work. My brother also bought a couple of your dad's trained horses. The last horse Grady bought from him beat me a couple of times in competitions. I've questioned my decision of introducing them more than once." Brody turned to Trace, "I'm looking for a horse for my son, Tanner. Like your son, mine wants to follow in my footsteps." Brody turned and looked at Charlie with appreciation, "I can tell he will make a fine cutting horse. Is Charlie for sale?"

Since the two men's conversation turned to business Finn excused himself. He didn't like where the conversation was going, so he didn't wait around for his dad's response. In his heart he already knew the answer. He headed back to the stable to cool Charlie off.

Trace's business had flourished thanks to the Maddox brothers and business was business. He nodded but was torn inside knowing Finn would be heartbroken. Finn and Charlie had become very attached. Trace understood the bond between a human and a horse. but this was part of the business. The part that never got easier. It was still difficult to turn the reins of one of his horses over to someone else. The two men came to an agreement on terms and price. After Brody left Trace went to find Finn.

Finn was sitting in the corner of his private stall. "You sold Charlie?" Finn couldn't stop his voice from breaking.

Trace nodded and walked away. There was nothing left to say.

CHAPTER FIFTEEN

The mild winter had come and gone. Signs of spring were everywhere. Early mornings were still Trace's favorite time of day. He stood leaning against the verandah post pensively scanning the horizon. The mountains offered a spectacular backdrop any time of the year, but this morning's view was serene. The air was still, like everything around him was waiting to catch its breath before another day unfolded. The Chinook arch had already formed to the west so Trace knew there was only a brief moment in time before the familiar westerly wind would sweep down from the mountains and howl across the land. He was feeling melancholy. He hadn't seen much of Riley or any of the Calhouns lately, and he missed them. Valley View had survived another busy calving season. Everyone had been grateful for the mild winter, but the land was dry. Trace had been busy with training new colts, as well as Finn. Trace smiled with inner pride. Not only was Finn going to be an excellent trainer, but he was also developing the same skills as Trace when it came to cutting. Most of the snow had melted in the foothills. Another couple of weeks and the training would be back outdoors. Trace tried to take Sundays off whenever he could. This wasn't always easy because ranching was an everyday job. It helped that Finn was doing some of his chores, as well as the training. Today the whole family, including Lola, was going over to the Walkers for an afternoon barbeque. The Ortiz family had also been invited; they had become like extended family to the Walkers.

Inside the house, Kit was alone in the kitchen. The kids were still upstairs in bed. It was nice having a few minutes to herself before bedlam erupted. Kit thought about her family as she puttered. The kids were growing up so fast. This year it was Kenzie who turned thirteen. Another milestone reached. Another teenager and Kit knew Kenzie would be a bigger challenge than her brother. Finn was now sixteen and driving. Lola was the good Samaritan who made herself available when Finn got his learner's licence, and she was the one who took him for his driver's test. The two of them had established a unique bond that began when she was homeschooling him. This time Finn was more than willing to spend time with her. Trace promised Finn that once he got his Driver's Licence, the old Ford pickup would become his. Even though it was dented and rusty, Finn was thrilled knowing he would have his own wheels along with a new sense of freedom. Finn had been saving the money he earned as an employee of Caballo Stables, knowing he had to pay for his own insurance. More than once he had been told responsibility came along with ownership. Then there was Benny Bear. Kit held back her motherly tears. She no longer had a baby and he made that very clear. He told the family he was too old to be called Benny Bear and he wanted to be called Ben. Kit would try to respect his newfound maturity and drop the Bear, but Benny would have to stay for a while. He may not be her baby anymore but he was only seven. Then there was Trace. Even after the many years they had been married, her heart fluttered thinking about him. Grabbing two coffees, Kit stepped outside and joined Trace. He smiled down at her as he took the coffee she handed him. She looked around at the beauty that surrounded them, "I love it here. I can't think of a better place to live."

"Well, city girl, you sure adapted to country life."

"Well, cowboy, there is no better life." Minutes later they heard voices. "I better go in and get breakfast. Benny must be going to grow again. I swear that boy is going to eat us out of house and home. Maggie says Rhett is the same." Kit smiled; grateful her children were healthy.

"I'll be right back; I'm going up to Ma's for a minute."

"See if she wants to join us for breakfast." Kit smiled as she watched Trace walk over to Lola's. Her husband was still one fine looking cowboy. Cowboy charisma. His swagger was still evident. Kit turned and headed into the house, happier than she could have ever imagined. "Kenzie, you can set the table while I start cooking. Set a place for Lita as well." Kit knew even if Lola had eaten, she would join them for coffee.

"Why do I have to do everything. Finn can do it for a change."

Kit hoped her daughter wasn't in one of her moods, "I asked you and we are in a hurry this morning. As soon as we're ready, we're going over to the Walkers for a barbeque."

Because Kenzie was looking forward to seeing her friend, she relented reluctantly, grumbling the whole time. She remained in a snit during breakfast and kept snapping at her brothers.

Finn elbowed Benny, "You better be careful with what you say to Kenzie, or she'll have one of her hissy fits."

Kenzie stuck her tongue out at him, a definite invite for further teasing. Finn chose to ignore Kit's warning and the squabbling continued. Finally, Trace cleared his throat loudly, a sign recognized by everyone that he had enough.

As soon as breakfast was done Kit began clearing the table and scooted the kids out of the kitchen. "Run upstairs and get changed and stay clean after you come back down. Kenzie, your attitude also needs changing. Don't make that face at me, young lady." Kit turned back to Trace and Lola, "Lately everything anyone says or does makes her mad, disgusted or embarrassed."

"Puberty," Lola said simply. "Finn was no different. We were just dealing with bigger issues when he was that age."

"She keeps trying to push the boundaries," Kit complained.

"Maybe it's time to widen them a little and allow her a little more independence," Trace commented casually.

Kit was surprised at how perceptive Trace could be at times. This would have to be a conversation for later.

Peace had been restored by the time they loaded up and left for the Walkers. Trace and Finn took Trace's truck while the rest piled into Kit's vehicle. Finn was excited because Trace was going to let him drive.

The Walker household was as busy as the Graysons. Pandemonium erupted as soon as they arrived. Kit and Lola went inside to see what they could do to help Maggie. Lola had brought homemade apple pie for desert and Kit had brought potato salad. The girls took off to the barn to play with the kittens. The two younger boys stayed back with their dads, who were enjoying cold beers on the deck. Quickly bored, they took off and went to play with Rhett's toys. Finn sat with the men waiting for Cruz.

Maggie and Kit were enjoying a moment in the kitchen. "I can't believe tomorrow is the first day of May. Two more months and school will be out," Maggie said as she began putting together a tray of appetizers.

"It's hard to believe next year is Finn's last year of high school."

"Does he know what he wants to do when he graduates?"

"He wants to work with Trace. He's a natural with horses like his dad. Trace was actually thinking about hiring an employee, but he said he would manage and take Finn on as a full-time employee if that's still what he wants to do a year from now."

"Matt's glad he hired Hector. They are such a nice family. Did you hear one of Valley View's full-time wranglers gave notice. He's getting married and moving to where his wife's family lives. Hector's brother is going to take his place. They aren't sure when he'll arrive. It could be another month or so. Hector said his brother is an experienced wrangler and a hard worker." Hearing a vehicle outside, Maggie looked out. "Everything is done for now and the Ortiz family has arrived. It's too nice a day to be stuck in the kitchen." Maggie grabbed the tray of snacks on her way out. Anna Ortiz and Lola had become friends. Lola went to their house once a week to help Anna with her English, focusing now on the written part.

Cruz and Finn high-fived each other and headed down to the corral. One of Matt's mares had a new foal that Finn was anxious to see. As they were crossing the yard, Finn said, "Ginger will foal this summer. She was sired by Diego, and we hope it's a colt to carry on Diego's strong lineage."

Both boys climbed up on the top rail and watched mother and foal frolic. "Matt says once school is out, I can help him, and he will pay me a wage. Maybe I can learn to train horses like you do."

Finn was excited for Cruz. He gave his friend an encouraging smile to boost his confidence. "We have another year before we graduate. Learn what you can over the summer. Matt's a great guy, you will learn a lot from him. Matt and my dad have been best friends since they were our age. I never had a best friend before you. Being a foster child, I never allowed myself to get close to anyone." A truth that could only be shared with a close friend.

Everyone enjoyed the day. The meal was a huge success as usual. Both women were surprised when Rhett and Benny asked for a second burger. On second thought, they settled on a hot dog instead, wanting to save room for dessert. The day flew by quickly. The adults continued to visit on the deck after the meal. All too soon it was time for everyone to head home. Tomorrow was a school day. The Ortiz family was the first to leave. It took longer for Kit to round up her kids. There was a definite nip in the air by the time they were leaving. "Thanks for an enjoyable day. It's our turn next."

Trace watched the storm clouds hanging over the mountains, hoping it would rain overnight. Rain would be welcomed by everyone. Large thunder clouds continued to gather as they drove home, a troubling wind pushing them closer. A clap of thunder boomed as a streak of lightning flashed across the sky.

Kit had taken the lead driving home. As they got closer to Lola Grande, they could see smoke billowing in the sky. When Trace passed and sped ahead, Kit knew his concern was the same as hers. Kit didn't say anything, not wanting to frighten the children, but Lola and Kit exchanged concerned looks. Was there a fire at Lola Grande? Unable to ignore her fears, she pushed down on the accelerator trying to keep up to Trace. Kit gripped the steering wheel tighter and sped down the road, her fears confirmed as they drew closer. The frantic beating of her heart increased as she drove into the yard. Lola was trying to keep the children calm but they were terrified by the flames coming out of the back of the barn. Trace and Finn were in motion. A feeling of dread spread through Kit's body.

Lola had already called 911 by the time Kit had parked. Knowing the kids were frightened, Kit followed them into the house. On her way in she turned the yard lights on. "Kenzie, I need you to be responsible tonight and take care of Benny. I want you both to get your pajamas on while I put on a movie. Finn is going to stay outside so he can help Dad with the horses. The fire department is on its way. There will be a lot of noise and activity outside, but you are safe in here. You don't have to be scared but I do want you to stay in the house. I'm going back outside to stay with Lita, but we are just outside on the verandah. Either Lita or I will come in and check on you later." Kit smiled as she hugged them, not wanting her fear to show.

Kit was relieved to see both Trace and Finn when she joined Lola on the verandah. The cold wind cut through her jacket. Shivering, Kit pulled it tighter before putting her hands in her pockets. Trace ordered

Lola and Kit to stay on the verandah. There was nothing they could do. The alarming sound of sirens brought comfort, but they still sounded so far away.

Trace was yelling to Finn, "I'm going in to save the horses. They have to be released before they're trapped inside their stalls. Try to head them to the far paddock when they come out. Do not come in with me. I'll be fine." Trace turned and ran into the barn. Fire was so uncontrollable. It didn't help that the wind had picked up, drawing the bright orange flames skyward through the dense smoke.

The sirens grew louder, and their lights lit up the sky as they drew near. Riley roared into the yard and slammed on his brakes, jumping out of the cab of his truck. "We heard the sirens. We all know anytime you hear a siren out here there's trouble. I hopped in my truck to help whoever was in danger. It wasn't until I was off the main road that I realized it was here. I called back to the ranch. Your dad is on his way, Kit."

Fear set in as Kit and Lola stood watching and waiting for Trace to come out of the barn. Trace had left the barn door open, and the frightened horses were escaping and taking flight. Kit's mind was racing, the rest of her was paralyzed with fear. Lola stood alongside Kit, praying Trace would be safe. Like Kit, she wondered why Trace hadn't come out. Fear was taking hold, every second that passed added to their anxiety.

The westerly wind fueled the flames, threatening the surrounding grassland. For now, the house was safe, as long as the wind didn't change direction. Finn walked over; his face covered in ash. Taking a deep breath of the cold night air, he croaked. "Dad must still be in the barn with Diego. All the other horses are out but most of them will have to be rounded up. They were terrorized and took off running in every direction. They were too scared to be led to the corral and too fast for me to rope any of them."

Riley detected real panic in Finn's voice. He tried to reassure Finn, "They won't have run far. We'll round them up and take them to Valley View and board them there." They looked over as two fire trucks roared into the yard. Buddy went and cowered in his doghouse, frightened by the sirens, lights and frantic activity.

Even though Kit was relieved to see the fire trucks, she was controlling her panic with great effort. *Trace said he would be fine. Please let him be fine.* The tightness in her chest made her realize she'd quit breathing.

Riley headed over to the fire truck and quickly returned. "The fire chief wants us to stay out of their way while they do their job. I told them Trace is still inside." They all felt helpless. Fear was suffocating them more than the smoke.

Inside the barn, Trace silently prayed the wind wouldn't carry flying embers across the dry grass to the house or to other outbuildings. He also prayed for his family to be safe. The flames had already jumped from the stored hay to the first stall. Fortunately, it was the empty stall that was Finns. The flames were licking their way along the floorboard, anxious to spread from stall to stall. He had to act fast. Trace ran to the back of the barn, frantically unlocking the latches as he ran by the stalls. He knew the fire would spread quickly since every stall had fresh dry hay. He heard the sirens but doubted they would arrive in time to save the barn. Despite the smoke and intense heat, he continued to free the horses. The burning boards allowed the flames to climb to the rafters above. The sound roared in his ears as he made his way from one stall to the other while he kept freeing the panicked horses. He led them in the direction of the door, swatted them hard on the flank and watched them run through the smoke to the open door to safety. The acrid smoke was much thicker. He was on his way to get Charlie, who was thrashing his hooves wildly against the stall. The frightened gelding danced in place, afraid to leave his stall. Trace pulled him out and swatted him hard and Charlie took off to safety. Relief swept over Trace. All of the horses had made it out safely except for Diego. Even though his stall had been unlatched he wouldn't leave Trace. "Let's get out of here, Diego."

Trace's eyes stung from the heavy smoke; his throat burned. Disorientated by the smoke and the dull roar of the fire, Trace hesitated. He needed all of his concentration to beat down the dizziness. The flames now ran across the rafters. Trace looked up when he heard the crack. He ducked as a large beam broke loose. Trace had no time to escape as another part of the roof collapsed and crashed down on him. Trace knew he was pinned; the beams lying across him too heavy to move. Trace coughed as he gasped for air. He could feel the heat of the fire intensify as it fingered closer, ready to grab hold as another rafter fell. He heard Diego's neigh. Trace knew Diego could have made it out. Instead, his beloved horse stayed and now lay next to him, unwilling to forsake his master. Trace closed his eyes and slipped into unconsciousness. Within minutes his laboured breathing was silenced. They died together.

Kit went into the house, concerned Kenzie and Benny might be scared by all the noise and commotion. Both had fallen asleep on the couch. The innocence of youth. Grateful they were able to escape through sleep, Kit went back outside. Finn had joined Lola. BJ was pulling into the yard and jumped out of his truck. Kit ran into her father's arms and broke down. "I'm so glad you're here, Dad. Will you go see what's happening?"

BJ could feel her trembling. "Stay here and I'll go find out what I can."

The two women watched BJ as he walked away and joined Finn and Riley, who were talking to the Fire Chief. Panic was evident on everyone's face, wondering why Trace wasn't coming out. Kit was sick with fear. Unable to stop herself, she began running toward the barn. She hadn't gotten far before strong arms grabbed her. One of the firefighters had stopped her and told Finn to take her back to the house and let them do their job.

The firemen worked fearlessly and quickly had the flames under control. As soon as they felt it was safe a couple of firemen went inside. Everyone's short-lived hopes were replaced with newfound fears when they came back out without Trace and waved Riley over.

Kit knew right away something bad had happened by the desperate way Riley looked at them and headed back. "Where's Trace?" Kit was unable to hide the panic in her voice. In her heart Kit already knew. With sickening certainty, she knew what Riley was going to say, and she couldn't breathe.

The silence was unbearable as they waited for Riley to speak. Riley never felt as helpless as he did in that moment. There was no way to prepare them for the devastating news. Riley looked down as he struggled to find his words. There were no words. He swallowed hard and finally spoke, "The Fire Chief said Trace was heading to the door, but he was pinned by a fallen rafter before he reached it. They found Diego lying beside him." His voice became so quiet that Kit prayed she heard it wrong when Riley said, "I'm sorry, Trace is dead." Their worst fears were realized.

At that moment, the world stopped and like Trace, for a moment Kit stopped breathing. Her life crumbled around her and a part of her died. "This can't be happening. Trace said he'd be fine." Kit's voice had dropped to an agonizing whisper. Life continued to be cruel. This nightmare was real. Kit's anguished sobs were smothered as BJ took his daughter into his arms. There were no words that would comfort her, so he just held her close. There was deep sympathy in BJ's eyes and a sharing of her pain. He could see how much Kit was suffering. They all were. Finn ran into Lola's arms. Riley stood alone, rigid, and silent, his eyes dark with grief.

Keeping his voice steady with difficulty, Riley continued, "The fire department and the RCMP will have to piece together the details of what happened tonight and what caused the fire. They need time to do their investigation but that won't be until tomorrow."

The officer who had been talking to the firemen came over. He looked at the others and suggested they go into the house. They were going to bring out Trace's body. Nobody moved.

BJ put his arms around Kit and turned her away when he saw two fireman carrying Trace's lifeless body out of the smoldering barn. Kit turned back. Her face paled as realism set in. Her legs threatened to buckle. It was only sheer willpower that kept her standing. Kit had to swallow hard to fight the build-up of nausea. Kit's heart shattered as her life's air expelled from her chest. Her body collapsed and she sat down on the steps. She put her head on her knees until the faintness passed. There was no way she could endure this kind of loss. Her mind fought to come to terms with the reality that in a matter of minutes her life with Trace was over. Her dreams with Trace vanished by the reality of life. Fate had again reared its ugly head. Kit was aware of fate. It can ambush you without warning. Once again, her life had changed forever.

Minutes later the structure of the barn collapsed. Lola could only shake her head in disbelief. Her face lost what little color it had. For an instant she let her own intense pain show. Even though her eyes filled with tears, she willed herself not to cry. Lola forced herself to be strong and maintain control. She knew how to lock deep hurt behind the invisible armor she had relied on in the past. She couldn't cry. Not yet. Lola would cry for her loss later.

Riley shoved his hands into the pockets of his jacket and hunched his shoulders in a momentary shiver. It felt like the devil himself just tapped him on the shoulder. Recovering his composure, Riley continued gravely, "I don't have a lot of details. One truck and the crew will stay through the night to watch for hot spots. There is still concern since the wind hasn't died down." Riley and Finn left as a fireman waved them over. The firemen wanted to know what to do with Diego's body. Riley and Finn knew Trace would want Diego buried on Lola Grande land but for now he would be taken out of sight away from everyone. The coroner's vehicle had already left with Trace's body.

When the two men headed back to the house, the RCMP officer stoically followed. Once they were all gathered, he shifted uncomfortably. He hated days like this. "I'm sorry for your loss. We'll be leaving now but will be in contact once we get the report from the Fire Inspector."

BJ stepped in and spoke for the family, who were still in shock. "Have any of the firemen said anything? Do they know what caused the fire? Could it have been arson?"

"They have been pretty closed mouthed but have been taking a lot of notes. They will be out tomorrow to begin investigating. They'll want to go through the ashes and find the source of the fire."

This drew a concerned look from BJ, "Do they think it was intentional?"

"That's not what I'm saying. It's routine follow-up." Nobody wanted to believe that someone would intentionally start a fire that would endanger the animals. Or worse. And it was worse. Both Trace and Diego were dead. No one knew if any of the other horses had been injured during their frantic escape.

BJ's face was solemn as he continued to take control. "There is nothing more we can do until daylight. I'll be back in the morning. The rest of you should go inside." He took his leave, dreading the news he would have to relay to the rest of the family. He knew how hard it would be for all of them in the weeks and months to come.

The family could no longer ignore the gruesome reality as they moved into the house in silence. It was evident they were dazed by the horror that surrounded them. Buddy wouldn't leave his post at the door. The loyal dog kept waiting for Trace.

Kit headed to the living room. Both children were sound asleep, the television still on. Kit chose not to disturb them as she covered them, kissed their cheeks, and went back to the kitchen.

"I need something stronger than coffee." Riley walked over to the liquor cabinet, pulled out Trace's whisky and poured himself a hefty shot.

Lola heard the pain in his voice. Lola went over and put on an urn of coffee. Riley noticed the hopeless set of her shoulders and the sadness in her eyes before she went and sat down. Something her pride would never allow to show under normal circumstances. Tonight, Lola was unable to hide her own grief. Riley went and sat down next to her. "One minute a person is here, living and breathing. The next minute they're gone." This was a big loss for Riley. He finished his drink and got up to get another one. He brought the bottle back with him.

Kit noticed how tired Finn looked. They all were. Finn's face was streaked with soot and his eyes were red from crying. The feeling of being forsaken returned from his past and for a moment he reverted back to that little boy with deep fears. He didn't want those old wounds opened up. What he wanted was to escape to his safe place, but it was gone.

It had been a long, exhausting night. The original shock that had overwhelmed them had been replaced by fatigue, but nobody went to bed. They sat hopelessly in the kitchen, numbed by the horror of what happened. Time passed unnoticed as they tried to come to terms with their loss. They were all confused and scared. This was going to change all of their lives. Nothing would be the same for any of them. Fate could be such a powerful force.

CHAPTER SIXTEEN

S ome things never change. Some things change forever. Yesterday had been a shocking day followed by a long sleepless night. Morning brought with it a new sense of reality. Life as they knew it had changed. Regardless of the shock, there was a lot they would have to deal with in the next couple of days. The first glimmer of dawn was lighting the sky to the east. By sun-up, it became evident how much damage had been done. All that was left of the barn was a pile of rubble surrounded by black soil where dry grass once grew. Riley and Finn left to go talk to the firemen. Throughout the night, they had taken them food and coffee. The firemen were beginning to pack up, confident all the hot spots were out, and would leave once the Inspector arrived to examine the fire scene and collect physical evidence. That would determine the cause of the fire and conclude if there was a suspicious source.

Kit's mind was on the difficult task ahead of her. She could bear the pain of loss. She'd already done that when she lost her first husband. It was the unbearable pain of telling her children their dad died in the fire she was struggling with. It broke her heart that her children would be introduced to death at such a young age. Kit was trying to stay calm while her world was spinning out of control around her, but her grief was so deep it took her breath away. Kit cried out in anguish, "How do I tell my children their dad is dead?" Kit's eyes darkened as unshed tears gathered. How could she explain this to her children when it made no sense to her?

Lola took Kit's hand, knowing today would be a difficult day. There was a sharing of deep pain. "No parent can protect their children from everything. We just have to be there for them when they need us. You and I will do it together." This was a family that needed her now more than ever.

Kit's breath caught when she heard her children stir. The heavy weight in the young mother's heart increased. Minutes later they came into the kitchen.

Kenzie entered first, with Benny right behind her. "Why is there still a firetruck outside? Isn't the fire out?" Kenzie looked at her mom, her eyes wide.

Lola answered, giving Kit another moment, "One truck stayed all night so they could monitor hot spots, but the fire is out."

Still concerned, Kenzie looked around the room. "Where is everyone?"

"Finn is outside with Uncle Riley."

"Where's Daddy?" Benny's eyes were wide-eyed and anxious. Both kids were desperate for assurance that everything was okay.

Kit became aware of the heavy silence and felt the tightness in her chest increase. She took a deep breath. She felt her mouth go dry as she leaned forward and placed her clasped hands on the table. Words failed her as she held back the tears that drowned the words before they reached her lips. She moistened her dry lips and realized she was trembling. Kit swallowed hard and tried again. This would be the hardest thing Kit would ever have to do. She could no longer shield her children from the truth. Reality at it's cruelest. She swallowed hard and tried again. When Kit finally spoke, her words came out in an agonizing whisper. With a torn heart, Kit explained, "Kenzie, Benny, listen to me. Something terrible happened. You know how much your daddy loved the horses. Last night Daddy had to go into the burning barn and try to save them. He was so brave and was able to save all of them except for Diego. Just before Daddy reached the door to come out with Diego, he was knocked down by a falling rafter. The roof collapsed and he got pinned and didn't make it out. Daddy died from the smoke before the fireman could get to him." Kit braced herself for their reaction.

Both kids stared at their mom in disbelief, followed by hopeless sobs. Lola reached over and took Benny into her arms. Kit gently wiped the tears from her daughter's cheeks as she pulled her close. Unbearable pain caused Kit's throat to grow all tight, "I can't make this better." Kit closed her eyes, unable to cope with the rising tide of emotions, and fought hard to hold back her tears. There was nothing more to say.

Kenzie stared accusingly at her mother, "You said Daddy would be fine."

So did your Dad. We both lied. Kit's tears now cascaded down the familiar trail on her own cheeks as her heart shattered into smaller pieces.

"This can't be happening," Kenzie cried out in despair as she turned and fled upstairs to her room, her brother right behind her. Kit wanted to do the same and have someone tell her the hurt would go away. She was helpless to stop her tears that continued to flow as she followed her children up the stairs.

After talking to both children, Kit went back downstairs and sat down at the table. Lola puttered around the kitchen, too distraught to remain idle.

Both jumped when there was a knock on the door and Maggie came in. Every time someone opened the door, the smell of smoke drifted in. Maggie walked in with a box of food. She had raided her freezer and set the box down on the counter.

Kit's eyes brightened briefly with gratitude. "I'm so glad you came."

Matt and Maggie had been devastated when they heard the news. "Riley called Matt first thing this morning. I still can't believe it's true. Matt knew I needed to be here with you, so he stayed home with the kids. I wish there was something I could say that would ease the pain you are having to deal with. I'm so sorry for your family." Maggie could see Kit was still dazed by what happened. "Where are the children?"

Tears glistened in Kit's darkly rimmed eyes; her face was stark white. "They are in their rooms. Finn is outside with Riley. I think they're talking to the firemen. I don't know what to do next. I feel like I've been knocked to my knees, and I can't get up."

The anguish in Kit's voice tore at Maggie's heart. She could only imagine the fear and grief they had to be experiencing. "For now, it's okay to lean on others. Let me take Kenzie and Benny to our place for a few days."

Kit was unable to swallow the lump in her throat, "I can't ask you to do that."

"You didn't ask; I offered."

Kit remained lifeless, confused, and desperate. "What about school?"

"Kenzie can ride the bus from our place with Lucy Rose. If you like, I can call the school to let them know what happened."

"You are so kind," Kit said sincerely. Maggie's offer was a tempting one, but Kit felt her kids needed her now more than ever. "I'll be fine. The kids need me."

"You are the most devoted mother I know, but the young ones don't need to be around all of this. Let us take Kenzie and Benny. We would take Finn as well, but I know he won't leave you. He will want to be here."

Kit's face remained blank. She was still in a state of shock. She tried to gather her thoughts, but they were so scattered she was unable to think clearly. Her head throbbed and her eyes burned with fatigue. Her initial reaction of refusal was now followed by a surge of relief. She knew she couldn't cope with everything, and the next few days would be very chaotic. Kit wanted to be strong and take care of her children but knew she was too exhausted and emotional to cope. Pride had to be set aside to make room for sound judgement. Maggie's offer was the best solution for the time being. "You're right. Bless you, Maggie."

With all the strength she could muster, Kit went upstairs. Kenzie was curled up on her bed with her favorite stuffed animal. Kit crawled up beside her and stroked Kenzie's hair after wiping away her tears. She dropped a light kiss on top of her daughter's head. They lay for a long time as Kit held her child in her arms.

"This isn't fair, Mommy. I'll never see Daddy again." Her expressive eyes were troubled. "Why is life so unfair? I have lost two daddies. Why do bad things like this happen?"

"I don't understand it either." Kit answered with a look of misery in her own eyes. She had lost two husbands. All she knew was life could change quickly and it wasn't always what you expected. This was beyond belief. "We don't always understand why something like this happens, but we still have to deal with it. We will get through this."

"Are you sure, Mommy?" Kenzie asked, a definite note of doubt in her voice.

Why should Kenzie believe her? She had told Kenzie her dad would be okay. Kit didn't answer. Instead, she told Kenzie about going to the Walkers. "There will be a lot of commotion around here for a couple of days. You and Benny will go with Maggie and stay there for a few days. Pack a bag while I go see Benny and pack one for him."

Kenzie wrapped her arms around her mother's neck and hugged her hard. "I'll take care of Benny. You take care of Finn."

Kit was touched by her daughter's concern. She sounded so grown up. It wasn't fair that sometimes children have to grow up too fast.

While Kit was upstairs with the kids, Riley came back in and stated, "BJ called. Most of the horses showed up at Valley View. He's going to take a couple of the wranglers and go look for the others. If any come back here, we'll take them over to Valley View. Doc also called. He'll go out to our ranch to check the horses. We'll board them there until..." Riley swallowed hard, "We'll board them there for now."

"When are you going home?" Lola asked.

"Not for a while. I'll stay and organize things outside. I'll wait and hear what the Fire Inspector has to say." Riley needed to make sense of what had happened. He needed to know how the fire started.

After Maggie left, Lola looked anxiously at her daughter-in-law. Kit's face was pale and drawn. "I'm going up to my place to shower. Why don't you do the same."

Kit pushed her coffee cup aside, "I don't understand why this happened. Why do some have to die so young? Trace still had his whole life ahead of him." Kit choked on her words, unable to continue.

"Tomorrow isn't guaranteed to any of us. This was God's will."

"God's will be damned," Kit cried out in anger, but immediately regretted her outburst.

Lola wondered how much Kit could take before she broke down. She knew this was not the time to get into it with Kit. Further conversation would be pointless. Lola felt Kit's pain and rage. It was no more than her own. Lola needed time by herself to release her own built-up emotions and personal grief. Lola had learned to cry when she was alone. Her eyes were dull and haunted as she walked up the stairs to her suite.

Lola knew how much Kit was suffering and she had remained strong for her and everyone else. Now that she was alone, Lola allowed herself to address her own grief. Trace had been a large part of her life, and she was aware of the strong bond they had. Riley had his own life at Valley View and had a strong relationship with the Calhouns because of the cattle business. When Riley married Shelby Calhoun, Shelby's grandparents retired to Black Diamond and Riley and Shelby moved into the main house. His life was independent from Lola Grande.

Lola stared absently out the window at the remaining rubble. All the work Trace put into building the barn and establishing Caballo Stables had literally gone up in smoke. She shifted her gaze to the mountains. She had worked hard to build a good life for herself and her sons. The Reed Ranch had sad history before it became Lola Grande. Perhaps the ghosts of the past did continue to linger. Even though her faith had once again been tested, her belief in God and his guidance would help her through this. Lola made the sign of the cross across her body, closed her eyes, and prayed. She prayed for Kit and her family. She prayed for Riley who lost his brother and best friend. Finally, she prayed for herself, asking God to give her the strength to get through the days ahead. Lola had done a lot of brave things in her life but that didn't mean she wasn't scared. Lola remained locked in her own private pain. Her son's death weighed heavily on her heart. A cry escaped and her tears began to flow. She had many reasons to cry in her lifetime, but this was the most painful. No parent should have to bury one of their children. After releasing her grief, Lola straightened her shoulders and wiped her eyes. She had to be strong. There was a family downstairs that needed her now more than ever.

Kit meant to go upstairs when Lola left but grief took over as she stood alone recalling the pain-filled moment they brought Trace's body out of the barn. It made it all real. Suddenly it was all too much. Unable to control her suffering, she sank to the floor, sobbing uncontrollably. Her life was unravelling around her, grief and confusion continuing to envelop her. For a moment Kit couldn't breathe, for the pain was unbearable.

That's where Doc found her. No one was around when he arrived and there was no response when he knocked and walked in. His own heart hurt for Kit, for he had heard her through the closed door. She looked up at him with such terror in her eyes. Doc had never seen someone look like this, as though part of her had died in front of him. Her tormented face bore the tracks of endless tears. He hated seeing Kit so broken.

The frantic despair in Kit's voice was evident, "I'm living in a nightmare. I keep thinking this is a horrible dream and I'll wake up any minute." She hung her head, struggling for control.

A shadow of pain crossed Doc's eyes as he heard the despair in her voice. He raised Kit up off the floor and drew her close, his face grim as he took her into his arms. Doc didn't want to let her go and felt a brief moment of guilt. For years he had loved another man's wife. From the day he met Kit, she not only intrigued him but had captured his heart, but she only had eyes for Trace. It didn't take long for everyone to see the immediate chemistry between Kit and Trace. Doc accepted that she loved Trace, but he hadn't moved on. All these years later he still loved her. Deeply. Secretly. His compassion drew him in, and he brushed a kiss on her forehead. His own voice was deep with emotion, "I'm here, Kit. How can I help?"

Tears still glistened in Kit's eyes. "There is nothing anyone can do. No one can bring Trace back to life. I can't imagine my life without him." Kit felt like her whole world was turned upside down.

Doc cleared the lump in his throat, "You're going to be okay."

Kit's reply was candid, "I'll never be all right ever again. You don't know the emptiness inside of me." Even Kit was surprised by the hardness in her voice. She took a deep breath as she pulled away. She hated to see the pity on Doc's face and there was nothing anyone could say to ease her pain.

Doc's heart twisted painfully, knowing Kit had to deal with this ugly twist of fate. He ached for Kit as he saw the obvious pain in her eyes, and he was determined to do everything he could to help her. "Where is everyone?"

Through trembling lips Kit managed to stutter, "Maggie Walker took Benny and Kenzie for a few days until things settle here. Lola went to her place to shower and make a couple of calls. Finn is outside with Riley." When Kit went and sat at the table Doc joined her. They were talking quietly when Lola returned.

Lola knew Kit hadn't left the kitchen. "Why don't you go upstairs and lie down for a while. If anyone else drops by they will understand your absence. I'll make sure no one disturbs you. There is nothing we can do right now."

Kit didn't want to go upstairs but agreed to go lie on the couch. It would give her time alone with no one hovering. The blankets the kids had used were still out. She grabbed one and wrapped it around herself. Kit closed her eyes and sought relief from the pain in her head and in her heart. The headache would pass; the pain in her heart would never go away. She listened to Doc and Lola in the kitchen with her eyes closed. Her mind fought to come to terms with her reality. Trace was dead and her life had changed forever.

Doc informed Lola he had talked to BJ and all the horses had been rounded up. "I stopped here first but I'm on my way over to check them. I don't know what else I can do to help but if there is anything just ask."

Lola was touched by his concern. "Thank you, Doc. You're a good friend. That's very kind of you."

Doc exhaled slowly, "I'm not doing it to be kind. Kit's not doing very well, is she?"

"She's been through a lot. Trace was her life."

"They had something special," Doc admitted softly. His face was solemn when he left.

When Kit heard Riley and Finn in the kitchen with Lola, she got up and joined them. It was early evening. She had drifted off but didn't feel rested.

Lola looked over, "Are you feeling better?"

"I'm okay," came the unconvincing response.

It was difficult but things had to be dealt with. Lola had been busy taking care of business. "I phoned the insurance company, and they started a claim. They will have an adjustor here tomorrow. They said once the fire department is finished with their inspection, we can begin the removal of debris. They want pictures taken for their file and pictures of the facility before it burned down."

Riley still had evidence of ashes on his face. "I'm heading home to shower and make some calls. Tomorrow will be another hard day. I've organized a work crew, and they will be here first thing in the morning." He glanced back at the charred remains of the horse facility as he climbed behind the wheel of his truck. He turned the key in the ignition and drove away. A mile down the road, he pulled over and wept. He was unable to forget the panic he experienced when he turned into Lola Grande and saw the fire. It was nothing compared to the fear when he realized his brother was trapped inside the barn. It only kept getting worse, but Riley never thought it would end like this. He wished he had a way of dulling the raw, agonizing ache within. He began pounding the steering wheel to release some of his anger.

The darkness of the night closed in around the ranch. The total opposite of the night before when the sky was lit up by a flaming inferno. The quietness was eerie.

Lola's voice was firm, "I'm going home for the night. You and Finn need to get some sleep as well." Kit didn't argue. Fatigue had set in for everyone.

Finn had already left the kitchen. He was unable to escape to his safe place. Instead, he sat alone in the living room. The television was on, but he was lost in thought. Finn couldn't shake off the haunted visions. He was filled with conflicting emotions, especially guilt.

Kit hesitated before entering when she heard Finn's weeping. It hurt to hear her son so tormented. Her own despair clutched at her throat every time she thought of life without Trace. She realized Finn was just as scared and confused as she was. Composing herself with difficulty, Kit went and sat next to her son. "I'm scared, too. I don't know what we'll do without your dad, but we will get through this."

The pain in Finn's voice was evident as he confessed, "It's my fault Dad is dead. I should have gone in after him."

Kit hated seeing the anguish on her son's face. Her heart ached for Finn as she took him into her arms. "We have all experienced that guilt, but we can't blame ourselves. Your dad's death wasn't your fault or my fault. It was a tragic accident, but you still wonder if you could have done something different. Your dad did what he needed to do. That's who he was. Things like this happen. That's life. We can't continue to ask why, and we have to keep on living. This is something we can't change."

"You're right about that," Finn said bitterly.

It was the break in his voice that caused Kit to feel the familiar sting of tears. She bit her lip trying to hold them back. "Go to bed and try to get some sleep. Tomorrow is going to be another difficult day for all of us. I'll be up shortly."

Finn was about to protest but it would be useless. He was physically and emotionally exhausted. With more willpower than strength, Finn headed upstairs.

After Finn left, Kit remained seated in silence. Time passed unnoticed. When she finally went up, she checked on Finn. He had left his light on, just like he did when he was frightened when he was little. Kit was glad he had fallen asleep. She walked out, leaving the light on to protect Finn from his fears. She went to her room and closed the door. Kit wished it was that easy to close her mind. She stared at the empty bed and shuddered. Tears blurred her eyes, her empty bed a reminder of her loss and she was alone. A future with Trace was never to be. Kit paced around the bedroom. There was nowhere to hide from the pain. Kit couldn't image her life without Trace.

Life could be cruel and unfair at times, but this was unbearable. Tragedy heaped upon tragedy. Once again, she was dealing with another loss. Death always seemed to overshadow her life. Once again, she was a widow. The loss of the others was nothing compared to this. Trace was her life. She wasn't sure if she could ever be happy again. Sorrow weighed heavy on her heart, and she vowed she would never open that part of her heart again.

Exhaustion swept through Kit, leaving her feeling lonelier than ever. Grabbing one of Trace's shirts, she smelled it up close. The scent of Trace was comforting so she changed into it and climbed into bed. Once in bed, Kit pulled Trace's shirt tighter. She allowed herself to remember how it had been with Trace. Kit had experienced the man's love and had lost it and the emotions that ensued were unbearable. Loving him and being loved by him had been the most glorious experience of her life. A sudden wave of unbelievable pain enveloped her, but it wasn't physical. Scary what grief could do to a body.

Kit looked at the clock on the end table. Time could move forward but there was no going back in time. She could turn off the light, but she couldn't turn off her thoughts. Kit willed herself to block out the images without success. Many thoughts later, Kit curled into the fetal position, closed her eyes, and prayed for sleep to take her. In time it did, but it was a disturbing sleep. Kit awakened, her cry of terror echoing in the room. A long time passed before she slept again and when she did, she was unable to escape the nightmare that returned. Even sleep didn't allow her an escape. She felt like she had fallen into a dark abyss and couldn't find her way out. She turned and reached for Trace for help. Feeling cold sheets, her eyes flew open. Reality was back. She was alone. Kit lay for a long time staring at nothing while trying to absorb what happened. She lay there and cried some more. The light had disappeared from her life. She reached over and turned the bedside light on, understanding Finn's need to keep his light on. She finally drifted off again, stirring occasionally. A pattern that lasted throughout the night.

CHAPTER SEVENTEEN

Finn was doing what needed to be done. With the sun peeking over the horizon, he drove over to Valley View to check the horses for himself. Doc Parker arrived shortly after. Only one of their own horses had cuts on his front legs from the barb wire. He had obviously been the lead horse that went through the fence while escaping. Doc gave a couple of the horses a mild sedative to calm them after their frightening experience. Knowing how quickly news could spread, Finn spent the morning calling his dad's clients, explained their situation. He reassured the owners that a vet had tended all the horses, and they were fine. With Doc's permission, he gave the clients his number. It had been an emotional morning coping with his dad's business.

On his way home, Finn drove the property, needing to focus on the matters at hand. He found the spot where the horses had broken through in their flight of terror. Finn heard Riley drive up and Riley saw the desperate look in the young boy's eyes.

Riley asked, his expression concerned, "How are you holding up? Are you okay?"

Finn's reply was unintentionally sharp, "I've been better."

"Me, too. I don't want you to shoulder yourself with the burden of responsibility you feel you have to take on. We would have sent one of our men out to fix the fence."

"I know. I needed time to myself, and Dad would want to keep the horses safe." Pain was evident in Finn's voice. He couldn't continue. That concern was what took his dad's life.

Riley could see the lines of strain on Finn's face. "Trace wasn't much older than you when our dad died, and our lives changed dramatically. Being the oldest, Trace thought he was now head of the Grayson family. When we got Lola Grande, he carried a high level of responsibility at too young an age. We had a ranch to run, and he also had started Caballo Stables when we still lived at Valley View. He worked extra hard because he wanted his own horse facilities so he could bring his horses to our ranch. Lola Grande and Caballo Stables became Trace's obsession. We don't want that for you. Trace was proud, too proud to ask anyone for help so there were times he struggled when he didn't have to. You can't be like that. You're a fine young man, Finn, but you can't do this on your own. We are in this together, including the Calhouns. They helped us when we first took over our ranch and they are going to help us again. It's not your fault but you are short-handed at the ranch right now. Don't refuse the help from others like Matt and Doc. That's what friends and neighbours do."

Finn nodded his head, not trusting himself to speak.

"When will you start training at Valley View?" Riley's question was intentional, a lead into further conversation.

Finn gave Riley a guarded look, "I'll start training after Dad's funeral. Brody Maddox was here a few weeks ago and watched me train. He said it was evident that Dad had trained me with the same skills and patience he did when training horses. Brody will let everyone know that Caballo Stables is still operating and will continue to recommend Caballo Stables and me within the industry. I have to carry on for Dad." He couldn't let his dad down.

"With an endorsement from Brody Maddox, you will continue to be busy. You know you will have to spend more time at Valley View than you will at Lola Grande. Besides that, you still have school for a few more weeks. Don't let pride get in the way. Trace couldn't do it all on his own and neither can you." Riley continued, his voice grave as he expressed his concerns, "You still have one more year of high school."

Finn kept his eyes down, struggling for control, knowing Riley was right. Finn swallowed his pride and gave a nod of submission. Some of the fatigue disappeared from Finn's eyes and the boy's shoulders sprung up as if released from an invisible load. After Riley left, Finn took his time fixing the fence. When he was done, he leaned against the fence post as he struggled to collect himself. He didn't want to go home and face reality.

It was early, daylight was just breaking when Kit heard Finn leave. She guessed he was heading over to Valley View. She wasn't concerned about Finn's absence, but she was concerned about him. She lay awake for a long time struggling with her emotions. She wanted to scream but knew if she started, she couldn't stop. She was back on a runaway roller coaster that was going too fast. Her life was out of control, and she couldn't find the brakes. All she could do was hold on tight. A new fear surfaced. What if the ride never ended? Kit struggled to drag herself out of bed and headed to the shower. She felt numb, but she couldn't lock herself away. Life wasn't that simple. Kit frowned as she looked at herself in the mirror. She was a pitiful sight. Kit walked away. What did it matter?

The quiet of the early morning held an eerie feeling. It was unusual for her children not to be in the kitchen first thing in the morning. Kit stepped outside. Although the night was over and the birds had returned to sing their morning song, Kit felt she was shrouded in darkness. The gentle breeze carried the smell of stale smoke, smothering the usual fragrant smells of spring. The acrid scent made her nauseous. She could only image how suffocating it had been for Trace. Kit, in turn, was being suffocated by her grief and heartache. She pulled herself away from her deep thoughts. The forecast for rain by late evening would be welcomed. It would settle the ashes and clear the smoke. It would not wash away her grief.

When Lola came down, Kit could see that Lola hadn't slept well either. They entered the kitchen together. "Have you had breakfast?"

Kit shook her head. The thought of eating turned her stomach.

Kit's manner concerned Lola, but she refrained from comment. "I've had a busy morning. The insurance company called. The adjustor will be out today. They want a copy of the report from the Fire Department confirming the barn was a total loss." Lola had spoken to Andy Shaw. He was also on his way out to pick up the original blueprints for the horse barn. They were stored in Trace's office in the old barn. "If Andy's quote is fair, the insurance company will approve him as the Project Manager for the rebuild." Andy and his crew had built her suited garage and the original horse facility and riding arena. Both Trace and her had been pleased with his work. He was an honest and fair contractor.

Kit had agreed to let Lola deal with the insurance claim. Kit knew it wasn't fair, but she was glad Lola had taken control. Kit knew she wasn't coping.

"Riley is on his way over. He will take charge of the men as they show up to help. The insurance company agreed to the removal of the debris but asked us to keep track of the men and their hours worked."

Forcing herself to help, Kit offered to do up some trays and put them out on the counter. Neighbours had already dropped off food along with condolences and offers of help. These acts of kindness would continue over the next few days, and the Graysons were grateful. "Tell Riley to let the men know there's coffee on all day and to come in and help themselves to a bite to eat whenever they want." The activity outside would only intensify throughout the day.

Kit took a call just as Lola rose to leave. Kit put her hand up to stop her. "That was the RCMP. They are on their way out. The Fire Chief provided them with their final report. They are bringing us a copy. They want to ask a few more questions and share the results of the report."

"I'll tell Riley when he gets here." Lola left and the phone rang again.

During the drive to Lola Grande, Riley decided to talk to his mom, knowing she would understand his concern for Finn. They had been down this road with Trace. She was just leaving the house when he pulled into the yard. "Ma, can I speak to you alone? I'm worried about Finn. He is pushing himself to make up for Trace's absence just like Trace did when Dad died."

Lola was impressed that Riley had stopped and talked to Finn. "Come upstairs where we won't be disturbed." How many times had Trace come to her for advice, especially when Finn had first arrived? Parenting never stopped. "I appreciate you being there for Finn. He still needs guidance. Beneath his tough, focused exterior, Finn is scared. He's like the young boy who showed up at the ranch, confused and unsure of the future. It will take some of us longer to work through our grief, but we are all suffering, Riley." Lola hadn't bothered to disguise the concern in her voice and was unable to hide her own grief.

"I better go. The men have started to arrive, and Finn just pulled in. It looks like the RCMP are right behind him. We'll come join you in the kitchen." Riley hugged his mom and took his leave, knowing it was time to talk to BJ as well to ask for help. Riley was also concerned about his mom. He'd never seen her look so frail.

The officer wasted no time once they were gathered in the kitchen, "The Fire Inspector has confirmed the fire started from the inside. The origin was where the hay bales were stacked in the back."

"Was it started on purpose?" Finn asked the question that was on everyone's mind.

The officer shook his head, "That has not been determined. After combing the ashes, the Inspector determined what caused the fire. You said no one here smokes. Do you know anyone who might have been here that smokes cigars? Any of your friends or neighbours?"

Kit shook her head to clear her mind when Jackson Beaumont's image appeared. He was known for his expensive fat cigars. Kit stared at the officer; fear mixed with disbelief. She tried to shake off the unwelcoming thought. Jackson was no longer of sound mind and his behaviour had been bizarre on more than one occasion, but would he do something like this intentionally? Was fear clouding her own sanity?

The officer pulled something out of an evidence bag, "We also found this lighter. Do any of you recognize it?" Kit gasped when she held the charred lighter in her hand. The initials JB were clearly visible. Her hand began to shake, and she felt nauseous. Kit had seen this lighter the first time she met Jackson.

Kit recalled the threats Jackson had made when Trace wouldn't sell him one of his horses and kicked both him and Olivia off his property. At the time, Olivia had reminded Trace her father was a very powerful man who would roll over him if he didn't get his way. Jackson's threat was more explicit and definitely threatening. He told Trace that because he crossed him, he would regret it. Trace wasn't intimidated by his threats, so he never backed down when confronted. Trace had become Jackson's enemy. It was common knowledge that Jackson went after those who crossed or defied him. Trace had done both. Everyone knew Jackson had a reputation for having a vile temper, but Kit couldn't believe that anyone would go to such extreme lengths as to intentionally start a fire, endangering both human and animal lives. Kit shared every occasion when Jackson had confronted or threatened Trace. It had been going on for years. Kit concluded with the most disturbing incident, "Jackson Beaumont verbally attacked Trace at a wedding we recently attended. Jackson was so outraged and out of control that it would have become physical if his family hadn't stopped him." Kit also shared the Hummer incident and her belief that it could have been intentional.

"We will follow up on the information you provided. Please keep all of this to yourself while we continue to investigate."

After the RCMP left and Riley and Finn went back to work, Kit and Lola remained in the house. Because of her conversation with Riley, Lola wanted to talk to Kit about her concern for Finn. She guessed that subconsciously Finn was experiencing the fear of abandonment. Another parent was gone from his life.

Kit listened intently and gazed at Lola with troubled eyes, "I've tried to get Finn to talk. He simply answers in monosyllables. Why won't he talk to me?"

"He may feel he can't because he doesn't want to upset you. He'll come to you when he's ready. Kids need time to work through their emotions, too. We have to remember that when Kenzie and Benny come back home."

They were interrupted by another call. The calls didn't stop, and more neighbours began dropping by with food and condolences. By the end of the day, Kit felt like a zombie going through the motions. Tomorrow would be another stressful day. Maggie would be bringing the kids home and she still had things to finalize for the funeral. It had been another emotional day.

*****

The morning sun filtered through the curtains as Kit woke. The house was quiet but that would soon change. Maggie would be bringing the kids home after lunch. Kit had missed them, but she was nervous.

Kit wasn't the only one who couldn't sleep. Lola looked out the window. The debris had been removed. She looked beyond to the empty corrals, a constant reminder of what happened. Seeing Kit's kitchen light on, Lola headed down to the main house.

Kit heard her footsteps outside and without thinking, she looked at the front door expecting Trace to walk in. Lola hated seeing the despair in Kit's eyes.

Kit invited Lola to join them for breakfast. Kit settled on toast even though she wasn't hungry. She knew she had to eat something if she was going to have the strength to get though the day. Finn left them as soon as he was done. Both women knew escaping was his coping mechanism. Kit was tense knowing the kids would soon be home. She wanted to tell them everything was all right. Instead, she had to prepare them for their father's funeral tomorrow. They would all have to find the courage to face the days ahead. This was real. This was life. This was death. This was unfair.

When Kit heard Maggie's vehicle pull into the yard, her stomach flipped. She didn't know what to expect, especially from Kenzie. As soon as the kids entered, they rushed over to their mother. Too young to understand everything, they were bewildered and frightened. Kit lifted Benny up and gently stroked Kenzie's cheek. Under normal circumstances, Benny would have squirmed, saying he was too big for such cuddles. Today, he leaned back for comfort. The kids had been traumatized when they saw the charred ground when Maggie pulled into the yard. They went up to their rooms. Kit promised to be up soon.

Maggie poured herself a coffee and joined the two ladies at the table. Maggie could tell by Kit's puffy eyes that she'd been crying. Her own eyes filled. She hated seeing her friend like this. "I am terribly sorry for your loss and all of this horror that your family has endured. Kenzie and Benny were good at our place, but it will be a lot different now that they're home. They were very quiet on the drive. Your kids are confused and scared."

So am I. "I appreciate your concern, Maggie. I'll go up and talk to them later. How do I even begin to help them?"

Years of living allowed Lola to say, "There are times, like now, when all you need to do is be there for them. You can't change things and you can't make it go away. Get through today and tomorrow will be better."

"How can it be better? Tomorrow we are burying their father." The silence that followed was uncomfortable. Kit immediately regretted her outburst and felt ashamed.

"We would do more if you'd let us," Maggie offered sincerely.

Kit was still embarrassed by her fit of temper. "You and Matt have already done so much. We are extremely grateful."

Another neighbour showed up to offer condolences and help, bringing with him a tray of baking. Maggie took her leave. She had to wonder how her friend would get through this.

*****

The funeral was difficult. Riley gave a beautiful eulogy honoring Trace, sharing many of their experiences and adventures together. He had spoken with such love, but his mournful voice often revealed his grief. The two brothers had a bond that nothing could shatter until death took it away. Kit was given Trace's ashes to take home. In time she would have her private farewell. Kit was glad it was over.

The Calhouns, and a few close friends like the Walkers and Doc Parker, came to the ranch from the service. Others would come and go throughout the day. Maggie walked over to Kit, "Is there anything I can do to help?"

"Ask Lola. She's in the kitchen taking care of everything. Keeping busy is her way of coping."

"How are you doing?" Maggie asked.

"I'm fine," Kit said, not wanting to admit how worn out she really was. She felt if one more person asked her how she was, she would scream. People kept showing up. Kit was tired and wished they would all go home. Everyone said having family and friends makes a difference. It did. It prolonged a trying day. On her way to greet new arrivals, Kit overheard someone say that even before the Graysons had taken over the Reed Ranch it had never been a happy place. Locals said it was overshadowed by bad luck. Kit knew the history of the ranch and wondered if it was true. Kit was beginning to feel faint. The smell of flowers was everywhere. There had been so many at the funeral that had been brought home to be added to the ones already delivered to the house. They were everywhere. Kit pressed her fingers to her temples, trying to massage away the headache that made her head feel as if it would explode.

Doc had been watching Kit throughout the day, often seeing spasms of emotion cross her face. She was now deathly pale except for the dark shadows under her eyes and the artificial color on her hollow cheeks. Doc's heart clenched with compassion. He walked over and took her arm, "You look like you need some fresh air." Kit was grateful for the support as he headed her outside. The drawn look on her face revealed how overwrought and tired she was. Kit was an empty shell with no spark of life. Doc's voice was sympathetic, "This has been an overwhelming time for you."

"This is familiar territory. I've lived this reality before," Kit said bitterly. Death always seemed to overshadow her life. "The difference is this time I'm carrying a heavier burden. I'm a widowed mother of three and I have a ranch to run." Bitterness was evident.

Knowing Kit's past, Doc understood her anger at fate. "Your friends are here for you to lean on and help."

Kit couldn't agree more. Everyone was sympathetic and supportive. They meant well as they expressed their condolences. Kit did feel grateful, but it had become overwhelming, and Kit felt suffocated by kindness. "I just want everyone to go home and leave me alone." She needed time alone to grieve. Trace's death had left her numb and cold. The funeral had brought no sense of closure. Kit had come to terms with her reality, but that didn't mean she was coping. "I better go back in and fulfill my role as the grieving widow." Doc flinched at her sarcasm.

By early evening everyone had left. Doc had stayed until the end. He followed Lola into the kitchen, "Is Kit okay to be left alone?"

"She needs time by herself, but she isn't alone. She has us. Thank you for coming but it has been a long day for all of us."

Once everyone was gone, and the children had gone to bed, Lola and Kit were alone in the kitchen putting things away. The day had been long and stressful. Kit's anger got the better of her and she cried out, "This has been so painful, and it isn't fair. It didn't have to happen." Getting mad felt better than mourning.

Lola's own shadowed eyes held Kit's sad ones, "Do you think this is any easier for me watching my family struggling. Every day, Trace is the first thing I think about and the last thing I think about every night." Lola turned and left. It had been an emotional day for everyone.

When Lola walked out, Kit felt abandoned. Along with the fatigue, the dull pounding in her head intensified. She headed up to her room. Kit entered, crossed the room, and placed Trace's urn on the dresser. Even though he was here with her, she was alone and she ached for Trace. Like the nights before, she grabbed one of Trace's shirts. Emotionally exhausted, she lowered herself listlessly onto her bed and crawled under the covers glad to end the day. Kit knew sleep would not allow her an easy escape. Unhappy thoughts caused her to toss and turn as she continued to face a future without Trace. Kit couldn't prevent Trace's image from tormenting her, the longing to hear his voice, the need for his touch. She wanted to turn into Trace's arms and have him hold her close. She missed the depth of feeling and soul-deep satisfaction that came from being with him. Kit was missing Trace, not just in her bed, but in every aspect of her life.

As Kit lay in bed, the events of the last few days became a jumble of thoughts in her head. Once again, fate had stepped in like a cruel intruder and she was having to face the challenge of a different life. Even though a vital part of her had died, she had to continue living despite the emptiness inside her. Depression and dark thoughts were out of character for Kit, but they kept pulling her down like thick quicksand. She was angry with herself for falling into such a dark place, but she couldn't find the strength to pull herself out. She would do anything to have her old life back but that wasn't a choice. Her mind had come to terms with her reality as she finally accepted the fact that Trace was dead. Now she had to figure out how to survive. Kit turned her face into the pillow and wept.

CHAPTER EIGHTEEN

Jackson Beaumont had gone downhill quickly in the last few weeks. Evelyn was concerned because her husband was having a bad day and was in a fowl mood. Days like this, no one knew what he would say or do. Evelyn and Olivia were in the office with him.

Jackson kept digging in his pocket. "Where is my damn lighter?" Olivia crossed over to his desk, opened the drawer, pulled out a lighter and lit his cigar. It was still one of the pleasures he enjoyed. "Where is my gold lighter with my engraved initials?" He turned to his wife, "Did you hide it again so I couldn't smoke?"

"Don't be ridiculous Dad. If Mom didn't want you to smoke, why would she leave a lighter in your desk drawer?" Olivia didn't go on; it would be useless. Some days were more frustrating than others.

Jackson leaned back in his chair. "It's amazing how much joy you get from a good cigar," he said, as he exhaled the smoke into the air.

Evelyn and Olivia were nervous waiting for the RCMP, who were on their way out to talk to Jackson. They were told not to tell him they were coming. They hadn't said anything, but Olivia wondered if it had anything to do with the fire at the Grayson ranch. Evelyn had called the doctor to come out in case Jackson would need to be sedated.

The doctor was in attendance when the RCMP arrived. The first thing the officer did was take out an evidence bag. Inside was Jackson's gold lighter.

Jackson smiled with glee like a child. "You found my lighter. Good job. And people say you are all a useless bunch of SOBs."

Olivia's face paled and she had to sit down. It was evident it had been in a fire. Her fears were becoming real and were confirmed a moment later.

"This was found in the remains at the Grayson Ranch."

The look in Jackson's eyes turned to blind rage. "That man needs to be arrested. Grayson stole my horses. Now he stole my goddamn lighter. He is a thieving bastard, and he hid my horses. They weren't there when I went to get them."

Disbelief was evident in Olivia's voice, "How did you get out there?"

"I drove myself. I'm not an invalid. You would be surprised what I can do when I have to. I went to get my horses, but I couldn't find them. Grayson must have known I was coming because he set a trap and I stumbled and fell. I dropped my cigar and couldn't find it. I keep losing things. Damn frustrating."

Evelyn was shocked, "The doctor took your Driver's Licence away months ago."

Jackson laughed. "As if that would stop me. I need to go out there again."

The doctor pulled the officer aside and talked to him in a low voice. The officer nodded. The doctor went over to Jackson and stood at the back of his wheelchair. "I'm going to take you to your room. The officer is finished asking you questions." He looked at Evelyn, "I'll give him a sedative and come right back. There is a lot to discuss in regard to what we just learned."

As soon as they left, the officer pulled out a plastic evidence bag and dumped the cigar ashes from the ashtray into it. He was sure it would be the same as the unusual ashes found at the scene. There was no doubt how the fire started thanks to Jackson's rant. "Your husband was involved in a serious offence. He is a danger to others as well as himself."

The doctor returned and the conversation became intense. It was stressful and upsetting for everyone. Big decisions were made that would affect every member of the Beaumont family.

Kit and Lola were both outside when the RCMP pulled into the yard. The same officers who had just been at the Beaumont ranch. They needed to share the information they had learned. Both women stopped what they were doing and walked over to the cruiser.

"As we told you, we'd follow up on the information you shared with us about the lighter. It was Jackson Beaumont's, and we are sure he started the fire. We can't prove it was intentional because he is mentally incompetent. Mr. Beaumont's doctor was in attendance and provided us with medical reports confirming he has Alzheimer's, and it has been aggressive. Documents by the doctor show he has been irrational and confused for months. According to additional reports Mr. Beaumont doesn't have long to live. Due to his mental state and other terminal medical conditions, we are not going to take him into custody."

It was impossible for Kit to hold back her anger. "So, he gets off scot free while we live the rest of our lives without a husband, father and son."

The officer shifted uncomfortably as the two women struggled with the news. "Mr. Beaumont is under house arrest and unable to leave the ranch. Arrangements are being made for a permanent form of lockdown in their home." The sergeant didn't say anything further. Justice wasn't always served. Such an unnecessary loss that affected so many lives.

*****

Hectic days of activity followed. Days that were surreal. Lola Grande was busy inside and out. A protective numbness helped Kit get through the lonely days that were followed by long, lonely nights. Neighbours continued to bring food. They were now storing food in Lola's fridge and the freezers were full. Kit knew it was an expression of kindness, but she was struggling through the social expectations. She wanted to escape her life but even her bedroom wasn't a place of refuge. Like Finn, she had nowhere to go.

It was early and the house was still as Kit passed through it on her way to the kitchen. She made herself a coffee and stepped outside. Dawn was slowly creeping over the horizon. Kit needed time alone to address the despair that continued to torment her. Everywhere she looked, Trace's presence was there. She could hear the wind crying through the trees, as if it shared her sadness. Kit felt she had no control of her future or her destiny. Fate kept interfering. Today she was filled with an incredible sense of emptiness. People didn't last long in her life. She was thoroughly miserable as she faced another lonely day. Kit hadn't been sleeping well, she wasn't eating well. Actually, she wasn't doing anything well. Despite her efforts, she kept struggling with her grief and anger.

Kit went inside, refilled her coffee, and went back out to the verandah. She sat in the wicker chair and watched Finn approach, Buddy at his heels. She needed to talk to him before he left for school. Kit was glad the kids had returned to school. It was a small step to returning to normal. She had scarcely seen Finn in the last few days. She could see the lines of stress in his face as he approached. Kit reached over to pat Buddy when he lifted his head for a familiar caress. She motioned for Finn to sit next to her. "You're up early. What's bothering you?"

Finn tried to push his troublesome thoughts away. He stroked Buddy's ears when he went over and put his head on Finn's lap. Finn looked up at his mom, "Buddy misses Dad, too." Finn swallowed hard, scared to reveal his deepest worry. It hurt too much to think about it. After a lengthy pause, he confessed, "What if something happens to you?"

Kit could hear the anguish in Finn's voice. She hadn't realized the hidden fears her son had. "You would deal with that, too. If I had worried every day that something bad would happen to your dad, I would have missed the joy each day brought. Sadly, bad things do happen. You and I have both experienced deaths before. It never gets easier, but we have to deal with it."

Finn's emotions spilled over, "It isn't fair."

Finn's sad tone and somber face were more than Kit could bear. "No, it isn't. Do you remember when you first arrived at Lola Grande? I told you a person has to learn to accept there is heartache and pain in everyone's life, and you can't let it control you. We have more strength than we realize to get through tough times, and in time we do."

"But it's damn hard," Finn admitted in defeat.

The pain in Finn's voice cut through Kit's own pain, and it was difficult to continue, "Life doesn't always work out the way you expect. Sometimes it keeps kicking you in the gut, and you have to dig deep to find your inner strength." Kit was still struggling. She didn't want a life without Trace.

With a moan of despair, Finn released his feeling of guilt. "If I could just tell Dad I'm sorry. I should have gone in when he wasn't coming out."

Finn turned away hoping his mom wouldn't see him wipe his eyes, but he couldn't hide the grief in his voice.

Her son's confession tore at Kit's already fragile soul. "When Buster Calhoun, Trace's mentor, and father figure, died, Trace retreated into himself. It wasn't a good thing."

"Then why are you doing it, Mom?"

Kit offered no response. When she spoke again, Kit forced lightness into her voice, hoping to dispel Finn's gloomy mood, "We're going to be fine. Give it time."

The worry lines between Finn's eyes had disappeared. "I'm okay, but I better get ready for school. I'm going to stop at Valley View before I come home."

It was almost dark when Finn got home. Kit stood quietly at the kitchen window, watching him walk up the drive. He looked so tall and mature. He was already a young man. Kit warmed a plate for him. When Kit set it in front of Finn, she knew he was as tired as he looked. Kit was worried about all the long hours he was putting in between the two ranches. "You're doing too much. You'll make yourself sick if you keep this up."

The extra work hours had taken it's toll on Finn's body. He was bone tired. He was mentally and physically beat at the end of every day. He had been pushing himself through gruelling days of training. Finn let out a heavy sigh, "It will be better when school is done. Before you ask, I am caught up. Just a couple more weeks." His eyes were expressionless when he fixed them on his mom, "The horses are my responsibility now."

"I told you your dad had to grow up too soon when his dad died. He was about the same age as you are. He believed he was now the head of the Grayson family. He carried such a high level of responsibility at too young an age. You have stepped up just like your father did. I don't want you to burden yourself with that same pressure. Tomorrow Lita and I are going over to Valley View to meet with my dad and Uncle Riley. We can't do this on our own. Not with dealing with the claim and rebuild and operating our ranch out of two locations. We are family, including the Calhouns, and we will get through this together with their help. It won't always be easy, and it may not always work out the way we think it should, but we will be okay."

The look of guilt remained on Finn's face. His voice broke, "I'm letting Dad down and everyone else."

A little ashamed, Kit found it difficult to speak. Tears welled in her eyes, but she didn't cry. "You feel you failed your dad. I feel I've been failing all of my children. Maybe it's time we let our guilt go. None of us is to blame for what happened." If they wanted to survive the nightmare that trapped them, they had to accept what happened. That acceptance had to include accepting outside help.

Lola and Kit were sitting in the office in the main house at Valley View with BJ and Riley. Everyone was there, except the one person whose opinion Lola respected and trusted most. Today was the first time they had all been together since the funeral. They were all nervous. Nothing had prepared them for the trauma of Trace's death. They were still reeling from the impact. This meeting wasn't going to be easy for anyone. The two men knew how much pride Lola had and Kit was no different. Regardless, several important issues had to be discussed.

BJ knew this would be an intense meeting. He looked directly at Lola, "C&G Ranching is a joint venture, and it's still the mainstay that maintains your ranch financially. The business relationship between Lola Grande and Valley View has not changed. Your ranch will continue to run the way it always has, but the next few months are going be a challenge."

Lola had to be honest with herself. Every day had been a challenge since the fire, and it wasn't going to change any time soon. They had been busy at Lola Grande, dealing with the funeral, investigators, and Insurance Adjustor. Things had changed drastically. They were just beginning to realize how much. It had been more stressful than she realized. The commotion of the rebuild would begin soon and it would get worse.

BJ got right to the point, "You will have to face more changes in the future but right now you have to deal with the immediate outcome of the fire and Trace's death. Things have to be sorted out and decisions have to be made. None of us want to think about it but it is time to take care of business. What's important right now is getting the horse facility rebuilt. Where are you at with the insurance company? Have any decisions been made in regard to the rebuild?"

"The original blueprints were stored in Trace's office. I've given them to Andy Shaw. The insurance company has agreed to use him because of our previous history."

BJ hesitated, making sure he had their full attention, "We have concerns about Finn. It's not just his dad's death he has to deal with. There is also Trace's horse business. Finn has to continue training full-time when school is out. He can train the horses here as long as he wants but he will be spending more time at Valley View than at Lola Grande. Keeping all the horses on our land for now makes sense. It's best to eliminate the stress the activity at Lola Grande would cause. While the horses are here, our men will tend to them, as well as all fence maintenance. Your concern right now is Lola Grande."

Riley had been watching his mom. He had never seen her look so fragile. His eyes darkened with concern, "Neither of you are in any position to take care of everything on your own." As soon as he said it, Riley knew he had phrased it wrong, and his mom made it quite clear that his remark was offensive to both of them.

Lola lifted her chin stubbornly and her voice was not only angry but indignant, "Don't be condescending. Let's get something straight right now. We are grown, capable women. You are not in charge of us."

Riley did not want to get into a heated discussion with his mother, but he didn't back down. "I didn't mean to offend either one of you. We're struggling with all of this, too. I miss Trace every day just like you do, but life goes on. There is no doubt that you can run Lola Grande without Trace, but you need our help through the next few months. Even though this situation is sensitive, we have to deal with it." The room filled with an oppressive silence.

If Lola wasn't so angry, she would have been impressed by the command her son had taken. A faraway look darkened her eyes as she allowed a flashback to the intense meeting that had resulted in the Graysons getting Lola Grande. By then Lola had become the strong, independent woman she was today. She was no longer intimidated by men. She had fought for her ranch then; she would fight for it today. "Trace isn't the only one who put sweat and blood into our ranch. I'm capable of doing it again. It is Grayson land and our heritage." Lola was angry at them, even knowing they were only trying to help.

"If you had let me finish before getting defensive, I was going to say this is going to be a busy time for both of you for the next few months. Kit, you are a full-time mother and right now Kenzie and Benny need you more than ever. Your main concern is the kids."

Experience had taught Kit being a single mom was hard enough when everything was going well. She nodded as she continued to sit there quietly.

"Ma, be reasonable. I remember how you were when the suited garage and horse facilities were being built. You know you're not going to be any different with the rebuild. So, you will oversee the project and work with Andy, like you did before." Great sorrow was in his eyes when he looked at his mother. He saw the hurt building. "Think about it, you don't have time to do everything on your own. Let's get through this the best way we can."

Lola knew the rebuild would be more involved than the original build. The contractor would take care of the structure, but it would require a lot of hours to list and price the contents lost inside the barn. Following that would be the ordering, and once the items arrived they would be placing everything back inside the new facility. Lola was trying desperately to swallow her pride, knowing she had to be realistic. So many things had changed.

The two men exchanged looks, concerned that in front of them sat two women who were too emotional to think clearly. Nobody said anything. The atmosphere remained strained.

Lola was used to making decisions, but Kit had an equal say in this. This was something that would affect all of them. Lola looked over at Kit. With a gesture of resignation, Kit nodded. She knew this would be the ideal solution for now. She continued to let Lola take control. Lola continued to struggle, "You should know by now I don't take charity."

BJ's anger was now evident, "This isn't charity. Not only do you have to deal with the claim but there will be strangers coming and going. That's the other thing we want to talk about. As you know, Mexico and Canada have an international agreement, so Mexicans can work in Canada. Hector Ortiz came here through The Federal Skilled Workers Program. This program allows skilled workers to migrate to Canada. His younger brother, Ricardo, has been accepted and is on his way. Matt says Hector is a hard worker and an honest man. Hector swears his brother is, too. We have agreed to take him on as a full-time employee of C&G Ranching. His employment will be handled by Valley View but, for now, he will work at Lola Grande." Before Lola could comment, he continued, "Your ranch will be busy with the rebuild. I spoke with Andy, and we have an agreement in place where Rio can help him out as well. Riley or I will bring him over when he gets here. He was going to live in the bunkhouse with Murphy, but having Rio live at Lola Grande is the perfect solution. It's unlikely that Jackson Beaumont would still be a threat, but the man is unstable and has been known to be ruthless and dangerous. I want a man on site for protection. Rio will be there to help when unexpected things happen."

Kit tensed at the mere mention of Jackson Beaumont. She took a moment to collect herself. This conversation had taken a turn she wasn't expecting. Up until now Kit had agreed with everything, but she was dead set against this new development. She looked at her dad in disbelief. Having some strange man living at Lola Grande was not the solution. Kit was usually reasonable, but she could be just as stubborn as Lola. "Lola and I are quite capable on our own. Besides, where exactly do you expect him to live?"

"Rio has a camper van he already lives in. He can use the bathroom facilities in the indoor arena. His living there won't be an imposition."

Anger reflected the pain Kit had been living with. There was more dread in her voice than anything else, "Like hell it won't." Having some man living outside their front door was not going to happen. Everyone was taken aback by Kit's unexpected anger.

BJ was not about to back down and was ready to conclude the meeting. "This is in everyone's best interest. It's not up for discussion. This temporary arrangement is necessary. There will be difficult adjustments to make and there will be other times when we will need to meet and discuss how to manage things moving forward. You will always be advised of everything. After the rebuild is completed, we can reassess the situation, but you know you can come to us for anything."

With a gesture of resignation, Lola agreed. BJ and Riley had presented a valid case so she would accept their help. "We are eternally grateful for your friendship and your help. Thank you." The meeting was over, but everyone knew it would be different moving forward.

Kit forced out a thank you she didn't mean. Although Kit's anger had subsided, she couldn't let go of the panic. There were too many big changes ahead of them. She wasn't sure how to deal with this. She just knew she couldn't change it.

It was a quiet ride on the way home. Both women were thinking about the meeting and the decisions that had been made for them. It had been a productive meeting, even though the meeting had not gone as expected. What was happening was a significant change for them. It was upsetting knowing they had no choice but to adapt. Lola broke the silence, "We will get through this stressful time. You and I are Grayson women. We have both dealt with challenges before and survived. We are strong and we will survive this too. We are going to make it work." Lola always did have a deep inner strength. Kit hoped she would find hers.

*****

Once again Lola was overseeing a major project at Lola Grande and would be working with Andy Shaw. It would give her purpose moving forward. She greeted Andy warmly when he arrived. Lola was relieved he was heading the rebuild. She felt like she had a friend in her corner for what would continue to be a traumatic ordeal.

Andy had not hesitated when Lola asked. He knew she was a detailed person from the first time they worked together. Trace had warned him his mother would not be pushed around. That had become evident quickly. Most days they worked without incident but there were the occasional days they butted heads. Even knowing this, Andy was ready to help. Despite the grimness of the situation, Andy was glad to see Lola. He could see this had been hard on her. "Thank you for insisting that I oversee the rebuild."

"I should be thanking you for accepting the job. I'm surprised you didn't hesitate, knowing what I'm like to work with," Lola said with a wry grin.

"You know the saying, the devil you know is better than the one you don't," Andy bantered back.

"When can you get started? We need to get this done."

Andy was familiar with her directness. "I'll have a crew here on Monday to start the basic groundwork, but I have a proposal to present to you. I went over Trace's original plans and reviewed my notes. Trace often said if he had to do it over, he would have added living quarters for a hired hand. He didn't realize how successful Caballo Stables would become in such a short time. There are also a couple other changes he would have made. I have done up a quote with the changes and one with the living quarters. If you agree to the addition, it will be more than the insurance settlement but now is the time to do it. It will take several weeks longer."

Lola appreciated Andy's candor. "I will discuss this with Kit and Finn tonight and give you our decision in the morning. Thank you for understanding how important it is to get started so we can get our lives back to normal." Right now, these were hardly normal times. Lola would also ask BJ and Riley to come over. She valued their opinion.

BJ and Riley came over after supper and they reviewed Andy's suggested changes and the option to include living quarters. The decision was unanimous. Trace had never settled. They wouldn't either. They would rebuild with living quarters. Hopefully, it would be the positive step for all of them to move forward and watch Caballo Stables business continue to grow.

Kit walked out with the others as they were leaving. Lola also called it a night and went upstairs to her place. Kit sat down on the top step and leaned against the verandah post. Most evenings a cool breeze would blow in off the mountains. Tonight, it had a bite to it. Kit remained outside even though the chilly wind made her shiver. The sky darkened as the sun dropped lower behind the mountains. She was tired by the time the lingering sunset disappeared. Kit stared out at the black night. She believed her future loomed ahead just as dark. Numb and cold, Kit got up and went inside where she sat alone unwilling to go up to bed. It wasn't until fatigue won out that she climbed the stairs. Moonbeams cast streams of light across the room. She hated facing another restless night unsuccessfully chasing sleep. It was after midnight before Kit was able to make her escape from reality by falling into a deep sleep. Sleep was her only escape. Trace still lived in her dreams, allowing her to remember the way he would make her feel.

CHAPTER NINETEEN

The sky began to lighten as Kit lay in bed, lifeless. She lay in a state of black despair and resentful of fate. With every passing day, she was struggling. She didn't have the energy to do anything. It took all of her effort to breathe. Kit was dreading another long day. With a lethargic sigh she threw back the covers and forced herself to get up. The warm rays of the morning sun drew her across the room to the window and looked out. It was hard to let go of her anger when every time she looked outside the changed landscape was an ugly reminder of her loss. The last few weeks had been a blur; the days overwhelming. Kit had been too distressed to think beyond her inner turmoil. The numbness was slowly ebbing, harsh reality taking its place. Today she was overtaken by an incredible sense of emptiness, and nothing seemed to ease the pangs of loneliness. Kit turned away.

Kit took her time in the shower and allowed the hot water to wash away some of her grief. Sadly, she couldn't wash away the dark shadows that remained under her eyes. Turning slightly, she caught her image in the mirror. She blinked hard seeing a pathetic stranger and felt ashamed. She was a pitiful sight. *Maybe today will be a better day. Probably not.*

Like Kit, Lola had difficulty sleeping since the fire, so she went downstairs and joined Kit for coffee. It was too early for the kids to be up. Lola was concerned about Kit and studied her as she sipped her coffee. Lola had been spending most of her time in the main house rather than upstairs in her suite. Lola understood the magnitude of Kit's loss. It was no bigger than her own. She usually kept her opinions to herself, but not when family was involved. There was no routine, and everyone was struggling to adjust to the changes around them and within themselves. These were stressful times as they tried to adapt to life without Trace. "I'm worried about you, Kit. You've lost weight and you're not getting enough sleep. I see your light on long after it's time for bed."

Kit didn't know which was worse, the nightmares when she was asleep or the nightmares when she was awake. She knew she had been struggling. "It's like I'm in a bad dream that plays over and over. I want this nightmare to end. I've tried shutting myself away thinking I can shut out the pain. I don't want to feel this way."

Lola always spoke her mind. "When you build a wall around yourself, it may keep out the grief, but it keeps out everything else. You can't escape reality. Life doesn't give us that choice. You can't hit pause. No matter how bad your heart is broken, the world doesn't stop while you deal with your grief. Life goes on and it only goes in one direction. You have to move forward."

Kit knew she couldn't lock herself away. Life wasn't that simple. Kit remained silent, not knowing what to say.

"I know you've had a hard time coping since Trace died. I have, too. It's such a shock at first you don't believe it. Death is a part of life and there is pain and heartache in everyone's life. Dealing with death is just one of life's harder lessons."

Kit had accepted Lola's directness over the years. Today it bothered the hell out of her. She interrupted; anger having taken hold. "My children were too young for this lesson. I can't handle what's happening."

"Bad things happen that you can't control. This is something that will not change. As difficult as this is, you must pull yourself together and go on."

Because Kit detected a note of criticism in Lola's voice, anger flashed in Kit's eyes. "That's what I'm trying to do. I'd sure like to know when it's going to get better."

"I don't know, Kit. Maybe tomorrow, or the next day, or the day after that. Just know, it does get better. You learn to accept the hurt, but you don't let it consume you. When you let life back in it takes over the hurt. The grief you're feeling right now isn't forever. Nothing is forever. Nothing good and nothing bad."

"I am trying to come to terms with everything but it's hard. Trace's death turned my world upside down. It changed my life. I've dealt with the shock; it's the injustice I'm struggling with. It didn't have to happen."

Lola could no longer hold back her own anger she'd been struggling with, "This isn't all about you, Kit. My life has also changed. I'm also heartbroken because I have to face a life without my son. It's not easy for any of us but your withdrawing is making it really difficult. Your family needs you now more than ever. Before you can take care of them you have to start by taking care of yourself."

Lola's words stung. Kit knew she wasn't the only one hurting but how could she help anyone when she couldn't even help herself? "I know that. I am worried about my kids. Finn was so brave those first few days but now he has withdrawn."

"Don't judge Finn too harshly. I'm sure he's angry, too. He needs time to process everything. He doesn't know what his role should be. Finn's life has changed much more than the younger kids. Give him time and be there for him when he's ready. He will need you."

Kit looked at Lola with distressed eyes, "Benny is too young to understand and has become very clingy. Kenzie, being older, understands more but she pretends everything is fine. It's like her dad is just away. The questions have started, and I don't know what to tell them. I feel everything I say makes things worse. I don't know what to do anymore," Kit confessed desperately.

"Just be there for them. That's all you need to do right now. Be honest and keep it simple but make sure they understand. You have to remember the kids will need to work through their emotions. Give them a chance to share their feelings and worries even if it comes out in anger."

"How can I make them understand when I don't understand?" Kit asked painfully.

None of them could live with this unhappiness that surrounded them and be okay. Lola had been strong through all of this but for some reason it was more than she could cope with today. Out of character, Lola snapped at Kit, "Your kids are missing their dad and can't understand why something so terrible happened. They are also missing their mom. You have to be there for your children. You don't have a choice. They need to know you are there for them at all times."

It became very quiet in the room. Kit was hurt by Lola's bluntness. "I've been here every day." Her eyes brimmed with unshed tears. She wiped at them furiously when they fell.

"Only physically. Emotionally you locked yourself away. Don't let your life be overshadowed by grief."

Startled, Kit attacked back, "Are you implying that I'm a horrible mother?" Part of Kit's anger was due to the guilt she felt knowing she was failing her children.

"No, you are a wonderful mother."

"It's exhausting trying to make everyone feel better only to realize you're failing." This knowledge frightened Kit. "It's like I'm full of anger every single day. I feel like screaming just to release it. I'm mad at God for his cruelty. I'm mad at Trace for dying. I'm mad at myself because I don't know what to do anymore. I know I'm not coping. I can't deal with my life right now. I need more time."

Lola's anger flared, "That's enough with the self-pity. The sooner everyone gets back into a normal routine the better. That goes for you too, Kit." Even though Lola understood Kit's loss and her anger, her own anger surfaced and coated the rest of her words, "I've never been one to wallow in self-pity or the past. It can't be changed." Lola had proven her strength when it mattered. She had never faltered throughout her earlier years of hardship and heartache, and she would remain strong now.

Kit had always admired Lola's incredible inner strength but today she took offense to what Lola was saying. "I've accepted what happened," she said defiantly.

Lola's voice took on a sharpness Kit hadn't heard before. "You're not dealing with it. We have to return to a normal life."

Trace's death had devastated Kit, and her life was turned upside down. "How? Everything is different. This has been unbelievable and there's this huge void in my life." Tears spilled down Kit's cheeks. "Do you think I want to feel this way?"

Lola's voice softened, taking away some of the hurt caused by the conversation, "There's going to be a period of adjustment for all of us but we have to maintain a routine so things can return to normal as soon as possible." Lola paused to let her words sink in. Kit was in a bad place right now. The poor girl didn't deserve this, but it didn't change the facts. Lola's look never wavered, even when Kit flashed her a hurt look. "You are and always will be a mother. That is what must matter, especially now. How do you think it makes your kids feel when you mope around? Parenting has to continue. Your kids still need responsibility. They also need accountability. It can't change because they lost their dad."

Kit knew Lola's comments were meant for her as well. "I hate this, Lola. I feel myself resenting Trace. He left me to cope with everything. The kids, their questions, their anger, my own anger. How can I help my kids when I can't help myself? Everything has changed for me." Bitterness coated every word as her voice trailed off while frustration sparkled in her eyes.

"It changed for all of us, Kit. Our family, as it was, will never be the same but we are still a family. We are going to work through these sudden changes one day at a time." Even Lola knew that was easier said than done. She was still struggling with moving forward. The older woman's eyes darkened with sorrow. "Death is difficult, especially when it comes too soon."

Kit was unable to control her anger. "It sure did for Trace, and I've had more than my share of having to deal with deaths."

"You and I have both made it through tough times and we can do it again. God doesn't give us sorrow without giving us the strength to bear it."

"Well, I haven't found mine. Maybe it's under the heavy burden I'm carrying. I didn't ask for all of this. I'm now a widowed mother of three children with a ranch to run, a business to save and a heart that won't heal." Kit glared back at Lola, failing to hide the hurt in her expressive eyes. The future of a lonely life angered her. "Anger may not get you anywhere, but it sure feels good to let it out." That said, Kit got up and walked away.

Even though nothing had been resolved, Lola felt better for having spoken her mind. Lola left and was on her way up to her suite when Doc pulled into the yard. She welcomed him as he climbed out of his truck. Doc had been dropping by on a regular basis. At first it was out of concern, but Lola knew now it was more than that. Anyone with eyes could see that Doc was in love with Kit. Lola guessed he had always been in love with her but kept it well hidden. Lola doubted that Kit realized how deep Doc's feelings were. As far as Kit was concerned, the vet was being a good friend. He had been a family friend for years.

Doc bent down to give Buddy a gentle pat on the head before greeting Lola, "It looks like they're making headway on the rebuild."

Things outside had settled with the arrival of Andy's crew, but they were still waiting for Rio Ortiz to show up. "There's been more good days than bad in regard to the rebuild. Not so much with us." The upheaval in their lives was wearing on all of them. Her fight with Kit had been upsetting.

"How's Kit doing today?"

"Not good. Sorry I can't chat. I have an appointment and I'm running a bit late. Kit's got coffee on at the main house. I'm sure she'll be glad to see you."

Kit stepped out of the house and waved. She knew Doc and Lola had been talking about her. Kit's head ached. Her conversation with Lola had been intense and upsetting. She knew she hadn't been fair to Lola, but her life hadn't been fair either.

Doc crossed the yard and greeted Kit casually, "How's it going?" He was concerned because she had slipped into a deep depression. Kit was finding it hard to accept losing Trace.

Kit managed a weak smile. "Fine," she assured him. She was sure Lola had said otherwise. "Let's sit on the verandah since it's nice out. I'll be right back with coffee."

Doc took the cup Kit handed him when she returned, "How are you really?" He noticed that the shadows under her eyes weren't as dark, but her eyes were still dull and haunted.

Kit was tired of trying to hide it. Tired of being worried over and pampered. She let out a heavy sigh. Anguish broke into her voice, "I suppose I'm still in shock. At first the pain was intolerable. Now my emotions have changed and I'm angry again at the injustice and at Trace. I feel myself resenting Trace for leaving me alone to deal with all of this. It's all up to me now." She was tired of wrestling with her emotions. The hurt faded from Kit's face, only to be replaced by intense sadness. She wondered how she would ever fill the void in her heart.

"I told you, I'm always here for you."

Kit knew Doc meant it. Knowing she had the support of family and friends wasn't enough. This was life and she had to deal with it. She just had to figure out how.

After Doc left, Kit went in to make supper. Although there hadn't been much of a routine, the evening meal remained the one constant. Tonight, Lola didn't come down for supper. Kit made a flimsy excuse. She hadn't seen much of Lola all day, and she knew it was intentional.

Unexpectedly, Kenzie brought up Father's Day. Finn shook his head at her. Kit didn't miss the silent look exchanged between them. They tried not to upset their mother.

Benny, too young to pick up on it, asked, "Do we still celebrate Father's Day when we don't have a daddy?"

Benny's question caught Kit off guard. She had been so self-absorbed in her grief she had forgotten it was Father's Day on Sunday. It hurt that her children no longer had a dad. Kit drew in a calming breath before answering, hoping she sounded more cheerful than she felt, "Let's celebrate right now and do something special to us. Let's take turns and say something wonderful we did with Daddy. Your daddy's death can't take our memories of him away." It was time to remember the good and let the bad go. Life moves on.

Benny looked up at his mom and smiled. Kit could already see he had the same charm as his father. He was Trace inside and out. Kit started, "Do you remember when ….." It helped talking about Trace and it was like he was there with them. They would not look back in sorrow. Instead, they'd remember the happy times and continue to share them, keeping Trace in their lives. They shared their memories, tears mixed with laughter.

"I wish we still had Daddy," Benny cried. Here sat a lonesome seven-year-old.

"He's in heaven with my first daddy." replied Kenzie, trying to console her brother.

"Maybe we'll get a new daddy like you did."

Kit gave Benny a reassuring smile before she kissed his anxious face. "I guess we'll just have to wait and see what happens." Kit was anxious to change the subject, "Let's do something different on Sunday. We can go to Calgary for a movie and pizza afterwards. We'll invite Lita."

Everyone cheered. Kit looked at Kenzie, "It's time to clean up the kitchen."

"Okay, Mommy."

Kit was surprised there was no argument. What had been an unpleasant day had ended surprisingly good. Kit smiled as she hadn't in weeks.

That night before bed, Kenzie crawled up next to her mom. "I wish Daddy was still here. I miss him every day. Sometimes I think if I wish hard enough, he'll come back."

"Wishing something doesn't make it happen." *I tried.* "We have to accept our loss and the changes that are happening. We are also changing as a result of this, whether we want to or not." Kit took a long pause before continuing, "I hate to admit I've slipped into a depression but I'm trying to get better. Remember when Finn became part of our family? Those first few months were difficult for all of us, but we adjusted. This is still a hard time for us. I promise you it will get better, and so will I."

Kenzie hugged her mom, "You don't have to worry, Mommy, I won't ever leave you."

After the kids were in bed, Kit went out to the verandah. She sat down and Buddy came and laid his head on her lap. "I know, I miss him, too." She gently stroked Buddy's ears before he lay down at her feet. Still reeling from the events of the day, Kit was feeling so low she felt like Trace was looking down at her and mocking her. In the moment she hated him. How dare he leave her. She didn't deserve the heartache. Her anger only lasted a moment, but nothing helped to ease the pangs of loneliness that grabbed hold.

Kit regretted her earlier outburst with Lola. She hated confrontations. They were extremely upsetting. Recalling much of what Lola said, Kit knew it was time to step out of her protective numbness and return full-time to the real world. A tinge of regret passed though Kit. She admitted she had spent too much time taking refuge in her room. She had spent days walking around like a zombie. Kit wasn't proud of her behaviour. She knew grief was normal but prolonged depression was unhealthy. It was time to find the strength to take care of herself if she was to find the strength to help her children. It was time to get back to being a mom. Her family needed her. She had obligations and responsibilities. Death didn't change that. She would have to try harder.

CHAPTER TWENTY

A new day was dawning. Kit went and leaned on the railing. She stared beyond the work site to the mountains. A pang of sorrow hit her, as it always did when she thought of Trace. When she first met Trace, she thought he was as rugged as the mountains and just as rigid. She soon found him to be a solid and upstanding man who was unmovable in his beliefs. She watched the rising sun's rays filter through the wispy clouds overhead. *Rays of hope starting a new day. Please give me strength so I can make this day better.* Kit was going to make an honest effort at returning to a regular routine. When she heard activity inside, she went in to start breakfast. It was a step forward, but she was a long way from acceptance. Lola didn't come down to join them for breakfast. It had been a couple of days since she and Lola had argued and the tension between them was still evident. Kit knew Lola was giving her time to process their conversation and take accountability again as a parent.

School would soon be out, and the kids would be home all day. Summer had always been Kit's favorite time of the year. Now she dreaded it because it would be so different. It would be one of continued change and chaos. She hated her life. As soon as the kids were off to school, Kit began cleaning up the kitchen. She was startled when there was a knock at the door and Maggie walked in. Kit was surprised to see her. "I'm not in the mood for company today."

Maggie was glad Kit was by herself in the kitchen. "Well, I didn't drive all this way just to turn around and go home." She poured herself a coffee and went and sat at the table.

"I'm not good company today," Kit confessed, refusing to join Maggie at the table.

"What do you mean today?" Maggie challenged. "You're exasperating at times. I've tried calling you for days and you don't return my calls. What's going on?" Maggie was worried about her friend. It didn't go unnoticed that Kit looked tired and drawn and had lost more weight. "You look terrible."

Kit knew she looked awful. "Thanks. Excuse me if I'm not looking my best these days. My whole life has changed and I'm all alone." Kit's voice broke and the tears she'd been holding back for days came. Tears she quickly blinked away.

"It just seems like that right now, but you have all of us. Me and Matt, Riley, the Calhouns, Lola."

Kit cut Maggie off before she got any further, "I don't have Trace. My children deserve to have a father. I deserve to have a husband. I already lost one. It isn't fair that I've lost another one. Fate keeps attacking me. Death has always been a part of my life, but nothing prepared me for this. My whole world has been torn apart. You don't know the emptiness inside of me. This is more difficult than anything you can imagine. In one day, my life was destroyed. This didn't have to happen and all I want to do is scream at the injustice of it all."

Maggie ignored Kit's rant. Like always Maggie kept it real, "You have to pull yourself out of your misery. You still have three children that need you. You have a friend who has missed you. Don't lock me out, Kit. If you start locking people out, you end up locking yourself away. Maybe you need some grief counselling."

The atmosphere was heavy between them. Throughout their friendship, Maggie had offered unsolicited advice. Kit didn't want to get into this right now. "I didn't ask for your advice, Maggie Walker."

Maggie was shocked by the hardness in Kit's voice. It didn't stop her from saying, "I've given up giving you advice, since you don't take it anyway. I will share a few facts with you. You're not the only one going through this. Matt misses his best friend every day."

Kit's anger was quickly replaced by bitterness. How could Maggie understand? She still had a husband. Kit's voice continued to rise, "You've made your point but let me ask you something. How would you feel if you suddenly lost Matt and you're all alone? You are the one responsible for running the ranch and raising your children on your own. How would you like to go to your room every night and lie alone in an empty bed?"

This was something Maggie couldn't comprehend and would never want to. Knowing being honest was more important than hurt feelings, Maggie continued, "I've never lost anybody close to me so it would be unkind to say I know how you feel, but we are in pain, too."

Pain was something Kit understood, for she had lived with it ever since that dreadful day. It was as familiar to her as the air she breathed. Grief coated Kit's words, "I feel like my life stopped that day, too."

Maggie remained frustrated, "I don't mean to be insensitive, but we've been over that. It was Trace who died, not you."

Kit was shocked by Maggie's bluntness. Unable to maintain eye contact, she turned away as many of Maggie's words struck a raw nerve. Deep down she felt a twinge of shame about her outburst.

Maggie's lips tightened in annoyance, "You never used to be like this, Kit."

"You're right. I used to be a happy married woman. Now I'm neither." Kit was well aware that sarcasm was ugly, but at the moment that's all she had as a defense. Bitterness turned to anger. "I don't need any help. I just want everyone to leave me alone." Kit turned away and looked out the window in an act of dismissal. Her voice was cold and detached when she turned back to Maggie, "Go home. I don't need anyone's pity."

Maggie fought back, not bothering to mince her words as they tumbled out, "No you don't. You have enough self-pity of your own." They glared at each other, tears rimming their eyes. When Kit blinked first, Maggie said with reservation, "I don't know who you are anymore, Kit Grayson." Without another word, Maggie got up and walked out the door. She knew no matter what she said it would be useless. It tore at Maggie's heart to see her friend like this.

I'm fine, Kit reassured herself as she looked out the window and saw Lola and Maggie going up to Lola's. *Just fine.* But everything was not fine. Kit had pushed the boundaries of their friendship. It was like she was fighting with everyone and losing. Kit knew she was being self-indulgent and was wrapping herself in self-pity, but she didn't know how to deal with this. Maggie's comments still hurt, and she hadn't recovered from her fight with Lola.

Up in Lola's suite, Maggie shared the conversation between her and Kit. "She won't discuss the fire and what happened to Trace. She was just angry. I don't know how to help her."

"Kit has a lot of anger she's struggling with. Anger can bring out the worst in anyone. Mix in the hurt and a person loses control. Everyone has to deal with grief in their own way. Right now, Kit is lashing out. She hasn't accepted what happened so she's struggling to deal with it. Her world has been deeply shaken and she is resorting to avoidance. She spends most of her time in the house."

Maggie couldn't hide her concern. She was frustrated because she wanted to help her friend but didn't know how. "I'm worried about Kit. She looks so fragile."

Lola recognized Maggie's concern. "She's stronger than you think. Right now, Kit's caught up in her anger. She still needs time before she can let it go. Kit's having a difficult time because a big piece of her life is missing. Trace was her life. She will have to pick up the pieces before she can start to put her life back together. There's nothing we can do for her right now. It takes time to accept before you can heal," Lola said, as much to herself as to Maggie. Lola knew in time they would all survive their personal grief.

"I feel like I've lost two friends. Trace and Kit. This has been horrible for you, too. You lost your son."

"No one understands another person's grief. Everyone has to deal with grief in their own way. Life still goes on. We'll be okay." She didn't know if she was trying to convince Maggie or herself. Sorrow weighed heavily on her own heart.

Maggie could see that Lola was upset and clearly worried about Kit. Lola had unwillingly revealed the depth of anguish she also carried since Trace's death. When Lola turned away, Maggie knew this topic was over, "How are things around here otherwise?"

Lola was grateful for Maggie's empathy. "Now that the rebuild has started there is added commotion all around so it's hard to settle. We've been waiting for Hector's brother to arrive. Kit's not happy about him living here at Lola Grande." The rebuild filled Lola's days and gave her purpose. She was grateful to have something else to think about and occupy the long days. Like Kit, the nights were long.

"How do you feel about it?"

Lola had regained control of her emotions, "I have come to terms with the circumstances. It's a change we have to deal with until the rebuild is done. Has Hector said anything to Matt when his brother will be here?"

"Hector says he should arrive any day now. I'm sorry your family has all of this to deal with. Unexpected obstacles always add unwanted stress. Take care, Lola."

It was late afternoon when Doc drove in. Kit was usually glad to see him, but after her fight with Maggie she would have preferred to be alone. She didn't go out right away to meet him. She needed a minute to put on her protective shell. By the time Doc was coming up the walk Kit was sitting on the verandah waiting to greet him.

Doc dropped into the chair next to her. A close study of Kit's face revealed her ongoing struggle and the sadness that overwhelmed her. His heart ached to see her like this but there was nothing he could do for her. "How are you?"

Kit couldn't hide her look of despair. "If I said I was fine I'd be lying. I don't know who I am anymore. I'm consumed by bitterness, drowning in sorrow and angry at life. Aren't you glad you asked?" After taking a deep breath, Kit was less angry, but her words remained bitter. "I'm adjusting but I'm struggling. As a parent, I have obligations and responsibilities that I haven't been doing very well. Can you believe I forgot that Sunday is Father's Day? What kind of mother am I? The kids miss their dad but being young they look to moving on. Benny said maybe next year they would have a new daddy."

Doc smiled sadly; he would love to fill that vacant role. He wondered if he could now win her love if he dared to try. When Trace was still alive, their professional relationship would have been affected. Besides, they were all friends and Doc had a high regard for the sanctity of marriage. It was on the tip of his tongue to confess his true feeling, but this wasn't the time. He knew it was too soon. He would wait a while longer. He'd been waiting for years. Doc would continue to be there for Kit in her time of need.

Kit wasn't proud of her recent behaviour. "Lola and I had an argument a couple of days ago and Maggie was here this morning. We also had a fight. Are you sure you want to stay? You might be round three."

"Sorry, verbal sparing is not on my agenda today," he declared, wanting to make her laugh.

Kit did laugh, taking away some of the hurt caused by her earlier conversation with Maggie. The light banter made her feel better. "Trace could always make me laugh. He could also make me mad. I'm mad at Trace for dying and I'm mad at myself because I don't know how to cope."

"You can and you will get through this. You're made of strong stuff, Kit Grayson."

"Trace used to tell me that." Kit smiled but she managed to look twice as sad. Kit could see that Doc was sad and said as much. Of course, he was missing his friend. Little did Kit know that she was the main reason for the sadness in his eyes.

Doc could see her heartache. Hearing the anguish in Kit's voice affected Doc. He wanted to reach out and erase the sad shadows still lurking in her eyes. Doc's suppressed feelings for Kit surfaced and he gave her hand a gentle squeeze, "You're someone special, Kit. I have such admiration for you considering everything you've had to endure. Time heals, so it will get better."

Kit could feel the pity in Doc's touch. She knew he was being sincere. How many times had she told her children that? In their own time they would heal, but how much time would it take?

Kit's face had taken on a familiar look and Doc guessed she was thinking about Trace. Even now, it was like Trace was still there between them. Kit was lost in her thoughts, her face showing the anguish the painful memories brought back. Kit turned to Doc and the haunted look was back. "One loses all that is familiar, all that matters. Suddenly, you're all alone even when you are surrounded by people. I can't ever repay you for the support you've given our family over the years and especially since Trace died."

Kit's voice had registered her hurt and Doc flashed her a compassionate smile. He had been struggling in silence with his feelings. "Life isn't always fair for anyone." Meaningful words that impacted lives again and again.

Kit hadn't failed to notice Doc's look of concern. "Don't worry. Even though it's difficult to put this tragedy behind me, I'll be alright. Time has dulled the sharp pain." Kit wasn't sure if she was admitting that to him or herself. Kit lowered her eyes, but her long lashes couldn't hide the misery that continued to overcome her. She wasn't the same Kit.

Their deep friendship allowed them to sit in companionable silence. It was peaceful. The workers had gone home for the day. Doc had planned just a short visit on his way home from an out-of-office appointment in the area and here it was almost supper time. He rose to leave, not wanting to overstay his welcome. He gave Kit a friendly kiss on the cheek. It had become part of his departure since Trace died.

It had been nice to have Doc's company. She appreciated the comfortable relationship she had with him. Kit was grateful for his non-judgemental friendship. Maggie's unexpected visit earlier had upset her. What did if matter? Nothing mattered anymore.

CHAPTER TWENTY-ONE

Kit pulled her hair back in a low ponytail. She hadn't been to a hairdresser since before Trace died, so she really needed a trim. She had hardly been anywhere, but at least now she wasn't locking herself away in her room. The old Kit was slowly emerging, having worked her way out of her heavy depression. Today, she was going to spend the morning in Trace's office. She would do what she could to help Lola find receipts for the inventory that was lost in the fire. Even though Lola was in charge of the rebuild project, Kit tried to help where she could. It wasn't a normal routine, but it was life as it was. Both the tack room and Trace's office were located in the old barn but there was still a lot of equipment in the new barn that had to be replaced. Kit shook her head when she walked into Trace's office. It was bad enough her life was a mess. For someone who was anal about his tack room, Trace was a slob in his office. She stared at several stacks of paper piled on his desk. Invoices, receipts, yellow stickies with notes and phone numbers written on them. It reminded her of when she arrived at Valley View and helped the Calhouns get through their paper mess when their bookkeeper quit unexpectedly. Kit sighed heavily; she had managed to get through that so she would manage to get through this. One piece of paper at a time.

After spending a few hours in Trace's office, Kit felt like she had made little headway. Feeling frustrated and claustrophobic, Kit decided to take a break. Everything in life seemed to be in a state of upheaval. Deep in thought, she rounded the corner of the barn as she headed back to the house, and bumped into a solid wall of muscle, knocking the wind out of her. A stranger towered over her. The man was an intimidating figure, over six feet of solid muscle.

"Hey, are you all right?"

The man's deep, dark voice startled Kit. The hair on her neck raised as she squinted in the bright sunlight. She was not happy seeing a stranger on her land. Buddy, who had tagged along with Kit, jumped up to greet him and yipped to get attention. When the stranger bent down to pet him, Buddy licked his hand. *Fine watch dog, you are.* Kit stepped back and shot the intruder a suspicious glance. "Who are you and what are you doing here?" Kit pushed back her tumbled hair that had fallen loose.

"My name's Ricardo Ortiz but everyone calls me Rio. I've been hired by BJ Calhoun, the boss man at C&G Ranching." Angry, gray eyes looked up at him as she openly inspected him.

Kit was aware of everything about him. The stranger was dark-skinned, with eyes as black as coal. His face was weathered from sun and wind, light crease lines at the corners of his eyes. There was a quality of roughness in his lean, hard features. The dark stubble covering his strong jaw only emphasized the chiselled planes of his face. A small scar over his eyebrow added interest to his rakish features. The imperfection enhanced his masculine appeal. Everything about him was rough and rugged. He was so blatantly macho. Kit could tell he was sure of himself. When he turned from her, she was shocked to see his hair was braided and hung down to his waist. Kit was too shocked to speak. This was the man hired to help them at Lola Grande. This was the man who was going to be living on site. Kit was more aware of him than she would have liked. It was disturbing. "What are you doing here?" Kit asked again. Her expression was far from friendly.

If Rio noticed Kit's stunned response, he didn't react. "Just following orders."

Kit's eyes widened a fraction, her shock replaced by confusion, "Who's giving you orders?"

Despite Kit's cold and detached attitude, Rio picked up on her conflicting features. "Riley told me to meet him here," he replied calmly.

"Well, you're on Lola Grande land and neither BJ Calhoun nor Riley Grayson is the boss here. Nobody told us you would be here today. Why didn't Riley call or bring you here himself?" Kit struggled to keep her voice civil, but she was unable to hide the fact his appearance had unnerved her. She knew her reaction to him had been rude, but Kit didn't like being put at a disadvantage.

Rio's eyes, dark and dangerous, held her gaze. He couldn't understand why she was giving him such a hard time. "You can ask him when he gets here. Is Mrs. Grayson around?"

"I'm Mrs. Grayson." The atmosphere remained strained as Kit maintained eye contact.

Rio's eyebrow raised sightly as he stared at her with open curiosity. How could he know she was one of the Mrs. Graysons. He expected someone older. Rio smiled in hopes of softening the scowl on her face, but that only earned a glare. Rio's eyes lost his steely look, now replaced with a hint of amusement as he hooked his thumbs in his faded jean pockets and studied her. He took in all of her, from her luscious auburn hair glowing in the late morning sunlight right down to her flip-flops. A plain T-shirt was tucked in at a narrow waist, and her worn jeans were ripped through at the knees. Her face was make-up free. The woman in front of him looked like a teenager. Her mysterious gray eyes were intense, but they had no life in them.

Kit and Rio stood there and stared at each other. Distrustful of the stranger. Kit's posture remained rigid. "There are two Mrs. Graysons," Kit informed coldly. *Where the hell is Riley?*

"Is the other Mrs. Grayson as distrustful as you?" Rio's lean frame revealed a trace of irritation.

Just then, Lola appeared, "I'm worse."

Two for two. Double damn. Rio wondered what he had gotten himself into.

Kit was relieved that Lola showed up. Fortunately, Riley also pulled into the yard. Kit verbally attacked Riley the minute he stepped out, "Why didn't you call and give us a heads up? Actually, why weren't you here first?"

Riley, the jerk, grinned as he tipped his hat back, which annoyed Kit even more. "Rio was at his brother's, so I asked him to stop here before coming over to Valley View since it was on the way. I thought I'd be here before Rio arrived, but I had to take an overseas call just as I was leaving. Rio, meet my mother, Lola Grayson, and this spitfire is my sister-in-law, Kit Grayson."

Rio confessed, "I thought she was one of the kids."

"She does behave like one on occasion." Rio joined in when Riley laughed. Lola knew better than to laugh.

Riley's teasing only fueled Kit's smoldering anger, while bringing a flush to her cheeks. Indignation surfaced and she gave Riley a dirty look.

Rio's gaze returned to the older Mrs. Grayson, who told him he could call her Lola as she extended her hand in welcome.

Kit fumed. How could Lola accept this stranger so readily?

Rio shook his head, "Senora Grayson, my mother would turn over in her grave if I was disrespectful."

"We aren't very formal here. Would you be okay calling me Mrs. G?"

"Only if you insist."

Kit continued to scrutinize Rio. Verbally, the man was smooth, but his manner was bold. Physically, he wasn't as tall as Trace, but he was just as formidable. There was something imposing about the man, who was a couple of years older than Kit, but Kit refused to be intimidated by another cowboy with attitude. The man oozed charm, but she remained immune to him. "You may call me Kit." Kit kept her voice deliberately cool, and didn't offer her hand. She did not like Rio Ortiz.

Riley looked at Rio, "Maybe you're having second thoughts now that you've met Ma and Kit."

I wish. Kit wanted to be done with him.

Reading her mind, Rio stared Kit down. "You can't get rid of me that easily. I said I'd help out." He knew the younger woman in front of him was trouble. He hadn't missed the open hostility in Kit's eyes. Hell, they might both be trouble, but he was staying and ready to work. These women were dealing with an agonizing loss, and Rio was determined to do anything he could to help.

"There is no point to delay since Rio has agreed to stay at Lola Grande. Rio will be bringing his van over tonight and will be staying on site as discussed. He will park his camper van beside the arena and use the bathroom in there to shower. He won't disturb you."

He already disturbs me. He had since the moment Kit met him.

"I'm going to take Rio over to introduce him to Andy before we head back to Valley View."

Indignation surfaced when Rio winked at her. Head high, Kit turned and walked away, wanting nothing to do with any of them. Kit knew Rio Ortiz's presence would prove frustrating.

Lola decided to set the men in front of her straight. "That woman who just left is the bravest, fiercest woman I've ever known. Don't sell her short and don't misjudge either one of us. We are the bosses here. This is the Grayson ranch, not the Calhoun ranch." That said, Lola turned and left.

Riley knew her last comment was more for him than for Rio. Riley gave Rio a word of caution as they went to find Andy, "We operate Valley View and Lola Grande together in a joint venture with the cattle, but otherwise Lola Grande operates independently. The Grayson women think they can handle anything so are struggling with this situation. They are tougher than they look. Tough, but fair. They aren't happy about you being here, but they will come around."

Rio's expression darkened. A sense of apprehension shivered down his spine. What had he gotten himself into? He wasn't sure if he should have agreed to this or not.

Kit had been anxious all day because of her initial reaction to Rio. Right after supper she went outside to wait for him. This was something they had no control over and there were going to be some challenging days ahead. She was going to have to accept it and get used to it. Rio's temporary residency was unavoidable, but she would remain cautious. Trust had to be earned. Kit walked over to the arena when Rio pulled into the yard.

Rio stepped out, wanting to know where Kit wanted him to park.

"Nice unit." Instead of the beat-up van she expected, it was only a couple of years old and definitely a high-end unit.

Rio hadn't missed the look of surprise on Kit's face when he pulled in. "Judging me again? You probably thought I lived in a dilapidated van that would break down any minute."

Once again, Rio had a disturbing effect on Kit because he was right. There was a draw to him despite the fact that his presence annoyed her. Kit decided to make an effort, "For some reason we seem to have gotten off on the wrong foot."

The reason is standing right in front of me. Rio recognized behind the cool exterior was a frightened young woman. Rio remained guarded.

"Thank you for letting me come over tonight to get settled. I wanted to be here when Andy arrives tomorrow morning."

Kit showed him where to park and left, giving him time to settle. Kit hated to admit she felt a little relief knowing he was living on site. She wasn't sure why. For weeks Kit had been sleeping fitfully. That night she slept through the night for the first time since the fire.

CHAPTER TWENTY-TWO

It was still early when Kit went out to the verandah to enjoy the peace and quiet before the rest of her household started their day and the workers would arrive. The smells of summer surrounded her, fresh cut grass, the fragrance of surrounding flowers, and pure mountain air. She took in the sights and sounds around her, grateful to have moved past the pain that had held her in its grip for too long. She was doing better every day. Her thoughts were interrupted by movement over by the riding arena. She was surprised to see Rio crossing the yard to his van. Kit sat quietly watching him. He carried himself with a definite swagger, his stride long and slow. Everything in her life seemed to be in a state of upheaval and now Rio was coming and going whenever and wherever he felt like it. It was obvious he had just showered. He was bare-chested, and his wet hair hung loose to his waist, shining like molten lava cascading down a mountain of muscles. Dormant feelings stirred as Kit continued to look. Her eyes slid appreciatively across the taut power of his chest and down his strong arms, taking in the corded muscles in his broad shoulders. She was surprised, not shocked, at the number of tattoos he had. There was no denying that Rio had a strong physical attractiveness, and the aura of power was more than well-developed muscles. Kit had to admit to herself she found his strong dark looks dangerously enticing. He was igniting the desire she missed from Trace. Heavy thoughts, no longer of Trace, were disturbing her. In the moment, she hated Rio even more because he reminded her of Trace.

Kit headed indoors. It was the beginning of another work week. Finn would be up soon and heading over to Valley View. He was still putting in long days until they could bring the horses home. The crew was making great progress on the rebuild, but Kit was tired of the ever-present workers milling around. The ranch had been a beehive of activity for weeks. After breakfast, Kit followed Finn outside and watched him leave. She looked over and saw Lola and Rio heading over to where Trace's truck had been parked since the fire. The hair on her neck raised, wondering what was going on. Curiosity drew her over. She couldn't believe it when Lola handed the keys to Rio just as she got there. Kit was enraged. No one had driven it since Trace's death and Rio Ortiz sure as hell was not driving it today. "Give me those keys," she yelled as she grabbed them out of his hand. A thousand emotions were raging through Kit, causing her hands to shake.

Kit's abrupt manner bothered Rio, but he also heard the panic in her voice. Knowing the circumstances of Trace's death helped him to guard his words and not react. "Good morning," he said with false brightness.

Lola took the keys from Kit and calmly stated, "I want Rio to pick up an order in town."

"It's Trace's truck." Kit's voice was barely a whisper.

"You know very well the ranch vehicles belong to Lola Grande." Lola gave Kit a warning look to back down, which Kit ignored.

Kit knew she was being unreasonable. She didn't care. "I know that, but Trace was the only one who drove this truck."

Under Lola's cool exterior was a strong businesswoman. Personal feelings had to be set aside. Lola was unsuccessful in keeping her annoyance out of her voice, "Not anymore."

Kit was usually reasonable, but she was also stubborn. She glared at Rio, her face angry. "Why can't you take Andy's?"

Lola was unable to hide the tone of annoyance in her voice, "Andy isn't here until noon, and I need that order here before he arrives. Everyone is doing what they can to keep this project on schedule."

Kit knew Andy had made their rebuild top priority and had even brought in a second crew. Still, she had no problem hanging onto her anger. Through pursed lips, Kit said, "He can't drive Trace's truck. Let him take yours."

Lola frowned at Kit's stubborn tone. They didn't clash often but when they did neither would back down.

Rio stood there listening to two head-strong women do battle. It didn't look like either one of them was going to back down. Instead of being uncomfortable, he was amused.

Despite the fact that Rio remained silent, his penetrating look was boring into Kit, making her madder. Rio saw the pain beneath Kit's anger. Only then did he feel bad.

Lola handed the keys back to Rio, "I would like you to leave now. The sooner you get back with that order the better." Her tone was dismissive, devoid of the emotions she was feeling, "Come find me when you get back."

"Yes, ma'am."

Kit saw Rio's pity as their eyes locked. Tears of frustration blurred her vision. It took all her inner strength to hold them back. She had lost this battle but the war between them was far from over.

It seemed like every encounter with Kit Grayson was a conflict. Rio took his leave. He knew better than to cross Lola Grayson. As he walked away, he reminded himself he was here for a reason. This family still needed him.

Kit stormed off to the office, leaving Lola stunned and speechless. Kit seated herself at Trace's desk and drew a deep breath to collect herself. Tears stung her eyes, anger and hurt mixing together.

Kit was rubbing her neck in frustration when Lola walked in. "Can I have a minute?"

Kit's tone was clipped and resentful, "No." Kit was in no mood for a lecture.

That one word spoke volumes but Lola choice to ignore it. Her own anger had surfaced. Getting straight to the point, Lola said, "I also have a temper, Kit. Fortunately, time has taught me how to control it. I suggest you work on yours."

Lola had spoken with underlying authority. Kit was usually reasonable, but she was also stubborn so chose to ignore Lola's warning. She knew her behaviour was childish, but she didn't care. Unshed tears glistened in her eyes. She bit her lip to prevent them from falling. "You weren't fair."

"Is that so. Do you think it's fair that you keep taking your anger out on Rio? Your behaviour just now was uncalled for. Your actions were pure emotion. Back off and give that poor man a break." Lola's tone matched the coolness in her eyes.

Kit couldn't ignore the truth of what Lola was saying. It was as if her control would snap, and she couldn't get it back. Kit hung her head in shame, for this knowledge frightened her. She drew a deep breath and took a moment to collect her whirling thoughts. "Everything is changing. Nothing is normal anymore." Kit wondered if things would ever be normal again.

Unaffected by the resentment in Kit's voice, Lola continued, "I don't care. Change happens. Deal with it."

Not knowing how to respond, Kit looked away. She shifted uncomfortably before saying, "You made your point. I'm sorry I overreacted."

"When are you going to stop being angry at everyone?"

"Obviously, not today." There was a hint of humor in Kit's sarcasm and Lola felt better. Humor often helped a person get through difficult times.

"Trace always said you were stubborn. Is there something else bothering you?"

"Just the man himself." Kit had the decency to look uncomfortable. She wasn't ready to give in.

"There appears to be underlying tension between you two."

Kit gave Lola an exasperated look, "I hate having Rio here."

Lola understood. She put her hand on Kit's shoulder in a comforting gesture, "Even if Rio leaves it will never be the way it was."

The fight went out of Kit. She knew she had gotten wound up over nothing. Her actions were reflective of her ongoing struggle with her emotions, and she had let her temper get the better of her. The stern lecture from Lola was deserving. Lola left but Kit remained in the office. She sat back and took several deep breaths and felt her rage die down. Kit knew it was unfair to keep snapping at Rio every time they spent five minutes together, but she would have bitten off her tongue before admitting it. She willed her mind to stop thinking about Rio, but it refused.

Kit heard Rio return. She would recognize the sound of Trace's truck anywhere. She was unable to ignore the jab of pain in her heart. Kit remained hidden in Trace's office, not wanting to cross paths with Rio.

Rio was grateful that Lola was talking to Andy when he returned and there was no sight of Kit. He handed the package and truck keys to Lola and headed into the new barn without saying a word. Even though the confrontation had passed, it still bothered him. He knew it was best to keep his distance.

As soon as Andy was finished talking with Lola, he sought out Rio. "Is everything all right?"

"No. What's with the Grayson women?" Rio shared the incident over Trace's truck. "Neither of them backed down from each other." He was sure if it had been two men it would have become physical. That would have been a sight to see. Rio had to smile in spite of himself.

Andy shook off Rio's concerns, "The Grayson women are strong and courageous. They have both endured a major loss they are still dealing with. You just witnessed that both Grayson women are as stubborn as they come."

"You and Mrs. G. seem to get along well."

Andy had experienced Lola's uncompromising strength of will and her stubbornness many times during the original build. She had constantly pushed his buttons. He had come to recognize the focused side of her personality and was no longer bothered by her frankness. "We do now but it was a challenge when we met. I pissed her off the very first day. Under her cool exterior lies a fiery temper. In no uncertain terms she let me know she was the boss at Lola Grande and would oversee the project. Just like she is now. She gradually earned my respect, and I earned her trust. Lola still likes to have control. To my surprise, she is less demanding, but Lola can be very intimidating."

That's putting it mildly. "I may not have been here long, but it didn't take me long to figure out who the boss is."

"Lola may be the boss, but you don't want to mess with either one of the Grayson women. You mess with one Grayson, you deal with them all. Are you having trouble with Kit?"

"Since the day we met. It would be nice to experience a day without a verbal sparing match. I knew from the beginning this was a difficult situation, but I thought given time Kit's animosity toward me would disappear. I don't know what I've done to offend her. What's with Kit?"

"You remind her of her husband. Kit is struggling with Trace's death and all the changes that ensued. It's such a terrible loss when someone dies unexpectedly, and his was such a traumatic death. It didn't have to happen."

With her composure somewhat restored, Kit headed back to the house to start supper. She had stayed working in Trace's office all afternoon, wanting to avoid everyone. When she got close to the house, Kenzie and Benny were in the front yard arguing. As soon as Kenzie saw her mom, she began whining, "Benny was up in my room without permission and took my new video game. Tell him to leave my stuff alone."

Kit let out an exasperated sigh, *I don't need this right now.*

Kenzie glared at her brother as she continued to fume, "I'm going to start locking my door so you can't come in."

Kit didn't want to overreact. "Benny, you know better. Go up to your room and I'll be right up."

"You can't make me."

Rio, who was walking by and overheard, reacted, "Listen, partner, that's no way to talk to your mom." No child should disrespect their mother.

Benny was confused and angry. He felt everyone was turning on him, "Mom doesn't care. She doesn't care about anything anymore."

"Benny Grayson, I told you to go to your room. Kenzie you can go in and peel potatoes for supper." Frustrated from earlier, Kit turned on Rio and snapped, "Mind your own business." The sudden anger in Kit's voice confused the kids because they didn't know who she was maddest at. Both kids took off, leaving Kit and Rio glaring at each other.

Rio was controlling his temper with effort. He was beginning to tire of her attacks. "What's your problem?"

Kit's voice took on a steely edge, "Don't interfere with my personal life and there is no problem, and I don't like your attitude."

"Well, I don't like yours either," Rio countered. Her attitude verged on abrasive most days but this time it was more than he could tolerate.

Rio's sarcasm fueled Kit's underlying anger. She wanted to be done with him. "I should never have gone along with this stupid idea of having you here." Her eyes were angry and resentful.

Rio called her on it, "Why did you agree if you don't want me here?"

Keeping her voice as even as possible she glared at him, "I was outnumbered. If it was up to me, you'd be long gone. You butt in when you have no business to interfere. Just do your job and stay away from me and my family."

"You're the boss lady."

Kit's eyes narrowed as she placed her hands on her hips. Her voice remained cool, "That's right and you are the hired help who seems to forget what his position is around here."

Rio ignored the insult she hurled at him. Twice in one day was more than any man could tolerate. Once again, she had gotten under his skin. A hostile look crossed his face, making it clear that she had struck a nerve. It took effort not to retaliate. Over the years Rio had learned it was best to hold his temper. He turned and stomped away, digging deep for control with every step he took. Moving forward he would have to keep his guard up.

Trembling from the unpleasant exchange, Kit remained outside. She was forced to admit that Rio bothered her just like Trace used to. At times, he had the same cocky attitude. Maybe it was a cowboy thing. She knew Trace would be enjoying her discomfort if he was here. Kit hated the fact that Rio had upset her again. She hated that Rio could make her react so quickly in anger. With determination she dismissed the man from her thoughts. Kit walked into the house. Responsibility called.

Rio was muttering under his breath in Spanish when he entered the old barn. "Una muter frustrante." He didn't know Finn was inside.

Finn laughed. "Mom is definitely one frustrating woman. So is Lita. You've only had to deal with the two of them for a few weeks. I've been answering to them for years."

Rio patted Finn in understanding. "You understand Spanish?"

Finn nodded, "I also speak Spanish fluently. I've been taking Spanish online for school since I was twelve. Your nephew, Cruz, and I are best friends. Every once in a while, we'll spend the whole day speaking Spanish to remain fluent. It also bugs our siblings." Finn liked Rio and they had started to form a bond. "Do you mind if I ask you about your tattoos? I heard most of them have a special meaning for the person who gets one."

Rio unbuttoned his shirt enough to show Finn the one on his right shoulder. It had three dots and three lines. "My dad, my brother and I all have this one. It translates to "my crazy life." It represents the struggle of the underprivileged and the minorities. Our people have survived humble beginnings and ridicule from others." Rio showed Finn the cross with cascading roses across the left side of his chest. "Hector and I got this when our mother died. Roses were her favorite flower, and the cross represents her strong Catholic faith. She went to church every week. I know she prayed a lot for me and my brother to keep us safe and out of trouble. Her prayers were answered but she forgot to pray for herself. She was a giving woman who gave up everything for her family and worked too hard. She died too young, like so many." Rio paused for a moment, concerned the topic of death might still be a sensitive subject. "The rose is also a symbol of love and passion. The flower itself is beautiful but the thorns can hurt. Roses and women are a lot alike. I'm sure your dad warned you about women. You can't live with them, and you can't live without them. And you will never understand them."

"Are you talking about my mom again?" Finn asked with a grin.

"She's making it difficult to be here, that's for sure." What bothered Rio more than anything was the fact he didn't know how to change it.

"Mom is struggling with my dad's death. She really misses him. We all do."

"I've heard nothing but good about your dad. He taught you well. I've seen you train when I've been over at Valley View. You're very good, Finn. I have no doubt you will honor your father." Rio ended the conversation. It had become a little too heavy for both of them.

CHAPTER TWENTY-THREE

Mother Nature brought the beauty she always did, bringing color and life back into the world. For Kit, the beauty had been overshadowed by Trace's death and for too long her world was cloaked in darkness. The old Kit was slowly emerging as she worked her way out of her heavy depression. The dark shadows had disappeared from under Kit's eyes now that she was sleeping through the night. For weeks, her family had been her salvation, making her days tolerable. Kit once again began to appreciate the gift of today and all she had to be grateful for. Days passed quickly. Nights were still long.

There were still stressful times as they adapted but life had settled into a routine and Kit had to admit it was a positive thing for all of them. Lola continued to have her evening meals with the family, but she was spending more time at her own place. For a change, Lola had joined them for breakfast. When they were finished, Kit went out to feed Buddy, while Lola remained at the breakfast table talking with the kids.

Kenzie, who was as direct as her mother, asked her grandmother, "I know it's okay to cry because Dad died. Is it okay to laugh?"

"Why do you ask?" Lola wondered where this was coming from.

"Because Mom doesn't anymore," Kenzie said sadly.

Overhearing their conversation, Kit hung her head, angry with herself for allowing her grief to consume her. It was time to accept life as it was and start living. Even though the spark had gone out of her life, she had to move on. Kit remained outside. Since her fight with Lola, Kit had processed what Lola had said to her and Kit thought she was doing better.

Obviously, she had to try harder. Something still needed to change. She had to figure out what. Kit put a smile on her face and walked back into the kitchen. As soon as she entered, the kids scattered.

Lola began clearing away the remains of breakfast. Kit stepped in and helped her. When they were finished Kit asked, "Do you have a few minutes? I can't deny my emotions have been in turmoil, and I've handled things badly for too long. I have gotten stronger mentally and time has dulled the sharp pain. That's a large part because of your tough love. It hurt at the time, but I do understand what you were saying. I just wasn't ready to listen at the time."

Lola met Kit's gaze and responded with her usual directness, "I'm sorry I hurt you, but I'm not sorry for what I said."

Lola's apology surprised Kit. It made Kit sad. She didn't want Lola to be sorry for being honest because she cared. "This has been just as hard on you. How do you manage?" Kit knew Lola was dealing with a lot, just like she was.

"We have more strength than we realize to get through difficult times. I get through the day and hope that tomorrow will be better. Usually, it is. It is going to be okay," Lola promised.

"Maybe, but not for a long time." A lull fell before Kit admitted, "Some days are better than others." She had finally achieved a level of resignation, which was helping her to feel emotionally stronger.

Lola smiled compassionately, "Sadness and pain exist for all of us throughout our lives. Your whole life was turned upside down when Trace died. The important thing to remember is you know you are strong enough to deal with this. You can keep going long after you think you can't. In time, you learn to live with the hurt. Then when you think you've gotten through it and you start to heal, you find it still hurts. But you don't let it consume you. As you let life back in, it takes over the hurt. The pain we're feeling right now isn't forever. I told you before, nothing is forever. Nothing good and nothing bad. Traumatic events like this do test your faith." Both women were silent. They had been suffering through great aching hurts they would choose to forget but never would.

Kit's eyes glistened with unshed tears, "I don't know what we'd do without you."

"That's one thing you don't have to worry about. Trace will also always be with us. Just look at Benny. He is the spitting image of his dad and I'm seeing more of Trace's mannerisms."

"Another up-and-coming cocky cowboy."

"Could be." Both ladies laughed as Benny walked in wearing one of Trace's old cowboy hats. It was good to laugh again. It brought them an odd sense of comfort. In that treasured moment it was like having Trace back again.

Lola looked at Kit in understanding. "You'll find a way to keep Trace in your life while at the same time letting him go and moving forward. You will learn to live without him. It takes courage to live, and we know how brave you are. You always impressed my son with your strength and courage. Life will be different for all of us as we move forward."

"I miss Trace so much. I miss his quick kiss on my cheek. I miss being in his arms. I even miss the things he did that drove me crazy. I wish …" Kit stared at Lola through her tears. "Nothing is ever going to be the same again, is it?" The words caught in Kit's throat, and she began to pace.

Lola looked at Kit through her own tears. She also missed her son. "No, it's not. Life is constantly changing, and we change with it. Life goes on."

"Without knowing you were here for me I'd still be locked away hanging onto my anger. I'm slowly working my way through my grief. I'm sorry it took so long. I know you are also grieving."

"Of course, I am. So is Riley, and the Calhouns, and our friends. Maggie is hurt that you keep pushing her away." By the serious expression on Kit's face, Lola knew where Kit's thoughts had gone.

Kit knew it was time to go see Maggie. "Would you mind watching the kids? I have another apology to make." Kit had to stop thinking of lives that were gone and turn her mind to those around her. It was time to let her everyday world back in. Despite the fact she was a single parent, she had a wonderful family to turn to for support. She also had a wonderful friend who she had been ungracious to since Trace died. Kit wanted their friendship back the way it was, and it was up to her to make amends.

Kit hadn't been to the Walker ranch since the fire, an unconscious act of avoidance. She was anxious when she drove into the yard. She hadn't called in case Maggie told her not to come. Kit walked up the steps and knocked.

Maggie invited her in, but her manner was cool. "I just poured myself a coffee." Maggie opened the cupboard door and grabbed another cup and joined Kit at the table. "This is an unexpected surprise."

Kit was silent for a moment. She was nervous and wasn't sure how to begin. Kit looked at Maggie with a look that begged her to understand. "Trace was taken from me in a heartbeat, and it felt like my own heart stopped that day, too. You lose more than the person. For a while you lose part of yourself. I really struggled because it didn't have to happen. My anger kept making me lose control and I've been lashing out at everyone. I have accepted what happened and am learning to deal with my grief with less anger. The hard part is over. Acceptance does allow one to move forward." There was less bitterness in Kit's voice.

They had known each other too long for Maggie to remain offended. "Well, I'm glad you finally came to your senses. It took you long enough to come and apologize. I've missed you." Maggie's understanding smile erased all of the charged tension between them.

It gave Kit the courage to continue, "When Trace died people kept asking me what they could do to help. I kept telling everyone I was fine, and I could manage on my own. I'm sorry, Maggie. I pushed a lot of people away. I hope you will forgive me."

Maggie hadn't missed the slight tremor in Kit's voice, and she also detected a change in Kit's voice since last time. Gone was the anger that was close to hysteria. Time had calmed Kit's wrath. "I watched you the day of the funeral. Even though you were suffering, you remained strong for your children. Now you are strong for yourself and coping without Trace."

"I am stronger, but I still struggle to cope. Most days are better. I'm ashamed to say I've made it all about me and wallowed in self-pity. I'm ashamed of how I treated you."

"I knew you were struggling. I didn't handle it right either, and I've missed my best friend. I felt I had lost you as well as Trace. I didn't know how to help you, so I stayed away. I'm so glad you came today."

"Grief doesn't excuse my behaviour. I know grief is normal but prolonged depression can be unhealthy. I was in a dark place for too long.

I hope there are no hard feelings between us. I said some awful things to you. Please forgive me."

"Friendship isn't always easy. A true friend is someone who knows all about you and is there for you especially in the hard times. We have all said things that hurt, and later come to regret it. Despite that, we will always be there for each other."

"I miss Trace so much. It hurts that he was taken from us too soon but I'm learning to live without him." Once Kit had accepted Trace's death, her life got easier.

"I miss him, too, and so does Matt. He's been lost without his best friend. I felt like I also lost my best friend. Don't shut your friends out. Your life isn't over; it's just different. Your husband is dead. You're not."

"I am doing better but it has been rough." The fact that Kit could talk about Trace and what happened had become part of the healing process.

"Good for you but you still look like hell." They both laughed and it eased the tension between them. It was true. Maggie grabbed her phone and made a quick call. Five minutes later she had booked a spa day for the two of them and wouldn't take no for an answer.

Kit made no objection. It would be nice to escape reality for a while.

When it was time to leave, Kit again thanked Maggie for being a true friend and not giving up on her. The two friends embraced, and Kit left knowing she could make it through anything with a friend like Maggie by her side.

*****

Kit had worked her way out of her heavy depression. Time had allowed her to emerge from the darkness that had engulfed her. Now that she was emotionally stronger, she decided today was the day to put closure to the part of her life she hadn't dealt with. There was a huge matter she needed to address to release the deeper anger still simmering inside her. The reason behind so much of her misery. She wanted it gone, along with the bitterness. Kit knew she had to deal with the Beaumonts.

Lola knocked and entered Kit's kitchen. Kit looked different today. It was like sunlight once again filled the room. Kit had allowed her hair to hang loose in soft waves that framed her face. She had applied full make-up and was dressed in a casual summer frock. Time outdoors had given Kit more color. She was definitely looking better and at that moment Lola knew Kit would be all right. "Do you have time to share a pot of tea?"

Kit shook her head as she closed the dishwasher door. She knew Lola wasn't going to be happy with what she was about to say. "I'm going to the Beaumonts to speak to them about the fire started by Jackson. I'm taking back control of my life."

"What do you mean you're going over to the Beaumonts? What do you expect to achieve by doing that?"

"You said anger doesn't allow a person to move forward. Life is too short to carry around anger and bitterness. I need to do this if I want to escape the nightmare of what happened. I need to see Jackson Beaumont face-to-face and tell him exactly how his actions affected our family. Hopefully, it will put an end to this resentment."

"Confrontation isn't the answer, Kit."

There was a determined look in Kit's eyes. Her voice rose in exasperation, "No, but closure is. I haven't been able to get by this. I've carried my resentment at the injustice of what happened for months. I need it gone. So, if you'll excuse me, I'm ready to leave. I don't think I'll be gone long."

Lola knew there was no way she could persuade Kit to change her mind.

Kit was anxious driving to the Beaumonts. She knew this confrontation wouldn't be easy. She had to swallow hard to supress her fear as she drove through the iron gates and up to the house. The stately home was exquisite, but it had a look of being cold and vacant. There was no activity anywhere on the property. She hesitated before getting out of her vehicle when she parked in the drive. She didn't want to be here. Facing the Beaumonts was terrifying. Her shoulders were tense, and she had a headache. Kit took a deep breath, hoping it would help. It didn't. The knots in her stomach twisted. Kit unbuckled her seat belt with shaking hands, and her anxiety kept building as she forced her legs to move and climb the steps to the front door.

Olivia opened the door when Kit knocked. "Why are you here, Kit?" Her voice was cool and impersonal, but she couldn't hide the fear in her eyes. Olivia forced herself to keep eye contact.

Kit took an anxious breath. She struggled to keep her voice from shaking, "This isn't a social visit and I'm not leaving until I see your father."

Kit wanted to confirm for herself what state Jackson Beaumont was in and confront him about his actions.

Olivia's manner remained cold, "My father no longer receives visitors. You know he's sick. He only has moments of lucidity or coherent communication. We keep the doors locked at all times for more than one reason. His recent fear is someone is going to break in and kidnap him. Here at home, he is settled and safe."

Renewed anger intensified the throbbing in Kit's temples. "Trace should have been safe at his home, but your dad changed that. He changed all of our lives."

There was a hint of despair is Oliva's voice, "My father's life has changed too. Besides the ugly disease of Alzheimer's, he has cancer. He has been given only a few months to live." Olivia had made no move to let Kit in.

Evelyn appeared, "Don't be rude, Olivia. Come, Kit. Jackson is in his office. He doesn't work anymore but he likes to sit in his familiar environment. Other than his bedroom, it is the only room that seems to bring him comfort, and the occasional memory. They are few and far between and gone in a flash. I'm very sorry for your loss. My prayers have been for your family as you recover from such a tragic loss."

Olivia stepped aside to let Kit in and led the way. Kit noticed the interior of the home was immaculate, but it felt cold and impersonal. The splendor of it didn't make it a home. She wondered what it must have been like growing up here. Without a word, Kit followed them to Jackson's office. The office was large and expensively furnished. Kit's eyes were drawn to the formal self-portrait of the man himself that hung on the wall behind his desk. At the time it was taken, Jackson Beaumont was a very distinguished-looking man. Today, he was a frail-looking man sitting hunched over in a wheelchair by the window. Kit studied him closely. The old man's face was expressionless, his eyes vacant. This was not what Kit expected.

Olivia stepped forward and took her father's hand. "Daddy, you remember Trace Grayson. This is his wife, Kit."

Kit moved forward and stood directly in front of Jackson, "I want to talk to you about the fire we had at our ranch." Even though Kit had never been intimidated by this man, she couldn't hide the tremor in her voice. She hated the fact that he had an effect on her today.

There was a brief moment of clarity when Jackson looked directly at Kit and spoke, "That man has always been a pain in my ass."

Kit's eyes went wide with shock, then narrowed with fury. She boldly held his gaze, "His name is Trace, and your actions took him away from us. Because of you my children have no father."

Jackson's gaze flickered and for a second an evil grin crossed his face, and his eyes were as clear as ever. In that brief moment of silent communication Kit confirmed Jackson Beaumont knew exactly what he had done and had no remorse. His glee sickened her.

Evelyn went and stood behind her husband. Always the southern lady she remained polite, "It was nice to see you again. I'm sorry it wasn't under better circumstances. Now, if you ladies will excuse me, I am going to take my husband to his room. This conversation has been very upsetting for all of us."

Kit could hear Jackson's evil laugh echo down the hall as Evelyn wheeled him away. Kit turned on Olivia and asked her if she knew what her father had done.

Olivia had the decency to flush with shame and nodded. Kit deserved the painful truth, "We both know how much my dad hated Trace, but he began confusing facts with reality. After speaking with Dad's doctors, they don't think he knew what he was doing."

"Don't kid yourself, Olivia. Your father knew exactly what he was doing. He has had a vendetta against Trace since he threw your dad off the ranch years ago. You were there that day so you can't deny it. Your dad has been out to get Trace since then. I know he tried forcing Trace's truck off the road, thinking he was the driver. You saw how he verbally attacked Trace at Dixie Dawson's wedding. Who knows what else he has tried to do? How can you defend him?"

"He is my father. I know what he did was wrong. He may not be in jail, but he is imprisoned in his home and in his mind." This was the most forthright Olivia had been with Kit.

There was no sympathy or compassion when Kit spoke, "Your father deserves to sit in this house until the day he dies. Then I hope he burns in hell, so he feels what it was like for Trace when he died in the burning barn."

"When did you get so hard-hearted, Kit?"

"The day Trace died. Your dad might as well have taken my life, too."

"My father was driven by his hatred for Trace. In his confused mind he blamed Trace for everything, even my failed marriages. He began to believe if I had married Trace first, my life would have been happy. He may have been right."

Kit's eyes remained as cold as ice. "Trace was involved with you a long time ago. Trace chose to marry me and adopt my daughter as his own. Together, we had a son, who by the way is the spitting image of his father. As a family, we adopted Finn, who made our family complete. Trace was happy with the choice he made. You meant nothing to him."

Olivia's eyes narrowed as she attacked back, "I may be a divorcee, but you, poor Kit, are a widow." Olivia could be as cold and unfeeling as her father.

Kit's responded spitefully, "At least I had a happy marriage. You missed out on a really good man."

"Get the hell out of our house," Olivia hollered.

Kit was ready to take her leave. With an air of finality Kit firmly closed the door, leaving behind the anger and resentment that had controlled her for too long. Her outrage was replaced with resignation.

Lola was waiting on the verandah when Kit returned. "Do you feel better?" When Kit didn't answer she asked, "Are you okay?"

Kit drew a deep breath and sat down. Other than confirming the fact that Jackson had started the fire, intentionally or not, her actions resolved nothing, and she felt like she had stooped to their level. Nothing in her life felt right anymore. "I'm fine. My confrontation didn't feel as satisfying as I thought it would. Seeing Jackson Beaumont was a shock. He is a shell of the powerful man he was. He is nothing more than a pathetic old man who is lost in his own mind. He did have a moment of clarity and so did I. Jackson could never let go of his anger toward Trace. I have to let go of my anger toward Jackson and his family. The past is the past. It can't be changed. I have to accept this in order to move forward." Kit had survived a traumatic experience that had mentally and physically exhausted her. By confronting Jackson, she had laid to rest the last of her demons. Kit had come to terms with what happened. She had left her anger behind, but the injustice of Trace's death remained. It hurt knowing Trace lost his life due to an ill deed by a sick old man.

"You really are an amazing woman, Kit Grayson."

"I guess I take after you."

CHAPTER TWENTY-FOUR

Lola detected a positive change in Kit since the confrontation. She knew Kit was stronger now that she had closure with the Beaumonts, but Kit still needed to put closer to another part of her life before she could really move on. There was no tactful way to approach the subject, "Have you gone through Trace's things yet?"

Kit immediately shrank from the question. She wasn't angry, knowing Lola was asking out of concern. Silence fell between them as Lola waited for an answer to her intended question. Kit understood this needed to be done. It wasn't the first time she would pack up a husband's things, but Kit didn't know if she was ready. Tears sprang into Kit's eyes when she broke the uncomfortable silence, "I don't want to let Trace go." Kit turned away for a moment and then with a small gesture of resignation she turned back to the person who was living through her own personal grief. In a calmer voice, Kit continued, for she knew this, too, had to be faced to find peace. "I haven't had the emotional strength to do it."

Lola spoke softly, "You told me you were stronger, and I've seen it for myself. For heaven's sake, you took on the Beaumonts. You have to move forward with this as well. The sooner you deal with Trace's things, the better. You continue your healing process by letting go. Trace is gone. He's not coming back. It's time."

"You're right."

Lola chose her words carefully, "Even though our loved ones aren't here with us, they are always in our hearts. You hold onto the good thoughts, the happy memories. Those precious moments that made up your life together and let the rest go. You will get through this part of saying goodbye as well."

The pain was once again evident when Kit confessed, "I have tried but as soon as I go to start I feel like my world is closing in around me. It actually hurts to breath." Kit turned away, not wanting to let Lola see her look of despair. This had been an intense conversation. Lola left to allow Kit time to process.

After lunch, Kit headed upstairs. She knew Lola was right. It was time. She had put off too many things. It was time to get both her house and her life in order. Kit knew where she had to start. She forced herself to rein in her emotions as she walked into the ensuite to remove all the items that were Trace's. When she took the lid off his aftershave, she inhaled deeply and felt his presence. Her loss overwhelmed her, as real as if it had just happened. "You don't know how hard this is. You don't know how much I miss you." It took all Kit's effort to let go. After she was done, she scrubbed everything down, top to bottom and stepped back into the bedroom. She sat down on the corner of the bed and cried.

Struggling through her grief, Kit went back to her task. Time passed unnoticed until the last of Trace's personal items had been packed into boxes to take to Good Will. On the bed were the personal items that would be passed down to her children. She packed them up and placed them in the corner of the top shelf in the closet. Kit had done what needed to be done. The familiar ache came, as she knew it would. Another person in her life was neatly packed away. She left a couple of Trace's shirts hanging in the closet. Every night since Trace's death Kit changed into one of his long-sleeved shirts before climbing into bed. She would pretend his arms were wrapped around her. She knew it had to stop. Maybe tomorrow. Kit crossed to the dresser and picked up their wedding picture. Loneliness and grief grabbed hold. She missed what they should have had. She frowned as she looked at Trace. "I'm trying so hard to be strong for everyone so we can get through this. I am facing my fears like you did after we met. Your fear of commitment vanished, and we began building our future together. This wasn't how our story was to end. We were supposed to live happily ever after." Nothing had gone the way Kit thought it would. They were supposed to spend their lives together, forever. Forever had its own timeline. For them it didn't last long. Fate had stepped in and taken Trace from her life.

Memory after memory assaulted her, bringing a flood of emotions. Kit paused, trying to deal with the unexpected wave of sorrow brought on by the memories. Kit moved to the corner of the dresser where Trace's urn sat. Not a day had gone by that she hadn't thought of Trace. He still lived in her dreams, allowing her to remember the way he would make her feel. He had been the centre of her life. The last farewell would be the hardest. She would ride out to the ridge with Trace's ashes and let him go. Kit's heart twisted and the familiar ache washed over her. A wound that hadn't quite healed. Kit turned the wedding ring on her finger as her eyes became blinded by tears. She had experienced this man's love and had lost it. Once again, Kit was experiencing the sensation of drowning, and she began taking deep breaths. The tears began to flow, and she wondered if a person could drown in their own tears. Her instinct of survival kicked in even knowing it meant living another lonely day. She wiped the tears from her eyes and walked out of the room. Trace's ashes remained on the dresser next to the wedding picture. They would be scattered when the time was right.

*****

Kit stepped into the early morning brightness and felt the gentle breeze caress her cheeks, like Trace often did before he would kiss her. She smiled. It was as if Trace was giving her permission to let him go. It was a perfect day for a horseback ride in the country. With grim determination, Kit called her dad and asked him to saddle up one of the horses, then headed over to Lola's to see if she would watch the kids. Kit had taken the time to grieve and was ready to let Trace go. Today was the day she would say her final farewell to Trace and scatter his ashes. It was time to move forward, even though heartache remained a constant companion. Confronting the Beaumonts and packing up Trace's personal belongings had let more healing in. Now it was time to say goodbye and let Trace go.

Riding always brought Kit pleasure. She enjoyed the feeling of freedom she experienced on horseback. Kit felt exhilarated and revitalized as she broke into a gallop, thundering across the fields, glad to escape her reality at home. A day away from the demands of her family and daily pressures.

She needed today for her and Trace. One last time before letting go. The fresh air felt invigorating. The dry wind carried the scent of the trees and grass, and wispy clouds drifted overhead. Kit rode out to the rise that had often brought Trace peace while growing up. It had always been Trace's special place. The place that mattered the most in his life and fulfilled his dreams. His reason for living, for breathing. The place that had always been his place of refuge.

Kit topped the gentle bluff and for a moment she expected Trace to ride up beside her on Diego. Her breath caught as it always did as she took in the magnificent view sweeping in all directions. She sat for a moment before dismounting, letting the silence encompass her, enjoying the stillness surrounding her and the natural beauty in front of her. Sunbeams filtered through the gathering clouds. She enjoyed the warmth on her skin as she tipped her face to the sun and let herself become absorbed into the silence. She wanted no pain, no anger, no worries. Just this moment. Nothing more. The sense of stillness was broken by the wind in the trees. Kit again felt the cool breeze caress her face and felt Trace's presence. It was as if he too was saying goodbye. As Kit gazed out, a peace derived from the timelessness of the land embraced her. There it was, lying low in the wide valley between the lower ridges of the mountains. Lola Grande. Trace loved every acre spread in front of her. This was Trace's reason for living, for breathing. This was where the Grayson dream came to life, the putting down of roots and establishing their heritage. Kit brushed away the tears that had sneaked past her guard. This was where Trace had allowed himself to dream, to grieve, and dream again. Now it was her turn to grieve, and in time, dream again. There was a moment of regret in her eyes. She shivered but it wasn't from the cold. It was from the dark memories that haunted her. An old ache gripped her. She was sorry for the bad things she said and all the things she never said. Kit looked up, thinking that people drift in and out of your life like clouds in the sky. Just like clouds, they drift on and are suddenly gone.

Kit closed her eyes attempting to focus her thoughts, but they were on a course of their own. Deep emotions flowed through her. She wanted to remember everything about Trace, but she was afraid that time would make her forget more than just the pain. She wanted to cling to the past, despite the sorrow that had never left. The familiar ache came over Kit as she knew it would. Her mind was no longer on the beauty surrounding her. It was on days past. It all came rushing back. The ghosts from her past pushed their way through. Kit was soon lost in remembering. She remained lost in thoughts and let the memories flow, allowing her mind to wander down the familiar trail of memories. She relived scenes over and over as she sat alone, her mind flipping through the treasured memories knowing her and Trace wouldn't be making any more together. She knew in time the memories would only become more precious. She smiled as she recalled the early sparks that had ignited the relationship between her and Trace and let love in. She remembered how quickly their love for each other had developed. Kit's eyes darkened with sadness. Today, she had to let that love go. She still felt the longing for her husband who she had treasured and lost. It was here that Kit revealed her deep feelings to Trace. Their love for each other continued to flourish. She smiled at memories of happier times with Trace. The wonder of their falling in love and the depth of their love. Suddenly the tears came, all the tears that hadn't found their release. Kit let the grief come so she could let it go.

The gentle breeze teased her hair. She lifted her hand to tuck a loose strand behind her ear. Kit sighed heavily, unaware of how long she'd been lost in the past. Time had ceased to exist as the hours passed. Kit shook her head to clear it as she returned to the present. There were tears clinging to her long lashes. Kit emptied her head, unwilling to allow herself to dwell on the unhappy memories that had invaded. The time had come to pick up the shattered pieces of her life and move on. She would make new memories without Trace. Life goes on. To the west the mountains stood unyielding against the horizon. Fine shafts of sunlight filtered through the clouds. Kit took a deep breath of the crisp mountain air. In the distance thunder rumbled. Like life, the storm would come, and the storm would pass, and the sun would again shine. Kit shifted her position and looked to the east. It had rained and a rainbow arced across the land. Her eyes lingered on the rainbow, as Trace's words seemed to echo around her, "Ma says rainbows are a reminder to continue through the hard times. It provides us with hope." In response, Kit quietly whispered, "Thank you, Trace. Continue to watch over our family." Today the rainbow provided Kit with the new hope she needed. Her life could begin again. The serene beauty of her surroundings worked its magic. The black sorrow was behind her. Peace settled over her, a peace that comes from accepting the inevitable. The symbolic rainbow was the perfect farewell. Her faith had been tested. Today, it had been restored.

Kit had been through a loss that had knocked her to her knees. It had taken a long time to recover. She was grateful to have worked through the self-pity and could again appreciate what she still had in her life. Kit looked out, allowing the beauty of her surroundings to dispel the sense of anxiety that gripped her. Kit was ready to leave the past behind. The heartache, the promises, all the unfulfilled dreams that had been part of their journey. Her journey wasn't over. Just the part she shared with Trace. She took another deep breath. This one for courage to complete the task ahead. Kit picked up Trace's urn. Her hands were shaking as she clasped the urn and held it to her chest. Kit knew she would only have closure by literally letting Trace go. It was time to release Trace's ashes. She opened the urn and with clear eyes Kit watched as the wind picked up the ashes and disbursed them across the land. The ridge and the valley below would be Trace's permanent resting place. A tranquil calm surrounded Kit as she scanned the horizon one more time. It was a relief to let go. Even though leaving Trace was the most difficult thing she had ever done, it allowed for a new beginning and acceptance of her life and whatever it would bring. Having said her painful goodbye, Kit gathered herself up and left.

CHAPTER TWENTY-FIVE

Kit had emerged from the darkness that had engulfed her. Now that her eyes were no longer clouded by despair, she could again appreciate the beauty of a new day. She felt alive and the world around her was beginning to brighten. She was sleeping through the night, no longer troubled by heavy emotions, or haunted by disturbing dreams. The sparkle of life had returned to her eyes. Yesterday, Kit had spent a long time thinking about her and Trace. She had allowed herself to grieve and let go. Kit sighed with contentment, having found acceptance. She was ready to move forward.

Today was a beautiful Alberta summer day, a clear blue sky overhead as the sun shone down warming the world around her. A new season was unfolding in front of her very eyes. Seasons change from one to another. Life also changes. She was now having to change from one season of her life to another without Trace. She refused to take the darkness with her.

Kit had taken the kids over to the Walker ranch so they could have a play date. Matt and Maggie had bought their kids a trampoline, so Kenzie and Benny were eager to go. Kit and Maggie were catching up while they watched the kids as they jumped and screamed and laughed. It was music to Kit's ears. She smiled at Maggie, "Just like old times. Thank you for being here for me. I don't think I would have gotten through this without you."

Maggie had seen the return of her dear friend. Back was the sparkle of life in Kit's expressive eyes that had been sad for too long. Maggie had to admire Kit for her incredible strength. She had seen Kit struggle and survive. Maggie knew Kit had found acceptance and had worked through her depression. It would take longer to work through her grief, but time would help her with that, too. Kit had begun to come alive and no longer isolated herself at the ranch. "It would have taken longer if I hadn't kicked you in the ass. By the way, I like your new haircut. It's quite a bit shorter." Kit's luscious auburn hair had been cut to just past her shoulders and her natural waves were back.

"Trace liked it long."

"I'm glad you can talk more freely about Trace."

Kit's eyes misted over. "I find it helps and the days are getting easier." Nights were still long and lonely. She hated the feeling of loneliness.

"How is the rebuild going?"

"According to Andy it's ahead of schedule. I guess having Rio on site has been an asset."

"Rio reminds me of Trace."

"You have got to be kidding. Rio is nothing like Trace." The man irked Kit to no end, but if she was being honest, she was grateful that he was at Lola Grande every night.

"Rio is definitely different. He's very attractive in a savage way."

Kit rolled her eyes. "You are a married woman, Mrs. Walker."

"But I'm not blind. Rio may look uncivilized but according to his sister-in-law he's well-educated and well-travelled. He's been to a lot of different countries over the last few years."

Kit had to wonder why such an educated man was working as a labourer. "Maybe he's running from a dark past."

Kit's sarcasm surprised Maggie. "Boy, you really have judged Rio unfairly."

Kit became defensive, "Have you and Lola been talking about this?"

"No. Why?"

"She said basically the same thing. Rio and I definitely got off to a bad start and it hasn't gotten any better. He struts around like he owns the place. The man is an arrogant idiot."

Now Maggie was amused. "I remember you saying those same words about Trace. Maybe you'll learn to like him when you get to know him better."

"Maybe when hell freezes over."

"With a frigid attitude like that it might happen sooner than you think," Maggie said with a wry grin.

"Very funny."

"Matt says he's a good guy. It must be nice having a man around the place again."

"Having Rio around feels like an intrusion. The sooner he's gone the better. Besides, Doc usually drops by on his way home to check on us. He's a good friend."

Maggie spoke without thinking, "Now that Trace is gone, I'm sure Doc would like to be more than that. Doc has been in love with you since the day he met you."

Kit looked startled. Maggie was obviously losing her mind. "You don't know what you're talking about. Doc has always been just our friend. Mine and Trace's." Kit took a moment for introspection; she knew Doc had been attracted to her when they first met but that was years ago. Did he still have feelings for her? Kit hoped she wasn't the reason he never married. She had enough guilt to deal with. This put a new spin on her life and definitely complicated things. Doc had always been the tender veterinarian Kit cared for as a friend. What was he now? It scared Kit if what Maggie said was true and he wanted to be more than friends. Kit shook her head and forced herself back to the present and tried not to put too much significance on what Maggie had said about Doc.

A strange look crossed Maggie's face. "My God, you really didn't know."

All the color left Kit's face. She had to swallow a moment of panic, "Do you think Trace knew?"

"Are you kidding. From the day Trace met you he only had eyes for you. Matt and I left the Calhoun barbeque the year you arrived and said Trace had been snared, hook, line, and sinker. All you had to do was reel him in."

Kit laughed, "He may have been hooked but he put up one heck of a fight." Anxious to change the subject, Kit looked over at the kids who were now spraying each other with the hose. "Thanks for having us here today. I know I should have all of you over for a barbeque or something, but it doesn't seem right without Trace. At least here I don't feel like a fifth wheel." It was different being single, so the social part of her life had changed. In truth, it was non-existent.

Maggie dared to bring up Doc again. "Doc would love to fill that vacant spot. Who knows, maybe even Rio is interested? It seems to me your reaction to Rio was very much like your reaction to Trace when you met him. Maybe fate has stepped in again and brought Rio into the picture for more than one reason."

Maggie's comment put Kit on the defensive, "Rio Ortiz is the hired hand. Nothing more." Kit gave Maggie an exasperated look, "You may be a romantic fool but you're not very subtle as a match maker. Give it up."

Maggie knew she should drop the subject, but she wasn't done. "It's okay, Kit. You're still young and some would even say a good catch."

Kit was not amused by Maggie's continued attempt at humor. Kit couldn't bring herself to think about those things. "I don't need to complicate my life right now with any man." Even though she no longer put up her protective shell, Kit's emotions were still raw. This conversation was upsetting. "My heart still hurts when I think of Trace. Maybe it always will. I thought Mike's death was the worst thing that could happen to me. Then Trace died and I felt like I died that day, too. I could never go through a loss like that again. I'm not looking for sympathy, just stating facts." Kit didn't want to discuss being a widow and she certainly wasn't about to consider dating options. "Trace took a piece of my heart with him. I miss him every day. I miss his cocky attitude and sexy grin. I miss his strong arms around me, and him telling me everything will be okay. I've had so many bad days and no Trace."

Maggie put her teasing aside, "You have to get on with your life, because if you don't, you lose a little of yourself every day. That doesn't mean you have to find yourself another husband. Just be open to the possibility there may be another suitable man out there."

"I didn't ask for your advice, Maggie Walker."

"I don't know why I even try to give you advice since you never take it anyway. What are you going to do? Shrivel up and become an old maid? You're not moving on with your life."

"You're right. I'm still learning to deal with my changed life. Besides, I do not need a man to move on with my life."

"You told me more than once that you are lonely. I'm not suggesting you get married tomorrow, but it's okay to date."

This was a conversation Kit wasn't ready to have.

When Kit refused to comment, Maggie knew not to pursue the subject. She just wanted her friend to be happy again.

*****

Finn spent most Sundays at home instead of at Valley View. Missing his dad, he puttered in the tack room reflecting on his earlier days here. He was feeling guilty knowing Benny wouldn't have the kind of relationship he had with his dad. What if Benny wanted to learn how to train horses and learn about the business their dad had started. Would he be able to fill that role? More guilt surfaced. He decided to go find Benny and Kenzie. Finn tried to set time aside with his siblings, just like their dad used to. It wasn't that he had to. He knew it strengthened their bond without their dad.

Kit could hear voices outside and was surprised to see Rio sitting on the steps with Kenzie on one side and Benny on the other. Finn was leaning against the railing post. Rio appeared relaxed and at ease with the children. Kit hadn't intended to eavesdrop but when she kept hearing her name she went and stood at the screen door and listened. It made Kit realize how much they were missing their dad and how much her depression had affected her children.

Kenzie was as outspoken and honest as her mother, "We are all sad, but Mommy's heart was broken when Daddy died. She goes outside so we can't see her cry, but we know. Her eyes are always red when she comes back in. Mom does smile more now but she still has sad eyes."

Rio was surprised at the awareness from such a young girl, but Kenzie was right. Kit's eyes often had a haunted look.

"We used to have so much fun as a family. In the summer we would go fishing and Mom would pack a picnic." They were all missing their dad.

Kit didn't listen long. The kids, Lola, even the dog, were more at ease with Rio than she was. She turned away and began making supper. She could no longer hear what they were saying but there was never a lull in their conversation, and it was often accompanied with laugher. Kit felt lonelier than ever.

Rio enjoyed the children. Kenzie was a spitfire, who was full of life and loved attention. Benny was a young boy wanting a father figure. Then there was Finn. More man than boy. Up until now Rio didn't realize there was a void in his own life.

Kenzie chatted continuously, "Dad said there is always something to do on a ranch. Mom says it's no different being a mother. There is something to do every day as a parent as well. She does work hard and she's a good mom. She's just struggling right now. You know our dad was well-known for his training of cutting horses and so is Finn. Did you take after your dad?"

Rio smiled and nodded.

Benny was at such a curious age, "What do they call cowboys in Mexico?"

"They are called vaqueros, which means native cowboy. They have superior roping and herding skills. My father was one of the best I've seen. He began earning wages before he was a teenager because he started developing his riding skills at a young age."

"I used to barrel race and I was good at racing. My horse, Tilly, got too old so if I continued, I would have had to train a new horse. I didn't want that kind of commitment anymore. I want to spend time with my friends doing the things they do. I was racing most weekends in the summer, so I missed out on birthday parties and sleepovers. I did miss racing for a little while, but I made the right choice even though I was good at it."

"I'm sure you were." Rio had no doubt especially if Kenzie was half as determined as her stubborn mother.

Benny looked up at Rio, "Now that I'm pretty good at riding, Daddy was going to start training me this summer. I want to learn just like Finn did."

"I'll help you," Finn said.

"Nah, you're too busy." Benny sounded close to tears.

"Maybe I can help you learn the basics for now," offered Rio. By now, Rio knew it was best to be on guard with Kit. He hoped he hadn't crossed another of her invisible lines.

Kit went outside to get the kids for supper just as Lola was approaching. "Supper's ready. Come in and wash up."

Lola smiled at Rio, "Would you like to join us?"

It appeared that Rio had captivated Lola as well as her children. Good thing Kit was immune to his charm, but the spontaneous invite upset Kit.

Seeing the look of panic on Kit's face, Rio smiled warmly at Lola as he declined, "Maybe another time."

Kit turned abruptly and went inside. She poured herself a glass of water and drank it down quickly to compose herself. She looked over at Trace's chair at the head of the table. No one had sat there since Trace died. These were the unexpected moments that tormented her.

That night at supper it was all about Rio. Kit could understand her kids fascination with the man. He was unlike anyone they had met.

Finn looked at his mom, "Rio reminds me a lot of Dad and shares his beliefs. He says the cowboy code of conduct is to live each day with courage, take pride in your work, and finish what you start. Dad said the same thing."

"That's not all it takes to be a cowboy," Kit stuttered due to Finn's comparison to Trace.

Benny shook his head and declared emphatically, "He is a real cowboy, Mom."

"How do you know he's a real cowboy?" Kit questioned.

"He wears a belt buckle he won in a rodeo. That's how he got the scar over his eye. An ornery bull bucked him off. He also plays a guitar and sings cowboy songs. Can we have a bonfire like we used to? Then he can show you."

One, two, three…..

Lola's interruption saved Kit from counting to ten. "Maybe we can plan something soon but right now the men are all busy. We'll wait until the rebuild is done and the horses are brought back home."

Kit smiled at her, thankful for the reprieve. Lola knew her so well. This was something she had to process before she considered doing it. Her kids were growing very fond of Rio. Their lives were complicated enough without having those kinds of feelings added into the mix. Kit was drawn back into the conversation when Benny said Rio had lots of tattoos, something Kit already knew.

"Rio says tattoos usually have a special meaning." Benny looked at his mom with a serious expression, "Can I get a tattoo when I'm big like Rio?"

"We'll see," she said, offering a mother's standard answer. When Finn looked over at her with a questioning look, she quickly mouthed, "No way."

Finn knew his mom wouldn't agree to him getting a tattoo, but it didn't stop him from considering it.

Rio. Rio. Rio. Kit mentally counted through to ten, something she'd been doing a lot more of since Rio arrived.

CHAPTER TWENTY-SIX

Everyone was waiting for Ginger to foal. She had been brought in from pasture but was still at Valley View. Finn and Rio were over at the empty corral deep in conversation. Kit walked over to let Finn know supper was almost ready.

Finn turned to his mom, "I want to bring Ginger back here to foal."

Finn didn't have to explain why. Kit understood the importance of his request. It was time to focus on the fine lineage of horses belonging to Caballo Stables and that would start with the last foal sired by Diego. "Is it her time?"

"She's close. Probably in the next day or two."

"Why don't you and Rio hook up the trailer after supper and bring her home. She can stay in the birthing stall and after she foals, they can be moved to the small paddock. Bring some fresh feed as well."

"Are you fine if Rio attends her birth."

Rio shook his head, "I'm here if you need help but this is a special time to be shared by you and your mother." He turned and walked away.

Kit was bewildered by his words and the gentleness in his tone. Despite the fact that this man confused her, she felt herself warming toward the hired hand. It made her realize she didn't know much about him.

There was a feeling of excitement at the supper table. The kids were elated when they heard about Ginger. Finn was anxious to get going, so had a hard time sitting still. Kit looked at him and smiled, "Go. I'll do up a plate for later." Lola laughed. The boy was halfway out the door before Kit finished speaking.

Kit went out when they returned. She was surprised at how gentle Rio was with Ginger as he backed her out of the trailer.

Finn took the reins from Rio, "I'm going to get Ginger settled in the birthing stall. She's ready, Mom."

Kit heard the excitement in his voice. He sounded just like his dad. "I'll let Lita know and I'll be right back." She heard Rio say he would be close if Ginger got into trouble and wished Finn well as he walked away.

This wasn't Ginger's first foal, so she delivered a couple of hours later with no problems. Her foal was a beauty. Strong with beautiful lines like Diego. Kit saw the look on Finn's face and began to cry. "This colt is yours. Yours to name, yours to rebuild our stock with." Kit stroked Ginger's slender neck. "Ginger stole my heart the first day I saw her. She was Trace's horse and had just delivered Jasper. I see the same look on your face that Trace saw on mine. Your dad gifted me Ginger when we married. There was a big red bow around her neck the day of our wedding. I don't have a bow and we don't have your dad, but I know he would gift you this foal if he was here." Now they were both crying. "Do you know what you want to name him?"

"Phoenix," Finn answered without hesitation. "We studied Greek mythology in history. The Phoenix represents destruction and power. Diego's foal has risen from his ashes and will carry on Diego's fine lineage." Just then the newborn found his legs and stood. Once he was up, he raised his head and snorted. The magnificent foal was spirited like his father. Life after death.

When Finn called Rio to come in and see Phoenix, Kit left to share the good news with the others. The birth of a new foal was always something to celebrate. She also felt Finn and Rio needed time together. They had developed a bond over the horses like Finn had with Trace. Kit was learning to accept change in more ways than one. Life had to go on for everyone.

Rio patted Finn on the back. "He's a beauty. Did you name him?"

Finn beamed with pride as he nodded, "Phoenix."

"Strong name."

"It's symbolic to us as a sign to continue with Caballo Stables and rise above the ashes that could have destroyed Lola Grande and our family."

Rio knew how proud this family was. He felt a deeper connection sharing a moment like this. It seemed like the Grayson family kept drawing him in. Rio had a phoenix tattoo on his back. For him it characterized strength of mind and the desire for life and hope for a happy and bright future. Rio hoped this family would find their happiness.

Finn was expecting the vet when he drove into the yard the next day. Doc always came by when a new foal was born. Doc was excited for the Graysons. This foal was the beginning of a new line to build on. He found Finn in the birthing stall with Ginger and her foal. Doc appreciated the fine stock Trace's horses delivered. This would be the last foal from Trace's prize stallion. The foal was healthy, strong, and black like his father.

When Doc was done, he headed up to the house. Kit was standing on the steps waiting. Kit, whom he'd always loved. Doc had always been able to hide his deep feelings for Kit but with Trace gone it was getting harder. Maybe now he had a chance with her.

Kit was still exhilarated by the birth of Phoenix. "I'm going to take a break. Care to join me for a beer on the verandah before you head home?" The air was hot and dry driven by a wind that had no coolness.

A beer sounded refreshing. Doc had no other appointments so was quick to agree, always glad to spend time with Kit. They had been friends for years and their paths often crossed professionally and socially. As usual, they kept the conversation light, but today there was a strange feeling of discomfort. The change was subtle, but it was there. He wondered if Kit had guessed how he felt.

"I can't repay you for the support you've always given me and the kids. Especially since Trace died. Thanks for coming by today."

"Ginger's foal is strong and healthy. Trace would have been proud. Another fine horse for Caballo Stables to continue the fine lineage you are known for."

"You continue to be a good friend, Doc."

Doc decided it was time to make his feelings clear. "I have cared for you all these years. I would like to be more than a friend." His voice was husky with emotion.

Kit saw the longing in his eyes. His confession made a painful smile come and go on her face. Kit's voice cracked when she stated, "I have already been a widow twice. Maybe I'm a jinx to any man who marries me." Her attempt at humour failed miserably. Kit didn't want to give Doc false encouragement. Her words were gentle when she spoke, "Now isn't the time. Maybe it never will be." Kit knew she had hurt him by the pained expression in his eyes. "My heart still hurts when I think of Trace, but I have accepted what happened and am getting on with my life."

Kit's comment was encouraging to Doc. "Can we be friends? We can keep things casual and go from there."

Kit smiled reflectively. That was how it started with Trace. Kit placed a hand on Doc's arm. "We already are. I would be sad to lose you, too."

Doc couldn't stop himself from asking, "Am I wasting my time?"

Kit let out a slow breath as she looked at him. "If you care for me like you think you do, you'll give me time. You're a good, kind, honest man, and that would be more than enough for any woman. What I need more than anything right now is your friendship." Her changed life was still difficult at times. She didn't want to complicate it. Doc smiled, but Kit saw his eyes remained somber as he got up to leave.

Doc knew he shouldn't have gone there. It was too soon. Walking away, Doc warned himself to go slow. Kit was still vulnerable. He wasn't about to give up though. If he didn't act now, he knew he would regret it for the rest of his life.

Kit watched until Doc's taillights disappeared down the road. She knew it wouldn't be fair to start a relationship with him. She valued their friendship too much to do that. Kit knew he was someone she could always rely on. Was it time to look at him as more than the tender veterinarian who had been a family friend?

CHAPTER TWENTY-SEVEN

K it had just stepped outside when she saw Lola getting into her vehicle. She waved and Lola rolled down her window. "Do you know where Rio is? I want to apologize to him." That was a lie. Apologizing to the cocky cowboy was the last thing she wanted to do. Kit cleared her throat, "I could have handled so many things better with Rio when he first got here. I was depressed and feeling sorry for myself, and I was angry at everyone and everything. Unfortunately, I was too angry to think clearly. I kept lashing out at everyone, especially Rio."

Lola didn't comment but thought Kit's apology was long overdue. The poor girl did struggle with stubbornness. "Andy sent him to town. He should be back by noon. I'm going over to visit with Anna but will be back by supper."

Kit looked up at the clear blue sky, "The weather is perfect today. Why don't we plan a wiener roast tonight with the kids, since they keep asking?"

"Are you going to invite Rio."

"Only if he accepts my apology," Kit said teasingly. "The kids would be thrilled, and we will find out if he really is a singing cowboy." Both women laughed.

Kit was annoyed. Here she was ready to apologize, and Rio wasn't around. Nothing with this man was ever easy. Kit was on a mission when she heard Rio return. She wanted to talk to him before she lost her nerve. She entered the old barn and found him in the tack room. Everything was neat and tidy. Another indication that Rio had the same work ethic as Trace. There were as many similarities to Trace as there were differences.

Rio stiffened when he saw Kit approaching. He knew his future here was unpredictable now that the rebuild was almost done. The feeling of uncertainty hung in the air between them. Rio could tell Kit had something serious on her mind.

"I want to talk to you, Rio."

"Fine, but I only have a minute. The boss lady doesn't like me standing around chatting."

Kit cleared her throat, "I need to apologize to you."

Rio lifted a surprised eyebrow. He certainly hadn't expected this. He wondered what in particular she wanted to apologize for since there were so many times she'd been rude. "I don't need an apology that isn't sincere." Rio remained skeptical.

Kit's tone changed because he put her on the defensive, "I wouldn't give one if it wasn't. Obviously, you bring out the worst in me." *Just like Trace used to.*

"Thank God, I thought this was your best." Rio was serious.

This was harder than Kit thought it would be. She took a deep breath before continuing, "My bad behaviour has been uncalled for on too many occasions. It became a habit. I'm sorry. I was in a bad place, but I've finally managed to let go of my anger."

There was a long pause while Rio decided whether or not to accept her apology. "I'll get over it. I learned a long time ago what other people think is not nearly as important as what I think. What made you change your mind?"

Rio was not making this easy. "I don't know. Maybe it took time to see you for who you are instead of looking through my grief. It clouded my vision for a long time. I was stuck in a very negative place caused by a traumatic turn of events. Life changing events. I didn't know how to cope. I know it sounds like I'm making excuses, but I really am sorry."

A genuine smile curled the corner of Rio's mouth, momentarily softening his features. "Fine, I forgive you. Was that so hard?"

Kit looked Rio squarely in the eyes and responded honestly, "No, I've had a lot of practice apologizing lately."

Rio knew this hadn't been easy for Kit. "I better get back to work."

Kit looked up at Rio and gave him one of her sassy grins. "That's right. The boss lady doesn't like anyone standing around doing nothing." With the overdue apology out of the way, Kit left. For some reason she didn't mention the wiener roast. She needed a few minutes to process what had happened between them.

*****

It had rained during the night. The land was freshly washed from the rain and a moist, earthy scent still hung in the air. Finn headed out right after breakfast. Kit knew Finn was struggling with something and in time he would talk to her. Kit felt sorry for her son; so much had changed for him in his life. He still didn't have his safe place to escape to. Soon.

Finn was over at the corral watching Ginger and Phoenix. It wasn't long before he was leaning against the railing lost in thought as he stared off into space. Over the past few days his thoughts had turned more to the future of Caballo Stables. The rebuild was done and the workers were gone. The remainder of the work now fell on them. He rubbed the back of his neck to ease the built-up tension; strain lines were beginning to show on his face. At times it was overwhelming because there was always something else to do. Finn knew he could get through the summer, but he still had another year of school. He went in search of Rio. He was turning more and more to Rio, like he used to with his dad. An hour later, Finn walked into the kitchen. Kit and Lola were talking about the upcoming changes when the kids would be back in school. They were both concerned about Finn.

Finn saw the concern on their faces. "I overheard you talking. I've been thinking about the future as well. The barn is done. Rio is putting in long hours now that we have access to the rebuilt facility. It will take a few days to get the inside set up. Stalls need to be prepared; the everyday equipment needs to be placed where it belongs. By next week we will be bringing the horses home, and I can start training again at Lola Grande." Finn was anxious to bring the horses home. There had been so many long days. Finn knew there would be new challenges ahead to keep his dad's dream alive. Finn's expression was deadly earnest. "I figured out what needs to be done to move forward and how to do it. I want you to listen to my plan without interrupting."

Kit looked at Lola. Now what.

"Dad was young when he had his dream and his belief in himself allowed others to believe in him as well. It didn't happen overnight. It took work and commitment. Graysons aren't afraid of hard work. I am a Grayson. Thanks to Dad, Caballo Stables has credibility in the industry. Brody Maddox's support has been a positive endorsement. We didn't lose any existing business because of the fire. After I graduate, I will commit full-time to my role as a trainer. I love this life, and this is what I want to do. Dad and I talked about it many times and he was going to make me a full-time employee after graduation. I'm not too young to take on the business and you know I'm responsible."

"Your dad was very proud of your skills. We all are. You have also earned a good reputation, or you wouldn't have been able to keep all of your dad's clients."

Finn's face was set, and his eyes were grim. With strong belief, Finn declared, "Dad is gone but his dreams aren't. I want to keep them alive. The Grayson name means something in these parts, and Caballo Stables was Dad's mark on something that was to stand for generations. Dad had a reputation for being an excellent horse trainer. I will do my best to live up to his reputation. Caballo Stables is also well known for fine stock. We will continue on with the breeding. We lost Diego as a stud horse. Fortunately, Phoenix was sired by Diego, so he has strong lineage in his veins. He will be raised as a stud horse. Meanwhile, Rebel will continue to fulfill that part of the business. He already has a good reputation as a stud horse."

Kit nodded, "Of course you'll continue on with Dad's dreams. Your dad molded you into a fine young man."

"I have to be realistic. I still have one more year of school, so I won't take new clients. I will continue to train and board the horses we have under contract." He turned to face Lola, knowing this would be another big change for her as well, if she agreed. "If you are open to homeschooling me again, I can manage this."

Lola could hear the determination in his voice. She was willing to consider this but felt she had to ask, "Don't you want to graduate with your friends?"

"I still will. I have talked with the principal and my guidance councillor. The school is willing to work with me, due to our situation. I can Facetime and email with my teachers when needed but I won't attend classes. When necessary, I can participate in Zoom sessions."

"Are you going to be as much trouble as you were the first time I homeschooled you?" teased Lola.

Finn grinned, "I'm out of practice but I'll do my best." They all laughed.

Kit was proud of her son, "Whatever lies ahead, we'll get through it together. We've managed so far."

"I'm glad you said that, Mom. I appreciate all that Uncle Riley and the Calhouns have done for our family but with Rio here every day I feel confident we can fulfill everyone's expectations without outside help." Since the arrival of Rio, a great weight had been lifted from Finn's shoulders and it felt good to rely on Rio. "There's a lot to do at our own ranch. I want to hire Rio full-time for the next year so I can concentrate on school and Caballo Stables. He will be paid out of the business. He can move into the addition and help around here as needed. If Rio agrees to stay, he will no longer have an affiliation with C&G Ranching."

This conversation wasn't at all what Kit expected. She was still struggling with her feelings about Rio, "That man has lived a transient lifestyle. He'll probably take off again." Kit knew it was an unfair accusation, but she didn't care. She may have warmed up to Rio, but she didn't know if she could trust him. Kit couldn't bear to see Finn lost and vulnerable again if Rio up and suddenly left. Her son would be devastated.

Finn was surprised by his mom's response but there was much more to discuss. "If he does, we hire someone else. But I know he'll stay," Finn said with confidence.

Kit had a feeling her son had already talked to Rio.

Finn continued, "We can all agree there is always something to do around here. There's a lot to take care of on our own ranch besides operating Caballo Stables. There are things that must be done every day. We need to stay on top of things like Dad did. That's where Rio can help us. Andy says Rio is a handy man to have around because he can do anything. He works hard and doesn't quit until the job is done. Rio can also help me with the horses. He has a firm but gentle nature with them."

Kit had to admit that Rio had already proven to be a hard worker and the kids liked him. She just wasn't sure she wanted Rio to be a permanent part of their lives. She wasn't about to promise anything. Kit understood Finn's plan, but this wasn't as simple as Finn made it sound.

Finn was determined, and his eyes rested on his mother, "These are huge changes, but they are necessary to move forward and I'm thinking long term. You taught us a lot of lessons, especially when you want to make a point. Fairness was one of them. Give Rio a chance."

This time Kit didn't know what to say.

Lola took Kit's hand. "Life reshapes our lives in unexpected ways. We have all experienced major changes that were out of our control, but we have always moved forward. Caballo Stables was Trace's dream. Finn has the same desire as his dad. Since moving to Lola Grande our views have never been short-sighted. Trace is gone but his dreams for Lola Grande are still alive."

Finn looked at his mother. "When I arrived here you told me life isn't always fair, and God guided me here for a reason. I think God guided Rio here as well."

Neither woman could hide their admiration for this young man. Kit's gaze lingered on her son, who was at that painfully awkward age between childhood and adulthood. Fate was pushing him into adulthood with both hands. Finn had become a man overnight. Kit smiled in spite of herself. "How did you get so wise, young man?" Kit asked proudly.

"I am a Grayson and I do listen to you and Lita."

Kit's eyes welled, "When you first came here as a foster child, I told you bad memories fade and get replaced with happy ones. Look how far we all came since then. Your dad would be impressed by the young man you've become. Lita's right. Life can only beat us up if we let it. We have one challenging year to get through, but we can, and will, if we stick together. This too will pass." There was nothing left to consider. Finn had presented a solid case with valid points. With a gesture of resignation, Kit agreed.

Finn's relief was overwhelming. Some of the stress lines disappeared from his face as if he was released from an invisible load.

Kit strolled across the yard to the corral knowing Ginger and Phoenix would welcome her. She crossed her arms on the top rail, her chin resting on them as she watched both horses wander over. Her mind drifted to when Ginger became hers. Trace always teased her she had fallen in love with Ginger before she had fallen in love with him. Kit smiled reflectively. He was right. It was a happy reminder of a blissful period in her life. Kit missed the emotions Trace always evoked, the depth of their feelings for each other, the soul deep satisfaction of their love. Recalled memories no longer brought bitterness, just a sense of loss of something precious. A wave of sadness washed over her, and tears gathered. Kit stood against the rail, a forlorn figure limp with unhappiness as she remained locked in the past. Ginger nickered softly to gain Kit's attention. With gentle fingers Kit stroked the mare's forehead while she talked softly. Ginger flicked her tail and welcomed the gentle petting. Hearing Rio approach, Ginger pranced off to the far side of the corral, her young foal behind her.

Rio usually tried to keep a safe distance from Kit, but it kept getting harder as he got to know her. He had never felt this kind of draw for any woman, so he found himself strolling over to where she stood. His feelings for Kit were stronger than simple attraction. They went deeper than he cared to admit. If he denied it, he was only fooling himself. How was he to know he would end up falling in love with her, which was stupid. Her husband may be dead, but her heart still belonged to a dead man. She was still Mrs. Trace Grayson. Rio wished he'd met Kit under different circumstances. His dark eyes filled with genuine concern. "Are you okay?"

Rio's voice broke through Kit's drifting thoughts. Lost in thought, Kit hadn't heard Rio approach. She couldn't give him the satisfaction of seeing her cry. Kit blinked hard but was so overwhelmed by her misery her tears spilled before she could hold them back.

Rio knew Kit was tougher than she looked so he was taken aback by her tears. All he had ever seen from her was control and anger. This was a different side that aroused his sympathy as well as his curiosity. The wind came up whipping her hair in all directions. Rio gently tucked it behind her ears. He knew it would feel like silken strands. Another tear escaped and Rio gently brushed it away.

Kit saw a warmth in his eyes that caused her pulse to quicken. It had been a long time since her senses had stirred. His action brought an odd sense of comfort, but it was so intimate Kit quickly pulled away. She averted her face to hide the sudden panic she was feeling.

Rio misread her actions. "Why do you hate me?" His question was simple and direct.

For a moment they stood in silence before Kit declared, "I don't hate you. I hate the reason you are here. Life became complicated."

Rio intentionally held her gaze, "It doesn't have to be." Wanting to break the tension, Rio turned his gaze to the horses. They stood side by side watching Phoenix romp. Rio's gaze focused on the high-spirited colt as he pranced freely. Phoenix revealed his heritage and high spirit. "Tell me about the magnificent horse that sired Phoenix. He really is a superb foal."

Kit became reflective. There was a hint of sadness in her smile as she explained her connection to Ginger before moving on to Diego. The expression in Kit's eyes was one of profound sorrow. "Trace and Diego had an extraordinary bond, an unexplainable connection. Diego was a temperamental stallion. Both Trace and Diego were headstrong, which often defined their relationship. Trace's beloved stallion died with him in the fire. Phoenix was sired by Diego and is the last of what was to be a dynasty of prize horses. Hopefully Phoenix will carry on the strong blood line of his father. Diego had undeniable fine lineage." The young colt picked up his ears and turned his head toward the voices. Phoenix snorted as if he knew he was the topic of conversation. He whinnied and pranced off.

Their eyes met and Kit felt an intense wave of longing. Her senses stirred, a physical reaction she couldn't control. Her heart was beating too fast; her flushed cheeks indicating inner turmoil. When Rio took a step closer, she felt that aching need to be in a man's arms. The tug on her heart pulled harder. She tried not to respond to him when everything inside her urged her to. She wanted to feel alive again. Kit held her breath for a moment before she tilted her head back and looked into Rio's eyes. She closed her eyes, her lips parting. They were caught up in the moment. Rio knew he shouldn't, but he couldn't help himself as his lips found her. As soon as the moment of desire for Rio came, it passed. Kit knew it was not completely due to the man in front of her. The desire within came from the longing for physical contact, something she had been missing. There was no way she was going to let Rio know how much it affected her.

The tension of the moment was broken by the arrival of Finn. Rio excused himself and sauntered off, whistling without a care. Kit wasn't sure why it bothered her. She watched Rio cross the yard as he headed to the stables. She couldn't help but wonder about this man. Conflicting emotions surfaced. Kit's heart was still beating too fast. She warned herself to be careful, knowing she was vulnerable.

"Are you okay?" Finn asked.

"I will be." Today had definitely taken an interesting turn.

Together they walked back to the house. They sat outside side by side and watched the lingering sunset as it painted the distant mountains various shades of purple. The night air was scented with the fragrance of pine as it drifted in the air. The quiet of the night had settled over the land. Serenity surrounded them and they sat enjoying the peace it brought with it.

It was Finn who broke the silence. "Does it hurt to talk about Dad?" Finn asked, revealing his own hurt.

Kit nodded, but admitted it was getting easier. Talking about Trace had become part of the healing process. The black sorrow was behind her. She wept less. "Even though our lives fell apart when Dad died, we are healing as we move forward and accept the changes in our lives. Lita always says if this is God's plan, he will give us the strength we need and will guide us. Tomorrow is a new day."

Finn remained reflective, "With renewed hope. When I first arrived here, you told me life isn't always fair, but it does get better. We will get through this, too. Good night, Mom."

Kit sat alone. She was glad she had grabbed her sweater, as the night air was cool. Where had the summer gone? It wouldn't be long, and the kids would be back in school. Except for Finn. He wasn't a kid anymore. As agreed, he would homeschool his final year and focus on Caballo Stables. Loneliness lingered. Some days Kit had to try harder not to succumb to it. Every night her thoughts turned to Trace. Tonight, her gaze drifted to Rio's camper van and her cheeks grew hot. Thinking about Rio felt like a betrayal to Trace. She had let Rio see how vulnerable she was. but more than that his kiss had ignited buried emotions. She felt more confused than ever. Kit huddled in the cool night, aware that gathering storm clouds had turned the sky dark gray. Could she weather another storm in her life because she felt there was another one brewing. When the rain began to fall, she headed inside.

CHAPTER TWENTY-EIGHT

S ummer had flown by. Today was the annual Calhoun Labour Day barbeque. It was always an event to look forward to. It was more than a barbeque. It was a festive event that was considered to be one of the social events of the year in the surrounding community.

The thought of facing everyone for the first time since Trace's death had Kit anxious. Other than coffee with Maggie, she hadn't been out socially since Trace died. Kit was dreading having to go but she knew it was important for her and her family to attend. Kit's spirits were low. Her changed life was still difficult at times. With trepidation, Kit loaded up her family and headed to Valley View. Even though Rio had been invited, he decided to stay at Lola Grande. He didn't want to meet a bunch of strangers. Kit wished she could stay home as well.

They were welcomed by her dad and Sadie. BJ knew this would be a difficult day for the Grayson family, especially his daughter, so he wanted to be there. Kenzie and Benny took off as soon as they saw their friends.

Laughter and music filled the air. It was like every other Labour Day barbeque, but not for Kit. Trace's absence screamed above everything else. She wasn't as emotionally prepared for today as she thought she was. It was all too much. It was too soon.

Doc had also been watching for the Graysons to arrive. Kit was pleased to see her friend as he made his way over. "I'm glad to see you and your family here today. It wouldn't be the same without you." Doc flushed, realizing how insensitive his comment was. It wasn't the same for them without Trace. He hoped he would find time later to talk to her alone. Kit drew comfort having them there for support but knew it wouldn't last long and she would have to face others on her own.

"Lola is coming up to the house. We're going to have a quiet visit over a pot of tea before we mingle. It's long overdue. Would you like to join us?"

Kit hugged her grandmother, grateful for a means of escape but she shook her head. Her grandmother and mother-in-law had a strong friendship and Kit was sure Lola would like time alone with Sadie.

Just like old times, Sadie and Lola sat at the kitchen table. "A cup of tea is just what I need, as well as my friend to talk to. One who understands how hard this has been. Talking to you always makes me feel better." Lola smiled, but it wasn't her usual smile.

Old hurt was evident on both their faces. History had a way of repeating itself. They had shared a lot over the years, and they had experienced a major loss together when Buster died. For a moment they were both caught up in the past.

Lola shook her head to escape the dark visions. It didn't help. Trace's death weighed heavily on Lola's heart. She had been so strong through all of this, but for some reason today it was more than she could manage. Her voice was thick with emotion when she confessed, "I miss Trace every day. There are days I expect him to walk out of that damn barn like nothing happened. This was such an unexpected loss for me. Like Kit, I'm struggling to work through the anger, knowing it didn't have to happen. Trace should be here with us. He has left such a huge void in our lives."

What had happened was a big change for both families. Sadie tried to comfort Lola. The elderly lady's eyes were sad when she said, "We have lived long enough to accept there is loss in everyone's life and you don't let the heartache and pain consume you. Everyone has their history of sadness. Life taught us acceptance but we both know it takes time to let it go. This, too, will pass, and we will get through this dark time. We have more strength than we realize to get through difficult times and you are the strongest, most resilient woman I know."

Lola was moved when Sadie clasped her hands in hers. "I'm tired of having to be strong for everyone. I've been doing it all my life." This was the most honest statement Lola had ever said out loud.

Kit hated the sympathetic looks whenever she looked someone's way. She braced herself every time someone approached her. Many had been at Trace's funeral and were once again wanting to express their condolences. She would be glad when the day was over. Kit was relieved when Shelby strolled over with her daughter Callie. Kit smiled down at Shelby's adorable little girl, "Callie's getting to be such a big girl."

"Mom is glad to have a little girl around here again. Everyone missed Kenzie and her antics when you married Trace and moved to Lola Grande."

"Callie is the same age Kenzie was when we arrived. They grow up so fast."

"There's nothing like a three-year-old to keep you grounded. This child keeps me running from sun-up to sun-down. Fortunately, she has more of Riley's temperament than mine." Callie scooted off to play with the other kids.

"There's nothing like three children around you everyday to keep it real." Kit choked on her words. It was hard enough when she had Trace there for support. She missed him every day.

"We must have been out of our minds when we decided to have another one," joked Shelby as she touched her stomach. "My doctor told me on my last visit everything looks good, but it would be a good idea to have a suitcase packed. I'm ready for our son to get here."

Kit hugged Shelby. She had to close her eyes as the urge to cry swept over her due to mixed emotions, "Life goes on, doesn't it. Another life to replace the one that was lost. I couldn't be happier for you and Riley."

Shelby knew Kit was being sincere. It broke her heart to see Kit so sad. Shelby saw Riley, who was now holding Callie and waving to get her attention. Their daughter seemed to be upset. "I need to go and console Callie before she drives her daddy crazy. She may be a daddy's girl but we both know there are times when all they want is their mommy."

Right after the meal Kit made her escape to wander down memory lane. She needed to grieve a little longer. Kit headed over to the secluded area where she and Trace had their wedding. It had been one of the happiest days of her life. This was where they had exchanged their wedding vows and became a family. They had a beautiful family together and that's what she had to keep her focus on even though a large part of her life was gone. Her family would continue to help her move forward. Kit moved on down to the corrals, still wanting to be alone.

Throughout the day, Doc couldn't stop himself from glancing Kit's way as she mingled. He felt such an overwhelming need to protect her. His gaze again wandered over the crowd until he spotted her by herself at the corrals. He was working his way over to go to her when he noticed BJ appear at her side. Doc jammed his hands into his pockets and headed over to the bar.

There was no way BJ could forget the terror in Kit's eyes the night of the fire. He looked at her closely. The terror had been replaced by grief. It was like the life had gone out of his poor daughter's life and he couldn't make her better.

Kit straightened her shoulders and wiped her eyes. "I feel Trace's presence everywhere. I know nothing is exactly what you think it will be, but I never expected this. Change is difficult, especially when it's not by choice. I am learning to cope, and I will be okay." Kit knew she was strong enough to survive anything fate threw at her. That didn't make it easier.

"We all need to work through this sudden change to our lives. You and I have done that before."

Kit started to giggle, "Like the day I showed up here unannounced, telling you I was your daughter and made you a grandfather?"

BJ nodded, "That was a big one. It left some of us reeling for a long time. It has been more than a blessing to have you and Kenzie as part of our family."

Kit did not miss the look of regret in his eyes. He had missed out on so much not knowing he had a daughter for so many years. Kit smiled reflectively, "That's how I met Trace. We never know what the future holds."

"That's life. Unexpected events change our lives. Change is good and bad. We just have to learn to embrace it. I'm glad you had the courage to come find us." His daughter had been brave to come today. "Rely on that courage as you continue to move forward. I told you I will always be there for you, Kit. That hasn't changed."

Kit knew it was time to call it a day. Being around so many people was too much. "Will you be offended if we leave early?"

"Of course not. I know it has been difficult for you today."

"I promise I won't allow Trace's death stop me from moving forward but I'm still heartbroken." Kit walked back to the party with her dad, arm in arm. There were no complaints as she rounded up the troops. It had been a traumatic day for them as well.

CHAPTER TWENTY-NINE

Kit's life was back in balance. For a long time, the one side weighed heavy with loss. Once she started putting good things on the other side it didn't take long for the weight to shift. She had family and friends and there was Lola Grande. The world around her was again familiar to the sight. Caballo Stables was in full operation, Finn was busy training, and their horses were grazing on Lola Grande land. Kit was able to look forward with a clear vision, not one that was clouded by loss. This was the start of a new journey down a familiar road. Kit was grateful to be back in a regular routine she silently described as her new normal.

Summer had flown by. The kids were back in school. Thanksgiving and Halloween were just around the corner. Finn was doing his schooling in the evenings and weekends. During the week he was training the horses while Rio took care of running Lola Grande and helping Finn when needed. Rio had accepted Finn's offer and had moved into the living quarters and became a full-time employee. His job with Valley View was over. Actually, it never existed. Although the last few months had been emotional and challenging, within a few weeks the Grayson family and Rio Ortiz had settled into a comfortable routine. They had adapted to life without Trace and Rio's permanent presence at Lola Grande. Having Rio here was making a difference. Finn's plan for Caballo Stables had been set in motion and it was working out better than Kit expected. Kit still felt guilty. Finn carried such a high level of responsibility at too young an age. Responsibility may build strength of character but it's not always easy.

Autumn was definitely in the air. The days were getting shorter and cooler. Most mornings were chilly but warmed by mid-afternoon. Rio had spent the morning chopping wood, stocking up for the winter ahead. Kit wandered out to the verandah when he was done. The sun shone bright, and the temperature had warmed. "Thank you for tending to our wood. We should be good for the winter. Finn has gone to meet a possible new client, another referral by the Maddox brothers. Lola is over at your brother's visiting with Anna, so it's just you and me. Would you like to join me for lunch on the verandah?" Kit had to admit Rio had remained a mystery. Over the last few weeks, Kit had dropped her guard to give Rio a chance since he was now part of their lives, but he had remained reserved with her and she knew it was her fault. Today was a good opportunity to find out more about him if he was willing to open up. She knew so little about him. The man was still a mystery.

Since Kit's apology, Rio found her attitude toward him to be much nicer. As a result, things had become more comfortable between them. Her invite seemed sincere. "That would be nice. I'll join you as soon as I wash up."

Rio held the door for Kit while she carried the tray and set it down on the table between them. He waited for Kit to sit first. He was so different from what she first thought. Rio was respectful and had proper manners. "Make yourself comfortable."

Rio took the chair indicated. Buddy dropped down at Rio's feet. "You're a good old boy, aren't you, Buddy."

"Traitor." Kit laughed at Buddy's betrayal of loyalty.

"At least he welcomed me that first day. I had no idea what I was getting myself into and there were days I wondered why I stayed." Rio didn't want to put Kit on the defensive, so he quickly changed the subject. All mothers like to talk about their children so that's where he went, "You have wonderful kids."

"I'm proud of all of them. I believe your being here has helped them get through what could have been an even harder time. Thanks for the time you spend with them. I hope they aren't bothering you."

Rio wasn't used to kids, but time here was changing that. He was starting to feel protective of this family. Being around the Grayson kids made him want a family. He was ready to settle down in more ways than one. This realization was more comforting than disturbing. "It's got to be hard on them without their dad. I can see how much they are missing Trace, especially Finn. I'm sorry for all you have been through."

Kit was surprised to see Rio's look of compassion and it touched her. "They're coping but there have been some hard days. Father's Day was a tough one for all of us. I think a little hero worship has set in with Benny in regard to you. He wants to be grown up. Kenzie thinks you're cool. Her words. Once her world stopped reeling, she returned to the spitfire we know and love but she has also entered a more challenging stage. Kenzie is strong-willed like me."

Rio didn't miss the pride in Kit's voice as she talked about her children. It was obvious Kit was a loving mother. "Finn is a fine young man who has taken on a very important role. He seems to have adjusted to fitting in both school and training."

Kit's concern about this hadn't disappeared. Worry clouded her expression, "Did you regret not going to university after you graduated? I don't want Finn to feel regret."

Rio raised a surprised eyebrow, "Gossiping about the hired help?"

Rio's comment caused Kit to become defensive, "Your name may have come up. Fine, we have gossiped about you, and Anna filled Maggie in on some of your past."

Rio grinned. "You know I don't care what people think." He had never allowed others to get too close to have it matter. "In answer to your question, I didn't know what I wanted to do when I graduated so the answer is no. Instead, I bought my first camper van and took to the open road. It was an old, dilapidated van just like the one you expected me to drive in with that first day. You judged me on my looks and let's not forget your reaction to my van. I'm sure you thought I stole it. Rest assured; I have never done anything illegal."

Kit had the grace to blush. She really had been judgemental. Now that she knew Rio better, her outlook had changed. Kit knew she had judged him unfairly.

"It offered me the freedom I wanted. Living in a camper van gave me a roof over my head and allowed me to live a nomadic lifestyle. It was a simple and inexpensive way to live while I was trying to figure out what I wanted out of life. I had nothing holding me down. I had no commitments, no plans, no destination and had the freedom that went along with it. That was my life for years. It's interesting where life can take you if you're open to adventure. I've seen many incredible places. You're always seeing something new and meeting different and interesting people. I've had many adventures, not all good. I learned to tolerate the ignorance of others along with the appreciation for other lifestyles and beliefs. I usually did jobs where I could work outdoors. I worked on ranches, I've done construction, I even worked a season on a fishing boat. I've never been afraid of hard work."

Kit knew this to be true. Everyone had been singing his praises and she had seen it for herself. "I would think a nomadic lifestyle is lonely."

"It was at times."

"Were you happy?"

Rio's answer was vague, "Happiness is different things to different people."

Both remained relaxed as they sat eating their lunch. When they were done, Kit stole a glance at Rio's rugged profile. She had to admit Rio was a remarkably disturbing man. "You know about us. Are you willing to tell me a little about yourself and why you ended up here. You said you were looking for something. Did you find it?"

Rio stroked his mustache, a habit of his when the conversation became too personal. Kit smiled to herself. Trace always ran his hand through his hair. "I think I was looking for something more than what my dad had. I didn't realize I was running. It took me a long time to accept you can't run far enough or fast enough. You can't run away from your problems any more than you can run away from your past. It's a part of you. It's what makes you who you are, and I like who I am. I am honest, hard-working, and trustworthy."

Rio's voice had that expressionless tone Kit had come to recognize. He shared facts with little emotion, but she didn't miss the shadow that crossed his eyes.

"I returned home when our mother got sick so my father could continue working. Hector was no longer living at home, and he had a family of his own. I stayed home with Mom, and to pass the time, I started taking online courses. You asked me if I regretted not going to university. I may not have attended a university, but I earned a degree in Social Services. For a time, I worked in Criminal Justice. I wanted to help troubled children. I had seen so many growing up. It would have been easy to take that road as well, but I think our mom had a direct line to God himself. Even though the work was meaningful and gave me a new awareness, I found I preferred working with animals over people. They are less judgemental and usually happy to see you. There are no difficult questions to answer."

Kit knew the last remarks were intended for her and wondered if he would continue.

Rio didn't miss the look of regret in Kit's eyes, so continued, "After Mom passed, Dad wanted to take her back to Mexico to be buried with her family. I stayed and lived in his house, intending to only stay until he returned. When he was in Mexico, he met old friends and decided to stay. I could have joined him but that wasn't the life I wanted. Hector and I had always kept in touch, so I applied for a working visa like he did. I realized I was a cowboy at heart and knew there was opportunity for work here. I missed Hector and his family. Once my visa was approved, I left and began working my way to Alberta. I was coming here to re-establish my relationship with my brother and his family. I had every intention of settling down like Hector. I was just taking my time driving across country. Then Hector called me and told me what happened here at Lola Grande. Like everyone around here, Hector had a lot of respect for Trace and said you were a family in need. I came as soon as I could. Canada is a big country. I didn't realize how big it was and that's one of the reasons it took longer for me to get here." Rio looked at Kit having read her mind. "My nomadic days are over. This is where I belong. I'm not going anywhere. I'm back with family." The wide-open spaces of Alberta had settled into his being.

The conversation had become too personal and too serious for Rio. It was time to lighten the mood. "It was a fascinating drive, especially when the sky would clear, unveiling the Rocky Mountains. I saw the flat prairie transform to rolling hills that lay at the feet of those majestic mountains. The beautiful scenery seemed to grow right out of the massive rocks. I had seen pictures, but nothing compares to seeing them up close." Taking another look at the view, Rio understood why everyone loved it here. The mountains were serene and undisturbed in their magnificence and remained unchanged by the events of time. "It's like the land draws you in and doesn't let go. You quickly become tied to the land and the people living here. The countryside here is breathtaking. The landscape is ever changing just like the weather."

"You have yet to experience your first winter. It can blizzard so hard you can't see past your nose, and you're snowed in for days. Then the Chinook blows in across the mountains and warms the air and the snow seems to melt overnight." Kit looked out at the mountains, "It's a beautiful country, and we are lucky to live where we do. I never tire of the view around me as I breathe in the fresh mountain air."

Coming to Alberta had been life changing for both of them. They sat in silence for a while, both lost in their own thoughts. Sitting on the verandah brought back so many memories for Kit. How many times had she and Trace sat together and talked. She missed what they should have had. Rio didn't know where Kit's thoughts were but his were on the lady next to him. There was something different about Kit today. Her smiles came easier, and her eyes no longer had the haunted look. Her words came slowly at first, but she had opened up and shared her own story about how she came to Alberta and her ties to the Calhouns. She talked about her marriage to Trace, how he had adopted Kenzie, and how together they adopted Finn when he was a foster child. Together they became a family. Not a typical family but a loving one. Kit's eyes often clouded over with sadness. Talking about Trace brought back the ache.

Rio was fascinated by the woman beside him and wanted to know her better. "I thought you were awfully young to have a child as old as Finn. It's easy to make assumptions and prejudge people. I know you thought I was a poor immigrant looking to take advantage of the system or my family. Or both."

Rio's comment hurt. "I hate to admit it but you're right. I didn't want you here. I wanted my old life back. I wanted my kids to still have their dad. There was such a void in our lives and then you stepped in. I was so caught up in my anger and grief I was finding fault with everything in life, and I made you the scapegoat for my anger. I knew it wasn't fair, but I didn't care. I had no one else to take it out on."

Rio didn't miss the flash of hurt in her eyes. "I understand your anger. Never a good emotion because it's so hard to control and even harder to let it go."

This was the most personal their conversations had been. Up until today, they had always kept their conversation light. Over the next few hours, they exchanged stories. Rio discovered Kit was intelligent and had a sense of humor to go along with her quick wit. Her combination of inner strength and vulnerability intrigued him. There was a lot to learn about her. Kit was surprisingly comfortable with Rio, so she continued to pump Rio for more information, hoping to learn more about him. Spending time with Rio all afternoon helped her understand him better. They both remained open, and the afternoon passed unnoticed. They didn't realize how late it was until Lola came out to tell them supper was ready. She invited Rio to supper.

Rio's easy smile softened his features, "That's all right, Mrs. G. I couldn't impose."

"You wouldn't be imposing."

Rio was shocked. It was Kit who replied, and her smile reached her eyes, warming them. He said yes without thinking.

Lola wisely kept her thoughts to herself, but there was a quick flicker of amusement in Lola's eyes that Kit didn't miss. Kit gave Lola a warning look before she turned and led the way into the house. Kit's heart did an anxious flip as she told Rio to sit in Trace's chair. One more step of acceptance. The kids were thrilled to have Rio join them. Conversation flowed freely and happiness filled the room. The meal passed pleasantly and when they were done, they all sat around the table chatting. Kit's feelings were mixed. She knew a strong bond was forming with the kids and Rio. She reluctantly admitted it wasn't just the kids.

Rio offered to help clean up, but Kenzie was quick to inform him, "Everyone has chores around here. Benny and I clear the table and load the dishwasher. If there are pots and pans to be washed, Mom washes and I dry. Benny has to take out the garbage. Finn used to but he is too busy for that, and Benny has to learn responsibility."

Rio struggled not to laugh. Kenzie Grayson sounded so much like her mother.

Finn said he was going over to the new facility to putter. He declined Rio's offer to help. Finn wanted to set up an empty stall to call his own. He had missed his safe place.

Kit and Rio went back out to the verandah. Lola headed home on the pretext of needing to catch up on paperwork. Kit believed Lola did have paperwork to do but she questioned if Lola was using it as an excuse so Kit and Rio could be alone.

Their conversation remained easy flowing. Today had been a pleasant change from the sorrow that had held Kit in its grip for so long. Rio had drawn her in with his openness. He had brought down her guard and she had opened up. It wasn't long before Doc pulled into the yard. It had become a familiar habit to stop. It was later than his usual time, so Kit thought he wasn't coming. When Kit heard Doc release a heavy sigh, she wondered if he was working too hard.

The vet was tired. It had been a long day due to emergency surgery on a client's dog. He was looking forward to a relaxing visit with Kit. Instead, Rio was with her looking way too comfortable. Doc failed to keep his disappointment from showing. "Am I interrupting anything?"

Kit watched as the two men sized each other up. The smile faded from her face when she glanced over at Doc. Doc appeared to be jealous or was she reading something into what wasn't there. "Don't be silly. We just finished supper. Can I get you a coffee or a beer?"

"A beer would be great." Doc wondered if Rio had supper with the family or was it just coincidental timing that he happened to be here. There was a hint of annoyance in Doc's eyes. He was quick to recover but Rio noticed.

The awkward moment passed. The two men shook hands and Rio sat down and resumed his relaxed position. His manner was easy and confident. There was a self-assurance about the cowboy that irritated Doc. He would be glad when Rio was gone.

"Can I get you one, Rio?" When Rio nodded, Kit headed into the house.

Rio was in no hurry to leave. By spending more time around Kit, Rio felt himself becoming more enchanted with her even though she exasperated him more often than not.

Doc studied Kit when she handed Rio his beer. He could see familiar sparks between the two of them. He had seen them many times between Kit and Trace. Doc's face flushed with annoyance. His comment to Rio wasn't very subtle, "I thought now that the rebuild was done you would have moved on."

This was a side to Doc Kit hadn't seen before. He usually had a relaxed and easy manner. Maybe his behaviour was off because he was overtired. Kit was quick to respond, "Things have changed. Rio is now a full-time employee at Lola Grande and working with Finn. He is staying in the living quarters we added onto the horse facility."

Doc leaned back and tipped his hat away from his forehead. He tried to keep his expression indifferent, "I'm surprised you haven't mentioned this."

So was Rio, who heard the restraint in Kit's reply, "It all happened very quickly, and I didn't think it was important."

Doc was less than impressed. Now, on top of everything else Rio was staying and living permanently on site. When Rio first arrived, Doc was glad he was staying at Lola Grande for protection. Doc couldn't ignore the stab of jealousy, knowing the man had a distinct advantage. Trace had been bigger than life. Now there appeared to be another cocky cowboy in the picture. Doc had wanted to take it slow but that was going to have to change. It was a risk he was willing to take. He had nothing to lose. He had stepped away once. He wasn't about to do it again. Having known Kit for so many years, Doc changed the subject and began talking about friends they had in common, intentionally excluding Rio.

Rio knew Kit and the vet had history and how close they were. He had watched them from a distance many times. He also knew exactly what Doc was trying to do. It was a revealing moment in more ways than one. Rio realized he was in love with Kit Grayson and wanted to make his own memories with her. Rio also realized he had competition. First it was with a dead husband. Now it was with the long-time family friend who wanted to be more than a friend, and the good old vet was waiting in the background ready to make his move.

Doc finished his beer, "It's late. I should go." He wondered if it was too late in other ways, recalling the earlier sparks between Kit and Rio. Was it time to let Kit go for good? No, it was time to step up his game and fight for her. Their relationship hadn't gone anywhere because he'd been respectful of her loss. It was time to show Kit the real Jim Parker. He knew if he didn't fight for her this time, it would never happen. Was he willing to open himself up to the possibility of future pain, more disappointment, even heartache? He had no choice. He loved Kit.

Kit walked Doc to his truck. Expecting the usual friendly kiss on the cheek, Kit was surprised when Doc took her in his arms and kissed her solidly on the lips, once again revealing his deep feelings for her. Kit wasn't angry, just saddened. There was no catch in the area of her heart, rather a feeling of panic. Kit had never felt uneasy in his presence. Tonight, changed that. She struggled to even her breathing.

Doc sensed the shift in her mood, a subtle withdrawal. Unconsciously, Kit had defensively put her protective shell back up. A heavy silence fell between them before Doc climbed into his truck and drove away.

Rio decided it was time to leave as well. He got up as soon as Kit came back from saying good night to the vet. "Do I get to kiss you good night like the good old vet did?" teased Rio.

The look in Rio's eyes brought back the memory of his kiss. Kit ignored him as her cheeks flushed. Her gaze was drawn to his mouth, now curled in a lazy smile. If they were being honest, they could no longer ignore the chemistry between them. Even though Rio knew he shouldn't tease her, he didn't let it go, "Are you afraid to let me kiss you again, Kit?"

"Good night, Rio." Kit thought she couldn't trust Rio. It was herself she couldn't trust.

"See you in the morning, boss lady." Rio was deep in thought as he headed home. Spending time with Kit and her kids made him long for a family of his own. He smiled. This was the family he wanted.

Lola heard the men leave and looked out her window. Kit was alone on the verandah, staring out at the mountains that brought all of them peace. She prayed that Kit would find her peace. She knew Kit needed to sort out the tangled emotions she was struggling with. Lola also knew the two men who left would both have an impact on Kit's life moving forward.

The fleeting sunset was quickly fading behind the mountains. Kit sat deep in thought, a lone silhouette in the gathering darkness. Sitting alone brought the stark reality of her solitary existence. Kit watched the evening sky change colors, aware that it was symbolic. There would always be changes. As she listened to the comforting sounds around her, time passed unnoticed. By the time she went inside the kids were in bed, but the fire was still burning in the fireplace. Kit threw on another log and curled up in the chair. She let out a weary sigh as she stared pensively at the dancing flames and allowed the thoughts she had tucked away emerge. Her mind immediately went to Rio. He had cut and stored the firewood. She smiled, recalling how he had let Benny haul it by the wagon load so he could help stack it beside the house. Her kids idolized Rio. She tried to evaluate her feelings for both Rio and Doc. She cared about both men more than she cared to admit.

Kit couldn't deny that with Rio it was desire, something she hadn't felt since Trace died. It wasn't Rio's fault that he remined her so much of Trace. Was that the draw or was it the man himself? Her mind remained on Rio who confused and continually kept her guessing. Would he once again be drawn to the freedom of a nomadic life to fill his need for adventure and leave? Some people never change.

Kit smiled, thinking of Doc. Her dear friend was thoughtful, charming, and funny. He was a kind and decent man, and they shared the same strong values. Doc had a caring nature and was always considerate. Had she been leading Doc on unknowingly by relying on his friendship since Trace died? They had many things in common and they were comfortable with each other. She liked his quietness and gentleness. Kit had never had feelings for Doc but could that change if she gave him a chance? Doc had always been overshadowed by Trace as he stood in the background of their lives. With Trace gone, could she see Doc in a different light? To do that she needed to discover who the real Dr. Jim Parker was. Would she discover a different person behind his guise of indifference he had always worn due to a loyal friendship? Kit hadn't expected such passion in his kiss.

Even though both men were confident and independent they were two totally different men. Doc was loyal and settled. He had an established practice and a secure future. Rio had no deep roots. The time spent thinking of Doc and Rio reminded her of the aching void in her life. Kit felt a combination of emotions as she vowed not to remain caught in the past. Life was filling the emptiness in her heart with happiness. Could she put her life with Trace behind her and move on? Would there even be another man in her future? She would have to wait and see.

CHAPTER THIRTY

The days continued to get shorter, and winter would come too soon. The trees that were shades of green a few weeks ago had turned color, carpeting the land in an array of bright colors. Finn was out raking the lawn and had gathered a good pile. Benny jumped in, Kenzie right behind. Finn covered them with the scattered leaves and they were all laughing. Finn had been so good with both Benny and Kenzie. As busy as he was, he always made time to be together. Finn had done this since Trace died. Kit looked up when she heard a flock of geese overhead. Another sign of seasonal change. Seasons changing, just like life.

Kit and Lola had invited Maggie over for tea. Kit was upstairs when she arrived, so Maggie quickly asked Lola how Kit was doing.

Lola was happy to say Kit was almost back to her old self and the spark of life had returned to her expressive eyes. "Doc drops by most days on his way home. I think he would like to be more than friends." Lola knew Doc had feelings for Kit.

So did Maggie. "Kit doesn't love him."

"How do you know?" asked Lola.

"Because Trace was my life," Kit said as she entered the room. "You two can leave my love life out of your conversation."

"You don't have a love life," Maggie dared to say. "You won't let anyone in."

Kit pushed her hand through her hair in frustration and spoke without thinking, "Now I have two men knocking on my door." Knowing the rush of color now warmed her cheeks, Kit shared the fact that both men had kissed her in the last few days. "It's too soon," Kit said emphatically. In fact, she had vowed to never open that part of her heart again.

Lola smiled. She figured Kit was in for another big change in her life. "I guess that complicated things."

"More than you know. My mind is all over the place," confessed Kit.

Maggie, never one to hold back said, "If you feel something for either one of these men, or both, give them a chance. You'll know when it's right."

"If it's right," Kit corrected. She took a deep breath to collect herself. This was a conversation she wasn't ready to have. Conflicting emotions crossed her face, "I don't want to discuss this any further so can we change the subject?"

Maggie knew when to back off, "You probably haven't heard the latest gossip. Jackson Beaumont passed away. He was no sooner dead and buried and Evelyn Beaumont sold the ranch. She packed up and moved back to Texas. I think she wanted to escape what happened here."

This was interesting news, but it didn't console Kit. "What about Olivia?" Kit was curious, even though Olivia would no longer have any impact on her life.

"She moved to Calgary and is living in her mother's condo. She's running her dad's business. I've heard she's just as ruthless as her old man was. She's probably on the prowl for a new husband, as well."

A reflective look clouded Kit's large gray eyes. The mere mention of the Beaumonts caused her momentary bitterness. "Pity the poor man if she finds one."

After the ladies left, Kit puttered in the house but it wasn't long before she was deep in thought. The conversation earlier about dating disturbed her more than she cared to admit. She hoped Lola would have time to talk tonight. Kit often turned to Lola for advice. It just had never been in regard to her love life.

After supper, Kit headed over to Lola's. She wanted the privacy Lola's suite would offer. At Kit's, the kids were constantly around and interrupting as kids do without thinking. Tonight, there was a cool wind blowing in off the mountains as the sun was setting. The air was heavy, the kind that brewed into thunderstorms, and the gathering clouds to the west hinted at rain.

Lola greeted Kit warmly as she opened the door and could see Kit was anxious. She poured them both a coffee and joined Kit at the kitchen table. Lola had a feeling their earlier conversation about dating was troubling Kit. Choosing her words wisely, Lola bypassed the small talk, "Seasons teach us how to acknowledge change. Life teaches us how to accept change. Life can be complicated with twists and turns that can change one's life in an instant. You can't let it stop you from moving forward. It's okay to let Trace go and move on."

"I can handle twists and turns. I've been down that road. I am twice widowed. It hurts that Trace was taken from me too soon, but I'm learning to live without him." Trace's death had changed her life. It had changed her. Time had given Kit time to heal, and she was ready to move forward. She knew that's what Trace would want for her. For a moment Kit's eyes clouded over. Lola's understanding smile gave Kit the courage to continue, "Our conversation this morning has played on my mind all day. I'm confused and scared, but excited at the same time. I don't need a man in my life, but I won't keep my heart closed."

"Won't or can't?"

Lola was more aware than Kit realized. Like always, Lola kept it real, "The part of your life with Trace is over. Don't let what happened interfere with living your life. You made it through that darkness before. You can do it again. You don't have to forget how much Trace meant to you in order to move on. You're still young. Hopefully, you'll give love another chance. Falling in love with another man takes nothing away from what you had with Trace and Mike. Trust your feelings. Life has a way of working things out, so you'll figure it out."

"I know there's no guarantee that I won't get my heart broken again. That's always a risk when you care deeply about another person." There were many times Kit questioned if she'd feel love again after Mike died. Trace had taught her to love again. She would always treasure her years with Trace. Kit knew both Doc Parker and Rio Ortiz had feelings for her. Was she willing to open herself up to love again? The thought was as scary as it was exciting, but she still needed time to adjust to all of the recent changes in her life. "You were still young when your husband died, yet you didn't remarry."

Lola seldom shared her private life or her past. Today she was in a melancholy mood and began to share about days long gone. "We both know life can easily erase one's dreams with reality. I was young and naïve when I met Tom Grayson. Tom was a handsome devil, and I was flattered by his attention. He easily drew me into his web of illusions and quickly stripped me of my innocence with his charm. The tenderness he showed when he courted me disappeared as soon as we were married. Tom's manner became possessive. I was forced from my familiar world into a world of harsh reality. Sometimes life sucks you in before you realize it and before you know it you've lost a part of yourself that you think you'll never get back. That's the way I felt when Tom took me away from my family immediately after we married."

The older lady's eyes darkened with sorrow as her memories surfaced. The scars were deep because of Tom. Her words revealed her own heartache and were underlined by a weariness that made her look older than she really was. "It wasn't long before life was unlike anything Tom had promised. I discovered my husband was a hard-edged man who was addicted to gambling and whisky. A man who became confrontational when he drank and was unable to control his temper. Tom liked to use threats as intimidation but there were times he had violent tendencies. My marriage to Tom was difficult. A marriage that was never what I imagined for myself. I lived a life of broken promises and shattered dreams. My life became a seesaw of hardship and heartache. While my marriage had been a drastic mistake, my boys provided me with the love I needed. For the sake of my boys and my religious beliefs, I stayed with a man who was controlling and abusive."

Kit was heartbroken for her mother-in-law. "How did you endure staying married to a man like Tom?"

"I just did," Lola said flatly. Her expression remained deeply saddened, as she let out a heavy sigh. "When Tom died, our lives changed dramatically. After the initial shock, the changes were for the better. You don't stay in the darkness when you move forward. I have experienced sad things in my life. We all do. But I have been blessed despite the hardships. Because of the kind of marriage I had with Tom, future dreams of marriage were gone forever. I accepted being alone. You and Trace shared a solid marriage filled with love and happiness. True love is very precious and very rare."

Lola wondered what it would be like to be loved that strongly. She suddenly felt cheated. "Life has taught me acceptance. It wasn't until Tom died that I discovered my inner strength." Lola took Kit's hand, "You also have a strong inner strength."

"Trace called it stubbornness."

"Men say that because they are uncomfortable with strong women," Lola declared. The more they talked, the more Lola opened up. "Coming to Valley View changed everything and owning Lola Grande restored my sense of worth. Did you know it was my boys who named Lola Grande? It was their way of thanking me for everything I had done for them along with the sacrifices. They wanted to honor me for all the hard work and heartache I had to endure while I was married to their father. They said that kind of devotion needed to be recognized. We were able to restore the ranch and make our mark on our land. We were able to make the Grayson name mean something." Trace's death had devastated Lola. The older woman's eyes darkened with sorrow. Her voice cracked as her own pain surfaced, "We can't let death control us. My life will continue without Trace in it. Like you, I miss him every day. Your life isn't over. It's just different."

Kit held the other woman's gaze. Of course, Kit knew this, but she had already lost so much in her life. She closed her eyes and allowed burning tears to escape. "I'm afraid to have those dreams again."

"What would your life look like if you hadn't taken a chance with Trace?" Moments passed without a response. Lola took Kit's hands in her own. "It would look like mine. I know you and Trace have both felt sorry for me when I've stayed home alone, and you've gone out. I also know there were times I was included because you felt sorry for me. That's not a life Trace would want for you." Aware of Kit's inner turmoil, Lola continued, "Trace would want you to move on and keep your heart open. You have so much love to give. You will know when it's right because you will have found that man who you want to include in your life and the lives of your children. You won't see him as a replacement, but someone who fills a void and once again makes you complete. Let me give you some advice, dear. Get on with your life, because if you don't, you lose a little of yourself every day. You can stay locked in the past and swear to yourself that you'll never care that much for anyone else, because you think you can never live through that kind of pain again. When we love we open ourselves up to getting hurt, but the rewards are worth it."

Kit understood everything Lola was saying. She had similar conversations with herself. It helped to hear it out loud. Kit had picked up the shattered pieces of her heart and was working on putting it back together. Maybe she needed more time, but she would not keep it closed. "I always appreciate your advice." They both laughed knowing that was a lie.

Kit looked up. Trace now joined a host of others who had passed. Even though she missed them, she chose to remember the happiness she had with them, rather than the emptiness left behind. It was time to stop dwelling on dreams that were gone and turn to those around her. If her past had taught Kit anything, it was that she was strong enough to endure the changes life presented. Change didn't have to be bad. She would pass on to her children the biggest lesson life had taught her. Live life to the fullest every day. Changes will happen; learn to embrace them. Kit knew she had been blessed, so she would meet each new day with grace and thanks. New memories would be made. She would live in the present and look forward to the future. It would continue to be full of surprises, good and bad. Moving forward, she had to accept that. If that took on the form of a new love, Kit would welcome it. She paused, expecting to feel disloyal to Trace, but she felt nothing. She had moved on when Mike died, and she found love with Trace. She would always love Mike and Trace. Both men had been a significant part of her life. She was grateful for all they had added to her life. "It's funny what comes to mind. I remember when Trace proposed to me. He felt he didn't have a lot to offer. I told him love is the essence of what life is made up of. Trace and I had a good life. None of us know what the future has in store. All we need is the courage to move forward. You have taught me we also need faith." Kit admired Lola. "My grandmother said it does no good to brood on what might have been. She taught me a lot of lessons and she always kept it real. Just like you. You are always such a strong, courageous, and independent woman. One I have always admired."

"That's what Trace always said about you. I've struggled like everyone else. Life reshapes our lives in unexpected ways. You and I have both experienced major changes that were out of our control. We made it through tough times and will do it again. Tough times don't break us.

They make us stronger. I have learned a lot about death and the meaning of life. No one knows what tomorrow will bring or if there will be another tomorrow. Death is also a growing experience. Changes occur in our lives whether we want them or not. The only choice we have is how we react to them. Some things never change. Some things change forever. We live for today, let the past go and tomorrow will take care of itself. I know that's easier said than done. It doesn't mean you forget the past. Just don't let it keep you from moving forward. We don't always understand God's master plan. We follow with our faith even when life doesn't work out the way we plan. We aren't allowed to see into the future for a reason. You have to endure the pain as you pass through difficult times to reach the wonderful things beyond. God guided us here with his hand. This is our home and our land. Lola Grande is our future. We have to trust that God has another plan, and he will guide us again." Lola had wisdom only experience could give.

Kit knew Lola was right. Life had changed in many ways for all of them. This was their new reality, and they were adjusting. "I'm learning to accept what is. I try to remember the good and let the bad go. Dwelling on the bad does no good, it just drags you down into darkness where you can't see the beauty in life." Kit realized that life was a lot like ranching. The rewards were worth the hardship. She would go forward with courage and embrace her future and trust she could deal with anything, whatever it was. Changes had taken place, including within. Kit accepted that the gift of life is today with the hope of tomorrow. She didn't know what her future would hold. Kit did know she could cope with any tomorrow.

A feeling of contentment circled the two women. Lola smiled at Kit. "Life changes and so do we. The past is gone. We will continue to be presented with challenges. You and I need to be strong for the next generation. They are the future of Lola Grande. This ranch will remain in our family and the next generation will live on this land. Your children are the next generation of Graysons. God willing, there will be many more. Lola Grande belongs to all of the Graysons. This is our home. Not for a short time, but for a lifetime. It is our legacy. There was a reason God guided us both here many years ago." The two women looked at each other with eyes full of hope. Lola' voice filled with pride, "We are Graysons. We are Lola Grande."

INTRODUCTION
to
"THE WILLOWS"

Seasons change from one to the other. Life also changes. It had been a year since the fire at Lola Grande that took the life of Trace Grayson. The year had been difficult for all of the Graysons. There was always one challenge after another, but they had learned to cope. As life continued to change, they changed with it.

Kit Grayson had emerged from the darkness that engulfed her. Now that her eyes were no longer clouded by bitterness and anger, she could again appreciate the beauty of a new day. She had worked through her despair and refused to take the darkness with her. She again felt alive and the world around her was beginning to lighten. Lola Grande was again familiar to the sight. Caballo Stables was in full operation. Finn was busy training, and their horses were grazing on Lola Grande land. They had all adjusted to the changes. Life was back in balance.

That all changed the day Finn took a phone call from an unknow number. Kit watched Finn's face pale as he listened to a familiar voice from the past. "Yes, I remember the address. I will see you tomorrow at ten o'clock," Finn replied and hung up the phone. He looked at his mom and swallowed hard. "That was Mrs. Sloan from the Foster Agency. She wouldn't tell me anything over the phone other than the fact that it was important that we meet. I don't have a good feeling about this." Finn turned and walked out the door without another word.

Kit knew he was escaping to his safe place. She would have to wait until he was ready to talk, but she was uneasy. Nobody knows when a big change will happen in someone's life, but she knew they had been thrown another curve. Kit had a feeling their lives were about to change.

FATE CAN BE A POWERFUL FORCE

SO CAN FAITH

"TRILOGY OF TRIUMPH"

Hidden Secrets (Book One)
Calhoun Family

Four generations dedicated their lives to their ranch, Valley View. The lives of the family living at the original homestead changed dramatically when a stranger showed up looking for her father. Kit Bennett had always been told her father had died before she was born. Her life crumbled around her when she found her birth certificate and her mother's journals in the attic.

Lola Grande (Book Two)
Grayson Family

Trace Grayson had committed his youth to establishing his horse business and restoring his family ranch, Lola Grande. A thriving ranch means nothing without someone to share it with. When Trace Grayson and Kit Bennett married it was the happiest day of their lives. They planned a lifetime together, forever. Forever has its own timeline.

The Willows (Book Three)
Rodwell Family

Baxter and Genna Rodwell would do anything for their daughter, Laurel, who was suffering from traumatic mutism. They prayed a move to rural Alberta would be the miracle they needed for her recovery. Laurel hadn't spoken a word or shed a tear since the day her husband and young daughter were killed in an accident. Laurel was driving.

OTHER BOOKS BY

LINDA RAKOS

Beyond the Journey

Double Dare

Hidden Secrets

ABOUT THE AUTHOR

Linda Rakos was born and raised in Alberta
and now resides in High River
with her husband. Linda is a wife, a mother of two sons, and a blessed
grandmother to two wonderful grandsons.
Happily retired, she devotes her
time to her family and her writing. While writing her first novel, she
discovered how exciting it is to create characters, each one individual and
different. Meeting the challenge of describing
what she wants someone to see
with her words. To create emotions, strong
enough for someone to feel. Achieving
success with her first book, ignited her passion
that has taken her in a new
direction as she continues on this journey.